DEMONS NEVER FORGET . . . AND THEY NEVER FORGIVE!

By Kim Harrison

Books of the Hollows

THE OUTLAW DEMON WAILS
FOR A FEW DEMONS MORE
A FISTFUL OF CHARMS
EVERY WHICH WAY BUT DEAD
THE GOOD, THE BAD, AND THE UNDEAD
DEAD WITCH WALKING

And Don't Miss

HOLIDAYS ARE HELL
DATES FROM HELL

THE
OUTLAW
DEMON WAILS

KIM
HARRISON

An Imprint of HarperCollinsPublishers

EOS
An Imprint of HarperCollins*Publishers*
10 East 53rd Street
New York, New York 10022-5299

Copyright © 2008 by Kim Harrison
Excerpt from *White Witch, Black Curse* copyright © 2009 by Kim Harrison
"The Bespelled" copyright © 2008 by Kim Harrison
Cover art by Larry Rostant
ISBN 978-0-06-114982-5
www.eosbooks.com

First Eos paperback printing: December 2008
First Eos hardcover printing: March 2008

HarperCollins® and Eos® are registered trademarks of HarperCollins Publishers.

Printed in the U. S. A.

10   9   8   7   6   5   4   3   2   1

To the guy who knows the more things change, the weirder it gets.

Acknowledgments

I'd like to thank Mike Spradlin, not just for the idea of the title, but for his long-time support of the Hollows, precious in those first tender years and still greatly appreciated. And as always, my agent, Richard Curtis, and my editor, Diana Gill, whose combined attention and skills in bringing a world to life is prized all the more.

THE
OUTLAW
DEMON WAILS

One

———————

I leaned over the glass counter, squinting at the price of the high-grade redwood rods, safe in their airtight glass coffins like Snow White. The ends of my scarf slipped to block my view, and I tucked them behind my short leather jacket. I had no call to be looking at wands. I didn't have the money, but more important, I wasn't shopping for business today—I was shopping for pleasure.

"Rachel?" my mom said from halfway across the store, smiling as she fingered a display of packaged organic herbs. "How about Dorothy? Make Jenks hairy, and he could be Toto."

"No friggin' way!" Jenks exclaimed, and I started when the pixy took off from my shoulder where he'd been nestled in my scarf's warmth. Gold dust sifted from him to make a temporary sunbeam on the counter and brighten the drab evening. "I'm not going to spend Halloween handing out candy as a dog! And no Wendy and Tinker Bell either. I'm going as a pirate!" His wings slowed as he settled atop the counter next to the stand of low-grade redwood dowels suitable for amulets. "Coordinating costumes is stupid."

Normally I'd agree, but, silent, I drew back from the counter. I'd never have enough disposable income for a wand. Besides, versatility was key in my profession, and wands were one-spell wonders. "I'm going as the female lead in the latest vampire flick," I said to my mom. "The one where the vampire hunter falls in love with the vamp?"

"You're going as a vampire hunter?" my mother asked.

Warming, I plucked an uninvoked amulet from a vanity rack to size my chest up. I was hippy enough to pass for the actress I was trying to mimic, but my excuse of a chest wouldn't match her spell-enhanced bust. And it had to be spell enhanced. Naturally big-chested women don't run like that. "No, the vampire," I said, embarrassed. Ivy, my housemate, was going as the hunter, and despite my agreement that coordinating costumes was stupid, I knew Ivy and I would stop conversation when we walked into the party. And that was the point, wasn't it? Halloween was the only time doppelgänger charms were legal—and Inderland and the braver slice of humanity made the most of it.

My mother's face went serious, then cleared. "Oh! The black-haired one, right? In the slut outfit? Good God, I don't know if my sewing machine can go through leather."

"Mom!" I protested, though used to her language and lack of tact. If it came into her head, it came out of her mouth. I glanced at the clerk with her, but she clearly knew my mother and wasn't fazed. Seeing a woman in tasteful slacks and an angora sweater swearing like a sailor tended to throw people off. Besides, I already had the outfit in my closet.

Frowning, my mother fingered the charms to change hair color. "Come over here, honey. Let's see if they have anything that will touch your curls. Honestly, Rachel. You pick the hardest costumes. Why can't you ever be anything easy, like a troll or fairy princess?"

Jenks snickered. " 'Cause that's not slutty enough," he said loud enough for me to hear, but not my mother.

I gave him a look, and he simpered as he hovered backward to a rack of seeds. Though only about four inches tall, he cut an attractive figure with his soft-soled boots and the red scarf Matalina, his wife, had knitted him wrapped about his neck. Last spring, I'd used a demon curse to make him human-size, and the memory of his eighteen-year-old, athletic figure, with its trim waist and broad, muscular shoulders made strong from his dragonfly-like wings, was still very much in my memory. He was a very married pixy, but perfection deserved attention.

Jenks made a darting path over my basket, and a package of fern seed for Matalina's wing aches thumped in. Catching sight of the bust enhancer, his expression turned positively devilish. "Speaking of slutty . . ." he started.

"Well-endowed doesn't equal slutty, Jenks," I said. "Grow up. It's for the costume."

"Like that'll do anything?" His grin was infuriating, and his hands were on his hips in his best Peter Pan pose. "You need two or three to even make an impression. Fried eggs."

"Shut up!"

From across the store came my mother's oblivious "Solid black, right?" I turned to see her hair color shifting as she touched the invoked sample amulets. Her hair was exactly like mine. Sort of. I kept mine long, the wild, frizzy red just past my shoulders, instead of in the close cut she used to tame hers. But our eyes were the same green, and I had her same skill in earth magic, fleshed out and given a professional stamp at one of the local colleges. She had more education than I did, actually, but had few opportunities to use it. Halloween had always been a chance for her to show off her considerable earth magic skills to the neighboring moms with a modest vengeance, and I think she appreciated me asking for her help this year. She had been doing great these last few months, and I couldn't help but wonder if she was doing better because I was spending more time with her, or if she simply appeared more stable because I wasn't seeing her just when she was having problems.

Guilt slithered through me, and giving Jenks a glare at his song about big-busted ladies tying their shoes, I wove through the stands of herbs and racks sporting premade charms, each having a distinctive sticker identifying who had made it. Charm crafting was still a cottage industry despite the high level of technology available to smooth out the rough spots, but one tightly regulated and vigorously licensed. The owner of the store probably only crafted a few of the spells she sold.

At my mother's direction, I held each sample amulet in turn so she could evaluate my appearance. The clerk oohed and aahed, trying to push us into making a decision, but my mom hadn't helped me with my costume in years, and we were going to make an evening out of it, ending with coffee and dessert at some overpriced coffeehouse. It wasn't that I ignored my mom, but my life tended to interfere. A lot. I'd been making an effort over the last three months to spend more time with her, trying to ignore my own ghosts and hoping that she wouldn't be so . . . fragile, and she hadn't looked this good in a while. Which convinced me I was a crappy daughter.

Finding the right hair color was easy, and I nodded when my red curls turned a black so deep they were almost gunmetal-blue. Satisfied, I dropped a packaged, uninvoked amulet into the basket to hide the bust enhancer.

"I've a charm at home to straighten your hair," my mother said brightly, and I turned wonderingly to her. I'd found out in fourth grade that over-the-counter charms wouldn't touch my curls. Why on earth did she still have the difficult-to-make charms? I hadn't straightened my hair in ages.

The shop's phone rang, and when the clerk excused herself, my mom sidled close, smiling as she touched the braid Jenks's kids had put my hair in this morning. "That charm took me your entire high school career to perfect," she said. "You think I'm not going to practice it?"

Worried now, I glanced at the woman on the phone—the one who obviously knew my mother. "Mom!" I whispered. "You can't sell those! You don't have a license!"

Lips pressed tightly, she took my basket to the counter in a huff to check out.

Exhaling, my gaze went to Jenks sitting on the rack, and he shrugged. I slowly followed in my mother's steps, wondering if I'd neglected her more than I thought. She did the damnedest things sometimes. I'd talk to her about it over coffee. Honestly, she should know better.

Streetlights had come on while we had shopped, and the pavement glowed with gold and purple holiday lights in the evening rain. It looked cold, and as I went to the register, I adjusted my scarf for Jenks. "Thanks," he muttered as he landed on my shoulder. His wings were shivering, and they brushed my neck as he settled in. October was too cold for him to be out, but with the garden dormant and Matalina in need of fern seeds, risking a trip in the rain to a charm shop had been his only recourse. *He'd brave anything for his wife*, I thought, as I rubbed my tickling nose.

"How about the coffeehouse down two blocks?" my mom suggested as the dull *beep, beep* of barcodes being read clashed with the earthy smells of the shop.

"Grab some air, Jenks. I'm going to sneeze," I warned him, and muttering things I was just as glad not to hear, he flew to my mom's shoulder.

It was a marvelous sneeze, clearing out my lungs and earning a "bless you" from the clerk. But it was followed by another, and I hardly had time to straighten when a third hit me. Breathing shallowly to forestall the next, I looked at Jenks in dismay. There was only one reason why I would sneeze like this.

"Damn," I whispered, glancing out the huge front window—it was after sundown. "Double damn." I spun to the clerk, who was now shoving things into a bag. I didn't have my calling circle. I had cracked the first one, and the new one was sandwiched between spell books under my kitchen counter. *Damn, damn, damn!* I should have made one the size of a compact mirror.

"Ma'am?" I warbled, then accepted the tissue my mom handed me from her purse. "Do you sell calling circles?"

The woman stared, clearly affronted. "Absolutely not. Alice, you told me she didn't deal in demons. Get her *out* of my store!"

My mother let out a huff of annoyance, then her face turned

coaxing. "Patricia," she cajoled. "Rachel does not summon demons. The papers print what sells papers, that's all."

I sneezed again, this time so hard it hurt. Crap. We had to get out of there.

"Heads up, Rachel," Jenks called out, and I looked up to catch a cellophane-wrapped stick of magnetic chalk as he dropped it. Fumbling with the wrapper, I tried to remember the complex pentagram Ceri had taught me. Minias was the only demon who knew I had a direct line to the ever-after, and if I didn't answer him, he might cross the lines to find me.

Searing pain came from nowhere. Doubled over, I gasped at the assault and fell back from the counter. *What in hell? It isn't supposed to hurt!*

Jenks hit the ceiling, leaving behind a cloud of silver dust like an octopus inking. My mother turned from her friend. "Rachel?" she questioned, her green eyes wide as I bent and clutched my wrist.

The chalk slipped from me as my grip went numb. It felt like my wrist was on fire. "Get out!" I yelled, and the two women stared at me as if I had gone insane.

We all jumped when the air pressure shifted violently. Ears ringing, I looked up, my heart pounding and my breath held. He was here. I didn't see the demon, but he was here. Somewhere. I could smell the burnt amber.

Spotting the chalk, I scooped it up and picked at the cellophane, but my nails couldn't find the seam. I was torn between fear and anger. Minias had no business bothering me. I didn't owe him, and he didn't owe me. And why couldn't I get the damned wrapper off the chalk!

"Rachel Mariana Morgan?" came an elegant British accent I'd expect from a Shakespearean play, and my face went cold. "Where a-a-a-a-are you?" it drawled.

"Shit," I whispered. It wasn't Minias. It was Al.

Panicked, I looked across the store to my mother. She stood with her friend, neat and tidy in her autumn-colored outfit, her hair perfectly arranged, and the skin around her eyes just starting to show a few faint lines. She hadn't a clue. "Mom," I whispered, gesturing frantically as I put space between us. "Get into a circle. Both of you!" But they just stared. I didn't have time to explain. Hell, I didn't understand it myself. This had to be a joke. Some perverted, twisted joke.

My eyes went to the darting clatter of Jenks as he came to hover beside me. "It's Al!" the pixy whispered. "Rache, you said he was in demon prison!"

"Rachel Mariana Mo-o-o-o-orga-a-a-an," the demon sang, and I stiffened at the *tap-thunk tap-thunk* of his booted feet coming from behind a tall display of spelling books.

"Damn fool moss-wipe of a pixy," Jenks berated himself. "It's too cold to take my sword," he said in a mocking falsetto. "It'll freeze to my ass. It's a shopping trip, not a run." His voice shifted, becoming angry. "Tink save you, Rachel. Can't you even go shopping with your mom without calling up demons?"

"I didn't call him!" I protested, feeling my palms start to sweat.

"Yeah, well, he's here," the pixy said, and I swallowed when the demon peeked from behind the display. He had known *exactly* where I was.

Al was smiling with deep, taunting anger, his red eyes, their pupils horizontal slits like a goat's, peering over a pair of round smoked glasses. Dressed in his usual frock coat of crushed green velvet, he was a picture of old European grace, the image of a young lord on the verge of greatness. Lace showed at his cuffs and collar. His aristocratically chiseled features, with a strong nose and chin, were tightened in bad humor, and his thick teeth showed in an expression that anticipated dealing out pain.

I kept backing up, and he came out from behind the display. "Oh, I say. This is splendid!" he said in delight. "Two Morgans for the price of one."

Oh, God. My mother. Terror snapped me out of my shock. "You can't touch me or my family," I said while I tried to get the cellophane off the magnetic chalk. If I could make a circle, I might be able to trap him. "You promised!"

The tapping of his boots stopped as he posed to show off his elegant grace. My eyes measured the distance between us. Eight feet. Not good. But if he was looking at me, he was ignoring my mom.

"I did, didn't I?" he said, and when he sent his gaze to the ceiling, my shoulders eased.

"Rache!" Jenks shrilled.

Al lunged. Panicking, I backpedaled. Fear hit hard when he found my throat. I dug at his fingers, my nails gouging him as he picked me up to dangle me from his grip. His sculptured face grimaced at the pain, but he only tightened his fingers. My pulse pounded in my head and I went limp, praying he wanted to gloat a little before he dragged me back to the ever-after to hopefully just kill me.

"You can't hurt me," I squeaked out, not sure if the sparkles at the edge of my vision were from lack of oxygen or Jenks. *I am dead. I am so dead.*

A soft sound of satisfaction emanated from Al, a long, low rumble of contentment. He effortlessly pulled me close until our breaths mingled. His eyes were red behind his glasses, and the scent of burnt amber coursed through me. "I asked nicely for your testimony. You refused. I've no incentive to play by the rules anymore. You can thank your own shortsightedness for that. Me sitting in a tiny little cell." He gave me a shake to rattle my teeth. "Stripped of my curses and naked but for what I can say or spell. But someone summoned me out," he said maliciously. "And we have a deal that's going to leave you dead and me a free demon."

"It wasn't my fault you went to jail," I squeaked. The pulsing adrenaline hurt my head. He couldn't take me to the ever-after unless I let him; he'd have to drag me to a ley line.

Somewhere in my frazzled brain, something clicked. He couldn't hold me and go misty at the same time. Grunting, I pulled my knee up, connecting right between his legs.

Al grunted. Agony smacked into me as he flung me away and my back hit a display. I gasped for air, holding my bruised throat as packets of freeze-dried herbs sifted over me with light thumps. Sucking in the scent of amber as I coughed, I held up a hand to fend them off, angling my legs under me to stand. *Where is the chalk?*

"You sorry bitch of a succubus whore!" Al groaned, holding himself as he hunched over, and I smiled. Minias had told me that as part of Al's punishment for letting his old familiar go when she knew how to spindle line energy, he'd been purged of the accumulated charms, spells, and curses he had built up over the millennia. It left him, while not helpless, at least reduced to a limited spell vocabulary. Obviously he'd been in the kitchen recently, since his upper-crust Englishman persona was a disguise. I didn't want to know what he really looked like.

"What's the matter, Al?" I mocked, wiping my mouth to find I'd bitten my lip. "Not used to anyone fighting back?" This was freaking great. Here I was in a charm shop, and nothing was invoked but vanity charms and bust enhancers.

"Here, Rachel!" my mom cried out, and Al's head swung around.

"Mom!" I shouted when she threw something at me. "Get out!"

Al's eyes tracked it. I stiffened as a ·shimmer of black ever-after coursed over him, healing whatever I had damaged. But the magnetic chalk thumped safely into my hand. I took a breath to yell at her to get out again, and the shimmer of a blue-tinted ever-after circle rose up around her and the clerk behind the counter. They were safe.

An odd, unexpected sensation of ice swept through me, and I stiffened. It felt like the chime of a bell ringing through my bones. Oblivious, Al let out a roar and lunged.

Yelping, I dropped to the floor and out of his reach. From behind me came a crash as Al sailed over me and fell into the rack I'd knocked over. I had seconds. Arm extended, I sat on the floor and scribbled a circle, rolling back and away as a premonition honed by years of martial arts told me he was reaching for me.

"Not this time, witch," he snarled.

Eyes wide, I spun on my butt. My foot came up to kick, but he moved with an inhuman quickness and my boot struck his palm. I froze, lying on my back with my ankle in his grip and my scarf in my face. One good twist, and he'd break it. *Shit.*

Al had lost his glasses. His eyes glinted maliciously as he smiled, but before he could move, an explosion rocked through the store and blew out the windows. My hands jerked to my ears and I yanked my foot out of Al's grip. The demon's goat-like eyes were wide as he stumbled back, but his shock quickly became anger.

Frightened, I scrabbled to knock over another display. Packaged amulets rained down. The shush of tires against wet pavement became obvious as my hearing returned, the sound coming in through the broken window along with the calls of people. *What had my mom done?*

"Jenks!" I shouted, feeling the icy cool of a damp night. It was too cold. It might throw him into hibernation!

"I'm fine!" he exclaimed as he hovered in a red haze of dust. "Let's get the bastard."

I gathered myself to stand, then hesitated in a crouch when Jenks's gaze fixed on something over my shoulder and the pixy went white.

"Uh, bastards," he amended shakily, and a new fear settled in when I realized Al wasn't moving anymore either, but watching whatever Jenks was. In the hush of ambient street noise, a wave of burnt-amber, tainted ozone flowed over me.

"There's another demon behind me, isn't there?" I whispered.

Jenks's eyes flicked to mine and away. "Two."

Terrific. Jenks darted away, and I moved. I tripped on my scarf, then kicked backward when someone grabbed my leg. Their hold faltered, and dropping back to the floor, I spun. A yellow-clad arm reached for me. Gripping someone's shoulder, I swung my foot up as a fulcrum and flung him over me.

There was no crash; whoever it was had gone misty. *Three demons? What in hell is going on!*

Ticked, I got to my feet only to stumble when a blur of red darted in front of me. My eyes went to my mother. She was okay, fighting to get the clerk's arms off her as the woman panicked, safe in the circle as the store was ripped apart.

"You sent a rent-a-cop after me?" Al bellowed. "Nice try!"

I covered my ears when a pressure shift pulsed against me and Al vanished. The demon in red that had been headed for him skidded to a stop. Cursing violently, he flung his scythe in rage. It sliced through a metallic rack like it was cotton candy, and the display toppled as the clerk began sobbing.

Blinking, I stood and slowly backed away. Packets of amulets crunched under my feet. *Holy crap,* I thought; the monster looked like death having a temper tantrum, and I jumped when Jenks landed on my shoulder. The pixy had a straightened plastic-coated paper clip, and I found strength in that. So what if there were still two demons here? I could do anything with Jenks watching my back.

"Follow him!" the last demon shouted, and I spun, fearing the worst. *Please, not Newt. Anyone but Newt.*

"You!" I exclaimed, my breath exploding out of me in that one word. It was Minias.

"Yes, me," Minias snarled, and I jumped when the red demon with the scythe vanished. "Why, by the bloody new moon, didn't you answer me?"

"Because I don't deal with demons!" I shouted, pointing to the shattered window as if I had any authority over him. "Get the hell out of here!"

Minias's smooth, ageless face creased in anger.

"Look out!" Jenks cried as he took off from my shoulder, but I was way ahead of him. The demon was striding across the store in his yellow robe and funny hat, kicking charms and herbs out of the way. I backed up, the cries from the sidewalk telling me how close I was to the circle I'd scribed earlier. My pulse pounded and I felt myself sweat. This would be close.

Murderously silent, he came on, his slitted eyes a red so dark as to be almost brown. His robes unfurled as he moved, looking like a cross between a desert sheik's cloak and a kimono. Pace stilted, he reached for me, the light glinting on his rings.

"Now!" Jenks shouted, and I dropped out from under the demon's reach and rolled past the chalk line.

I was outside the circle; Minias was in it. *"Rhombus!"* I exclaimed, slapping my hand down on the chalk. My awareness reached out to touch the nearest ley line. Power surged through me and I held my breath, eyes watering as it flowed in unchecked, my desire for a quick circle letting the ley line energy fill me with an unusual force.

It hurt, but I gritted my teeth and held on while the forces equalized in the time it takes for an electron to spin. Pulled by the trigger word, my will tapped the memory of hours of practice, consolidating a five-minute prep and invocation into an eyeblink. I wasn't that good with most ley line magic, but this? This I could do.

"Bloody hell and damn your dame!" Minias swore, and I couldn't help but smile when the hem of his yellow robe swung to a stop. It was blurry from the molecule-thin sheet of ever-after that rose to trap him in my circle.

My breath slipped from me, and I sat back on my butt, my palms behind me on the hardwood floor and my knees bent as I looked at the demon. I had him, and the fading adrenaline was starting to turn into the shakes.

"Rachel!" my mother called, and I looked past Minias. She was frowning at the clerk. The woman refused to take down her protective circle, sobbing and crying. Finally my mother had enough, and with her lips pursed in the temper we shared, she shoved the woman into her own bubble, causing her to break it.

Out of sight behind the counter, the frazzled woman hit the

floor and wailed all the louder. I sat upright when the phone was dragged from the counter to thunk on the floor. Beaming, my mother stepped delicately around the scattered charms and spells, hands extended and pride flowing from her like a wave.

"Are you okay?" I asked as I took her grip and she pulled me up.

"Fantabulous!" she exclaimed, eyes bright. "Hot damn, I love to watch you work!"

I had crushed herbs all over my jeans, and I slapped at them to get the flakes off. There was a crowd at the broken window, and traffic had stopped. Jenks dropped to hover behind my mom, making the "crazy" motion with his finger, and I frowned. My mom had been more than a little off since my dad had died, but I had to admit this nonchalance at a three-demon attack was much easier to take than the clerk's noisy hysterics.

"Get out!" the woman yelled as she pulled herself up. Her eyes were red and her face was swollen. "Alice, get out and don't you ever come back! You hear me? Your daughter is a menace! She ought to be locked up and shunned!"

My mother's jaw clenched. "Shut your mouth," she said hotly. "My daughter just saved your butt. She drove off two demons and bound a third while you hid like a prissy girlie-girl who wouldn't know the right end of an amulet if it came out her ass." Color high, she turned with a huff and looped her arm through mine. The plastic bag of charms was in her grip, and it thumped into me lightly. "Rachel, we're leaving. This is the last time I shop in this pee-stained hole."

Jenks was grinning as he hovered before us. "Have I told you lately how much I like you, Mrs. Morgan?"

"Mom . . . people can hear you," I said, embarrassed. God! Her mouth was worse than Jenks's. And we couldn't leave. Minias was still standing in my circle.

Heels crunching on the merchandise, my mom dragged me to the door, her head high and her red curls bobbing in the breeze from the busted window. A tired sigh lifted through me at the wail of sirens. Great. Just freaking great. They'd want to haul me down to the I.S. tower to fill out a report. Demon summoning wasn't illegal, just really stupid, but they'd think of something, probably a bald-faced lie.

The I.S., or Inderland Security, didn't like me. Since having quit their lame-ass worldwide police force last year, Ivy, Jenks, and I had been showing up the Cincinnati division with a pleasant regularity. They weren't idiots, but I attracted trouble that just begged me to beat it into submission. It didn't help that the media loved printing stuff about me either, if only to feed people's animosity and sell papers.

Minias cleared his throat as we approached, and my mother halted in surprise. Clasping his hands innocently before him, the demon smiled. From outside came an increase in conversation at the approaching cruisers. The jitters started, and Jenks slipped between me and my scarf with that paper clip still in his grip. He was shivering, too, but I knew it was from the cold, not fear.

"Banish your demon, Rachel, so we can get our coffee," my mother said as if he was a nuisance like fairies in her garden. "It's almost six. There will be a line if we don't hurry."

The clerk steadied herself against a counter. "I called the I.S.! You can't go. Don't you let them go!" she screamed at the watching people, but thankfully none came in. "You belong in jail! All of you! Look at my shop. Look at my shop!"

"Put a cork in it, Patricia!" my mother said. "You have insurance." Coyly touching her hair, she turned to Minias. "You're nice looking—for a demon."

Minias blinked, and I sighed at his contriving smile and the bow that made my mom titter like a schoolgirl. The conversations at the broken window shifted, and when I looked at the street and the sound of approaching cruisers, someone's camera phone flashed. *Oooooh, better and better.*

Licking my lips, I turned to Minias. "Demon, I demand that you depart—" I started.

"Rachel Mariana Morgan," Minias said, stepping so close to the edge of the barrier that smoke curled up where his robe touched it, "you're in danger."

"Tell us something we don't know, moss wipe," Jenks muttered from my shoulder.

"I'm in danger?" I said snidely, feeling better now that the demon was behind a circle. "Gee, you think? Why is Al out of jail? You told me he was in custody! He attacked me!" I shouted, pointing to the destroyed shop. "He broke our agreement! What are you going to do about it?"

Minias's eye twitched and the barest rasp gave away his slippers scuffing the floor. "Someone is summoning him out of confinement. It's in your best interest to help us."

"Rache," Jenks complained. "It's cold and the I.S. is almost here. Get rid of him before they make us fill out paperwork until the sun goes nova."

I rocked back on my heels. Yeah. Like I was going to help a demon? My reputation was bad enough.

Seeing me ready to banish him, Minias shook his head. "We can't contain him without your help. He will kill you, and with no one alive to file a complaint, he'll get away with it."

A chill ran through me at the certainty in his voice. Worried, I glanced at the people at the window, then looked over the store. Not much was standing. Outside, traffic began to move as the amber and blue lights of an I.S. car started playing over the buildings. My gaze fell on my mom and I cringed. I could usually keep the more lethal aspects of my job from her, but this time . . .

"Better listen," she said, shocking the hell out of me, then clacked her heels smartly as she went to intercept the clerk's dash to the street.

A bad feeling knotted my stomach. If Al wasn't playing by the rules anymore, he'd kill me. Probably after making me watch him murder everyone I loved. It was that simple. I'd been living on instinct for the first twenty-five years of my life, and though it had gotten me out of a lot of trouble, it had also gotten me into just as much. And killed my boyfriend. So though every fiber of my body said to banish him, I took a slow breath, listened to my mother, and said, "Okay. Talk."

Minias pulled his attention from my mother. A sheet of ever-after cascaded over him, melting the formal yellow robe into a pair of faded jeans, leather belt, boots, and a red silk shirt. My face went cold. It was Kisten's favorite outfit, and Minias had probably picked it out of my thoughts like a cookie out of a jar. Damn him.

Kisten. The memory of his body propped up against his bed flashed through me. My jaw trembled, and I clenched my teeth. I knew I had tried to save him. Or maybe he had tried to save me. I just didn't remember it, and guilt slithered across my soul. I had failed him, and Minias was using it. *Son of a bitch demon.*

"Free me," Minias said mockingly as if he knew he was hurting me. "Then we'll talk."

I held my right arm as it throbbed with a phantom pain, remembering. "That's likely," I said bitterly, and the clerk jerked from my mother, her shrill voice hurting my ears.

Minias wasn't fazed, and he looked over his new attire with interest. A pair of modern, mirrored sunglasses misted into existence in his grip, and he placed them on the bridge of his narrow nose with a meticulous care to hide his alien eyes. He sniffed, and I felt sick at how much he looked like any guy on the street. An attractive, university kind of guy, who'd fit in on any campus as a grad student, or maybe a teacher still working for tenure. But his bearing was uncaring and slightly supercilious.

"The coffee your mother mentioned sounds equitable. I give my word I'll be . . . good."

My mother flicked her attention to the noisy street, and seeing her eyes glinting in approval, I wondered if this was where I got my need to live for the thrill. But I was smarter now, and putting a hand on my hip, I shook my head. My mother was nuts. He was a freaking demon.

The demon glanced over my shoulder at the sound of a car door shutting and a police radio. "Have I ever lied to you?" he murmured so only I could hear. "Do I look like a demon? Tell them I'm a witch that was helping you catch Al and I got in the circle by mistake."

My eyes narrowed. He wanted me to lie for him?

Minias leaned so close to the barrier of ever-after that it buzzed a harsh warning. "If you don't, I'll give the public what they expect." His eyes went to the people clustered at the window. "Proof that you deal in demons ought to do wonders for your . . . sterling reputation."

Mmmm. There is that.

The door jingled open. With a cry of relief, the clerk shoved my mother away and ran to the two officers. Sobbing, she draped herself over them, effectively preventing them from coming in any farther. I had thirty seconds, tops, and then it would be the I.S.'s decision as to what happened with Minias, not mine. No freaking way.

Minias saw my decision and smiled with an infuriating confidence. Demons never lied, but they never seemed to tell the truth either. I'd dealt with Minias before, finding that for all his considerable power, he was a novice when dealing with people. He had been babysitting the ever-after's most powerful, insane denizen for the last millennium. But clearly something had changed. And someone was summoning Al out of containment and setting him free to kill me.

Damn. Is it Nick? Stomach caving in, I put a fist to my middle. I knew he had the skill, and we had parted on very bad terms.

"Let me out," Minias whispered. "I'll hold myself to *your* definition of right and wrong."

I glanced across the demolished shop. One of the officers managed to disentangle himself when the clerk pointed at us, almost gibbering. Other people in uniform were filing in, and it was getting crowded. I'd never get a better verbal contract from Minias than that.

"Done," I said, rubbing my foot across the chalk line to break the circle.

"Hey!" an incoming suit shouted as my bubble went down. The spare young man whipped a thin wand from his belt and pointed it at us. "Everybody *down!*"

The clerk screamed and collapsed. From outside came the sound of panic. I jumped in front of Minias, hands up and spread wide. "Whoa, whoa, whoa!" I cried out. "I'm Rachel Morgan from Vampiric Charms, Independent Runner Service. I've got the situation under control. We're cool! We're all cool! Point the wand up!"

The tension eased, and in the new calm, my mouth dropped open when I recognized the I.S. officer. "You!" I accused, then started when Jenks catapulted himself from my shoulder.

"Jenks, no!" I shouted, and the room reacted. A unified protest rose, and ignoring the calls to halt, I lunged to get in front of the man with the wand before Jenks could pix him and somehow land me with an assault charge.

"You sorry-ass hunk of putrid fairy crap!" Jenks shouted, darting erratically as I tried to stay between them. "Nobody sucker punches me and gets away with it! Nobody!"

"Easy, Jenks," I soothed, all the while trying to watch both him and Minias. "He's not worth it. He's not worth it!"

My words penetrated and, with his wings clattering aggressively, Jenks accepted my shoulder when I fluffed my scarf and turned to the I.S. officer. I knew my face was as ugly as Jenks's. I hadn't expected to ever see Tom again—though who else would they send out on a call concerning demons but someone from the Arcane Division?

The witch was a mole in the I.S., working one of their most sensitive, highest-paying jobs while simultaneously laboring away as a peon in some fanatical black-arts cult. I knew because he had played messenger boy last year and asked me to join them. Right after he stunned Jenks into unconsciousness and left him to fry on my car's dashboard. *What an ass.*

"Hi, Tom," I said dryly. "How's the wand hanging?"

The I.S. officer backed up with his eyes on Jenks. His face reddened when someone laughed at him for being afraid of a four-inch pixy. The truth of it was, he should be. Something that small and winged could be lethal. And Tom knew it.

"Morgan," Tom said, nose wrinkled as he breathed in the burnt-amber-tainted air. "I am not surprised. Summoning demons in public?" His gaze traveled over the trashed store, and a mocking *tsk-tsk* came from him. "This is going to cost you."

My breath quickened when I remembered Minias, and I spun. True to his word, the demon was behaving himself, standing still as every incoming I.S. officer pointed their weapons, both conventional and magic, at him.

My mother made a puff of noise, her high heels clacking as she strode to him. "A demon? Are you insane?" she said as she tucked our purchases under an arm to take Minias's hand and pat it. I froze in shock. Minias looked even more surprised.

"Do you honestly think my daughter is so stupid she'd let a demon out of a circle?" she continued, her smile bright. "In the middle of Cincinnati? Three days before Halloween? It's a costume. This kind man helped my daughter repel the demons and got caught in the crossfire." She beamed up at him, and Minias delicately removed his hand from hers, curling his fingers into a tight fist. "Isn't that so, dear?"

Minias silently sidestepped away from my mother. I felt a tug on my awareness as something was drawn from the ever-after to this side of the lines, and Minias pulled a wallet from his back pocket.

"My papers . . . gentlemen," the demon said, giving me a smirk before he passed Tom what looked like one of those ID holders you see on cop shows.

The clerk slumped against the first officer, wailing. "There were two of them in robes and one in a green costume! I think that's the green one there. They trashed the store! They knew her name. That woman is a black witch and everyone knows it!

It's been in the papers and the news. She's a menace! A freak and a menace!"

Jenks bristled, but it was my mother who said, "Get a grip, Pat. She didn't call them."

"But the store!" Patricia insisted, her fear turning to anger now that I.S. officers surrounded her. "Who's going to pay for this?"

"Look," I said, feeling Jenks shivering between me and the scarf. "My partner is cold sensitive. Can we wrap this up? I haven't broken the law as far as I can see."

Tom looked up from reading Minias's ID. He squinted from the picture to Minias, then handed it to someone far older standing behind him with a curt, "Pull it."

Unease trickled through me, but Minias didn't seem to be troubled. Jenks pinched my ear when Tom moved to stand before me, and I jerked out of my reverie.

"You shouldn't have turned us down, Morgan," the witch said, so close I could smell a witch's characteristic redwood smell rolling off of him. The more magic you practiced, the stronger you smelled, and Tom reeked. I thought of Minias and felt a moment of worry. He might look like a witch, but he would smell like a demon, and they'd seen me let him out. *Crap. Think, Rachel. Don't react, think!*

"Somehow," Tom said softly, threateningly, "I don't think your friend Minias is going to have a record. Any record at all. Sort of like a demon?"

My thoughts scrambled, and I felt more than saw Minias ease up behind me.

"I'm sure Mr. Bansen will find my papers are in order," he said, and I shivered when a chill ran through me, pulled into existence from the draft of Jenks's wings.

"Holy crap! Minias smells like a witch!" the pixy whispered.

I took a deep breath, my shoulders relaxing when I found Minias did indeed lack the characteristic burnt-amber scent that clung to all demons. I turned to him in surprise, and the demon shrugged, twisting his hand. It was still in a fist, and my lips parted when I realized he hadn't opened his fingers since my mother had taken his hand.

Eyes widening, I spun to my mother to find her beaming. She'd given him an amulet? My mother was crazy, but she was crazy like a fox.

"Can we go?" I said, knowing Tom was trying to get a good sniff of him as well.

Tom's eyes narrowed. Taking my elbow, he pulled me from Minias. "That is a demon."

"Prove it. And as you once told me, it's not against the law to summon demons."

His face went ugly. "Maybe not, but you're responsible for the damage they do."

A groan slipped from Jenks, and I felt my face go stiff.

"She destroyed my store!" the woman wailed. "Who's going to pay for this! Who?"

An I.S. officer approached with Minias's ID, and while Tom held up a finger for me to wait, he talked to him. My mother joined me, and the people outside complained as an officer started to make them move on. Tom was frowning when the man left, and bolstered by his show of bad temper, I smiled cattily. I was going to walk out of here. I knew it.

"Ms. Morgan," he said as he slid his wand away. "I have to let you go—"

"What about the store?" the woman wailed.

"Can it, Patricia!" my mother said, and Tom grimaced as if he'd eaten a spider.

"As long as you agree that demons were here because of you," he added, "and you agree to pay for damages," he finished, handing Minias his ID back.

"But it wasn't my fault." My gaze scanned the broken shelves and scattered amulets as I tried to add up the potential cost. "Why should I have to pay for it because someone sicced them on me? I didn't summon them!"

Tom smiled, and my mother squeezed my elbow. "You're

welcome to come down to the I.S. and file a countercomplaint."

Nice. "I'll accept the damages." So much for the air conditioner fund. "Come on," I said, reaching for Minias. "Let's get out of here."

My hand passed right through him. I froze, but I didn't think anyone had noticed. Glancing at his irate face, I gestured sourly for him to go before me. "After you," I said, then hesitated. I wasn't going to do this at the coffeehouse two blocks away. Not with the I.S. buzzing like fairies around a sparrow nest. "My car is about five spots down. It's the red convertible, and you're riding in back."

Minias's eyebrows rose. "As you say . . . ," he murmured, rocking into motion.

Looking proud and satisfied, my mother snatched my purchases up, linked her arm in mine, and like magic the crowd parted to show us the door.

"You okay, Jenks?" I questioned when the cool of the night hit us.

"Just get me in the car," he said, and I carefully wrapped my scarf about my neck once more to snuggle him in.

Coffee with my mom and a demon. Yeah, that was a good idea.

Two

The coffeehouse was warm, smelling of biscotti and brewing beans. Jenks went to my mom's shoulder when I loosened my scarf, but I didn't take it off, not knowing if my neck showed Al's fingerprints or not. It sure hurt enough to. *Al is out? How am I going to shut this down?*

Gently rubbing my neck, I lingered at the door to watch Minias, Jenks, and my mother find their place in line. The heavy-charm detection alarm was glaring a harsh red—responding to Minias most likely—but no one in the crowded place was paying it any mind. It was three days before Halloween, and everyone was trying out their spells.

The demon looked tall beside my mother as she fidgeted. Her cream-colored leather clutch purse matched her shoes to perfection; I must have gotten my fashion sense from my dad. I knew I had gotten my height from him, putting me several inches taller than my mom and a shade shorter than Minias, even in my boots. And my athletic build had certainly come from my dad. Not that my mom was a slouch, but memories of afternoons at Eden Park and pictures from before he had died reassured me that I was as much my father's daughter as my mother's. It made me feel good, thinking that a part of him lived on though he'd been gone twelve years. He'd been a great dad, and I still missed him when my life got out of control. Which was more often than I liked to admit. Behind me, the irritating heavy-charm detector gave a final pulse and went dark.

Relieved, I eased up behind Minias, making his shoulders stiffen. He'd been markedly quiet in the car, giving me the creeps as he sat rigidly behind me while my mother sat sideways in her seat to watch him. She had disguised the scrutiny by trying to engage him in conversation while I called Ivy and left a message for her to run across the street and warn Ceri that Al was on the loose again. The demon's ex-familiar didn't have a phone, which was getting tiresome.

I was hoping my mother's light banter had been a ploy to ease the tension and not her usual out-of-touch-with-reality mentality. She and Minias were on a first-name basis now, which I thought was swell. Still, if he had wanted to cause problems, he could have done it half a dozen times between the charm shop and here. He was biding his time, and I felt like a bug on a pin.

My mother and Jenks edged out of line to ogle the pastries, and when the Were trio ahead of us finished ordering and moved off, Minias stepped forward, glancing indolently at the hanging menu. A man in a business suit behind us huffed impatiently, then went pale and backed up when the demon eyed him through his dark glasses.

Minias turned back to the counter attendant and smiled. "Latte grande, double espresso, Italian blend. Light on the froth, extra cinnamon. Use whole milk. Not two percent or half-and-half. Whole milk. Put it in porcelain."

"We can do that!" the kid behind the counter said enthusiastically, and I looked up. His voice sounded familiar. "And for you, ma'am?"

"Uh," I stumbled, "coffee. Black. That's it."

Minias looked askance at me, his surprise clear even through his dark glasses, and the kid behind the counter blinked. "What kind?" he asked.

"Doesn't matter." I shifted from foot to foot. "Mom, what do you want?"

My mother cheerfully hustled back to the counter with Jenks on her shoulder. "I'll have a Turkish espresso and a slice of that cheesecake if someone will share it with me."

"I will," Jenks sang out, startling the guy behind the register. He still had that paper clip sword with him, and it made me feel better.

My mom glanced at me, and when I nodded that I'd have some, too, she beamed. "I'll have that, then. With forks for all of us." She shyly looked to Minias, and the demon stepped back almost out of my peripheral vision.

The kid snuck glances at Jenks as he punched that in, announcing, "Fourteen eighty-five."

"We have one more person here," I said, trying not to frown, and Jenks landed on the counter with his hands on his hips. I hated it when people ignored him. And asking him to share simply because he wasn't going to eat much was patronizing.

"I want an espresso," he said proudly. "Black. But give me the domestic blend. That Turkish crap gives me the runs for a week."

"TMI, Jenks," I muttered while I yanked my shoulder bag forward. "Why don't you find a table? Maybe a corner without a lot of people?"

"With your back to the wall. You got it," he said, clearly doing better in the shop's moist, balmy climate. A sustained temp below forty would send him into hibernation, and though Cincinnati was regularly hitting that after dark, the stump he and his huge family lived in would retain enough heat to keep them warm until almost mid-November. I was already dreading his brood moving into the church Ivy and I lived in, but they would not hibernate and risk Matalina, his ailing wife, dying of the cold. Jenks was why I wore the scarf; it wasn't for my comfort.

Glad for the warmth of the shop myself, I unzipped my coat. I handed the kid a twenty, then dropped the change into the tip jar, making the businessman wait while I scribbled "client meeting" on the receipt and tucked it away.

Turning, I found my mother and Minias standing uneasily beside a table against the wall. Jenks was on the light fixture, the dust slipping from him rising in the bulb's heat. They were waiting for me to sit down before choosing their seats, so grabbing some napkins, I headed over.

"This looks great, Jenks," I said as I edged behind my mom to reach the chair against the wall. Immediately my mother sat to my left, and Minias chose the chair to my right, shifting it a foot back before sitting down. He was almost in the aisle; apparently we both wanted our space. I took the opportunity to remove my jacket, and my expression froze when the bracelet Kisten had given me slipped to my wrist. Pain hit, almost panic, and I didn't look at anyone as I tucked it behind the sleeve of my sweater.

I wore the bracelet because I had loved Kisten and still wasn't ready to let him go. The one time I'd taken it off, I found myself unable to tuck it away in my jewelry box next to the sharp vampire caps he'd given me. Maybe if I knew who had murdered him I could have moved on.

Ivy hadn't had much luck tracking down the vampire Piscary had given Kisten to as a legal blood gift. I had been sure that Sam, one of Piscary's lackeys, had known who it was, but he hadn't. The human polygraph test at the FIB, or Federal Inderland Bureau—the human-run version of the I.S.—was pretty good, but the witch charm I had around Sam's neck when Ivy "asked" him about it was better. That was the last time I helped her question anyone, however. The living vampire scared me when she was pissed.

That Ivy wasn't getting results was unusual. Her investigative skills were as good as my ability to get into trouble. Since the "Sam incident," we had agreed to let her handle our search, and I was getting impatient at her lack of progress, but my slamming vampires into a wall for information wasn't prudent. What made it worse was that the answer was buried somewhere in my unconsciousness. Maybe I should have talked to the FIB's psychologist to see if he could pull something to light? But Ford made me uneasy. He could sense emotions faster than Ivy could smell them.

Uncomfortable, I scanned the décor of the busy place. Behind my mother was one of those stupid pictures with babies dressed up as fruit or flowers or something. My lips parted and I looked at Jenks, then to the counter where the college-age kid managed the customers with a professional polish. *This was it!* I thought in a surge of recognition. This was the same coffeehouse where Ivy, Jenks, and I had agreed to quit the I.S. and work as independent runners! But Junior looked like he knew what he was doing now, sporting a manager tag on his red-and-white-striped apron and with several underlings to handle the nastier parts of running the place.

"Hey, Rache," Jenks said as he dropped down to dust my sweater with gold. "Isn't this the store we—"

"Yup," I interrupted him, not wanting Minias to be privy to more of my life than necessary. The demon was unfolding a paper napkin and meticulously settling it across a jeans-clad knee as if it were silk. Unease flowed through me as I remembered the night I decided to leave the I.S. Going clueless into an independent bounty hunter/escort service/jack-of-all-magical-trades runner service with a vamp had been one of the most stupid and best decisions of my life. It went along with Ivy and Jenks's opinion that I lived my life to find the edge of disaster so I could feel the rush of adrenaline.

Maybe I had once, but not anymore. Believing I had killed Jenks and Ivy with one of my stunts had cured me one hundred percent, and Kisten's death had slammed the lesson home, hard. And to prove it, I *wasn't* going to work with Minias no matter what he offered. I wouldn't repeat the past. I could change my patterns of behavior. I would. Starting here. *Watch me.*

"Coffee up!" the kid shouted, and Minias took his napkin from his lap as if he was going to rise.

"I'll get it," I said, wanting to minimize his interactions with everyone.

Minias eased down without a fuss. I gathered myself to stand, then frowned. I didn't want to leave him with my mother either.

"Oh, for God's sake," my mother said, standing to drop her purse loudly on the table. "I'll get it."

Minias touched her arm, and I bristled. "If you would, Alice, bring the cinnamon with you?" he asked, and my mother nodded, slowly pulling from his fingers. She was holding her arm when she walked away, and I leaned toward Minias.

"Don't touch my mother," I threatened, feeling better when Jenks took an aggressive stance on the table, his wings clattering menacingly.

"Someone needs to touch her," Minias said dryly. "She hasn't been touched in twelve years."

"She doesn't need to be touched by you." I leaned back with my arms crossed over my middle. My gaze went to my mother, who was flirting in an old-lady way with the counter kid, and I paused. She hadn't remarried when Dad died, hadn't even dated. I knew she intentionally dressed herself to look older than she was to keep men at a distance. With the right haircut and dress, we could pass as big sister, little sister. As a witch, her life span was a good hundred and sixty years, and while most witches waited until they were sixty before starting a family, she had had Robbie and me very early in her life, giving up a promising career to raise us first. Maybe we were accidents. Passion babies.

That brought a smile to my face, and I forced it away when I noticed Minias watching me. I straightened as my mom approached with a canister of cinnamon and her plate of cheesecake; the kid behind the counter was following with the rest. "Thank you, Mark," she said as he placed everything on the table and backed up a step. "You're a sweet boy."

I smiled at Mark's sigh. Clearly he wasn't happy with the title. He glanced at me, then Jenks, his eyes brightening. "Hey," he said as he tucked the tray under his arm. "I think I've seen you somewhere. . . ."

I cringed. Most times people recognized me, it was from the news clip of me being dragged on my ass down the street by a demon. The local news had incorporated it into their front credits. Sort of like that guy on skis pinwheeling over the finish line in the agony of defeat.

"No," I said, unable to look at him as I pulled the lid off my cup of coffee. *Ah, coffee.*

"Yes," he insisted, weight on one foot. "You've got that escort service. In the Hollows?"

I didn't know if that was better or not, and I looked tiredly up at him. I'd done escort service before, not *that* kind of escort service, but real stuff, dangerous stuff. I had a boat blow up around me once. "Yeah, that's me."

Minias looked up from shaking cinnamon on his coffee. Jenks snickered, and I bumped my knee on the underside of the table to make his espresso slop over. "Hey!" he shouted, rising up a few inches, then settled back down, still laughing.

The front door jingled, and the kid shot off his glad-to-have-you-here spiel and left. Minias was the only one listening.

My coffee was steaming, and I hunched over it while I watched the demon. His long fingers were interlaced about the white soup-bowl mug as if relishing its warmth, and though I couldn't tell for sure because of the sunglasses, I think his eyes closed as he took the first sip. A look of bliss so deep it couldn't have been faked slipped over him, easing his features and turning him into a vision of relaxed pleasure.

"I'm listening," I said, and a mask of nothing fell between us.

My mother quietly ate her cheesecake, her eyes flicking uneasily between us. I had the distinct impression she thought I was being rude.

"And I'm not happy," I added, making her lips press tightly. "You told me Al was contained." I lifted my coffee and blew across the top. "What are you going to do about him breaking his word and coming after me? What do you think will happen when this gets out?" I took a sip, forgetting for a moment where I was when it slipped down, easing my slight headache and relaxing my muscles. Jenks cleared his throat, bringing me back.

"You won't have a chance of luring anyone into any agreements again," I said as my focus cleared. "No more familiars. Won't that be nice?" I finished with a simpering smile.

His eyes on the delights of that fruit-baby picture, Minias sipped his drink with his elbows on the table and his mug propped up at mouth height. "This is much better this side of the lines," he said softly.

"Yeah," Jenks said. His espresso cup came up to his waist. "That burnt amber really sticks in your throat, doesn't it?"

A flicker of annoyance flashed across Minias, and a thread of tension entered his stance of relaxed idleness. I took a deep breath, smelling only coffee, cheesecake, and the characteristic redwood scent of a witch. I was sure my mom had slipped him a charm, and I wasn't looking forward to finding the cost of such an expensive amulet tacked on to the losses from the store. But if it kept him from smelling like a demon and causing a panic, I couldn't complain.

"Well, what do you want?" I said, setting my cup down. "I don't have all night."

My mom frowned, but Minias took it in stride, easing back in his stiff chair and setting his giant mug aside. "Al is being summoned out of confinement—"

"We figured that part out," Jenks said snottily.

"Jenks . . . ," I murmured, and the pixy walked across the table with his makeshift sword to the cheesecake.

"We've never run into this before," Minias said, hesitating as he took in Jenks's "whatever" attitude. "Because of his extraordinary amount of contact with this side of the lines, Al has arranged for someone to summon him every sundown. They get what they want, then release him without the compulsion to return to the ever-after. It's a win-win situation for both of them."

And a lose-lose for me. My thoughts flashed to my old boy-friend, Nick. Jenks eyed me over a chunk of cheesecake as big as his head, clearly thinking the same thing. Nick was a thief who habitually used demons as a source of information. Thanks to Glenn at the FIB, I had a copy of his file in my dresser's bottom drawer. It was so thick a monster rubber band barely kept it shut. I didn't like thinking about it.

"Someone's freeing a demon without compulsion to return to the ever-after?" I managed, my eyes lowered. "That's not very responsible."

"It's extremely clever. For Al." Minias's one elbow found the table as he took a draught.

I cringed, fully conscious of my mom listening quietly. "You think someone's doing this to kill me?" I finally asked.

Minias shrugged. "I don't know. Nor do I care, really. I sim-ply want it to stop."

A reproachful huff came from my mother, and Minias pulled his elbow from the table. "We can regain control of him after sunup," the demon said, his eyes hidden behind his glasses. "When the lines close to cross-traffic, he's snapped back to our side. Finding him then is just a matter of using his demon marks."

I pulled my hands from atop the table, my fingers pushing aside Kisten's bracelet to feel the raised scar. The demon mark had flared into pain just before Al showed up, and a new worry settled in beside the old ones. That's how Al had found me. Crap. I didn't like feeling like a tagged antelope.

"Al doesn't have access to a lab while in custody," Minias said, drawing my attention back. "So he only has simple, eas-ily performed curses, but he's exceptionally adept at line jump-ing."

"Well, he's been in someone's kitchen. He looks like he al-ways does, and I know that's not his natural form." *I don't want to know what he looks like. I really don't.*

Minias's head moved up and down once, and he swallowed his coffee. "Yes," he said softly as he leaned back. "Someone has been helping him. That he tried to take you tonight went a long way toward convincing me it wasn't you."

"Me?" I blurted. "You really think I'd work with *him*?" Then my fingers, gripping my coffee, went weak. Appearance charms didn't just happen in one night. That meant that Al . . . My eyes rose, and I wished Minias would take off his glasses. "How long has Al been slipping your containment?"

Minias's lips twitched. "This is the third night in a row."

Fear jolted me, and Jenks rose from the table, red dust slipping from him.

"And you didn't think I might want to know that?" I exclaimed.

In a smooth motion, Minias took off his glasses. His arm flat on the table, he leaned in to me. "How much effort do you expect me to exert?" he said tightly, and I blinked at the irate emotion reflected in his goat-slitted eyes. "We don't care if he kills you or not. I have no reason to help you."

"But you did," I said belligerently, thinking anger seemed better than fear. "Why?" Immediately Minias backed down, and seeing there was something here he didn't want to talk about, I decided I did.

"I was tracking Al," the demon said. "That you were there was merely helpful."

Jenks began laughing, and all eyes turned to him as he rose several inches. "You got sacked, didn't you," he said, and Minias stiffened.

My first impulse to protest died at Minias's stoic face. "You got fired?" The demon's reach for his oversize mug almost smacked Jenks in its quickness.

"Why else would he be tracking Al instead of watching TV with Newt?" Jenks said, flitting to the safety of my shoulder. "You got canned. Outsourced. Pink-slipped. Handed your walking papers. Given the go light. Slipped on the banana. Served the dead slug."

Minias put his glasses back on. "I've been reassigned," he said tightly.

Suddenly I was afraid. Really afraid. "You aren't watching Newt?" I whispered, and Minias looked surprised by my fear.

"Who is Newt?" my mother asked, dabbing a napkin at her lips and sliding the last half of the cheesecake to me.

"She's just the most powerful demon they got over there," Jenks boasted as if he had something to do with it. "Minias was her babysitter. She's more dangerous than a militant fairy on Brimstone, and she's the one who cursed the church last year before I bought it. Didn't twitch a wing. She's got a major burr up her ass about Rachel."

Minias bit back a snort, and I wished Jenks would shut up. My mother hadn't known about the "blasphemy incident."

"There are no female demons," my mother said, fumbling in her purse to bring out a compact and her lipstick. "Your father was very clear on that."

"Apparently he was mistaken." I picked up a fork but immediately set it down. I'd lost my desire for cheesecake about five surprises ago. Gut clenching, I turned to Minias. "So who's watching Newt?"

The demon's face lost all its amusement. "Some young punk," he said sullenly, surprising me with the modern phrase.

Jenks, though, was delighted. "You lost Newt one too many times, and they replaced you with a younger demon. Oh, that's beautiful!"

Minias's hand quivered, his fingers abruptly loosening on his mug when a soft crack rang out from the porcelain.

"Stop it, Jenks," I said, wondering how much of Minias losing his job was due to Newt slipping away on his watch, and how much was from the demon's inability to make impartial decisions regarding her security. I'd seen them together, and Minias clearly cared for her. Too much to lock her up when she needed it, probably.

"How do they expect me to seduce her and maintain her adherence to the law simultaneously?" he snarled. "It can't be done. Damned fool bureaucrats don't know the first thing about love and dominance."

Seduce her? I arched my eyebrows, but an icy sensation rippled through me at the glimpse of his anger and frustration. Silence, thick and uncomfortable, took over, making the surrounding conversation seem louder. Seeing us staring, Minias forced his tension from him. His sigh was so soft, I wasn't sure I hadn't imagined it.

"Al can't be allowed to flaunt the rules," he said, as if he hadn't just shown us the pain in his soul. "If I can contain him, I can return to supervising Newt."

"Rachel!" my mother exclaimed, and I turned to see a familiar mask of lighthearted ignorance on her. "He's a runner, just like you! You should go out to a movie or something."

"Mom, he's a—" I hesitated. "He's not a runner," I said, stopping just short of saying he was a demon. "And he certainly isn't date material." Guilt hit me. I'd pushed her, and she was slipping into old patterns. Cursing myself, I pulled my attention to Minias, just wanting to wrap this up and get out of here. "Sorry," I said to apologize for my mother.

Minias's face was still empty. "I don't do witches."

I had a hard time not finding offense in that, but Jenks saved me from making a total ass out of myself by buzzing his wings to gain everyone's attention.

"So let me get this straight," he said, hovering a breath above the sticky table with one hand on his hip, the other pointing that plastic-coated paper clip at Minias. "You lost your cushy babysitting job and are now trying to gain control of a demon who has limited power and resources. And you can't do it?"

"It's not a matter of gaining control over him," Minias protested indignantly. "We can catch him. We simply can't contain him after sunset. As I told you, someone is summoning him out of confinement."

"And you can't stop them?" I questioned, thinking of the charmed zip-strips that the I.S. used to keep ley line practitioners from jumping out of custody via a ley line.

Minias shook his head and his glasses caught the light. "No.

We catch him, confine him, and when the sun goes down, he pops out, rested and fed. He's laughing at us. Me."

I disguised my shiver by taking a sip of my coffee. "Any idea who's doing it?" My thoughts went to Nick, and the coffee turned to acid in my stomach.

"Not anymore." His boots scraped against the gritty floor. "Soon as I find out, they die."

Nice. Fumbling for my mom's hand under the table, I gave it a squeeze.

"Do you have any idea as to who might be helping him?" Minias asked next, and I forced myself to keep breathing.

Nick, I thought, but I wouldn't say it aloud. Not even if he *was* sending Al to hurt me—because if it was Nick, I'd take care of him myself. I could feel Jenks's eyes on me, wanting me to say it, but I wouldn't. "Why don't you just get rid of his summoning name?" I said, looking for other options. "You do that, and he can't be summoned out."

The skin visible past Minias's sunglasses tightened. He knew I wasn't saying something. "You can't throw away a password. Once you have one, it's yours." He hesitated, and I felt the gathering of trouble. "You can exchange it with someone else's, though."

The ribbon of tension around my chest squeezed, and all my warning flags went up.

"If someone exchanged names with him," Minias drawled into the conversation-rich air, "we could contain him. Unfortunately, because of his job, he's been very lax with his summoning name. There are an astounding number of people on this side of the lines who know it, and no demon will willingly take it." Minias stared at me. "They have no reason to."

My fingers tightened on my waxed paper cup, sure now I knew why Minias was sitting at a table sipping coffee with me. I had a password. I had a reason to trade. I had a major problem.

"So what does that have to do with my daughter?" my mother said, her voice thick with warning. Fear caused her to drop the scattered-thoughts image she used as a buffer to hide the damage my dad's death had wrought.

Minias adjusted his glasses to give himself time to weigh the emotions at our table. "I want your daughter to exchange passwords with Al."

"No fairy-crap way." The dust slipping from Jenks was a red so deep that it seemed black.

"Absolutely not," I echoed. I scowled and slid my chair back.

Unperturbed, Minias shook more cinnamon into his coffee. "Then he'll kill you. I don't care."

"Obviously you do or you wouldn't be here," I said sharply. "You can't hold him without my name. You don't care if I live or die. It's you you're worried about."

My mom sat stiff and miserable. "Will you remove her demon marks if she does this? All of them?"

"Mom!" I exclaimed, not aware that she even knew about my demon marks.

Green eyes full of pain, she took my cold fingers in hers. "Your aura is filthy, honey. And I do watch the news. If this demon can remove your marks and purge your aura, then you should at least find out what the consequences or possible side effects are."

"Mom, it's not just a password, it's a summoning name!"

Minias gazed at my mother with a new interest. "It's a summoning name that has no pull on you," he said. "The most that will likely happen is you fielding a few months of redirected calls to Al."

I took my hand from my mother's, not believing this was happening. "You said I had to pick a name no one could figure out, that if someone did, they could make my life miserable. Do you know how many people know Al's name? I don't, but it's more than know mine." Done with this, I pushed myself from the table. The chair scraped, and the vibration went all the way up my spine and made me shiver.

"That's the point, witch," Minias said, making the word an insult. "If you don't, you're going to die. I intervened tonight in the hope you'd be willing to come to an arrangement, but I won't do it again. I simply don't care."

Fear, or maybe adrenaline, sparked through me. Arrangement? He meant a deal. A deal with a demon. My mother's eyes pleaded with me, and Jenks lifted his poker, bristling. "Is that a threat?" he snarled, his wings going red with his increased circulation.

"A statement of odds." Minias set his cup down with a sense of finality. The napkin was next, folded and laid flat beside it. "Yes or no."

"Pick someone else," I said. "There are millions of witches. Someone has got to be more stupid than me and say yes. Give them a name and exchange it with Al."

He looked at me from over his shades. "You're one of two witches this side of the lines whose blood is capable of making a strong enough bond. Yes or no?"

Oh, back to the demon magic thing. Swell. "So use Lee," I said bitterly. "He's stupid." As well as aggressive, ambitious, and now a basket case from having been Al's familiar for a couple of months before I rescued him. Sort of. God, no wonder Al hated me.

Minias sighed and crossed his arms over his chest. A faint whiff of Brimstone tickled my nose. "He has too close a tie to Al," he said, his gaze on the ceramic mug cradled in his hands. "He wouldn't do it. I asked. The man is a coward."

My neck stiffened. "And if common sense makes me say no, then I'm a coward, too?"

"You can't be summoned," he said, as if I was being obstinate. "Why are you balking?"

"Al would know my name." Just the thought made my pulse quicken.

"You know his."

For one brief moment I considered it. Then the thought of

Kisten flashed through me. I couldn't take the chance. Not again. This wasn't a game, and there was no reset button. "No," I said abruptly. "We're done here."

My mother's shoulders eased and Jenks's feet touched the table. I was wire tight, wondering if this truce would last now that I had said no, whereupon he'd return to a normal demonic frame of mind and trash the place along with what was left of my reputation. But Minias finished his coffee in a final swallow, raising his hand and motioning for the clerk to make one more to go. He rose, and my held breath escaped. "As you want it," Minias said as he picked up the cinnamon and stood. "I won't be conveniently coming to save you a second time."

I was about to tell him where he could shove his convenience, but Al *was* going to show up again, and if I could call Minias to collect him, my chances of survival would increase—I thought. I didn't have to take Minias up on his offer, just survive until I figured out who was summoning Al and deal with him or her myself. Demon summoning wasn't illegal, but my foot in their gut a couple of times might convince them it was a really bad idea. And if it was Nick? Well, that would be a real pleasure.

"What if I think about it?" I said, and my mother gave me a nervous smile and a pat on my arm. *See, I can use my brain, too.*

Minias smirked as if he saw right through me. "Don't think too long," he said, accepting the paper cup Junior was extending to him. "I've gotten word that they caught him on the West Coast trying to ride the shadow of night into tomorrow. The pattern-shift indicates he has everything he needs and all that's left is implementing it."

I refused to show my fear, not swallowing though my mouth was dry.

Minias leaned close, the scent of burnt amber high in my imagination as his breath shifted my hair. "You're safe until the sun goes down tomorrow, Rachel Mariana Morgan. Hunt fast."

Jenks rose up on his dragonfly wings, clearly frustrated as he stayed just out of the demon's easy reach. "Why don't you just kill Al?"

Tucking the entire container of cinnamon into a jacket pocket, Minias shrugged. "Because we haven't had a demon birth in five thousand years." He hesitated, then shook his arm to cause an amulet to slip from his sleeve and fall into his fingers. "Thank you, Alice, for the use of your amulet. If your daughter is half as skilled in the kitchen as you, she would make a fine familiar."

Mom had made it herself? I thought. *Not simply invoked a pilfered one?*

The cloying scent of burnt amber rolled over me, and my mother blushed. It was obvious by the protests of the surrounding people that they had noticed the stench as well, and Minias smiled an empty smile behind the mirrored black glasses. "If you would banish me?"

I'd totally forgotten. "Oh. Sure," I mumbled as the people behind him turned with their hands over their noses in complaint. "Ah, demon, I demand that you depart here and return directly to the ever-after to not bother us again this night."

And with a nod, Minias vanished.

The people behind him gasped, and I waved. "University professor late for a class," I lied, and they turned, laughing at their fear and dismissing the stench as an early Halloween prank.

"Lord help you, Rachel," my mother said sourly. "If that's how you treat men, it's no wonder you can't keep a boyfriend."

"Mom, he's not a man. He's a demon!" I protested softly, pausing as she pocketed that charm. Clearly hair straighteners weren't the only thing she was trading to Patricia. Scent amulets weren't hard to make, but one strong enough to block out a demon's stench was highly unusual. Talk about your niche market. Maybe she was specializing in charms no one else bothered with to avoid competition—and thus lawsuits—from annoyed, licensed charm makers.

Eyes on my coffee, I said, "Mom, about those amulets you've been making for Patricia."

Jenks took to the air, and my mother huffed. "You're never going to find Mr. Right if you don't start playing with Mr. Right Now," she said, gathering everything up on her plate. "Minias is obviously Mr. Never, but you could have been a little nicer."

Jenks shrugged, and I sighed.

"I noticed he didn't offer to get the tab, though, did he?" my mother finished.

I took another swallow of my coffee and gathered myself to rise. I wanted to get home to my sanctified church before any more demons popped into my life with nasty solicitations. Not to mention I had to talk to Ceri. Make sure Ivy had told her Al was out.

As I slowly followed Jenks and my mom to the trash and then the door, my thoughts swung back to what Minias had said about no new demons being born for the last five thousand years. He was at least five thousand years old and had been assigned to monitor and seduce a female demon? And why no new demons? Was it because there were so few female demons left, or because having sex with one could be deadly?

Three

I set the stack of unopened desk organizers I'd bought last month on the scratched hardwood floor of the sanctuary, wincing at the high-pitched squeal of pixy children as they swarmed into the nook of my desk that I had just opened up. They weren't moving in for the winter yet, but Matalina was getting a jump on prepping my desk. I couldn't blame her for the fall cleaning. I didn't use my desk much, and there was more dust gathering than work done at it.

The urge to sneeze took me, and I held my breath, eyes watering until the feeling evaporated. *Thank you, God.* I glanced at Jenks at the front of the church, where he was keeping a fair number of his younger kids busy, and out of the way, with decorating the sanctuary for Halloween. He was a good dad, a part of him that was easy to overlook when he was out busting bad guys with me. I hoped I found half as good a man when I was ready to start a family.

The memory of Kisten—blue eyes smiling—swam up, and my heart seemed to clench. It had been months, but reminders of him still came fast and hard. And I didn't even know where the thought of children had come from. There wouldn't have been any with Kisten, unless we fell back on the age-old tradition of borrowing a girlfriend's brother or husband for a night, practices born long before the Turn, when to be a witch would sign your death warrant. But now even that hope was gone.

Jenks met my eyes, and a gentle dusting of gold contentment slipped from him as he watched Matalina. His pretty wife looked great. She had been fine all this summer, but I knew Jenks was watching her like the proverbial hawk with the onset of the cold. Matalina barely looked eighteen, but pixy life spans were a mere twenty years, and it made me heartsick that it was only a matter of time before we'd be doing this with Jenks as well. A secure territory and steady food supply could do only so much in lengthening their lives. We were hoping that by removing the need for them to hibernate they all would benefit, but there was a limit to what good living, willow bark, and fern seed could do.

Turning away before Jenks could see my misery, I put my hands on my hips and stared at my cluttered desk.

"'Scuse me," I said, pitching my voice high as I edged my hands among the darting shapes of Matalina's eldest daughters. They were chatting so fast that it sounded like they were speaking another language. "Let me get those magazines out of your way."

"Thank you, Ms. Morgan!" one hollered cheerfully, and I carefully pulled out the stack of *Modern Witchcraft for Today's Young Woman* out from under her as she rose up. I never read them, but I hadn't been able to turn down the kid on my doorstep. I hesitated with the stack in my arms, not knowing if I should throw them out or put them next to my bed to someday read, maybe, finally dumping them on the swivel chair to deal with later.

A fluttering of black paper rose up as Jenks flew into the rafters with a small paper bat trailing after him by a thin thread. The smell of rubber cement mixed with the spicy scent of chili slow-cooking in the Crock-Pot Ivy had bought at a yard sale, and Jenks taped the string to a beam before dropping down for another. The swirl of silk and four-part harmony pulled my attention back to my desk, now barren, making the tiny nooks and drawers a pixy paradise done in oak. "All set, Matalina?" I asked, and the tiny woman smiled with a duster made from the fluff of a dandelion in her hand.

"This is wonderful," she said, her wings a blur of nothing. "You are too generous, Rachel. I know how much of a bother we all are."

"I like you staying with us," I said, knowing I'd find pixy tea parties in my spice drawer before the week was through. "You make everything more alive."

"Noisy, rather," she said, sighing as she looked to the front of the church and the papers Ivy had spread to protect the hardwood floor from the arts and crafts. Pixies living in the church was a bloody nuisance, but I'd do anything to put off the inevitable another year. If there was a charm or spell, I'd use it in a heartbeat, regardless of its legality. But there wasn't. I had looked. Several times. Pixy life spans sucked.

I smiled wistfully at Matalina and her daughters as they set up housekeeping, and after rolling the top of the desk down to leave the now-traditional one-inch gap, I grabbed my clipboard and looked for somewhere to sit. On it was a growing list of ways to detect a demon summoning. In the margin was a short list of people who might want me dead. But there were safer ways to kill someone than sending a demon after them, and I was betting the first list would get me closer to who was summoning Al than the second. After I exhausted the local stuff, I'd look out of state.

The lights were high and the heat was on against the hint of chill in the air, turning the autumn night to a noon summer. The church's sanctuary wasn't much of a sanctuary anymore; the pews and altar had been removed even before I had moved in, leaving a wonderfully open space with narrow stained-glass windows stretching from knee height to the tall ceiling. My desk was atop the shallow stage up front, to the right of where the altar had been.

Back by the dark foyer was Ivy's seldom-played baby grand piano, and tucked into the front corner across from my desk was a new cluster of furniture to give us somewhere to interview prospective clients without dragging them all the way through the church to our private living room at the back. Ivy had a plate of crackers, cheese, and pickled herring arranged on the low coffee table, but it was the pool table my gaze lingered on. It had been Kisten's, and I knew that the reason I was drawn to it was because I missed him.

Ivy and Jenks had given the table to me on my birthday. It was the only piece of him Ivy had taken besides his ashes and her memories. I think she'd given it to me as an unspoken statement that he'd been important to both of us. He had been my boyfriend, but he had been Ivy's onetime live-in and confidant, and probably the only person who truly understood the warped hell that their master vampire, Piscary, had put them through with his version of love.

Things had changed radically in the three months since Ivy's former girlfriend, Skimmer, had killed Piscary and landed herself in jail under a wrongful-death charge. Instead of the expected turf war, with Cincy's secondary vampires struggling to assert their dominance, a new master vampire had stepped in from out of state, one so charismatic that no one rose to challenge him. I'd since learned that bringing in new blood was commonplace, and there were provisions set up in Cincinnati's charter to deal with the sudden absence of a city power.

What was unusual, though, was that the new master vampire had taken in every single one of Piscary's displaced vamps instead of bringing his own camarilla. The small bit of kindness cut short an ugly mess of vampire misery that would have put me and my roommate in serious jeopardy. That the incoming vampire was Rynn Cormel, the very man who had run the country during the Turn, probably had a lot to do with Ivy's quick acceptance. Respect usually came slowly from her, but it was hard not to admire someone who had written a vampire sex guide that sold more copies than a post-Turn bible, and had been president.

I had yet to actually meet the man, but Ivy said that he was quiet and formal, and that she was enjoying getting to know him better. If he was her master vampire, they were going to have a blood tryst at some point. Euwie. I didn't think they had yet, but Ivy was private about that sort of thing, despite her well-earned reputation. I suppose I should have been thankful he hadn't taken Ivy as his scion and made my life hell. Rynn had brought his own scion, and the woman was just about the only living vamp to come with him from Washington.

So after Kisten died, Ivy got a new master vampire, and I got a pool table in my front room. I'd known that a blood-chaste witch and a living vampire could never make it work in the long run. Regardless, I had loved him, and the day I found out who Piscary had given Kisten to like a thank-you card, I was going to sharpen my stakes and go for a visit. Ivy was working on it, but Piscary's hold on her had been so heavy the last few days of his existence that she didn't remember much. At least she no longer believed she had killed Kisten in a blind, jealous rage.

I eased myself up to sit on the edge of the table, smelling the scents of vampire incense and old cigarette smoke rise from the green felt like a balm. It mixed with the odor of tomato paste and the sound of melancholy jazz filtering in from the back of the church, bringing to mind my early mornings spent in the loft of Kisten's dance club, inexpertly knocking pool balls around while I waited for him to finish closing up.

Closing my eyes against the lump in my throat, I pulled my knees up to prop my heels against the bumper and wrapped my arms around my shins. The heat coming from the long Tiffany lamp Ivy had installed over the table beat on the top of my head, hot and close.

My eyes started to fill, and I pushed the pain down. I missed Kisten. His smile, his steady presence, just being with him. I didn't need a man to feel good about myself, but the shared feelings between two people were worth suffering for. Maybe it was time to stop saying no to every guy that tried to ask me out. It had been three months. *Did Kisten mean that little to you?* came an accusing thought, and I held my breath.

"Get off the felt," came Ivy's voice out of my swirl of emotions, and my eyes flashed open. I found her at the top of the hallway leading to the rest of the church, a plate of crackers and pickled herring in one hand, two bottled waters in the other.

"I'm not going to tear it," I said as I dropped my knees to sit cross-legged, loath to move since the only other place to sit was across from her. It was easier to keep our distance than deal with the building pressure of Ivy wanting to sink her teeth and my wanting her to, both of us knowing it would be a bad idea. We'd tried it once and it hadn't worked out well, but I was a get-back-on-the-horse kind of girl—even when I knew better.

Almost of their own accord, my fingers rose to my neck and the nearly unnoticeable bumps of scar tissue marring my otherwise absolutely pristine skin. Seeing my hand where it was, Ivy folded herself gracefully into a chair behind the plate of crackers. She shook her head at me, making the gold tips of her short, sin-black, lusciously straight hair glimmer, frowning at me like a ticked-off cat.

I pulled my hand down and pretended to read the clipboard now propped in my lap. Despite her grimace Ivy seemed relaxed as she eased into the black leather, looking pleasantly exhausted from her workout this afternoon. She was wearing a long, gray, shapeless sweater over her tight exercise outfit, but it couldn't hide her trim, athletic build. Her oval face still carried the glow of exertion, and I could feel her brown eyes watching me as she worked to quell the mild blood lust stirred by the spike of surprise that I had given off when she had startled me.

Ivy was a living vampire, the last living heir of the Tamwood estate, admired by her living vampire kin and envied by her undead ones. Like all high-blood living vampires, she had a good portion of the undead's strengths but none of the drawbacks of light vulnerability or the inability to tolerate sanctified ground or artifacts—she lived in a church to irritate her undead mother. Conceived as a vampire, she'd become an undead in the blink of an eye if she died without any damage for the vampire virus to repair. Only the low-born, or ghouls, needed further attention to make the jump to a damned immortality.

Moved by scent and pheromones, it was an ongoing ballet between us of want and need, desire and will. But I needed protection from the undead who would take advantage of me and my unclaimed scar, and she needed someone who wasn't out for her blood and had the will to say no to the ecstasy a vampire bite could bring. Plus, we were friends. We had been since working together in the I.S., an experienced runner showing a newbie the ropes. I'd, um, been the newbie.

Ivy's blood lust was very real, but at least she didn't need blood to survive as the undead did. I was fine with her sating her urges with anyone she wanted, seeing as Piscary had warped her such that she couldn't separate love from blood or sex. Ivy was bi, so it wasn't a big deal to her. I was straight—last time I checked. But after getting a taste of how good a blood tryst felt, everything was doubly confusing.

It had taken a year, but I finally admitted that I not only respected Ivy but loved her, too—somehow. But I wasn't going to sleep with her just to have her sink her teeth in me unless I was truly attracted to her and not just to the way she could set my blood burning, aching to fill the hole Piscary had carved into her soul, year by year, bite by bite. . . .

Our relationship had gotten complicated. Either I had to sleep with her to safely share blood, or we could try to keep it to a blood exchange alone and run the risk that she would lose control and I'd have to slam her against the wall to get her to stop before she killed me. In Ivy's words, we could share blood without hurt if there was love, or we could share blood without love if I hurt her. There was no middle ground. How nice was that?

Ivy cleared her throat. It was a small sound, but the pixies went silent. "You're going to damage the felt," she almost growled.

My eyebrows rose, and I turned to look at the table, already knowing its surface like the palm of my hand. "Like it's in such good shape?" I asked dryly. "I can't make it any worse. There's a dent in the slate the size of an elbow by the front left pocket, and it looks like someone stitched up nail gouges there in the middle."

Ivy reddened, picking up an old issue of *Vamp Vixen* that she had out for clients. "Oh, my God," I said, untwisting my legs and jumping off as I imagined just how gouges like that could get there. "I'll never be able to play on it again. Thanks a hell of a lot."

Jenks laughed to sound like wind chimes, and he joined me as I headed over for some of the pickled herring. The puff of leather was soothing as I flopped into the couch across from Ivy, dropping my clipboard beside me and reaching for the crackers.

"The blood came right out," she muttered.

"I don't want to know!" I shouted, and she hid behind her magazine. The cover story was SIX WAYS TO LEAVE YOUR SHADOW BEGGING AND BREATHING. Nice.

Silence slipped between us, but it was a comfortable one, which I filled by shoving pickled herring into my mouth. The tart vinegar reminded me of my dad—he had been the one who'd gotten me hooked on the stuff—and I settled back with a cracker and my clipboard.

"What have you come up with so far?" Ivy asked, clearly looking for a shift in topics.

I pulled the pencil from behind my ear. "The usual suspects. Mr. Ray, Mrs. Sarong. Trent." *Beloved city's son, playboy, murdering slicker-than-a-frog-in-a-rainstorm bastard Trent.* But I doubted it was him. Trent hated Al more than I did, having run into him once before to come away with a broken arm and probably a recurring nightmare. Besides, he had cheaper ways to knock me off, and if he did, his secret biolabs would hit the front page.

Jenks was jabbing the point of his sword into the holes of

the crackers to break them into pixy-size pieces. "What about the Withons? You did bust up their plans to marry off their daughter."

"Nah . . . ," I said, not believing anyone could hold a grudge for that. Besides, they were elves. They wouldn't use a demon to kill me. They hated demons more than they hated me. Right?

Jenks's wings blurred and the table was cleared of the crumbs he had made. Eyebrows raised at my doubt, he started layering herring bits on his tiny crackers, each the size of a peppercorn. "How about Lee?" he said. "Minias said he didn't trust him."

I set the arches of my feet on the edge of the coffee table. "Which is why I do." I *had* gotten the man away from Al. One would think that would be worth something, especially when Lee had taken over Cincy's gambling when Piscary died. "Maybe I should talk to him."

Ivy frowned at me over her magazine. "I think it's the I.S. They'd love to see you dead."

My pencil scratched against the yellow tablet. "Inderland Security," I said, feeling a ping of fear drop through me as I added them to the list. Crap, if it *was* the I.S., I had a big problem.

Jenks's wings hummed as he exchanged a look with Ivy. "There's Nick."

I unclenched my jaw almost as fast as it tightened up.

"You know it's him," the pixy said, hands on his hips as Ivy peered at me over the magazine, her pupils slowly dilating. "Why didn't you tell Minias right there? You had him, Rachel. Minias would have taken care of it. And you didn't say a thing!"

Lips pressed tight, I calculated the odds of me hitting him with the pencil if I threw it at him. "I don't know it's Nick, and even if it was, I wouldn't give him to the demons. I'd take care of it myself," I said bitterly. *Think with your head, Rachel, not your heart.* "But maybe I'll give the cookie a call."

Ivy made a small noise and went back to her magazine. "Nick's not that smart. He'd be demon fodder by now."

He was that smart, but I wasn't going to start a witch hunt. Or stupid-human hunt, rather. My blood pressure, though, had gone back down at her low opinion of him, and I reluctantly added his name to the list. "It's not Nick," I said. "It's not his style. Demon summoning leaves traces, either in collecting the materials to do it, the damage done while he's there, or the increase in educated young witches dying of unnatural causes. I'm going to check with the FIB and see if they've found anything odd the last few days."

Ivy leaned forward, knees crossed as she took a cracker. "Don't forget the tabloids," she offered.

"Yeah, thanks," I said, adding that to the list. A "Demons Took My Baby" story could very well be true.

Propping the tip of his metal sword on the table, Jenks leaned against the wooden hilt and let out a piercing chirp by rubbing his wings together. His kids flew up in a noisy flurry by the door, and I held my breath, fearing they were all going to descend on us, but only three came to a swirling, wing-clattering stop, their fresh faces smiling and their innocence beguiling. They were capable of murder, all of them. Down to his youngest daughter.

"Here," he said, handing a cracker to one of his sons. "See that your mom gets this."

"'Kay, Papa," he said, and was gone, his feet never having touched the table. The other two ferried the rest of the portions out in a well-organized display of pixy efficiency. Ivy blinked at the normally nectarivorous pixies descending on the pickled herring like it was maple syrup. They'd eaten an entire fish last year for an extra boost of protein before their hibernation, and though they weren't going to hibernate again this year, the urge was still there.

Sourly contemplating my new and improved list, I cracked the bottled water Ivy had brought me. I thought about heading into the kitchen for a glass of wine, but after glancing at Ivy, I decided to make do with what I had. The pheromones she was kicking out were enough to relax me as much as a shot of whiskey, and if I added to it, I'd probably fall asleep before two in the morning. As it was, I was feeling pretty damn good, and I wasn't going to feel at all guilty that most of it stemmed from her. It was a thousand years of evolution to make finding prey easy, but I felt I deserved it for putting up with all the crap living with a vampire brought. Not that I was that easy to live with either.

I tapped the eraser against my teeth and looked at my list. The Weres were probably out, and Lee. I couldn't imagine the Withons would be that ticked, even if I had busted up their daughter's marriage to Trent. Trent might be angry, though, seeing as I'd gotten him jailed for all of three hours. A sigh lifted through me. I'd built up a lot of animosity with some pretty big people in a remarkably short time. My special talent. I should concentrate on finding traces of demon summoning and go from there, rather than investigating people who might hold a grudge.

The dinner bell Ivy and I used as a doorbell bonged, startling us. A jolt of adrenaline pulsed through me, and Ivy's eyes dilated to a thin rim of brown.

"I'll get it," Jenks said as he flew up from the coffee table, his voice almost lost in the commotion his kids were making from the front corner of the newspaper-plastered sanctuary.

As Ivy went to turn down the music coming in from the back room, I wiped my mouth of cracker crumbs and did a quick tidy at the table. Ivy might take a job two days before Halloween, but if they were looking for me, they were going to be sadly disappointed.

Jenks worked the elaborate pulley system we'd rigged for him, and as soon as the door cracked, an orange cat streaked in. "Cat!" the pixy shrilled as the tabby headed right for his kids.

I bolted upright, breath catching as every pixy in the sanctuary was abruptly eight feet higher. Shrieks and calls echoed, and suddenly the air was full of little black paper bats dangling enticingly from thin strings.

"Rex!" Jenks shouted, darting to land right before the black-eyed animal, which was entranced and frozen by the overwhelming sensory input of twenty-plus dangling bits of paper. "Bad cat! You scared the fairy-loving crap out of me!" His gaze went to the rafters. "Everyone up there?"

A shrill round of "Yes, Dad," made my eyeballs hurt, and Matalina came out of the desk. Hands on her hips, she whistled sharply. A chorus of disappointed complaints rose and the bats fell. A flow of pixies vanished inside the desk, leaving three older kids to sit and dangle their feet from the rafters as casual sentries. One of them had Jenks's straightened paper clip, and I smiled. Jenks's cat patted one of the fallen paper bats and ignored her tiny master.

"Jenks . . . ," Matalina said in warning. "We had an agreement."

"Ho-o-o-oney," Jenks whined. "It's cold out. She's been an inside cat since we got her. It's not fair to make her stay outside just because we're inside now."

Her tiny, angelic face tight, Matalina disappeared into the desk. Jenks streaked in after her, a mix of young man and mature father. Grinning, I snagged Rex on my way to the door and the two shadows standing hesitantly in my threshold. I had no idea how we were going to handle this new wrinkle. Maybe I could learn how to make a ward to let people through but keep felines out. It was just a modified ley line circle. I'd seen someone do it by memory once, and Lee had put a ward up across Trent's great window. How hard could it be?

My smile widened when the light from the sign over the door illuminated who was there. It wasn't a potential client. "David!" I exclaimed when I saw him next to a vaguely familiar man. "I told you I was okay earlier. You didn't have to come over."

"I know how you downplay things," the younger of the two men said, his face easing into a few smile wrinkles as Rex struggled to get away from me. " 'Fine' can be anything from a bruise to almost comatose. And when I get a call from the I.S. about my alpha female, I'm not going to take that at face value."

His eyes lingered on the faint mark on my neck where Al had gripped me. Dropping the wildly wiggling cat, I gave him a quick hug. The complicated scent of Were filled my senses, wild, rich, and full of exotic undertones of earth and moon that most Weres lacked. I drew back, my hands still on his upper arms, peering into his eyes to evaluate his state of being. David had taken a curse for me, and though he said he liked the focus, I worried that one day, the sentient spell would risk my anger and take him over.

David's jaw clenched as he reined in an urge to flee that stemmed from the curse, not himself, then smiled. The thing was terrified of me.

"Still got it?" I said, letting him go, and he nodded.

"Still loving it," he said, dropping his head briefly to hide the need to run shimmering behind his dark eyes. He turned to the man beside him. "You remember Howard?"

My head bobbed. "Oh, yes! From last year's winter solstice," I said, wiggling my foot at Rex so she wouldn't come in and reaching to shake the older man's hand. His grip was cold from the night and probably poor circulation. "How you been doing?"

"I'm trying to stay busy," he said, the tips of his gray hair moving as he exhaled heavily. "I never should have taken that early retirement."

David scuffed his boots, muttering a quiet "I told you."

"Well, come on in," I said, waving my foot at the disgusted cat so she'd go away. "Quick, before Rex follows you."

"We can't stay." David hotfooted it inside, his old business partner quick on his heels despite his accumulated years. "We're on our way to pick up Serena and Kally. Howard is driving us out to Bowman Park and we're going to run the Licking River trail. Can I leave my car here until morning?"

I nodded. The long stretch of railroad track between Cincy and Bowman Park had been converted to a safe running surface shortly after the Turn. This time of year, you'd only find Weres on it at night, and the rails-to-trails path ran fairly close to the church before it crossed the river into Cincinnati. David had used the church as an endpoint before, but this was the first time he had the ladies with him. I wondered if it was their first long fall run. If so, they were in for a treat. To run full out and not get hot was exquisite.

I shut the door and ushered the men from the unlit foyer into the sanctuary. David's duster brushed his worn boot tops, and he took off his hat as he entered, clearly uncomfortable on the holy ground. As a witch, Howard didn't care, and he smiled and waved at the tiny hellos from the ceiling. I probably owed Howard a big thank-you—it had been his idea that David should take me as his new business partner.

David set his worn leather hat on the piano and rocked from heel to toe, looking every inch the alpha male, albeit an uncomfortable one. The faint hint of musk rose from the sturdy but graceful man, and his hand nervously ran across the hint of stubble the almost-full moon was causing. He wasn't tall for a man, standing almost eye to eye with me, but he made up for it in sheer presence. "Sinewy" would be the word I'd use to describe him. Or maybe "yummy," if he were in his running tights. But like Minias, David had a problem with the different-species thing.

He'd been forced to assume the title of alpha male for real when he accidentally turned two human women into Weres. It wasn't supposed to be possible, but he had been in possession of a very powerful Were artifact at the time. Watching David accept his responsibility left me both proud and guilty, since it was partly my fault. Okay, mostly my fault.

It would be a year come the winter solstice since David had started a pack with me, pressured into it by his boss and obstinately choosing a witch instead of a Were female so he wouldn't have to take on any new responsibilities. It was a win-win situation: David got to keep his job, I got my insurance cheap. But now he was an alpha for real, and I was proud of him for accepting it with so much grace. He went out of his way to make the two women he had turned with the focus feel wanted, needed, and welcome, taking every chance he could to help them explore their new situation with joyous abandonment.

But I was most proud of his refusal to show the guilt he lived with, knowing that if they knew how bad he felt for changing their lives without their consent, they might feel that what they had become was wrong. He had gone on to prove his nobility by taking the Were curse from me to save my sanity. The curse would have killed me by the first full moon. David said he liked it. I believed him, though it worried me. I appreciated David for everything he was and who he was becoming.

"Hi, David, Howard," Ivy said from the top of the hall, her hair freshly brushed and shoes now on her feet. "Can you stay for dinner? We have a slow cooker full of chili, so there's plenty." Ivy, however, just wanted to get in David's pants.

David had started at her voice. Shifting his long coat closed, he took a step back as he turned. "Thanks, but no," he said, eyes down. "I'm going for a run with the ladies. Howard might want to come back after dropping us off, though."

Howard mumbled something about a meeting, and Ivy turned to the stained-glass window and the moon, just shy of full but hidden behind clouds. Weres could change anytime, but the three days of a full moon were the only time it was legal to roam the city's streets on four paws, tradition turned to law by paranoid humans. What Weres did in their own houses, though, was their own business. The moonlit trail would be busy tonight.

Ivy's foot twitched like a cat's tail as she sat, turning her magazine over to hide the headline. I had to work to keep a straight face. It wasn't often that she was smitten enough by anyone to look like a high schooler with a crush. And it wasn't that she was obvious about it, but she was so closed with her emotions that any indication of attraction was as clear as finding love notes strewn on her bedroom floor. She'd probably recognized the sound of his car and had gone to tidy up, using the excuse of lowering the music.

"You should have called me when the demon showed," David said, edging to the door.

Jenks's wings clattered as he darted from the desk to the center of the room. "I was there to save her ass," he said belligerently, then added a belated, "Hi, David. Who's your friend?"

"This is Howard, my old partner," David said, and Jenks's head bobbed up and down.

"Oh, yeah. You stink for a witch. Whatcha been doing?"

Howard laughed, the sound echoing into the rafters and setting the pixies giggling. "Some freelance work. Thank you, Mr. Jenks. I'll take that as a compliment."

"It's just Jenks," the pixy muttered, giving Howard an unusual, cautious look as he landed on my shoulder.

Ivy was making eyes at David from over the crackers, and the small man started edging toward the door in earnest. "Do you want me to stay until sunup? Just in case?"

"Good God, no!" I exclaimed. "I'm on holy ground. I'm as safe here as if I was in my mother's arms."

"We've met your mother," Ivy said lightly. "That doesn't instill any confidence."

"What is this, pick-on-Rachel night?" I said, tired of it. "I can take care of myself."

No one said anything, the silence broken by a stifled laugh from the rafters. I looked up, but the pixies had hidden themselves.

"Guess what she's doing tonight?" Jenks said, leaving me to escort a quickly retreating David and Howard to the door. "Making a list of people who want to kill her, followed by ways to detect demon summoning."

"She told me." David retied his coat closed and headed for the door. "Don't forget to put Nick on there."

"Got him," I said, flopping into my chair and scowling at Ivy. She chased David away almost every time. "Thanks, Jenks," I shot at the pixy, but he wasn't listening as he opened the door for David and rose up out of the cold draft.

David turned at the threshold. Behind him, Howard was heading down the steps to an unfamiliar station wagon. Parked by the curb was David's gray sports car. "'Bye, Rachel," David said, the light over the door glinting on his black hair. "Call me tomorrow if I don't see you. Summoning demons usually results in a claim or two being filed. When I get back to the office, I'll see if anything unusual has come in."

My eyebrows rose, and I made a mental note to add insurance claims to the list. David worked at one of the largest on-paper insurance companies in the United States and had access to just about everything, given time. Actually, maybe I'd call Glenn at the FIB to see if they had any complaints recently. They kept great records to compensate for their utter lack of Inderlander talents.

"Thanks, I'll do that," I said as David followed his old partner out and shut the door.

Ivy frowned at the dark foyer, sipping her drink as one foot bobbed up and down. Seeing me track the motion, she forced it still. I jumped at the high-pitched burst of noise from my desk, eyes widening as four streaks of silver raced out from it and into the back of the church. A crash brought me around in my seat, and I wondered what had just fallen off the overhead rack in the kitchen.

And so it begins. . . .

"Jack!" came Matalina's shrill cry, and she zipped out of the desk after them. Jenks intercepted her, and the two had a rapid high-pitched discussion in the hallway punctuated by bursts of ultrasonic sound that made my head hurt.

"Honey," Jenks coaxed when she slowed enough that we

could hear them again. "Boys will be boys. I'll talk to them and make them apologize."

"What if they had done that when your cat came in!" she shrilled. "What then?"

"But they didn't," he soothed. "They waited until she was secure."

Hand shaking as she pointed to the back of the church, she took a breath to start in again, gulping it back when Jenks kissed her soundly, wrapping her slim form in his arms and body, their wings somehow not tangling as they hovered in the hallway.

"I'll take care of it, love," he said when they parted, his emotion so earnest that I dropped my eyes, embarrassed. Matalina fled to the desk in a dusting of mortified red, and after grinning at us in some masculine display of . . . masculinity, Jenks flew to the back of the church.

"Jack!" he shouted, the dust slipping from him a brilliant gold. "You know better than that. Get your brothers and get out here. If I have to dig you out, I'm going to clip your wings!"

"Huh." Ivy's long fingers carefully picked up a cracker. "I'll have to try that."

"What?" I asked, shifting to prop my clipboard up on my knees.

Ivy blinked slowly. "Kissing someone from agitation into bliss."

Her smile widened to show a slip of teeth, and a sliver of ice dropped down my spine. Fear mixed with anticipation, as unstoppable as jerking my hand from a flame. And Ivy could sense it as easily as she could see my embarrassed flush.

Pulling herself upright, she stood. I blinked up at her as she stretched, and brushing past me in a wave of vampire incense, she headed for the door as the doorbell rang.

"I got it," she said, her pace provocative. "David left his hat."

My exhaled breath was slow and long. Damn it, I was *not* an adrenaline junkie. And Ivy knew we weren't going to shift our relationship in either direction. Still . . . the potential was there, and I hated that she could flip switches in me as easily as I could flip them in her. Just 'cause you *can* do something, doesn't mean you *should*, right?

Exasperated with myself, I grabbed the empty cracker plate and headed for the kitchen. Maybe I needed a midnight run myself to clear my head of all the vamp pheromones in there.

"Cat in the house!" came Ivy's call, and then a different voice filtered in, stopping me cold.

"Hi, I'm Marshal."

If the mellow, attractive voice hadn't jerked me to a halt, the name would have, and I spun in the hallway.

"You must be Ivy," the man added. "Is Rachel in?"

Four

"Marshal?" I exclaimed as my thoughts realigned and I figured out who was standing in our threshold. "What are you doing here?" I added as I headed back.

He shrugged and smiled, and the cracker plate dangled from my hand as I pushed past a belligerent Ivy to give him a one-armed hug. Dropping back a step, I warmed, but damn, it was good to see him. I had felt really guilty watching him swim back to his boat last spring, having to go on hearsay that he made it back all right and that the Mackinaw Weres were leaving him alone. But not contacting him had been the best thing to ensure his anonymity and safety.

The tall, wide-shouldered man continued to grin. "Jenks left his hat on my boat," he said, extending the red leather cap to me.

"You did not come all the way down here for that," I said as I took it, then squinted at the dark shadow of an infant beard on him. "You've got hair! When did you get hair?"

Taking off his knitted cap, he ducked his head to show its fuzz. "Last week. I brought the boat in for the season, and when I'm not wearing a wet suit, I can let it all grow back." His brown eyes pinched in mock agony. "I itch like crazy. Everywhere."

Ivy had moved back a step, and setting the cracker plate on

the table beside the door, I took his arm and pulled him in. The scent of his short wool coat was strong, and I breathed it in, thinking I could smell gas fumes mixing with the strong redwood smell that meant witch. "Come on in," I said, waiting for him to finish wiping his boots on the mat before he followed me into the sanctuary.

"Ivy, this is Marshal," I said, seeing her with her arms crossed over her middle and David's hat in her grip. "The guy who got me out to the island at Mackinaw and let me run off with his diving gear. Remember?" It sounded stupid, but she hadn't said anything yet, and I was getting nervous.

Ivy's eye twitched. "Of course. But Jenks and I didn't see him at the high school pool when we returned his stuff, so I never met him. It's a pleasure." Dropping David's hat on the small table beside the door, she extended her hand, and Marshal took it. He was still smiling, but it was growing thin.

"Well, this is it," I said, gesturing to the sanctuary and the rest of the unseen church. "Proof that I'm not crazy. You want to sit down? You don't have to leave right away, do you? Jenks will want to say hi." I was babbling, but Ivy wasn't being nice, and she'd already driven one man out of the church tonight.

"Sure. I can stay for a minute." Marshal took his coat off as he followed me to the furniture clustered in the corner. I watched him take a deep breath of the chili-scented air, and I wondered if he'd stay if I asked. Plopping myself down in my chair, I gave him a once-over as Marshal eased his lean swimmer's body down to the edge of the couch. Clearly not yet ready to relax, the tall man sat on the edge with his arms flat on his legs.

Marshal was wearing jeans and a dark green pullover that had a backwoods look to it, the color going well with his honey-colored skin. He looked great sitting there, even if his eyebrows weren't grown in yet and he'd nicked himself shaving. I remembered how utterly in control he had looked on his boat, dressed in a swimsuit and an unzipped red windbreaker that showed skin so smooth it glistened and beautiful, beautiful abs. God, he had had nice abs. Must be from all the swimming.

Suddenly shocked, I froze. Guilt turned my skin cold, and I settled into my chair, heartache riding high where enthusiasm had just flowed. I had loved Kisten. I *still* loved him. That I'd forgotten for even an instant was both a surprise and a pain. I'd been listening to Ivy and Jenks long enough to know this was part of my pattern of getting hurt and then finding someone to hide the pain with, but I wasn't going to be that person anymore. I couldn't afford to be. And if I saw it, I could stop it.

But it was really good to see Marshal. He was proof that I didn't kill everyone I came in contact with, and that was a welcome relief.

"Uh," I stammered when I realized no one was talking. "I think my old boyfriend stole some of your gear before he went off the bridge. Sorry."

Marshal's wandering attention lighted briefly on the bruise on my neck before rising to my eyes. I think he recognized something had shifted, but he wasn't going to ask. "The FIB found my stuff on the shore a week later. No problem."

"I didn't have a clue he was going to do that," I said. "I'm really sorry."

He smiled faintly. "I know. I saw the news. You look good in cuffs."

Ivy leaned against the wall by the hallway where she could see both of us. She looked left out, but that was her own fault. She could sit down and join us. I flashed her a glance, which she ignored, then turned to Marshal. "You didn't really drive all the way down here to give Jenks his hat, did you?"

"No . . ." Marshal dropped his head. "I'm here for an interview at the university, and I wanted to see if you were jerking me around or if you really did have a job where you thought you could take on an entire Were pack alone."

"I wasn't alone," I said, flustered. "Jenks was with me."

Ivy uncrossed her ankles and pushed herself away from the wall an instant before Jenks zipped in, wings clattering. "Marshal!" the exuberant pixy shouted, dust slipping from him to make a sunbeam on the floor. "Holy crap! What the hell are you doing here?"

Marshal's jaw dropped. For an instant, I thought he was going to stand up, but then he fell all the way back into the couch. "Jenks?" He stammered. His eyes were wide as he looked at me and I nodded. "I thought you were kidding about him being a pixy."

"Nope," I said, enjoying Marshal's disbelief.

"What you doin' here, old dog!" the pixy said, darting from one side of him to the other.

Marshal gestured helplessly. "I don't know what to do. You were six feet tall the last time I saw you. I can't shake your hand."

"Just stick your hand out," Ivy said dryly. "Let him land on it."

"Anything to get him to stop *flying around*," I said loudly, and Jenks settled on the table, his wings going so fast I could feel a draft.

"It's great to see you!" Jenks said again, making me wonder just why we were so glad to see Marshal. Maybe it was because he had helped us when we really needed it at great risk to himself when he owed us nothing. "Crap on my daisies," Jenks said, rising up and settling back down. "Ivy, you should have seen his face when Rachel told him we were going to rescue her ex-boyfriend from an island full of militant Weres. I still can't believe he did it."

Marshal smiled. "Neither can I. She looked like she could use some help was all."

Ivy made a questioning face at me, and I shrugged. Okay, seeing me in a tight rubber suit might have swayed his decision, but it wasn't as if I had dressed up to romance help out of him.

Marshal's eyes darted to Ivy when she pushed herself into motion. Sleek and predatory, she eased onto the couch beside him, angling herself so her back was to the armrest, one knee pulled up to her chin, the other draped over the edge of the couch. Her magazine slid to the floor when she bumped it, and she pointedly set it on the table between us with the headlines showing. She was acting like a jealous girlfriend, and I didn't like it.

"Huh," Jenks said, a smile on him as he looked at me sitting with my hands clasped primly in my lap and that unusual amount of space between Marshal and myself. "I guess you can teach a young witch new tricks."

"Jenks!" I exclaimed, knowing he was talking about me distancing myself from Marshal, but the poor witch didn't have a clue. *Thank God.* Incensed, I made a snatch for the pixy, and the laughing four-inch man settled himself on Marshal's shoulder. Marshal stiffened but didn't move but for tilting his head and trying to see Jenks.

"You said you were here for an interview?" Ivy said pleasantly, but I didn't trust her mood as far as I could throw her. Which was about three feet on a good day.

Moving carefully as if Jenks might leave, Marshal eased into the cushions and away from her. "At the university," he said, showing signs of nervousness.

"What's the job?" Ivy questioned, and I could almost hear her think "Janitor?" Though not saying one cross word, she wasn't being nice, like I'd asked him to come over to betray Kisten's memory.

Marshal must have picked up on it, too, for he shifted his wide shoulders and tilted his head to crack his neck, clearly a nervous tick. "I'd be coaching the swim team, but once I'm on the payroll, I can put in for a real teaching position."

"Teaching what?" Jenks asked suspiciously.

At that, Marshal smiled. "Minor ley line manipulations. More of a high school course than anything else. A primer to bring deficient students up for the hundred-level classes."

Clearly Ivy wasn't impressed. But she probably didn't know that he had to be at a four-hundred level to instruct anyone in anything. I had no idea where my ley line proficiency put me, seeing as I was picking it up as I went along, learning what I had to when I needed it, not what was safe or prudent in a steady, progressive pace.

"Cincinnati doesn't have a swim team," Ivy said. "Sounds like quite a job to build one."

Marshal's head bobbed, and the stubble on it caught the light. "It will be. Normally I wouldn't even try for the position, but I earned my bachelor's here, and coming back feels right."

"Hey!" Jenks exclaimed, and I shivered in the draft from his wings. "You're a Cincy boy! What year did you graduate?"

"Class of 2001," he said proudly.

"Holy crap, you're almost thirty?" the pixy said. "Damn, you look good!"

"Almost? No, I'm past it," he said, clearly unwilling to divulge just how much. But since he was a witch, it didn't really matter. "It's the swimming," he said softly, then looked at Ivy as if he knew she was going to look up his records. "I majored in business management, and I used my degree to start Marshal's Mackinaw Wrecks." Disappointment flickered over him. "But that's not going to work anymore, so here I am."

"Too cold?" Jenks said, either ignoring that we were likely the reason it wasn't working anymore or trying to make light of it. "God, I froze my nuggie plums off in that water."

I winced, thinking Jenks's mouth was getting steadily worse. Almost as if he had to prove he was a man in front of Marshal, and the way to do it was to be as raunchy as he could. But I had heard the hint of blame in Marshal's words.

"The Mackinaw Weres found out you had something to do with me getting onto the island, didn't they," I said, knowing I was right when he looked at his water-stained yellow leather boots. *Shit.* "I'm sorry, Marshal," I said, wishing now I'd just knocked him on his head and stolen his stuff. At least he'd still have his business. I'd done the right thing, and it had hurt him in the long run. Where was the justice in that?

His smile was tight when he pulled his head up, and even

Ivy looked apologetic. "Don't worry about it," he said. "I didn't lose anything that mattered in the fire."

"Fire?" I whispered, appalled, and he nodded.

"It was time for me to come back," he said, one shoulder rising in a shrug. "I only started the diving business so I could build the capital to get my master's."

Ivy's fingers, drumming on the couch, went still. "You're finishing your degree?"

Saying nothing, Marshal ran his gaze over her as if estimating how great a threat she was and nodded. "Hey, I have to go. I've got a couple of apartments I'm looking at tonight, and if I don't show on time, the Realtor will probably figure it was a Halloween prank and leave."

He stood, and I found myself rising as well. Jenks darted into the air, grumbling about not having anything comfortable to put his ass on in the entire church before he landed on my shoulder. I wanted to go with Marshal so the Realtor wouldn't convince him to take a rattrap that would be noisy with humans after sunup, but he probably knew Cincinnati as well as I did. Not much changed fast, despite the size of the city. Besides, I didn't want to give him the wrong idea.

Ivy stood as Marshal shrugged into his coat. "Nice to meet you, Marshal," she said, then turned her back on him as she walked out. Five seconds later, I heard her taking the lid off the slow cooker, and a new wave of tomato, beans, and spices wafted out.

"Can you stay for dinner?" I found myself asking, not knowing why, except that he had helped Jenks and me, and I owed him. "We actually cooked tonight. Chili."

Marshal's eyes went to the top of the dark hallway. "No, but thank you. I'm having dinner with a couple of guys from school. I just wanted to bring Jenks his hat and say hi."

"Oh, okay." Of course he'd have friends here. I was being stupid.

I followed him to the door to see him out, my eyes landing on Jenks's leather cap, back after months of being with Marshal. I was glad to see him, and I wished he could stay, but it was tinged with depression from the guilt that I even wanted him to.

Glowing a hot gold, Jenks hovered at eye-height beside Marshal as I reached to open the door. "It's good to see you, Marsh-man," he said. "If it was warmer, I'd show you my stump."

The way he said it almost sounded like a threat, and I could see Marshal thinking about it as he slowly buttoned his coat, probably trying to decide if he was serious or not. I wanted to talk to Marshal alone for a moment, but Jenks wasn't leaving.

Jenks suddenly noticed that neither of us was talking, and when I made a face at him, he dropped in height. "If you want me to go, you just have to say so," he said sullenly, then darted off to leave a fading sprinkling of pixy dust to glow on the floor for a moment. My blood pressure dropped, and I smiled at Marshal.

"That was the most excellent charm I've ever seen," Marshal said softly, his eyes dark to take in the limited light in the foyer, "making him human-size, then small again."

"It's not half as excellent as the person who actually made it for me," I said, thinking that Ceri should get her just dues. "I just invoked it."

Marshal took his hat out of his wide pocket and put it on. I felt a twinge of relief when he reached for the door, then guilt that I'd enjoyed seeing him again. *God, how long will I have to live like this?* Marshal hesitated. Turning back, he searched my face. I silently waited, not knowing what might come out of his mouth.

"I, ah—I'm not interfering in something, am I?" he asked. "With your roommate?"

I grimaced, cursing both Ivy for her jealousness and Jenks for his protective nature. *God help them, were they that obvious?*

"No," I said quickly, then dropped my gaze. "It's not that. My boyfriend . . ." I took a breath and lowered my voice so it wouldn't break. "I just lost my boyfriend, and they both think I'll jump into bed with the first guy to come into the church simply to fill the ache he left behind." *A fear that is both understandable and at the same time unnecessary.*

Marshal shifted his weight back. "The guy that went over the bridge?" he asked quizzically. "I thought you didn't like him."

"Not him," I said, flicking my eyes to his and away. "My boyfriend after him. Kisten was . . . important to both Ivy and me. He died to prevent an undead vampire from binding me to him . . . I don't remember it, but I know he did. And I still . . ." I closed my eyes, a lump in my throat. "I still miss him," I said miserably.

I looked at Marshal, needing to see what he thought. His face was carefully blank of expression. "He died?" he said, and I nodded, looking away.

"I think I understand," he said as he reached to touch my shoulder, and guilt tweaked through me as I soaked in the support radiating from him. "I'm really sorry about your boyfriend. Um . . . I didn't know. I should have called before coming over. I'll just, uh, go."

His hand slipped away, and my head came up. "Marshal," I said, reaching to take his sleeve, and he stopped. I let go, then glanced behind me at the empty church, then back to him. I loved Kisten, but I had to try to start living again. The pain would ebb only if I pushed it out with something good. Marshal patiently waited, and I took a deep breath.

"I'd like to see you again," I said, miserable. "If you want. I mean, I really can't handle having a boyfriend right now, but I've *got* to get out of this church. Do something." His eyes widened, and I blurted, "Never mind."

"No, no!" he said. "That's cool." He hesitated, then shrugged. "To be honest, I'm not looking for a girlfriend either."

I kind of doubted that, but I nodded, grateful he pretended to understand.

"There used to be a place by the waterfront that had really good pizza," he offered.

"Piscary's?" I almost panicked. *Not* Kisten's old dance club. "Uh, it's closed," I said, which was the truth. The elaborate apartments underground were now the property of Rynn Cormel. And since he wasn't a partier, he had gutted the upper rooms and turned them into a day residence for his living guests and staff. But it still had one hell of a kitchen. Or so Ivy said.

Weight shifting to one foot, Marshal frowned in thought. "Don't the Howlers have an exhibition game this week? I haven't seen them play in years."

"I'm banned," I said, and he looked at me as if he thought I was joking.

"From the Howlers?" he said. "Maybe we could just have lunch or something."

"Okay," I said slowly, not knowing if I could actually do this.

His smile widened and he opened the door. "I have that interview tomorrow, but I was going to go look at some apartments before that. If I treat you to coffee, will you tell me which ones are overcharging me? Unless you're working . . ."

"Two days before Halloween?" I clasped my arms about me in the sudden chill. I hadn't expected to do anything this soon, and now I was having second thoughts. I thought of backing out on the excuse of needing to track down a demon summoner before sundown tomorrow, but I had to give my sources time to work. I stunk at research, and I knew enough people who enjoyed it to pass it off on them. "Sure," I reluctantly said. It was coffee. How bad could it be?

"Perfect," he said, and I froze when he eased forward. Before it could become a hug, or worse, a kiss, I stuck out my hand. Marshal tried to make his shift to my hand natural, but it was kind of obvious, and his fingers slipped from mine almost immediately. Embarrassed by my guilt and misery, I looked down.

"I'm sorry you're still hurting," he said sincerely as he stepped back onto the stoop. The light from the sign above the door made shadows on him. His eyes, when I met them, held a soft emotion, black from the low light, nothing more. "I'll see you tomorrow. About noon?"

I nodded as I tried to think of something to say—but my mind was empty. Marshal smiled one last time before taking the steps lightly and heading for the new-model, chrome-plated sport utility at the curb. Numb, I backed up into the church, my shoulder thumping painfully into the doorjamb and startling me back into reality. Heartache swelled as I shut the door and leaned back against it to stare into the sanctuary.

I had to start living again, even if it killed me.

Five

The soft click of teeth on the knob of my bedroom door stirred me, but it wasn't until a wet nose snuffled in my ear that I truly woke up, with a pulse of adrenaline that was better than chugging three cups of coffee.

"David!" I exclaimed, jerking upright and scooting back to the headboard, my covers pulled to my neck. "How did you get in here?" Pulse hammering, my panic subsided, turning to irritation when I saw his pricked ears and his doggy smile. My gaze slid to my clock. Eleven? Damn it, I had a good hour left before the alarm was going to ring. Irritated, I flicked the alarm off. No way would I get back to sleep now. Not after a Were's version of a wet willy.

"What's the matter? Your car not starting?" I asked the large, gangly wolf, but he only sat on his haunches and let his tongue loll as he stared at me with his luscious brown eyes. "Get out of my room. I have to get up. I'm meeting someone for coffee," I said, making shooing motions with one hand.

At that, David snuffed a negation, and I hesitated.

"I'm not meeting someone for coffee?" I said, ready to believe him. "Is Ivy okay? Is it Jenks?" Worried, I swung my feet to the floor.

David put his front paws, each as big as a saucer, to either side of me to keep me sitting. His breath was warm, and he gave me a comforting lick. He wouldn't get this close in his people skin, but wearing fur seemed to bring out the softer side of most Weres.

I eased back, deciding everything was okay. He didn't look worried. "Talking to you is like talking to a fish," I complained, and David huffed, his claws clicking on the hardwood floor as he got off my bed. "You want some clothes?" I asked, seeing as he probably hadn't woken me up for the hell of it. If it wasn't car problems, maybe he had forgotten to bring something to change into. "You might fit in Jenks's old stuff."

David bobbed his head, and after a brief thought of my almost-nakedness, I got out of bed and snagged my robe from the back of a chair. "I kept a pair of his sweats," I said as I shrugged into the blue terry cloth and tied it closed with an abrupt, embarrassed haste, but David had turned to the hallway, the perfect gentleman. Feeling awkward, I dragged a box down from my closet shelf and dropped it on my bed. Not that we had a lot of naked men in our church, but I wasn't going to throw out Jenks's old clothes from when he had been people-size.

The scent of Queen Anne's lace came to me when I wrestled the box open. Fingers searching through the cool fabric, my slight headache eased and the smell of growing things and sunshine rose high. Jenks smelled good, and it hadn't washed out.

"Here you go," I said when I found the sweats and extended them to him.

His brown eyes sheepish, David carefully took them in his mouth before padding to the dim hallway, the oak floorboards glowing with morning sun reflecting in from the living room and kitchen. Shuffling to the bathroom, I decided he had probably locked himself out of his car and change of clothes—which left me curious as to where the ladies were. David didn't seem to be distressed, and I knew he would be if either one of them had a problem.

Wondering how David knew I didn't have a coffee date when I hadn't even told him I had one to begin with, I shuffled into the bathroom and quietly shut the door to keep everyone who was sleeping, sleeping. It was nearing the golden hour of noon when the church went silent—Ivy and me asleep and the pixies just settling down for their four-hour nap.

Hanging on the back of the door, my costume thumped, and I quieted it, listening for the hum of pixy wings. I fingered the supple leather in the silence, hoping I would get a chance to wear it. I was pretty much churchbound after dark until I nailed whoever was sending Al after me. And Halloween wasn't a holiday to be missed.

Since the Turn—the nightmarish three years following the supernatural species coming out of the closet—the holiday had been gaining strength until now it was celebrated for an entire week, becoming the unofficial celebration for the Turn itself.

The Turn actually began in the late summer of sixty-six when humanity began dying of a virus carried by a bioengineered tomato that was supposed to feed the growing populations of the third-world countries, but it was on Halloween that we celebrated it. That was the day Inderland had decided to come out of the closet before humanity found us by way of the "why aren't these people dying?" question. It had been thought that Halloween might ease the panic, and it had. Most of the surviving human population thought it was a joke, easing the chaos for a day or two until they realized that we hadn't eaten them yesterday, so why would we today?

They still threw a bloody-hell tantrum, but at least it had been aimed at the bioengineers who designed the accidentally lethal fruit instead of us. No one had been so tactless as to make the holiday official, but everyone took the week off. Human bosses didn't say, er, boo when their Inderland employees called in sick, and no one even mentioned the Turn. We did throw tomatoes instead of eggs, though, put peeled ones in bowls and called them eyeballs, stacked them up on our porches along with carved pumpkins, and generally tried to gross-out the human population that wouldn't touch the no-longer-lethal red fruit.

If I was stuck in my church for the night, I was going to be ticked.

By the time I finished a quick morning prep and was headed for the kitchen, David was changed and at the table, with coffee brewing and two empty mugs waiting. The hat he had forgotten yesterday was beside him, and he looked good sitting there with a thick black stubble heavy on him and his long black hair loose and flowing. I'd never seen him so casual before, and it was nice.

"'Morning," I said around a yawn, and he turned to acknowledge me. "Did you and the ladies have a good run?"

He was smiling, his brown eyes showing his pleasure. "Mmmm. They headed home from here on paws, confident enough without me. That's why I'm here, actually."

I sat at my spot at the table, the bright sun and the scent of coffee making my head hurt. There was a stack of late-night newspapers opened to the obituaries that I'd gone through before bed. There had been nothing obvious, but Glenn, my FIB contact, was running the three young witches I'd found there through their database to see if they were known acquaintances. One had died of a heart attack at age thirty, another of a brain aneurism, and the third of sudden appendicitis—which had once been a common, pre-Turn expression for a magic misfire. Soon as I got this morning's edition, I'd pass any more likely candidates on to Glenn. He was working Halloween since he was a human and didn't celebrate it; he policed it.

"I thought you'd locked yourself out of your car," I said, and he chuckled.

"No. I would have just run the rest of the way home if I had. I wanted to ask you about a pack tattoo."

My eyebrows rose. "Oh?" Most Were packs had a registered tattoo, but I hadn't seen the need, and David was used to standing alone.

Seeing my reluctance, David shrugged. "It's time. Serena and Kally are confident enough to be on their own in fur, and if they don't have a sign of pack recognition, someone might think they're curs." He hesitated. "Serena especially is getting cocky. And there's nothing wrong with that. She has every right, but unless she has an obvious way to show her status and affiliation, someone will challenge her."

The coffeemaker finished with a hiss. I got up, eager for the distraction. I'd never given it much thought, but the tattoos that Weres decorated themselves with had a real and significant purpose. They probably prevented hundreds of skirmishes and potential injuries, allowing the multitude of packs that lived in Cincy to get along with minimal friction.

"Okay," I said slowly, pouring out the coffee into his mug first. "What were you thinking of?" *I don't want a tattoo. The damn things hurt!*

Clearly pleased, David took a mug when I came back and offered it. "They've put their heads together and came up with something with you in mind."

Images of broomsticks and crescent moons danced in my head, and I cringed.

The Were leaned forward, the pleasant scent of musk giving away his eagerness. "A dandelion, but with black fluff instead of white."

Oh, cool, I thought, and seeing my reaction, David smiled with one side of his mouth. "I take it that's okay, then?" he asked, blowing across his coffee.

"I suppose I ought to get one, too?" I asked, worried.

"Unless you want to be rude," he admonished gently. "They put a lot of thought into it. It would mean a lot to them if you would."

A breath of guilt wafted through me, and I hid it behind a gulp of scalding coffee. I hadn't done much with Serena and Kally. Maybe we could get our tattoos together. *Oh, God, I'm going to be a hundred and sixty with a flower on my ass.*

"You, ah, said I don't have a coffee date?" I said, changing the subject. "What do you know that I don't?"

David nodded to a scrap of paper in the middle of the table, and I pulled it closer. "Jenks let me in before he headed off for his nap," he said. "Matalina . . ."

His words drifted to nothing, and I looked up from Jenks's note. "What about her?"

"She's fine," he said, easing my worry. "But she was going to bed early, and there was no need for him to stay up to man the door if I was here, so I told him to go."

I nodded and turned my attention back to the note, uneasy about Matalina, but glad that Ivy and I had broken Jenks of answering the phone without taking a message. According to the note, Marshal's interview had been moved from tonight to this morning, and he wanted to know if we could get together at about three instead. Plenty of time to do something before Al started gunning for me after sundown. There was a number, and I couldn't help but smile. Below it was another number with the cryptic message JOB, and Jenks's reminder that rent was due on Thursday the first, not Friday the second or Monday the fifth.

"I should get home," David said softly as he rose and took another gulp from his mug. Hat in hand, he said, "Thanks for the coffee. I'll let Serena and Kally know you like their idea."

"Um, David," I said, and I saw his brow crease at the sound of Ivy moving about. "Do you think they'd mind if I went with them when they got their tattoos?"

His sun-darkened face broke into a smile, the faint wrinkles about his eyes deepening in pleasure. "I think they'd like that. I'll ask them."

"Thanks," I said, and he jumped at a bumping sound from Ivy's room. "You'd better get going unless you want to be here when she gets up."

He was silent as his face reddened. "I'll lope in to work later and check out the recent claims for possible demon damage. There won't be anyone in two days before Halloween, so I won't have to explain myself."

"This isn't illegal, is it?" I asked suddenly. "I've gotten you in enough trouble as it is."

David's smile was easy and a bit devilish. "No," he said, shrugging with one shoulder. "But why draw attention to yourself? Don't worry about it. If someone in Cincy is summoning demons, any claims will be odd enough to be flagged for investigation. At least you'll know then if it's a local threat. Help you narrow your suspects."

I drew my coffee closer and slumped into the hard chair. "Thanks, David. I appreciate it. If I can shut down the guy summoning Al, then I won't have to take Minias up on his offer." I didn't want a demon's summoning name, especially Al's. Unusable or not.

A sliver of worry slipped between my thought and reason, and I forced my smile to be light, but David saw it. Coming closer, he put a small but powerful hand on my shoulder. "We'll get him. Don't do anything with that demon. Promise?"

I winced, and David sighed when I didn't say anything. There was a soft creak of a door opening, and David started like a deer. "I'll, uh, bring Jenks's sweats back later, okay?" he muttered, then grabbed his hat and almost ran for the back door, red faced, as I chuckled.

Still smiling, I stretched for the phone and brought Jenks's note with the number for the potential job closer. I wasn't going to work until after Halloween, but it would be nice to have something lined up for the first of the month. Besides, I didn't have anything else to do this afternoon but surf the Net for local demon sightings and bug Glenn for his findings.

And that, I thought as I reached for the phone, *would only slow him down.*

Six

The muffled *thump, thump, thump* of the rubber seal of the revolving door overtook the street noise and turned into the echoing sound of sporadic voices as I entered Carew Tower. It had grown warm, so I'd left my coat in the car, deeming jeans and a sweater would be enough until the sun went down—and I'd be back in my church by then. Hoping I didn't lose my signal, I tried to catch what Marshal was saying as I held my phone to my ear and waited for my eyes to adjust to the dimmer light.

"I'm really sorry, Rachel," Marshal said, sounding embarrassed. "They asked me to come in early when someone canceled, and it wasn't like I could say no."

"No, it's okay," I said, glad I was my own boss, even if my boss was an idiot sometimes. Stepping inside, I shifted out of the foot traffic and took my sunglasses off. "I had an errand come up, so this might work out better anyway. You want to grab a coffee at Fountain Square?" *Three is good. Not breakfast, not lunch. A nice, safe hour with no expectations attached.* "The only thing is I have to be back on hallowed ground by sunset," I added, remembering. "I've got a demon gunning for me until I can figure out who's sending him to kill me and knock some sense into him or her."

As soon as I said it, I couldn't help but wonder if I was trying to drive him away. But Marshal laughed, quickly sobering when he realized I was serious. "Uh, how are your interviews going?" I asked to break the uncomfortable silence.

"Ask me in a few hours." He groaned softly. "I've got two more people to meet. I haven't kissed so much ass since I accidentally knocked a customer off the dock."

I chuckled, my gaze rising across the busy lobby to the signs directing people to the elevators. My smile ended with a flash of guilt, then I got mad at myself. I could laugh, damn it. Laughing was not saying I had cared for Kisten less. He had loved to make me laugh.

"Maybe we should try tomorrow instead," Marshal said softly, as if he knew why I was suddenly silent.

Tucking my shades into my bag, I headed for the express elevators. I was meeting a Mr. Doemoe at the observation deck. Some people just love the cloak and dagger. "There's a coffee cart at Fountain Square," I suggested with a bitter resolve. *I can do this, damn it.* It was right next to a hot dog cart. Kisten had liked hot dogs. A memory hit me—an image of Kisten in his snappy pin-striped work suit, leaning casually next to me against the huge planters at Fountain Square, smiling as he caught a drop of mustard from the corner of his mouth, the wind ruffling his hair and him squinting from the sun. I felt my stomach cave. *God, I can't do this!*

Marshal's voice intruded. "Sounds great. First one there buys. I take a grande with three sugars and a hint of cream."

"Black, straight up," I said, almost numb. Hiding in my church because of heartache was worse than hiding there because of a demon, and I didn't want to be that person.

"Fountain Square it is," Marshal said. "I'll see you then."

"You got it," I replied as I passed the security desk. "And good luck!" I added, remembering what he was doing today.

"Thanks, Rachel. 'Bye."

I waited until I heard the phone disconnect, then whispered, "'Bye," before shutting the phone and tucking it away. This was harder than I had thought it would be.

My melancholy trailed behind me like a shadow as I went

down the short hall, my thoughts slowly turning to the upcoming client meeting. *The roof*, I thought, rolling my eyes. Honestly, Mr. Doemoe had sounded like a mouse of a man when I called him earlier to set this up. He'd refused to come to the church, and I hadn't been able to tell by phone if he was nervous because he was a human asking a witch for help or if he was just worried that someone was out to get him. Whatever. The job couldn't be that bad. I had told Jenks to stay home since it was simply an interview. Besides, I was running errands, and dragging Jenks around when I went to the post office and FIB building was a major waste of his time.

My trip to the FIB had been productive, and I now had information on my original three witches plus an additional one from this morning's obituaries. Apparently two of the recently dead witches knew each other, seeing as they had joint prior arrests for the crime of grave robbing. I thought it interesting that the arresting I.S. officer had been Tom Bansen, the same nasty little twerp who had tried to arrest me yesterday.

This was looking easier all the time. Tom had all the motive he needed to call a demon to take me out—seeing as I'd told him to shove his little demon-summoning club last year. He also had the knowledge to do it, being high up in the I.S.'s Arcane Division. That in itself would make his demon-summoning hobby harder to trace and recruitment easy as he'd run into all sorts of black-art witches eager to make a deal. David was still checking recent claims for me, and if any of them pointed to Tom, the I.S. officer and I were going to have a chat. We might have a chat anyway.

I really didn't think it was Nick sending Al after me. I mean, I had misjudged his character badly, but actively sending a demon to kill me? My gaze unfocused in the memory of our last conversation, and as I turned the corner, I saw one of the express elevator doors closing. *Maybe I shouldn't have been so bitchy with him.* He had sounded desperate.

Jogging forward, I called out for whoever was in the elevator to hold it. A weathered, sturdy hand gripped the door at the last moment to wedge it open. I darted inside the otherwise empty lift, turning to the man to give him a breathless "Thanks." But my words caught in my throat and I froze.

"Quen!" I snapped, seeing the plague-scarred elf standing in the corner. He smiled without showing his teeth, and at the hint of amusement in his eyes, it all fell into place.

"Oh, hell no," I said, looking for the elevator panel for a button to push, but he was standing in front of it. "You're Mr. Doemoe? Forget it. I'm not working for Trent."

The older man hit the highest button, adjusted his weight, and clasped his hands before him. "I wanted to talk to you. This was the easiest way."

"You mean this is the only way, 'cause you know I'd tell Trent he can shove his problem up an orifice," I said.

"As professional as always, Ms. Morgan."

His gravelly voice was mocking, and knowing I was trapped here until we reached the upper floors, I slumped in the corner, not caring if I looked sullen for the cameras. I *was* sullen. I wasn't going to tap a line. You don't pull a gun unless you're going to use it—and you don't tap a line in front of a master of ley line magic unless you want to be slammed up against the wall.

Quen's smile faded. He appeared innocuous in his long-sleeved shirt and matching black pants, which looked vaguely like a uniform. Yeah, he was innocuous. Like black mamba innocuous. The man stood only a few inches taller than me in his flat, soft-soled shoes, but he moved with a liquid grace that put me on edge, as if he was able to see me react before I actually did. I was trapped in a tiny metal box with an elf skilled in martial arts and black ley line magic. *Maybe I should be nice. At least until the doors open.*

His complexion was marred by the scars a few Inderlanders had come away with from the Turn, and his roughened, dark skin only added to his presence. A vampire bite marked his neck, most of the white scar tissue hidden by his high black collar. Piscary had given the scar to him in anger, and I wondered how Quen was handling the new problem of having an unclaimed vampire bite, now that Piscary was truly dead. I had one, too, but Ivy would kill any vampire who broke my skin, and all of Cincy knew it. Quen didn't have any such protection. Perhaps the bite was why he wanted to talk to me—if this wasn't about a run for Trent.

Quen was Trent Kalamack's eminently skilled security officer, one hundred percent deadly, though I'd trust him with my life if he said he'd watch my back. Trent was just as dangerous without having earned my trust, but he did his damage with words, not actions—a stinking politician at his best, a murderer at his worst. The financially successful, attractive, charismatic hunk of man flesh efficiently ran most of Cincinnati's underworld and the northern hemisphere's illegal Brimstone trade. But what Trent could go to jail for besides being a murdering bastard—for which I'd gotten him incarcerated for all of three hours a few months ago—was his worldwide trade in illegal biodrugs. What really stuck in my craw was that I was alive because of them.

I'd been born with a fairly common genetic defect among witches, Rosewood syndrome, where my mitochondria kicked out an enzyme my body determined was an invader, the result being that I should have died before the age of two. Because my dad had secretly been working closely with Trent's dad trying to save his species at the time, Trent's dad had tinkered with the genetic makeup of my mitochondria, modifying something just enough that the enzyme would be ignored. I truly believe that he hadn't known the enzyme was what allowed my blood to kindle demon magic, and I thanked God the only people who knew it were me and my friends. And Trent. And a few demons. And whatever demons they told. And whomever Trent told. And Lee, of course, the only other witch Trent's dad had fixed.

Okay, so maybe it wasn't that good a secret anymore.

Trent and I were currently at an impasse, with me trying to put him in jail and him trying to buy my services or kill me—depending on his mood—and while I could bring the house down on him if I went public about his illegal biodrugs, I'd probably end up in medical confinement in Siberia—or, worse yet, surrounded by salt water like Alcatraz—and he'd be back on the streets and campaigning for reelection in less time than it takes a pixy to sneeze. That's just the kind of personal power the man had.

And it is really irritating, I thought, shifting my weight to my other foot as the elevator dinged and the doors slid open.

Immediately I got out and jabbed at the "down" button. No way was I going to go through the halls to the closet-size secondary elevator and up to the roof with Quen. I was impulsive, not stupid. Quen ghosted out as well, looking like a bodyguard as he stood in front of the elevator doors until they closed again.

My eyes went to the camera in the corner, its friendly red light blinking. I'd stay there until another car arrived. "Don't touch me," I muttered. "There isn't enough money in the world for me to work for Trent again. He's a manipulative, power-hungry, spoiled only-child who thinks he's above the law. And he kills people like a homeless man opens a can of beans."

Quen shrugged. "He's also loyal to those who have earned his trust, intelligent, and generous to those he cares about."

"And those he doesn't care about don't matter." Hip cocked, I silently waited, getting more annoyed. *Where in hell is the elevator?*

"I wish you'd reconsider," Quen said, and I jerked back when he pulled an amulet from his sleeve. After giving me a high-eyebrow look, he turned a slow circuit, attention lightly fixed on the redwood disk glowing a faint green. It was probably a detection amulet of some kind. I had one that would tell me if there were any deadly spells in my vicinity, but I'd quit wearing it when it kept triggering the anti-theft wards in the mall.

Apparently satisfied, Quen slid the amulet away. "I need you to go into the ever-after to retrieve an elven sample."

I laughed at that, and anger flickered over the older man. "Trent just got Ceri's sample," I said, pulling my shoulder bag tight to me. "I'd think that would keep him busy for a while. Besides, you couldn't pay me enough to go into the ever-after. Especially not for a chunk of two-thousand-year-old dead elf."

One of the elevators behind me dinged, and I backed up to it, ready to make my escape.

"We know where a tissue sample is. We just need to get it," Quen said, his gaze flicking behind me as the doors opened.

I backed into it, standing so he couldn't follow me. "How?" I said, feeling secure.

"Ceri," he said simply, fear flashing in the back of his eyes.

The doors started to close, and I hit the "open" button. "Ceri?" I questioned, wondering if this was why I hadn't seen much of her lately. She knew I hated Trent, but she was an elf and he was an elf—and seeing as she had been born into royalty and he was a zillionaire, it would be foolish to think that they hadn't had some contact the last few months, whether they liked each other or not.

Seeing my interest, Quen took a more confident stance. "She and Trent have been having tea every Thursday," he said softly, sneaking a guilty glance at the hallway. "You should thank her. He's absolutely obsessed with her even as her demon smut terrifies him. I think that's part of the attraction, actually. But he's starting to consider that demon smut might not equal a bad person. She saved my relationship with him. She is a very wise woman."

She ought to be, seeing as she had over a thousand years of servitude to a demon. The doors started closing again, and I hit the button for a few more seconds. "Everything went to hell when Trent found out you use black magic to protect him, eh?"

Quen didn't shift, even maintaining his sedate breathing, but his very stillness told me I was right.

"So?" I said belligerently.

"So he's starting to entertain the thought that you might be trustworthy, too. Will you at least consider it? We need the sample."

The reminder of my own demon-smut-laced soul bothered me, and I jabbed at the "close" button. No freaking way. "Get back to me later, Quen. Like a hundred years later."

"We don't have a hundred years," Quen said, desperation entering his voice. "We have eight months."

Oh, shit.

I pushed myself into motion, my shoulder bag catching on the doors as I shoved my way past them. Quen had moved back. His lips were tightly pressed, as if he wished he hadn't had to say that to get me to listen. "What do you mean, eight months? As in one less than nine?"

Quen said nothing. Didn't even look at me. And I didn't dare touch him.

"He got her pregnant?" I exclaimed, not caring who heard me. "The son of a bitch! The stinking son of a bitch!"

I was so angry, I was almost laughing. Quen's jaw had clenched so tight his pox scars stood out white and stark. "Will you do it?" he said stiffly.

"I want to talk to Trent," I said. No wonder Ceri was avoiding me. The woman was recovering from a thousand years of demon servitude, and Trent goes and gets her pregnant! "Where is he?"

"Shopping."

My eyes narrowed. "Where?"

"Across the street."

He was shopping. A hundred to one it wasn't for baby booties or a car seat. Remembering Marshal and our coffee date, I glanced out the cloudy window to estimate the time. It couldn't be much past one o'clock. Plenty of time. Unless this was a ruse and Trent was going to try to kill me—in which case I might run a little late.

I hit the "down" button hard, and the elevator doors opened immediately. Shopping? He was shopping? "After you," I said, and followed Quen into the lift.

Seven

The thin heat from the sidewalk vanished when I turned the corner and entered the shadow of tall buildings. "Where is he?" I said, holding my hair out of my face when I looked to Quen. He was beside and a little behind me, and it gave me the creeps.

The quiet, powerful man pointed with his eyes across the street, and when I followed his gaze, I felt a wash of apprehension. OTHER EARTHLINGS COSTUMER, INC. Holy crap, Trent was picking out a Halloween costume?

I pushed myself into motion and headed for the exclusive costumer. Well, why not? Trent had parties to go to like anyone else. Probably more of them. But Other Earthlings? You needed an appointment just to walk in, especially in October.

Hesitating at the curb, I felt Quen's presence slide up behind me. "Will you stop guarding me?" I muttered, and Quen made a little start.

"Sorry," he said, then hastened to catch up when I crossed in the middle of the street. I caught him glancing at the crosswalk and snickered. *Yeah, me bad.*

After a moment's hesitation at the brass BY APPOINTMENT ONLY sign, I reached for the door only to have someone from inside pull it open. The doorman looked seriously brain-dead when I entered, but before I could say anything, an older woman in a crisp peach skirt and jacket click-clacked to us, the sound of her heels muffled when they found the thick white carpet. "I'm sorry. We're closed to walk-ins," the woman said, her face a mix of cool professionalism and polite disdain at my jeans and sweater. "Would you like to make an appointment for next year?"

My pulse quickened and I cocked my hip at her obvious but unspoken opinion that hell would freeze over before I'd ever have enough money to buy even a complexion charm from them. I took a breath to demand to see their hair straighteners, knowing their claim to be able to straighten any hair wouldn't be able to touch mine, when Quen settled in behind me, too close for my comfort.

"Oh! You're with Mr. Kalamack?" she said, only the faintest blush marring the aged whiteness of her complexion.

I glanced at Quen. "Not really. I'm Rachel Morgan, and I've got something to say to Mr. Kalamack. I understand he's here?"

The woman's mouth dropped open, and she came forward to take my hands. "You're Alice's daughter?" she said breathlessly. "Oh, I should have known. You look just like her, or you would if she wouldn't spell herself down. It is *such* a pleasure to meet you!"

Excuse me? She was pumping my arm up and down enthusiastically, and when I looked at Quen, he seemed as mystified as me.

"We don't have any openings today, sweetheart," she said, and I blinked at her familiarity. "But let me talk to Renfold. He'll stay late for you. Your mother's straightening charms have saved our reputation *too* many times."

"My mother's hair straighteners?" I managed, grabbing her wrist and extraditing my hand from hers. I was going to have to talk to my mother. This was so not-good. Just how long had she been making bootleg charms?

The woman, Sylvia, according to a name tag outlined in green pearls, smiled and winked at me as if we were grand friends. "You don't think you're the only person who has difficult-to-charm hair?" she said, then reached to touch my hair fondly as if it were a thing of beauty, not a constant bother. "I will never understand why no one is satisfied with what nature gives them. I think it's wonderful that you appreciate yours."

"Appreciate" wasn't the right word, but I didn't want to stand here and discuss hair. "Uh, I need to speak to Trent. He's still here, right?"

The woman's surprise that I was on a first-name basis with the eminently eligible bachelor flashed across her face. She glanced at Quen, who nodded, and with a soft "This way, please," she led us through the store.

I felt better now that we were moving, even if the staff was whispering as Sylvia led us along a wandering path through racks of scrumptious clothing. The store smelled wonderfully of expensive fabrics and exotic perfumes, plus the snap of ozone that said ley line charms were made and invoked here. Other Earthlings was an all-encompassing costumer, supplying the clothes, prosthetics as needed, and charms to make anyone into anyone else. They weren't online, and the only way you could get their products was to make an appointment. I couldn't help but wonder what Trent was going for, costume-wise.

Quen was behind me again, and Sylvia led us past a small back counter and to a short hall with four doors. They were set back like the entries to high-class hotel rooms, and from behind the last, I could hear Trent's voice.

The soft murmur of it went right to my middle and twisted something. God, he had a beautiful voice: low, resonant, and rich with unexplored undertones—like shadowed moss in the sun-dappled woods. I was certain his voice contributed to how well he did in the city elections—if the generous donations to underprivileged children and hospitals weren't enough.

Clearly not hearing anything in Trent's voice but words, Sylvia knocked smartly on the door and entered without waiting for an invitation. I hung back and let Quen go in ahead of me. I didn't like being burst in upon by rude salespeople, and they did sell clothes here. And while seeing Trent in his tighty-whities would make my decade, I'd found out long ago that I couldn't stay mad at a man wearing nothing but underwear. They looked so charmingly vulnerable.

The rich smell of wool and leather struck deeper as I entered. The lights were low at the perimeter of the comfortably warm, low-ceilinged room, helping to hide the open cupboards filled with racks of costumes, hats, feathers, wings, and even tails—things that ley line charms couldn't easily create. To my right in the shadows was a low table holding wine and cheese, to my left a tall screen. Smack in the middle and under can lights was an ankle-high round stage cradled in the lee of a trifold mirror. Low racks of amulets surrounded it, the wood structures having the smoothness and color of hundred-year-old ash. And in the center of it all was Trent.

He wasn't aware I was in the room, clearly trying to fend off the overenthusiastic attentions of the witch helping him try on ley line amulets. Beside him was Jon, his freakishly tall lackey, and I bristled, remembering him tormenting me when I had been a mink trapped in Trent's office.

Trent frowned at his reflection and handed the clerk an amulet. His hair flashed back to its usual transparent whiteness that some children have, and the witch began babbling, deducing that he wasn't doing well. Trent was clean shaven and comfortably tan, with a smooth brow, green eyes, that gorgeous voice, and a cultivated laugh. A politician through and through. He wasn't much taller than me when I was in heels, wearing his thousand-dollar silk-and-linen suit with the VOTE FOR KALAMACK pin well. It accented his trim form, making me believe he actually got out and rode his race-winning horses more than once every new moon when he played The Huntsman in his fenced-in, old-growth planned forest.

He gave the witch a professional smile as he refused another amulet, his unworked hands gesturing smoothly. There were no rings on his fingers, and seeing as I broke up his wedding by arresting him, it was likely it would stay that way, unless he was going to make an honest woman of Ceri, which I doubted. Trent lived by appearances, and him publicly joining with a demon's ex-familiar covered in smut any witch could see with their second sight probably didn't fit into his political agenda. He hadn't seemed to have a problem knocking her up, though.

Trent ran his fingers over his carefully styled hair to flatten a few floating strands as Sylvia approached. Shifting my shoulder bag forward, I said loudly, "That suit would look better with a burping pad."

Trent stiffened. His eyes flicking to the mirror, he searched the shadows for me. At his side, Jon pulled himself upright, the distasteful man holding a thin hand to his eyes to see through the glare. The witch at his feet fell back, and Sylvia murmured an apology, flustered, as her most valuable client and the daughter of one of her suppliers glared at each other.

"Quen," Trent finally said, his voice now hard but no less beautiful. "I don't doubt you have an explanation for this."

Quen took a slow breath before he started forward. "You weren't listening, Sa'han. I had to try another method to bring you to see reason."

Trent waved the clerk away, and Jon strode across the room to flick on the main lights. I squinted as light blossomed, then smiled cattily at Trent. He had regained his composure remarkably fast, with only the slight tightening of the skin around his eyes giving away his annoyance. "I was listening," he said, turning. "I choose to think other than you."

Stepping from the stage, the multimillionaire shook his sleeves down. It was a nervous reaction he had yet to break himself of. Or maybe his jacket was too tight. "Ms. Morgan," he said lightly, not meeting my gaze. "Your services are not required. You have my apologies for my security officer wasting your time. Tell me what I owe you, and Jon will draft you a check."

That was kind of insulting, and I couldn't help my snort. "I don't charge if I don't do the run," I said. "Unlike *some* people." I held my arms over my chest as a flicker of annoyance crossed Trent's face and vanished. "And I didn't come here to work for you," I added. "I came because I wanted to tell you to your face that you're a lowlife, manipulative bastard. I told you if you hurt Ceri that I'd be ticked. Consider yourself warned." Angry was good. The pain from losing Kisten disappeared when I was angry, and right now, I was pissed.

The witch who had been helping him gasped, and Sylvia started for me, rocking to a halt when Trent lifted his hand to stop her. God, I hated that—as if he had given me permission to call him names. Ticked, I tilted my head, waiting for his response.

"Is that a threat?" Trent asked softly.

My gaze went to Jon, who was grinning as if my saying yes would please him immensely. Quen's expression had gone dark. He was mad, but what had he really expected me to do? Still, I did want to get out of here on my own power and not at the end of an I.S. leash, arrested for harassment . . . or whatever Trent wanted. He might own the I.S. now that Piscary was gone.

"Take it any way you want," I said. "You are scum. Absolute scum, and the world would be better without you." I wasn't sure I truly believed that, but it felt good saying it.

Trent thought for all of three seconds. "Sylvia, if we might have the room?"

I stood, smug, as the room emptied with soft murmurs of apologies given and reassurances offered.

"Jon," he added as Sylvia headed out, "see that we are not disturbed."

Sylvia hesitated by the open door, then vanished into the hallway to leave the door open. The older man's craggy face went pale. He was being gotten rid of, and he knew it.

"Sa'han," he started, cutting it short when Trent's eyes narrowed. *What a sissy-pants.*

Jon's thin, long hands clenched as he shot me a look and left. The door shut softly behind him, and I turned to Trent, ready to blast him. I wasn't about to air Ceri's dirty laundry where it might get into the tabloids, but now, I could really say what I thought.

"I can't believe you knocked Ceri up. God, Trent! You are unbelievable!" I said, gesturing. "She is just starting to rebuild herself. She doesn't need this emotional crap!"

Trent glanced at Quen. The security officer had taken a wide-footed stance before the closed door, his arms loose at his sides and his face lacking emotion. Seeing his nonchalance, Trent stepped back onto the stage and began sifting through the charms. "None of this is your business, Morgan."

"It became my business when you romanced information from my friend, knocked her up, then asked me to do something you're afraid to," I said, taking offense at his cavalier attitude.

Trent bent over the metallic ley line charms as he watched me through the mirror. "And what have I asked you to do?" he said, his voice rising and falling like a gust of rain.

My blood pressure spiked, and I stepped forward, halting when Quen cleared his throat. "You are despicable," I said. "You know the chances that I'd go into the ever-after to help Ceri are a hundred times better than me going to help *you*. I'd hate you for that if nothing else. How cowardly is that? Manipulating someone into doing something you're afraid to do yourself. A stinking coward, not willing to help your kin except for when you're safe and secure in your little underground labs. You're a mouse burger."

Trent straightened, surprised. "Mouse burger?"

"Mouse burger," I stated again, arms crossed and hip cocked. "A weenie little man with the courage of a mouse."

A faint smile quirked the corner of his lips. "That sounds funny coming from a woman who dated a rat."

"He wasn't a rat when we dated," I shot back, face flaming.

Trent's attention went to his image in the mirror, and he pulled the pin on the ley line charm to invoke it. A shimmer flared through his aura, making it visible for an instant as the illusion took over. I snorted; Trent now looked like he had gained twenty pounds of muscle, his coat seeming to bulge with the illusion. "I didn't ask for your help with retrieving a sample of elven tissue," he said, turning sideways to see himself and frowning at the result.

Behind me, Quen shifted uneasily. It was a small motion, but it rang through me like a gunshot. The request for help could have been Quen acting on his own. He'd done so before.

"Well, Quen did, then," I said, knowing I was right when Trent's attention flicked to the security officer through the mirror.

"Apparently," Trent said dryly. "But I didn't." Grimacing, he felt his face. It looked like he'd been pumping iron, bulgy and ugly. "I don't need your help. I will go into the ever-after myself and retrieve the sample. Ceri's child will be healthy."

I couldn't stop my laugh at the mental image of Trent standing in the ever-after, and the man reddened. Relaxing, I slumped into one of the cushy chairs by the wine and cheese and sat with my feet spread wide. "I can see why you came to me," I said to Quen. "You think you can handle the ever-after?" This was directed at Trent. "You wouldn't last a minute. Not a freaking minute." I eyed the cheese. I hadn't eaten anything since this morning, and my mouth started to water at the sharp scent. "The wind might muss up your hair," I said lightly.

Quen stepped from the door. "So you'll go in his stead?"

Reaching for a cracker, I hesitated until Trent grimaced. But he hadn't said I couldn't have it, so I snapped the cracker in two and ate half. "No."

Looking like a steroid poster boy, Trent frowned at Quen. "Morgan doesn't need to be involved in this." His gaze went to me. "Rachel. Leave."

As if I ever do anything *he tells me to do?*

Trent's fingers sifted through a display of amulets, choosing one that added eight inches to his height. The fake bulk thinned a little, but not much. I could feel the tension rise as I stayed where I was. Quen would have to work to get me out of here, and I knew he'd rather wait until I was ready. "Lowlife Romeo," I said, taking another cracker and adding a piece of cheese. "Slime of the earth. I knew you were a murderer, but knocking up Ceri and abandoning her? That's pathetic, Trent. Even for you."

At that, Trent turned. "I did nothing of the kind," he said, his voice rising. "She is getting the finest care. Her child will have every opportunity."

I smiled. It wasn't often I could get him to lose his professional edge and act his age. He wasn't much older than me, but he got precious little chance to enjoy his wealthy youth.

"I'll bet," I said, egging him on. "Who are you trying to be here?" I asked, gesturing to the charms. "Frankenstein's monster?"

His neck went red, and Trent took off the height and weight charms. "You're embarrassing yourself, not me," he said, once again his usual size and shape. "I offered to move her into my compound. I offered to put her anywhere she liked from the Alps to Zimbabwe. She chose to stay with Mr. Bairn, and whereas I might object—"

"Bairn?" I gasped, jerking upright, my fake indolence vanishing. "You mean Keasley?" I stared into Trent's mocking green eyes. "Leon Bairn? But he's dead!"

Trent was positively smug. Showing me his back, he rifled through a rack of earth charms and watched his hair shift color. "And whereas I might otherwise object—"

"Bairn did the investigation on your parents' deaths," I interrupted, thoughts scrambling. "And my dad's." *Bairn is supposed to be dead. Why is he across the road pretending to be a kind old man named Keasley? And how did Trent know who he was?*

His hair now an authoritative gray, Trent frowned. "And whereas I might otherwise object," he tried again, "Quen assures me that between Bairn and two pixies—"

"Two!" I blurted. "Jih took a husband?"

"Damn it, Rachel, will you shut up?"

My attention fixed on him, and I hesitated. Trent's face was longer, kind of creepy. He had the bulking-up charm on again, but with the extra height, the roundness had been lost. I blinked at him, then closed my mouth. Trent was giving me information. That didn't happen very often. Maybe I should shut up.

I forced myself to recline in the chair, pantomiming zipping my mouth shut. But my foot was jiggling. Trent watched it for a moment, then turned to the mirror.

"Quen assures me that Ceridwen is as safe in that nasty little hole of a house as she would be with me. She's agreed to receive medical attention at my expense, and if she's lacking anything, it's because she has stubbornly refused to accept it."

The last was said rather dryly, and I couldn't help my rueful smile as Trent studied his reflection, clearly not pleased with what he saw. I understood completely. Though mild mannered most times, when Ceri set her mind to something, she was quietly adamant, then aggressively so if she didn't get her way. She had been born into royalty, and I had a feeling that apart from having to be submissive to Al when she was his familiar, she had pretty much ruled the rest of his household. Until her mind had broken and she lost the will to do anything at all.

Trent was watching me when I met his gaze, clearly bewildered at my fond smile. Shrugging, I ate another cracker. "What are her chances for a healthy baby?" I asked, wondering how guilty I was going to have to feel about my refusal to go into the ever-after.

A silver-haired Trent went back to the ley line charms. He was silent, and I imagined he was weighing his words carefully. "If she had a child with someone from her own period, chances would be good that her child would be healthy with a minimal amount of genetic intervention," he finally said. Choosing another ley line charm, he invoked it. A shimmer cascaded over him, and his height grew by almost three inches. Tossing the invocation pin aside, he kept the charm.

His fingers among the shards of metal, he almost whispered, "Having a child with someone of our generation, the chances of a healthy child are only marginally better than anyone else's without intervention. Though some of the repairs my father and I have managed are hooked into mitochondrial DNA and therefore passed from mother to child, most aren't, and we are limited by the health of the egg and sperm at the time of conception. Ceri's reproductive capabilities are excellent." His eyes met mine, every drop of emotion gone. "It's those of us who are left that are failing her."

I wouldn't look away, though guilt smacked me a good one. Trent's father had kept me alive by modifying my mitochondria. Even if I conceived a child with a man who carried Rosewood syndrome, our child would survive, free of the genetic aberration that had been killing thousands of witches in infancy for millennia. My attention rose from the half-eaten cracker in my hands. It seemed unfair that elven efforts could save a witch but not the elves themselves.

Trent smiled knowingly, and I dropped my gaze. He had to guess where my thoughts were, and it made me uncomfortable that we were starting to understand what drove each of us, even if we didn't agree on each other's methods. Life had been easier when I had been able to pretend I couldn't see shades of gray.

"Who are you trying to be?" I said suddenly, trying to change the subject and gesturing at the amulets so he knew what I was talking about.

Quen shifted into a more comfortable position, and Trent sighed, going from successful business executive to embarrassed young man in an instant. "Rynn Cormel," he said hesitantly.

"It's awful," I said, and Trent nodded as he looked at his reflection.

"Yes, it is. I think I should try for someone else. Something less . . . ominous."

He started taking off charms, and gathering myself, I lurched out of the chair and brushed my sweater free of crackers. Leaving my shoulder bag on the table, I headed to the open closets. "Here," I said, giving him an oversize black suit coat.

"That's too big," he said, but he took it. The only charm he still had was the earth charm that turned his hair gray, and the silver gave him a more distinguished look.

"It's supposed to be big. Just put it on," I griped, watching as he shuffled out of his linen coat and handed it to me. A puff of scent rose as I took it, and I breathed deeply. Sort of a mix of mint and cinnamon . . . with a little bit of crushed leaves and, oh, was that a hint of leather from the stables? Damn, he smelled good.

Trying not to be obvious about my sniffing, I draped it over one of the amulet racks and turned to find Trent wearing the coat. The sleeves covered his hands but for his fingertips; it was clearly too long. The starkness of the black fabric looked bad with his complexion, but when I was done with him, it would be perfect.

Trent moved to take it off, and I waved for him to wait. "Try this," I said, handing him a ley line charm to add about six inches of height. He could make up the rest with his shoes and it wouldn't cost him beaucoup bucks. The usual rate was a thousand dollars an inch, but here it was probably more.

He put the charm on, but I didn't wait to see the result, already back among the amulets and the more familiar earth charms. "Longer, longer . . . ," I muttered. "Don't they have these in any order? Ah. Here it is." Pleased, I turned, almost smacking into him. Trent backed up, and I extended the charm. "This will add a few inches to your hair. Hold on." I shuffled through the clutter, found a finger stick, pricked my finger, and while Trent watched, invoked the amulet with three drops of my blood.

"Now try it," I said.

Trent took it, his silver-enhanced hair growing the instant his fingers encircled the redwood disk. Unlike ley magic charms, earth magic needed to be touching the skin, not just within a person's aura.

"Okay . . . you don't want a bulk-up amulet," I directed. "You don't need muscles, you need mass." I turned with the proper ley line charm. "Try this," I said, and he silently took it, his weight seeming to grow to match his new height. I smiled as I eyed my efforts. It was a delicate balancing act, one I'd practiced with my mom for the better part of two decades before I'd moved out. And having this much variety at my fingertips made it a real pleasure.

"Rynn Cormel's facial structure is kind of spare," I murmured, fingers dancing through the ley line charms. "We don't want to mess with your weight-to-height ratio, so if we add a few years with an age amulet, and then add a complexion charm to remove the wrinkles . . ." I quickly chose the age ley line charm, then hesitated. If it were me, I'd spring for the earth magic complexion amulet rather than a ley line spell of illusion in case someone touched my face. Then I shrugged. Like anyone would be touching Trent's face at a party? And a second ley line charm joined the pile.

"Your chin needs to be longer . . . ," I murmured, rifling through the labeled ley line charms. "Get rid of the tan. A wider brow, thicker eyebrows. Shorter eyelashes. And ears . . ." I hesitated, my focus blurring as I brought the undead vampire's face to mind. "His ears don't have much of a lobe and are round." I glanced at Trent. "Yours are kind of pointy at the top."

He cleared his throat in warning.

"Here," I said, invoking the charms I had selected as I dropped them one by one into his hand. "Now let's see what you look like."

Trent slipped them into a pocket, and I turned to the mirror. Slowly I smiled. Trent said nothing, but Quen swore softly, his steps unheard on the carpet as he came forward.

I went to a drawer marked GLASSES and, after shuffling

around, pulled out a pair of modern wire-rims. I gave them to Trent, and when he put them on, Quen whistled low and long. "Morgan," Quen said, shooting me a wary but impressed glance. "That is fantastic. I am going to install a few more charm monitors in the hallways."

"Thank you," I said modestly, beaming. I stood beside Trent and admired my handiwork. "You need teeth, yet," I said, and Trent nodded slowly, as if worried he might break the spell if he moved too fast. "Are you going with caps or a charm?" I asked.

"Charm," Trent said absently, turning his head to get a better glimpse of himself.

"Caps are more fun," I said, inordinately pleased. There was an entire bin of teeth charms, and I went ahead and invoked the ley line spell and dropped it into his pocket.

"And you would know that how?" Trent asked slyly.

"Because I have a pair," I said, refusing to show any pain about Kisten in front of Trent, but I couldn't meet his eyes.

Done, I stood beside Trent as he smiled at the illusion of longer teeth. Somewhere along the line, I'd joined him on the stage. Not wanting to get down and look subservient, I quieted my sudden nervousness at how close we were. And neither of us was trying to kill or arrest the other. Huh. How about that?

"What do you think?" I asked, since I had yet to hear Trent's opinion.

Standing beside me, Trent, who now had distinguished gray hair, a thin, almost hollowed face, six more inches, and fifty more pounds, shook his head, looking nothing like himself and everything like Rynn Cormel. Damn, I should have gone into showbiz.

"I look just like him," he said, clearly impressed.

"Almost." More pleased than I wanted to be by his approval, I invoked and handed him one last ley line charm.

Trent took it, and my breath caught. His eyes had gone pupil black. Hungry vampire black. A shiver rose through me. "Holy crap," I said, pleased. "Can I play dress-up, or what?"

"This is . . . impressive," Trent said, and I got off the stage.

"You're welcome," I said. "Don't let them overcharge you. There are only thirteen charms there, and only the two for your hair are earth magic and not pure illusion." I glanced at the plush surroundings, deciding that they wouldn't sell temporary ley line spells with a reduced life. "Maybe sixteen grand for the entire outfit if they put it all in two charms. You can triple that considering who you're buying them from." Doppelgänger charms were legal on Halloween, not cheap.

Trent smiled, a truly vampiric smile, charismatic, dangerous, and oh-so-seductive. Oh, God. I had to get out of there. He was hitting all my buttons, and I think he knew it.

"Ms. Morgan," Trent said, his suit rustling as he followed me off the stage. "I do believe you're betraying yourself."

Swell. He totally knew it. "Don't forget to pick up a charm to change your scent," I said as I went to get my shoulder bag. "You won't be able to match Cormel's individual smell, but a generic scent charm ought to fool everyone." I plucked my bag up, then turned, taking one last look at him. *Damn.* "Everyone except those who know his scent, of course."

Trent glanced at Quen, who was still staring in disbelief. "I'll keep that in mind," Trent muttered.

I headed for the door, my pace faltering when Quen said, "Rachel, please reconsider?"

My good mood crashed, and I stopped two feet from the door with my head bowed. Quen was asking, but I knew he was asking for Trent. I thought of Ceri and the happiness a healthy child would bring her, the healing that could come of it. "Trent, I can't. The risk—"

"What would you risk for your child to be healthy?" Trent interrupted, and I turned around, surprised at the question. "What would any parents do?"

Tension pulled me stiff, and hearing the accusation of cowardice in his voice, I hated him more than I ever had before. I'd never thought about children much until I met Kisten, and then it had always been with a melancholy sadness that they wouldn't have his beautiful eyes. But if I had a child? And that child was suffering as I had in my past? Yeah. I'd risk it all.

Trent seemed to see it in my eyes and a hint of victory quirked his lips. But then I thought of Al. I'd been his familiar once. Sort of. And it was hell on earth. That was assuming he wouldn't outright kill me. I wouldn't chance it. I was going to think with my head this time and not be goaded into a stupid decision by Trent pushing my buttons—and I wasn't going to feel guilty about it either.

A shiver lifted through me and was gone. Lifting my chin, I stared until the disgust I directed at him made his eye twitch. "No," I said, my voice shaking. "*I won't.* I go in the ever-after, and Al will pick me up three seconds after I tap a line. After that, I'm dead. It's that simple. You can save your own damn species."

"We don't need Morgan's help," Trent said, his voice tight. But I noticed he'd waited until I refused before he said it. Ceri wasn't the only stubborn elf, and I wondered if Trent's new desire to prove his worth came from his trying to impress her.

"This isn't my problem," I muttered, hiking my shoulder bag up. "I have to go."

Feeling ugly, I opened the door and walked out, bumping Jon in his gut with my elbow when he didn't get out of my way quick enough. I had never cared about Trent's grand plan to save the elves before, but this wasn't sitting well with me.

I consoled myself that Ceri's child would survive whether they had a thousand-year-old sample from her or a two-thousand-year-old sample from the ever-after. The only difference was the amount of tinkering that they would have to do to the child.

My mouth twisted into a grimace as I remembered my three summers spent at Trent's father's Make-A-Wish camp for dying children. It would be stupid to believe that all the children there were on the roster to save. They were a living camouflage for the few that had the money to pay for a Kalamack cure. And I would give anything to have escaped the pain of making friends with children who were going to die.

The chatter of the people up front changed when they caught sight of me, and I waved so they'd leave me alone. I stormed to the door, not caring if Jon thought his boss had gotten the best of me. I didn't stop or slow down until my feet reached the sidewalk.

Street noise hit me, and the sun. Slowing, I remembered where I was and did an about-face. My car was the other way. I didn't look up as I passed the front window, hiding my eyes as I dug my phone out of my bag. Bothered, I hit the return-last-call number to tell Marshal I had a friend emergency and I'd let him know if I couldn't make Fountain Square by three.

I had to talk to Ceri.

Eight

I cut a sharp left into the carport, taking it fast because of my lingering anger at Trent. Habit alone kept the paint unscratched. I loved my car, and though I was jamming the gearshift like an Indy 500 driver, I wasn't going to do anything to hurt my mobile icon of independence. Especially after finally getting my license back and the dent I didn't remember putting in the car repaired. Fortunately the church was in a quiet residential area, and only the sixty-year-old oaks lining the street saw my ugly temper.

I hit the brakes sharply, and my head swung forward and back. A perverse sense of satisfaction filled me. The grille was four inches from the wall. Perfect.

Grabbing my bag from the backseat, I got out and slammed the door. It was edging two. Ceri was probably still asleep, seeing as elves kept the same sleeping habits as pixies when they could, but I had to talk to her.

I heard the dry clatter of pixy wings when my feet hit the walk, and I swung my hair out of the way for whomever it was. My money was on Jenks; it was his habit to stay awake with the few kids on sentry duty, sleeping odd hours when everyone else was up.

"Rache," Jenks said in greeting, his swooping dart to land on my shoulder shifting at the last moment when he saw my sour expression. Hovering, he flew backward in front of me. I hated it when he did that. "Ivy called you, huh?" he said, his attitude one of affronted righteousness. "It's in the eaves in the front. I can't wake the damn thing up. You need to use a spell or something."

My eyebrows rose. *It's in the eaves?* "What's in the eaves?"

"A gargoyle," Jenks said angrily, and my alarm vanished. "A clumsy-ass, pimply-faced, big-footed gargoyle."

"Really?" I said as I stopped right there and peered up at the steeple, not seeing the gargoyle. "How long has it been here?"

"How the hell should I know!" he shouted, and I realized that was where his anger was coming from. Someone had slipped through his lines, and he didn't like it. Jenks saw my smile, and he put his hands on his hips as he hovered backward. "What's so funny?"

"Nothing." I pushed myself into motion, making a left on the sidewalk to go to Keasley's instead of the church. Jenks's wings hummed when I took the unexpected direction, and he hastened to catch up. "We'll talk to him or her tonight, okay?" I said, wanting to get Ivy's take before we made any sweeping decisions. "If it's young, it's probably just looking for somewhere to hang."

"They don't hang, they lurk," he muttered, wings clattering aggressively. "Something's wrong with it, or it would be with its kin. They don't move, Rachel, unless they did something really bad."

"Maybe he's a rebel like you, Jenks," I said, and the pixy made a tiny huffing sound.

"Where are we going?" he asked shortly as he turned to look at the church behind us.

Immediately my bad mood returned. "To talk to Ceri. I ran into Trent trying on costumes."

"What does that have to do with Ceri?" Jenks interrupted, as protective of the small but self-assured woman as I was.

Toes edging the drop off of the curb, I pulled myself to a

stop so I could watch his expression. "He got her pregnant."

"Pregnant!"

The shrill shout was punctuated by a flash of dust I could see even in the strong afternoon light. "It gets better," I said, stepping into the empty street and heading for the tired, sixty-plus-year-old house Ceri and Keasley shared. "He wants me to go into the ever-after to get a sample so their child will be born without any effects of the curse. Tried to guilt me into it." *And it almost worked.*

"Pregnant?" Jenks repeated, his angular face showing his shock. "I gotta smell her."

The scraping of my boots on the pavement faltered. "You can smell it when someone's pregnant?" I said, somewhat appalled.

Jenks shrugged. "Sometimes. I don't know about elves." He darted to the sidewalk, then back to me. "Can you walk a little faster? I'd like to get there before the sun sets and that thing in the eaves wakes up."

My gaze went three houses down to find Keasley outside enjoying the fall weather, raking leaves. Great, he'd seen me tear into here like a bunny on fire. "Jenks," I said suddenly. "I'm going to do the talking. Not you."

"Yeah, yeah, yeah," he said, and I fixed my gaze on him with a threatening sharpness.

"I mean it. Ceri might not have told him yet."

The hum of his wings dropped in pitch, though he didn't lose a millimeter of height. "Okay," he said hesitantly.

My boots hit the sidewalk and the dappled pattern of sun that made it through the colored leaves still clinging to the dark branches. *Keasley is Leon Bairn?* I thought as I looked him over. Leon was the only other person besides me to quit the I.S. and survive, though he'd apparently had to fake his death to do it. I was guessing that Trent knew it because he had helped. He would have been about fifteen then, but just coming into his parents' legacy and eager to show his stuff.

I glanced at Jenks, remembering how mad the pixy had

been when I hid from him that Trent was an elf. If Keasley was Leon, then he was a runner. And Jenks wouldn't violate that trust for anything.

"Jenks, can you keep a secret?" I said, slowing when Keasley saw us and stopped his work to lean on his rake. The old man suffered from arthritis so badly that he seldom had the stamina for yard work, despite the pain charms Ceri made for him.

"Maybe," the pixy said, knowing his own limits. I gave him a sharp look, and he grimaced. "Yeah, I'll keep your lame-ass secret. What is it? Trent wears a man-bra?"

A smile quirked my lips before I grew serious. "Keasley is Leon Bairn."

"Holy crap!" Jenks said, a burst of light glowing against the bottom of the leaves. "I take the afternoon off, and you find out Ceri's pregnant and sharing a roof with a dead legend!"

I grinned at him. "Trent was chatty today."

"No fairy-ass kidding." His wings went silver in thought. "So why did Trent tell you?"

I shrugged, running my finger against the thump-bump of the chain-link fence surrounding Keasley's yard as I walked. "I don't know. To prove he knew something I didn't? Did Jih tell you that she's shacked up with a pixy buck?"

"What!"

His wings stopped and my palm darted out with a flash of adrenaline, but he caught himself before he could drop into my palm. Jenks hovered, his face a mask of parental horror. "Trent?" he squeaked. "Trent told you?" And when I nodded, he turned his gaze to the front gardens of the house, just starting to show the grace of a pixy presence even in the fall. "Sweet mother of Tink," he said. "I have to talk to my daughter."

Without waiting for my reply, he darted away, only to jerk to an abrupt halt at the fence. Slipping several inches in height, he yanked a pixy-size red bandanna from a pocket and tied it about his ankle. It was a pixy's version of a white flag: a promise of good intention and no poaching. He'd never worn it before when visiting his daughter, and the acknowledgment of her new husband had to be bittersweet. His wings a dismal blue, he zipped over the house to the backyard where Jih had been concentrating her efforts on building a garden.

Smiling faintly, I raised a hand to Keasley's hail, opened the gate, and entered the yard.

"Hi, Keasley," I called, looking him over with a new interest born of knowing his history. The old black man stood in the middle of his yard, his cheap sneakers almost hidden by leaves. His jeans were faded by work, not distressing stones in the wash, and his red-and-black plaid shirt looked a size too big, probably gotten at discount somewhere.

His wrinkles gave his face texture that made his expressions easy to read. The tinge of yellow in his brown eyes had me worried, but he was healthy apart from old age and arthritis. I could tell that he'd once been tall; now, though, I could look him eye to eye. Age was beating hard upon his body, but it had yet to touch his mind. He was the neighborhood wise old man and the only one who could give me advice without triggering my resentment.

But it was his hands that I liked the most. You could see how he had lived his entire life in them: dark, spare, knobby with stiffness, but not afraid of work, able to stir spells, stitch vampire bites, and hold pixy children. He had done all three in my sight, and I trusted him. Even if he was pretending to be something he wasn't. Didn't we all?

"Good afternoon, Rachel," he called, his sharp gaze coming back from the roofline and Jenks's disappearing trail of pixy dust. "You look like a piece of autumn in that sweater."

I glanced down at the black-and-red pattern, never having thought about it before. "Thanks. You look good out here raking. Your knees doing okay?"

The old man patted the worn spots, squinting in the sun. "They've been better, but they've been a lot worse, too. Ceri's been in the kitchen a lot lately, trying things out."

I slowed, my feet still on the cracked walk to the front porch. Grass had encroached upon it until it was only eight inches wide. "I suppose," I said softly, "chasing bad guys all your life can really damage a person. If they aren't careful."

He didn't move, going still as he stared at me.

"I, uh, talked to someone today," I said, wanting to hear it from him. "He said—"

"Who?" he rasped, and my face lost its expression. He was frightened. Terrified, almost.

"Trent," I said, pulse quickening as I came forward. "Trent Kalamack. He acted like he's known for a long time." My shoulders tensed, and the dog barking nearby made me nervous.

Exhaling long and slow, Keasley replaced his fear with a relief so deep I could just about feel it. "He has," he said, a shaky hand going over his tight, graying curls. "I have to sit down." He turned to his house. It needed new shingles and paint in the worst way. "Do you want to sit for a moment?"

I thought about Ceri, then Marshal. Then there was the gargoyle Jenks was going on about, too. "Sure."

Keasley made his slow way to the sagging porch steps, propping the rake against the rail before easing himself down in stages with a heavy sigh. A basket of cherry tomatoes decorated the railing to be given out for trick-or-treat, and two pumpkins waited to be carved. I gingerly sat beside him, my knees even with my chest. "Are you okay?" I asked hesitantly when he didn't say anything.

He looked at me askance. "You know how to get an old man's heart going, Rachel. Do Ivy and Jenks know?"

"Jenks," I said, guilt pinching my brow, and he raised a hand to tell me it was all right.

"I trust he will keep his mouth shut," he said. "Trent gave me the means to stage my death. Actually, all he gave me was the DNA-doctored tissue to smear over my front porch, but he knew."

Gave him tissue? There's a nice thought. "Then you really

are—" My words cut off when his twisted hand landed warningly on my knee. In the street, five sparrows fought over a moth they had found, and I listened to them squabble, hearing in his silence his request that I not even say it. "It's been over a decade," I finally protested.

His eyes tracked the birds as one gained the moth and the rest chased the bird across the street. "It doesn't matter," he said. "Like a murder charge, the file stays open."

I followed his gaze to the church Ivy and I shared. "That's why you moved in across from the church, isn't it?" I asked, remembering the day. Keasley had saved my life by removing a delayed combustion charm someone had slipped me on the bus. "You figured if I could survive the I.S.'s death contract, you might find a way, too?"

He smiled to show his yellowing teeth, and he pulled his hand from my knee. "Yes, ma'am. I did. But after seeing how you did it?" Keasley shook his head. "I'm too old to fight dragons. I'll stay Keasley, if you don't mind."

I thought about that, cold despite the sun on us. Becoming anonymous was just something I couldn't do. "You moved in the same day I did, didn't you? You really don't know when Ivy rented the church."

"No." His eyes were on the steeple, the top hidden behind the trees. "But I watched her patterns close that first week, and I'm guessing she'd been there for at least three months."

My head was going up and down. I was learning a lot today. None of it comfortable. "You're a good liar," I said, and Keasley laughed.

"Used to be."

Liar, I thought, and then my mind drifted to Trent. "Uh, is Ceri up? I have to talk to her."

Keasley shifted to look at me. In his tired eyes was a deep relief. I had learned his secret and freed him of the necessity to lie to me. But what I think he was the most grateful for was that I didn't think any less of him for it.

"I think she's asleep," he said, smiling to tell me he was glad I was still his friend. "She's been tired lately."

I'll bet. Giving him a smile, I stood and tugged my jeans straight. I'd long assumed that Ivy had moved in before me, having only pretended to move in the same day to ease my suspicions. Now that I knew the truth, I might confront Ivy about it. Maybe. It didn't necessarily matter—I understood her reasons, and that was enough. Sometimes, just let sleeping vamps lie.

I extended a hand to help Keasley rise. "Will you tell Ceri I came over?" I asked as I held his arm until I knew he had his balance.

The porch creaked behind us, and I whipped my head around. Ceri was standing behind the closed screen door, in a sweaterdress that made her look like a young wife from the sixties. A jumble of emotions hit me as I took in her somber, guilty stance. She didn't look pregnant. She looked worried.

"Did Jenks wake you?" I said in greeting, not knowing what else to say.

She shook her head no with her arms crossed over her middle. Her long, translucent hair was done up in a complex braid that needed at least two pixies to manage it. Even through the screen I could see her cheeks were pale, her green eyes wide, and her narrow chin raised defiantly. Though delicate and petite, her mind was resilient and strong, tempered by a thousand years of serving as a demon's familiar. Elves didn't live any longer than witches, but her life had paused the moment Al took her. My guess was she'd been in her midthirties. She was barefoot, as usual, and her purple dress had black and gold accents. They were the colors that Al made her wear, though admittedly, this wasn't a ball gown.

"Come in," she said softly, vanishing into the dark house.

I glanced at Keasley. He had a wary sharpness to him, having read my tension and the shame she was hiding under her defiance. Or maybe it was guilt.

"Go on," he said, as if wanting us to get this over with so he'd know what was the matter.

Leaving him, I went up the stairs, my tension easing as the shelter of the house accepted me. I didn't think she'd told him yet—which meant I'd been seeing guilt.

The screen door squeaked, and now, knowing Keasley's past, I was sure the lack of oil was intentional. The scent of redwood struck me as I followed the sound of her fading steps down the low-ceilinged hall, past the front room, the kitchen, and all the way to the back of the house and the sunken living room, added on at some point.

The older house muffled outside sounds, and I stood in the middle of the back living room. I was sure this was where she had gone. My gaze traveled over the changes she'd made since moving in: asters arranged in Mason-jar vases, live plants bought off the sale rack and nurtured back to health clustered at the lace-curtained windows, bits of ribbon draped over mirrors to remind wandering spirits not to cross into them, yellowed doilies bought at yard sales decorating the padded arms of the couch, and faded pillows and swaths of fabric disguising the old furniture. The combined effect was clean, comfortable, and soothing.

"Ceri?" I finally called, not having the slightest idea where she was.

"Out here," she said, her voice coming from beyond the door, which was propped open with a potted fig tree.

I winced. She wanted to talk in the garden—her stronghold. Great.

Gathering myself, I headed out to find her seated at a wicker table in the garden. Jih hadn't been tending it very long, but between the enthusiastic pixy and Ceri, the tiny space had gone from a scuffed-up scrap of dirt to a bit of paradise in less than a year.

An old oak tree thicker than I could get my arms around dominated the backyard, multiple swaths of fabric draped over the lower branches to make a fluttering shelter of sorts. The ground under it was bare dirt, but it was as smooth and flat as linoleum. Vines grew above the fence to block the neighbors' view, and the grass had been allowed to grow long past the shade of the tree. I could hear water somewhere and a wren singing as if it were spring, not fall. And crickets.

"This is nice," I said in understatement as I joined her. There was a teapot and two tiny cups on the table, as if she had been expecting me. I would have said Trent had warned her, but Keasley didn't have a phone.

"Thank you," she said modestly. "Jih has taken a husband, and he works very hard to impress her."

I brought my attention back from the garden to focus on Ceri and her anxiety. "Is that where Jenks is?" I asked, wanting to meet the newest member of the family myself.

A smile eased her tight features. "Yes. Can you hear them?"

I shook my head and settled myself in the bumpy wicker chair. *Now, what would be a good segue? So, I hear Jih isn't the only one who's been knocked up. . . .*

Ceri reached for the teapot, her motions wary. "I imagine this isn't a social call, but would you like some tea?"

"No, thanks," I said, then felt a tug on my awareness as Ceri murmured a word of Latin and the pot began to steam. The amber brew tinkled into her tiny cup, the click of the porcelain sounding loud among the crickets.

"Ceri," I said softly. "Why didn't you tell me?"

Her vivid green eyes met mine. "I thought you'd be angry," she said with desperate worry. "Rachel, it's the only way I can get rid of it."

My lips parted. "You don't want it?"

Ceri's expression blanked. She stared wonderingly at me for a moment. "What are we talking about?" she asked cautiously.

"Your baby!"

Her mouth dropped open and she flushed scarlet. "How did you find out . . ."

My pulse had quickened, and I felt unreal. "I talked to Trent this afternoon," I said, and when she just sat there, staring at me with her pale fingers encircling her teacup, I added, "Quen asked me to go into the ever-after for a sample of elven DNA that predates the curse, and I wanted to know what the rush was. He kind of blurted it out."

Panic filled her, showing as her hand flashed to set her cup down and grip my wrist, shocking me. "No," she exclaimed softly, eyes wide and breath fast. "Rachel, you can't. You can't go into the ever-after. Promise me right now that you won't. Ever."

Her fingers were hurting me, and I tried to pull away. "I'm not stupid, Ceri."

"Promise me!" she said loudly. "Right now! You will not go into the ever-after. Not for me. Not for Trent. Not for my child. Never!"

I wrenched my wrist away from her, taken aback at her extreme reaction. I had been in the ever-after before, and I wasn't about to go back. "I told him no. Ceri, I can't. Someone is summoning Al out of confinement, and I can't risk being off hallowed ground after sunset, much less go to the ever-after."

The pale woman caught her emotions, clearly embarrassed. Her eyes flicked to my reddened wrist, and I hid it under the table. I felt guilty about the stand I was taking to stay out of the ever-after, even if it was a smart decision. I wanted to help Ceri, and I felt like a coward. "I'm sorry," I said, then reached for the teapot, wanting a cup of something to hide behind. "I feel like a pile of chicken crap."

"Don't," Ceri said shortly, and my eyes met hers. "This isn't your war."

"It used to be," I said, my thoughts going to the widely accepted theory that the witches had abandoned the ever-after to the demons three thousand years before the elves gave up. Before that, there was no witch history except what the elves remembered for us, and very little elf history either.

Ceri intercepted my reach for the teapot, pouring it out for me and carefully handing me the cup and saucer with the grace of a millennium of practice. I accepted it and took a sip. It wasn't coffee, but I could still feel the caffeine rush, and I eased into the wicker and crossed my legs. I had time, and Ceri, nervous and flustered, clearly was in no state for me to leave yet.

"Ceri," I said, putting a tone of pride in my voice. "You're something else. If I found out that I was pregnant unexpectedly, I'd be falling apart. I can't believe Trent did this to you."

Ceri hesitated over her cup, then took a delicate sip. "He didn't."

I shook my head. "You can't take the blame for this. I know you're a grown woman and you make your own decisions, but Trent is devious and manipulative. He could charm a troll out of her bridge if he tried."

A faint rose color tinged her cheeks. "I mean, it's not Trenton's child."

I stared at her. *If it isn't Trent's . . .*

"It's Quen's," she said, her eyes on the swaths of fabric fluttering overhead.

"B-But . . ." I stammered. *Oh, my God. Quen?* Suddenly his awkward silences and stiff looks meant something completely different. "Trent never said anything! Neither did Quen. They just stood there and let me believe—"

"It's not their place to say anything," Ceri said primly, then set her teacup down with a sharp clink.

The breeze shifted the wispy strands of her hair that had slipped her braid as I realigned my thinking. That's why Quen had gone behind Trent's back to ask for my help. That's why he'd seemed guilty. "But I thought you liked Trent," I finally managed.

Ceri made a face. On me it would have looked ugly; on her, it looked comely. "I do," she said sourly. "He is kind with me, and gentle. He is clever with words and quick to follow my thoughts, and we enjoy each other's company. His bloodline is impeccable . . ." She hesitated, her eyes going to her fingers, now sitting still in her lap. A deep breath lifted through her and was gone. "And he won't touch me without fear."

My brow furrowed in anger.

"It's the demon smut," she said distantly, shame in her gaze darting about. "He thinks it's the bloody kiss of death. That I'm filthy and foul, and that it's catching."

I could not believe this. Trent was a murdering drug lord, and he thought Ceri was dirty?

"Well," she said sourly, as if she'd heard my thoughts, "technically he's right. I could slough it off on him, but I wouldn't." Her eyes came up to find mine, dark with unshed misery. "You believe me, don't you?"

I thought back to Trent's reaction to black magic, and my jaw clenched. "Yeah. Yes," I amended. "He won't touch you, huh?"

Ceri's expression went pleading. "Don't be angry with him. Bartholomew's balls, Rachel," she cajoled. "The man has a right to be scared. I'm mean, I'm nasty, overbearing, temper driven, and I'm covered in demon smut. The first time we met, I knocked Quen out with a black charm and then I threatened him."

"The man was trying to drug me with an illegal charm!" I said. "What were you supposed to do? Ask him to play nice?"

"Quen understands," she said, her eyes watching her still fingers. "I don't have to explain myself or my past to him." Her head came up. "I don't even know how it happened."

"Uh," I murmured, sensing a story coming that I really didn't want to hear.

"I agreed to meet with Trent. I wanted to apologize for threatening him," she said. "I wanted to hear how his genetic treatments are keeping our species alive when magic could not. The afternoon went surprisingly well, and his gardens are so lovely—silent, but lovely—so we had tea the following week, and I told him of my life with Al." A tear spilled over and ran a quick path to her jawline. "I wanted him to know so he'd understand that the demon smut wasn't a sign of one's morals but simply a mark of imbalance upon one's soul. I thought he was beginning to understand," she said softly. "We even laughed at a shared jest, but when I touched him, he jerked back, and though he apologized and turned red, I saw the entire afternoon was a sham. He was entertaining me because he felt he needed to, not because he wanted to."

I could see it clearly in my mind. Trent was slime.

"So I finished our tea, playing the part of a courtesan entertaining the son of a potential ally," she said, and I felt her hurt pride and the shame her words couldn't hide. "I thank God that I saw his true feelings before . . . my heart softened to him."

Ceri sniffed, and I handed her one of the cotton napkins she had arranged about the teapot. Though she said she didn't care for him, I saw that it had wounded her deeply. Probably too far for Trent to ever make amends to the self-admittedly overly prideful woman.

"Thank you," she said, dabbing at her eyes. "Quen drove me home that afternoon as usual. He had witnessed the entire miserable affair, and when I fled his car to find solace in my garden, he followed me, taking me into his arms and telling me I was beautiful and pure. Everything I wanted to be. Everything I know I'm not."

I wanted her to stop, but she had to tell someone. And I knew how she felt, wanting to be loved, accepted—only to be reviled for things she couldn't control. A hot tear spilled over and ran a quick path to my chin when Ceri's eyes rose to mine, red and swimming.

"I spend time with Trent now simply so that Quen may escort me there and back," she said softly. "I think Trent knows it, but I don't care. Quen is confident and secure in his mind. When I'm with him, I feel beautiful and unsullied. I didn't have the ability to say yes or no to a man's attentions for a thousand years," she said, her voice gaining in strength. "I was a thing to Al, something to teach to showcase his talents, and when Quen stirred my passions after a particularly trying engagement with Trent, I realized I wanted more than his gentle words."

My throat was tight when her gaze found mine. *Kisten.* I knew what she meant, and he was gone. Utterly gone.

"I wanted to give myself to a man who would give himself in return," she said, pleading for understanding when I had already given it. "Not just sharing the ecstasy our bodies could bring each other, but sharing our thoughts as well. Quen is a good man," she said as if I would deny it. "He will instill my child with a proper frame of beliefs. I'd rather have as my husband a man of mixed birth who accepts me than a pure-blood who, deep in his soul, thinks I'm tainted."

My hand went out, finding hers. "Ceri—"

She pulled away, apparently thinking I was going to argue with her. Nothing could be further from the truth. "Quen is as noble as any man in my father's court," she said hotly.

"And more honorable than Trent," I said, cutting her argument short. "It's a good decision."

Relief cascaded over her, melting the tension and widening her eyes. She went to say something, then stopped. Steadying herself, she tried again, managing a high, squeaky "Would you like some more tea?"

My cup was full, and I smiled back. "Yes, thank you."

She topped it off, and I took a sip, hearing a new understanding in the cricket-filled silence between us. I knew what it was like to seek that feeling of being wanted—though I was going to play it smart with Marshal, I was the last person to say she should have been stronger. Stronger for what? What was she saving herself for? And I knew Quen would be honest with her. He probably needed an understanding soul as much as she did.

"I saw Quen today," I said, and her expression grew eager, telling me she loved him. "He looks good. Worried about you, I think." God, I felt like I was in high school, but who else did

Ceri have to bubble and overflow with? The woman was in love and couldn't tell anyone.

"I'm fine," she said, flustered.

Smiling at seeing her in such a state, I settled back with my tea. I had some time yet before I had to go. Marshal could wait. "Have you given any thought to moving closer to him?" I said. "Trent offered to put you up in his . . . compound."

"I'm safe here," she said softly, eyes lowered, telling me she had considered it.

"I wasn't thinking about safer," I said, laughing. "I just don't want Quen coming over here all the time. Parking his big-ass limo at the curb. Driving in and out at all hours. Waking me up at sunrise when he beeps his horn for you to come out."

She blushed delicately. "I'm going to stay with Keasley."

My smile faded, and though I didn't want her to leave, I said, "You could both go."

"Jih and her new husband . . . ," she protested, but I could see her desire to be closer to Quen.

"I bet Trent would let pixies in his garden if you asked," I said with a smirk, imagining the man covered in them. "Quen is trying to convince Trent how good pixies are at detecting intruders." *Brand-new gargoyle in our eaves aside.* "And Trent is trying to impress you, even if he's as ignorant as a duck." Her eyebrows were high in speculation, and I added, "He insists *he's* going into the ever-after to get that tissue sample."

"He can do more good in his lab," she said caustically.

"That's where he belongs," I agreed, taking a sip of tea. "Little mouse burger."

Ceri's eyebrows went up, and she lost her stiff, formal stance. "I'm safe here," she reaffirmed. "Nothing will harm me or Keasley. I have defenses that I can raise in an instant."

I didn't doubt it, but demons were able to pop in anywhere but holy ground. "There's Al to think about," I added. "He's gone rogue. Ivy told you, yes?"

She nodded, eyes on the distant vines, and I felt a frown come over me. "Someone has summoned him out of confinement and let him go three nights in a row," I said sourly. "David is checking the incoming claims to see if it's someone local out to get me, or if it's just Al giving some nameless idiot a wish per night to let him go." My lips pressed together and I thought of Nick. My gut said no, and I was going to believe that.

"He tried to kill me last night," I said. "While I was shopping with my mom."

"K-Kill you?"

My attention swung back at her faint stutter. "He says he's got nothing to lose, so he's not going to hold to his agreement to leave me or my kin alone." I hesitated. "Does that mean I can teach anyone how to spindle line energy?" Demon immunity for keeping our mouths shut had been the deal.

"He said he wasn't going to hurt you," she said, looking rightly frightened. "I mean, they aren't going to let him get away with breaking his word, are they? Did you call Minias?"

I let out a puff of air, not eager for the bill from the charm shop to hit my desk. "I didn't have to. He showed up and chased him off," I said, wondering whether, if I asked, if she would come over and sleep in the sanctuary until they found a way to contain Al. "Minias doesn't even care that Al's breaking his word. He's only upset that he's slipping their cell. They pulled Minias off babysitting Newt and put him on demon-catching detail." I looked up, seeing an almost panicked look on her face.

"It's not that Al's breaking his word that's got them in a tizzy," I said. "It's that he's escaping. Minias expects *me* to exchange names with Al so he can't be summoned out of confinement."

"Rachel, no!" she cried, shocking me as she reached across the table. *"You can't!"*

I blinked, surprised. "I wasn't planning on it, but if I can't find out who is summoning Al and letting him go, it might be the only way to get my nightlife back."

Ceri drew away, her hands clasped in her lap, sitting very straight.

"Why in the Turn's sake would I take Al's name when all I have to do is kick some demon-summoner's ass?" I muttered, and her narrow shoulders relaxed.

"Good," she said, seemingly embarrassed at her strong outburst. "You don't need to deal with them. I'll help you if you need it. Don't go to the demons even if you need to exchange names with Al. I'll find the curse for you."

Curse. Yeah, it would be a curse I needed to save my neck again. I was really going to have to put some effort into getting Al's get-out-of-jail-free card away from him. "I can't believe they put him in jail just for letting you live knowing how to spindle line energy," I mused, taking a sip of tea and startling myself when it wasn't coffee. "Stripped him of his accumulated potions. Everything. No wonder he wants me dead."

"If it got out, it would limit their pool of familiars," she mumbled, obviously wanting to drop the subject.

"Yeah, well, he's got someone cooking spells for him. He was his usual crushed-green-velvet self. I swear, if it's Nick, I'm going to kick his butt back off the Mackinac Bridge. That is, if Al hasn't chewed it off him by then. That demon is going to kill me if I'm not careful."

"No," Ceri rushed. "Al wouldn't. It's got to be a bluff. He said—"

Her words cut off and my focus sharpened on her suddenly distressed, almost panicked features. My runner training kicked in, and my heart pounded. *"He said." Ceri had talked to him? To Al?*

"You?" I stammered, scrambling to my feet. "You're summoning him?"

"No!" she protested, her face going whiter. "Rachel, no. I'm only making appearance charms for him. Please. Don't be angry."

Aghast, I tried to find words. "He's been loose every night for three days, and you never told me!"

"He said he wouldn't attack you!" she said, standing. "I thought you were safe. He *can't* attack you! He promised."

"He *did* attack me," I shouted, not caring if the neighbors heard me. "He's going to freaking kill me because he's got nothing to lose. And you're making him curses?"

"It's a good deal!" she shot back. "For every thirteen, he takes a day's worth of smut off of me. I've already lightened my soul by a year."

I stared at her. She was voluntarily making Al curses? "Well, merry freaking good for you," I snapped.

Her face flashed red in anger. "It's the only moral way I can get rid of the smut," she said, the loose strands of her hair starting to float. "He promised me he wouldn't go after you." Her eyes widened, and she put a hand to her upper chest, her mood shifting like a kite. "They want you to help capture him? Rachel. Don't say yes. No matter what they offer. If Al has gone rogue, he will be as slippery and devious as a stingray. You can't trust him now!"

Like I ever have? "I can't trust him *now*?" I exclaimed. "What kind of game is this when the rules keep changing!"

Ceri appeared affronted as she looked me up and down. "Well, did he actually hurt you?"

"He picked me up by the neck and shook me!" I shouted. She was defending him. She was defending Al!

"If that was all he did, then whether he broke his word might be open to interpretation," she said sharply. "He is bluffing."

I do not believe this. I freaking do not believe this. "You're siding with him!"

"I am not!" she exclaimed, red spots showing on her cheeks. "I'm telling you how their law system works. If there is a loophole, they'll allow him to use it. And I only made him disguise charms. I would never do anything that might hurt you."

"You're working for Al, and you didn't tell me!"

"I didn't tell you because I knew you'd get angry!"

"Well, you were right!" I yelled, heart pounding. "I got you free of him, and now you're right back at it again. Just another potential familiar who thinks they're smarter than a demon."

Ceri's red face went ashen. "Get out."

"With pleasure."

I don't even remember walking through the house. I do remember storming down to the walk because I jumped when the screen door slammed behind me. Keasley was sitting on the steps, three pixies on his hand. They flew up when the door banged, and he turned to look at me. "All set between you two . . . ladies?" he said, his eyes widening when I stomped past him and a frustrated scream from the backyard echoed over the neighborhood. There was a booming noise, and the pixies yelped at the sudden pressure shift. Ceri was throwing a tantrum.

"Congratulations, Jih," I said as I jerked to a halt at the bottom of the steps. "I'd like to meet your new husband properly, but I don't think I'm welcome here anymore." I turned to Keasley. "If you need me, you know where I am." Saying nothing more, I left.

My pulse was fast and my breath was short. I felt my expression turn ugly when Jenks joined me, flying at eye height.

"Uh, Rache? What's up? Is Ceri okay?"

"Ceri is ju-u-u-ust fine," I muttered, slamming the latch to the chain-link fence down and chipping a nail. "She's always fine. She's working for Al."

"She's summoning him out of confinement!" Jenks squeaked.

"No, she's making appearance curses for him to get the smut off her soul."

I paced across the street, and at his continued silence, I looked up. His tiny face was pinched and he seemed torn. "You don't see a problem in that?" I said in disbelief.

"Well . . . ," he hedged.

I did not believe this. "That's how it starts, Jenks," I said, recalling my days as an I.S. runner bringing in witches who had gone wrong. "Then it's one black curse that he promises to use for a good reason, and he offers so much in return that you can't resist, then another, then another, and then you're his familiar for real. Well, if she wants to throw her life away again, that's not my problem."

Jenks flew beside me silently, then spoke. "Ceri knows what she's doing."

My feet found the wide, worn steps of the church, and I stopped. Storming in like this with me out of control was asking for trouble. Ivy's blood lust was triggered by high emotions, and I knew better. Turning, I looked across the street at Keasley's house. A red film enveloped the oak tree, making it look like it was on fire. People were coming out of their houses to gape at the phantom flames as Ceri raged, but I knew she wouldn't hurt the tree.

"I hope so, Jenks. I really hope so."

Nine

Hush. Quiet," one of Jenks's kids said in a loud whisper. "You're scaring her."

A chorus of denials rose, and I smiled at the eager little pixy girl standing on my knee, her wings blurring for balance and her pale green silk dress drifting about her ankles. I was sitting cross-legged on the floor beside the couch in the sanctuary, covered in pixy kids. Colorful fabric billowed in the breeze kicked up by their dragonfly-like wings, and their dust was making me glow in the late-hour dusk. Rex was under Ivy's piano, and she didn't look scared. She looked predatory.

The small orange cat was crouched by a polished leg, her tail twitching, her ears pricked, and her eyes black in a classic pre-stalking posture. Matalina had relented in her stand, having admitted herself that even their smallest child could outfly a cat's pounce, and after Jenks pointed out that Rex wintering indoors wouldn't allow them to become lazy sentries, the cat's place inside was assured.

The theory now was that if the pixy kids, whom Rex loved, could get her to come to them while they were with me, Rex might start to like me, too. Nice thought, but it wasn't working. Rex hadn't liked me since I used a demon curse to go wolf. I had returned back to myself with pristine skin and no fillings, but I'd rather have freckles than the demon smut that had come along with the unexpected makeover. Not to mention Rex might willingly let me touch her. I think she was waiting for me to change into a wolf again.

"This isn't working," I said, turning to Jenks and Matalina, who had perched on my desk in the heat of the lamp to watch the drama unfold. The sun had set, and I was surprised Jenks hadn't moved everyone out to the stump, but maybe it was too cold tonight. It was either that or he didn't want his kids outside when that gargoyle was lurking about. I didn't know why Jenks was so upset. The thing was only a foot tall. I thought he looked kind of cute on the edge of the roof, and if I could go outside, I'd try to coax him down—now that he was probably awake.

"I told you that wouldn't work," Jenks said snarkily. "You'd better utilize your time coming up to the belfry and talking to that hunk of rock."

Better utilize my time? It *was* the gargoyle. "I'm not going to lean out the belfry window and shout at him," I muttered when the pixies squealed. "I'll talk to him when he comes down. You're just mad that you can't make him leave."

"She's coming. Rex is coming!" one shrilled loudly enough to make me wince, but the cat was only stretching, settling in for a good long stare session. That's all she did—stare at me.

"Here, kitty, kitty, stupid kitty," I coaxed. "How's my little chicken-ass feline today?" I crooned, holding out a hand as I sat on the floor. One of Jenks's daughters walked down the plane of my arm, her own hand outstretched. "I'm not going to hurt you, you sweet little bundle of asinine, orange-furred, Were-toy of a cat."

Okay, maybe that was harsh, but she couldn't understand me, and I was tired of trying to get her to like me.

Jenks laughed. I would have been embarrassed by my word choices, but his kids had heard worse from their dad. And in fact, the pixies ranging about me had taken up my crooning, singing insults heavy on the earthy vulgarity.

Disheartened, I let my arm fall and sent my eyes past the hanging paper bats to the stained-glass windows, the colors muted from the late hour. Marshal had called to tell me that he was still stuck in interview hell and wouldn't be able to have coffee. That had been hours ago. The sun was down now, and I couldn't safely leave the church lest I become demon bait.

My jaw tightened. Maybe someone was trying to tell me it was too soon. *I'm sorry, Kisten. I wish you were here, but you're not.*

The buzzing of my vibrating phone cut through the pixy chatter, and they all flew up and away when I stretched to reach my bag on the nearby couch. As I lay almost flat, my fingers brushed my bag and I yanked it down. I sat up with an exhalation, flipping my hair back and digging out my phone. The number was unfamiliar. Marshal's landline, maybe?

"Hi," I said casually, seeing as it was my cell and not the business phone. Realizing I was covered in pixy dust, I slapped at my jeans to get it off.

"Rachel," came Marshal's apologetic voice, and the pixies clustered by the desk hushed themselves so they could hear. Rex stretched and padded over to them, now that they weren't sitting on me, and I frowned at her. Stupid cat.

"Hey, I'm sorry." Marshal continued to fill the silence. "I don't know why they're taking so long, but it looks like I'm not going to get out of here for a few hours more."

"You're still there?" I asked, glancing at the dark stained-glass windows and thinking that what time his interviews ended didn't matter anymore.

"It's down to me and one other guy," Marshal rushed to say. "They want to make a decision today, so I'm stuck trying to impress the hell out of these people over pasta and sparkling water."

Resigned to another evening alone with the pixies, I picked at the edge of my chipped nail and wondered if I had a file in my bag. Rex was on her back, the pixies hovering just out of her playful, lethal reach. "No problem. We'll do it some other day," I said as I rummaged for the file, disappointed even as I was sort of relieved.

"I must have met with six people already," he complained. "Honest, they told me it was going to be a two-hour interview when I came down here."

My fingertips brushed the rough surface of a file, and I tugged it out. Three quick swipes, and the damage was smoothed out. If only it were that easy for everything else.

"I've got to be done by midnight," he continued at my silence. "You want to go out to The Warehouse for a beer? The guy I'm interviewing against says they let you in free this week if you come in costume."

My gaze slid to the dark windows as I slipped the file away. "Marshal, I can't."

"Why—" he started, then went silent. "Oh," he continued, and I could hear him kicking himself. "I forgot. Um, I'm sorry, Rachel."

"Don't worry about it," I said. Feeling guilty about my relief, then determined to get past it, I took a slow breath, steadying myself. "You want to come over when you're done? I've got some reports to go over, but we can play pool or something." I hesitated, then added, "It's not The Warehouse, but . . ." God, I felt like a coward, hiding in this church.

"Yes," he said, his warm voice making me feel a little better. "Yeah, I'd like that. I'll bring dinner. You like Chinese?"

"Mmmm, yes," I said, feeling the first hints of enthusiasm. "No onions?"

"No onions," he acknowledged, and I heard someone in the background call his name with authority. "I hate to keep saying this, but I'll call you when I'm done."

"Marshal, I said don't worry about it. It's not like it's a date," I said, remembering Kisten's calm acceptance of my breaking our arrangements because of last-minute runs. He had never gotten upset, maintaining the belief that when he had to do the same, I'd respond in kind. It had worked, and now I could take a lot of last-minute cancellations before I let it get to me. Marshal had called. He couldn't make it. Case closed. Besides, it wasn't like we were . . . anything.

"Thanks, Rachel," he said, sounding relieved. "You're something else."

I blinked fast, remembering Kisten saying the same thing. "Okay, um, I'll see you later then. 'Bye, Marshal," I said, making sure my voice didn't betray me. Unclenching my fingers from the top of my right arm, I hit the "end" button and closed the phone, torn between feeling good at Marshal's last words and depressed at the reminder of Kisten.

Knock it off, Rachel, I thought, taking a cleansing breath and tossing my hair.

"'By-y-y-y-y-ye, Marshal," Jenks mocked from the safety of my desk, and I turned—just in time to see Matalina backhand him on the shoulder.

"Jenks," I said wearily as I lurched to a stand. "Shut up."

Matalina rose, her wings a pale pink. "Jenks, dear," she said primly. "Can I see you in the desk for a moment?"

"What . . . ," he complained, then yelped when she pinched his wing and jerked him through the crack of the roll-top desk. The kids cheered, and their eldest daughter grabbed the hand of the youngest, flying the toddler away from the desk and to some pixy distraction.

Smiling at the thought of a seasoned warrior being dragged about by his just-as-deadly wife, I straightened my legs, which ached from being motionless so long on the hardwood floor. I really needed to do some stretches to loosen up, and I wondered if Marshal liked to run. I'd be willing to get him an early-hours runner's pass for the zoo just for the company. No expectations, no hidden agendas, just someone to do something with. Kisten had never run with me. Maybe it would help if I did different things—for different reasons.

I scooped up my bag and headed to the kitchen and my reports, my mood changing to one of surprising anticipation as I planned out my night. Marshal could tell me all about his interviews, and I could tell him all about my demon death mark. Ought to make for interesting conversation over rice. And if that didn't scare him away, then he deserved everything he got.

Going sourly introspective, I slapped at the pixy dust on me again as I entered the hall. The dust glowed briefly from the friction as it sifted from me to light the darker space. I passed the old his-and-hers bathrooms converted on Ivy's side to a conventional bathroom, and to a bathroom/laundry room on my side. Our bedrooms had once been clergy offices, and what was now the kitchen and living room had been added on to provide the long-absent congregation with a place to prepare and serve church suppers.

I leaned into my room to throw my bag onto the bed, and my cell phone rang again. Digging it back out, I sat on my bed to take my boots off and flipped the top open. "Back already?" I said, letting my voice hint at my anticipation. Maybe Marshal was done.

"Sure, I only had to check three days of records," David's rich voice said, startling me.

"Oh! David!" I·said, getting one lace undone and kicking my boot off. "I thought you were Marshal."

"Uh, no . . . ," he drawled, the question clear in his voice.

Phone tucked between my shoulder and my ear, I swung my other foot up. "Just some guy I met up in Mackinaw," I said. "He's moving to Cincinnati and coming over for dinner so neither of us have to eat alone."

"Good. It's about time," he said with a small laugh, and when I cleared my throat in protest, he continued. "I've been through the recent filings. There's been a spate of interesting claims out at the smaller cemeteries."

As I worked the laces one-handedly, my fingers slowed. You could get just about all the parts you needed to do black magic from any charm shop, but the ingredients were regulated, and oftentimes people just collected their own. "Grave robbing?"

"Actually . . ." There was a rustling of papers. "I don't know. You'd have to go to the FIB or the I.S. for that, but there's been a statistically large increase in the amount of damage to small cemeteries, so you might want to keep a closer eye on yours. Only the active ones have been hit so far. Damage to monuments, broken gates, cut locks, ruts in the landscape. It could just be kids, but someone stole the equipment to dig up the comfortably dead. My guess is someone is setting themselves up for a long-term commitment, either to supply black witchcraft and demon summoners on a commercial basis, or just themselves. You should check with your FIB guy. I won't hear about grave robbing unless something's been damaged or stolen, seeing as we don't insure the truly dead."

"Thanks, David," I said. "I've been talking to Glenn already." My gaze slid to the four reports on my dresser, sandwiched between the perfume bottles. "I'll ask him if any bodies are being moved out. I appreciate you checking." I hesitated, kicking my second boot off. "You didn't get in trouble, did you?"

"For working before Halloween?" he said around a guffaw. "Not likely. I do have one thing before I let you go. I've got a minor-damage claim that came in from a woman just outside the Hollows. I'm not scheduled to be the field adjuster for it, but if I can trade, do you want to come with me and check it out? An entire basement wall is bowing out from water damage. It could be a typo, seeing as water bows walls in, not out, but even so, we haven't gotten much rain in months."

I leaned across the space to my dresser and brought my FIB reports over. "Where is it?"

There was a soft shuffling of paper. "Ah, hold on." There was another moment of silence. "Nine thirty-one Palladium Drive."

A quiver started in my belly as I snatched the reports off my dresser and the addresses leapt out at me. *Bingo.* "David, get that claim. I'm looking at the obituary of the guy who owned that house. And get this. He had a record of grave robbing while in college."

David's laugh was low and eager. "Rachel, my boss ought to

be paying you for all the money you're saving him. The damage was demon wrought?"

"Probably." Damn, this was coming together nicely. I deserved a night off. And if I stayed in my church, I'd live through it. *Please, don't let this be Nick.*

"Oka-a-a-a-ay," David said, his voice tight and eager. "Promise me you won't move tonight. I'll see about getting the claim, and we'll go from there. You need anything? Ice cream? Popcorn? I want you to stay in your church."

My head shook, though he couldn't see it. "I'm fine. Let me know when you're ready to go out. The sooner, the better."

His thoughts already on other matters, he growled a good-bye. I wasn't much better, mumbling something before I hung up and headed for the kitchen. I loved kicking ass, but the next best thing was making the spells that made kicking ass easier.

I was deep in anticipation when I found the hall, my mind already going over what I'd want to take to confront experienced demon summoners specializing in ley line manipulation. Heavy magic-detection charms . . . maybe a disguise amulet for that precious moment of distraction that could be the difference between falling down or staying upright . . . a couple of the zippy strips Glenn had traded me for ketchup that kept ley line witches from tapping a line and using ley line magic. I was going to have a busy night.

The hallway was dark, and I jerked to a halt just past my door, frowning. Ivy had put up a sign dangling by threads from the ceiling; clearly Jenks had assisted her. God help her, she had used a stencil, and I snatched at the yellow poster board, reading BEYOND THIS POINT, THERE BE DEMONS in bright red lettering. Crap on toast. I had forgotten about that.

When Jenks had bought the church from Piscary's estates, he had insisted I pay to get it resanctified, and though I had protested, I eventually agreed to keep the back end of the church unsanctified, as it had been originally. Not all of our clients were living, and Ivy said that interviewing the undead on the porch steps was unprofessional. The result was the kitchen and back living room weren't holy. In the past, Al had always seemed to know when I stepped from secure ground, and after my wrist had flamed in agony before he showed up to trash Patricia's charm shop, I figured I knew how he did it. *I have to get rid of this thing*, I thought, gently rubbing the raised scar. As I hesitated in the dark, weighing my risk, the front doorbell rang.

Immediately I spun on my heel. "I got it!" I shouted before Jenks could leave the desk. He and Matalina got precious little time alone as it was. They may have gone into the desk arguing, but I knew they wouldn't end that way. The man had fifty-four kids.

Rex skittered past me when I burst into the sanctuary at an easy jog, the fluffy-tailed cat thinking I was going for her. It was too soon for Marshal, and if it was some early trick-or-treaters, I was going to mess with their minds. I hadn't even gotten my tomatoes yet.

I slapped Ivy's sign down upon her piano for her to find, then padded into the dark foyer in my stocking feet. I paused to let my eyes adjust to the close darkness of the narrow room between the sanctuary and the front door. One of these days, I was going to invest in a drill and peephole.

Ready to give whoever was begging early some grief, I pushed the heavy wooden door open, and the yellow glow of the light illuminating the sign above the door spilled in. A soft scuff of dress shoes drew my attention, and I crossed my arms over my middle as I saw who it was, whose Jag was idling at the curb.

"Well, well, well," I drawled, seeing Trent in full costume. "It's a little early for trick-or-treats, but I might have a few pennies to give you."

"Excuse me?" the spell-enhanced, rather imposing man said. His charmed-brown eyes widened, and he turned to his car in a rustle of silk and linen, taking off a smart-looking hat to show off his mid-length black hair, restyled to Rynn

Cormel's latest photo. Man, he looked good, slightly older, taller, and somehow more sophisticated. Sort of like the reverse card of himself, dark where he was usually light and vice versa. Same build, though: trim and lean—nice. I liked tall.

The black overcoat he had on went down to his ankles and contrasted beautifully with his new pale complexion, as I'd known it would. He had taken my advice and picked up a charm to change his scent, and the delicious aroma of vampire eased over me, mixing with a hint of expensive cologne. He wasn't wearing the glasses, but they peeked out from the top of an exterior breast pocket of his coat. A gray cashmere scarf fluttered about his neck, and I noticed it matched his shoes, now a nice flat black instead of his usual shiny ones.

"Wow," I said, cocking my hip and putting my hand against the door frame to prevent him from coming in, "they even did the voice. I didn't think they could do that. How much did that set you back?"

Trent brought his attention down from the bats hanging in the sanctuary to give me a closed-lipped smile from under his raised eyebrows. They were thick and black, very unlike his pale wisps, and it made reading his emotions easier. He looked highly amused as his smile widened, showing a slip of long canine. He'd gone for the more realistic caps, and I felt an unhelped pulse of adrenaline dive to my middle at the mix of vampiric threat and lure. I wondered if that was why Trent was standing on my doorstep—trying to get a rise out of me. Or maybe he was rethinking his stellar decision to go into the ever-after and thought showing me his twenty-thousand-dollar costume would impress me.

Suddenly wishing I'd never helped him, I blanked all the emotion from my face except for a bothered annoyance. "What do you want?" I said snidely. "Is this about Ceri? You know, letting me walk out of there thinking you got her pregnant was low even for you. If I wasn't going to go into the ever-after for you then, I sure as hell wouldn't work for you now." Yeah, I was mad at Ceri, but I was still her friend.

Trent's eyes fixed on me, his pupils widening slightly in surprise. "I'm very glad to hear that, Ms. Morgan. Avoiding Mr. Kalamack is one of the items I wanted to talk to you about."

I froze, alarmed. Not only had his voice lacked its musical cadence, but the accent was very New York.

The sound of a car door opening jerked my attention past Trent to the curb. The man getting out of the driver's side wasn't Jonathan or Quen. No, this guy was bigger, with wide shoulders and arms as big as my legs. I could tell by his grace that he was a living vampire. Trent didn't employ vampires unless absolutely necessary. The man in black pants and a stretchy black T-shirt by the car crossed his arms over his chest and fell into a parade rest that looked threatening even at forty feet away.

Swallowing hard, my gaze returned to the man on my stoop. I didn't think it was Trent anymore. "You're not Trent, are you," I said, and I flushed when he flashed me the beautiful smile Rynn Cormel was known for.

"No."

"Oh, God, I'm sorry, Mr. Cormel." I stammered, wondering if I could make this any worse. Ivy's number one was standing on our doorstep, and I'd just insulted him. "Ivy's not here right now. Do you want to come in and wait?"

Looking utterly alive, the man threw his head back and laughed, long and deep. I warmed. Damn it, he was undead. He couldn't come in on holy ground. And asking him to wait had been stupid. Like he had time to wait for my roommate?

"I'm sorry," I blathered, wanting to curl up and die. "You're probably really busy. Would you like me to tell her you called? I can try to reach her cell." My thoughts flashed to the vampire dating guide he had written to help increase a shadow's life expectancy. It was currently shoved to the back of my closet.

Ivy had given it to me on our second night sharing the same roof so I'd quit pushing her vampire buttons. Reading it had been an education, one that left me wide-eyed and a little ill. Some of the stuff they did in the name of pleasure . . .

Rex appeared at my feet, pulled out from the depths of the church by the scent of vampire, something she associated with Ivy. The stupid cat rubbed against me by mistake before going to twine about Cormel's feet. Shaken from my musings, I lunged for her, and when she spat at me, Mr. Cormel picked the cat up, crooning to the animal as he looked at me from between her ears.

Rynn Cormel had run the world during the Turn, his living charisma somehow crossing the boundaries of death to give his undead existence an uncanny mimicry of life. Every move was a careful study of causality. It was highly unusual for so young an undead vampire to be so good at mimicking having a soul. I figured it was because he was a politician and had had practice way before he died.

"Actually," he said, "it's you I've come to see. Did I catch you at a bad time?"

I choked on my breath, and the corners of his mouth rose in amusement. What did Ivy's master vampire want with me? "Uh . . . ," I said, backing up into the black foyer. He was an undead. He could ask anything . . . and if he insisted, I wouldn't be able to say no. Oh, God. Table 6.1. Had he really . . . I mean, you have to *try* stuff before you can print it, right?

"It will only take two minutes of your time."

I breathed a little easier. Everything in the guide would take at least twenty minutes. Unless he was working on a sequel. HOW TO NAIL YOUR SHADOW AND LEAVE THEM BREATHING IN TWO MINUTES.

Letting the cat slip from his arms, he brushed at his somehow immaculate coat. Rex continued to purr and twine. Her attention went behind me, and the clatter of pixy wings became obvious. "Rachel, it's getting late," Jenks said, his voice high and preoccupied. "I'm moving everyone out to the stump for the night." But his entire demeanor changed when he came wing to shoulder with me.

"Holy crap!" he swore, pixy dust sifting from him to make sunbeams at my feet. "Rynn Cormel? You gotta be pissing on my daisies! Rache!" he exclaimed, flying an erratic path between us. "It's Rynn Cormel!" Then he stopped as if he'd been nailed to the air. "I'm giving you fair warning, Mr. Cormel. If you bespell Rachel, I'll open up your head for the sunshine to come in."

I cringed, but the dignified man clasped his surprisingly ugly hands before him and gave Jenks a respectful nod. "Not at all. I want to talk to Ms. Morgan. That's all." He hesitated, and I flushed when his gaze dropped to my stocking feet. "Is there a more comfortable place . . ."

Oh, God. I hate it when this happens. "Um," I hedged, then winced. "Would you mind coming around the back, Mr. President? We have two unsanctified rooms for our undead clients. I'm really sorry for asking you to come in the back door, but the majority of our clients are living."

"It's just Rynn," he said, smiling as if he were Father Christmas. "I was never sworn in, actually." He rocked back and glanced at his bodyguard. "I'd be happy to join you in back. Is it just that way?" he asked, leaning to his right.

I nodded, glad Ivy and I had put in a slate walk, then wondered if we had gotten the trash out this week. Crap, I hoped so. "Jenks, if it's warm enough, could you escort Mr. Cormel?"

A flash of dust slipped from him, and he darted outside. "You bet." He flew down the stairs and then back up. "This way, please."

His tiny voice was sarcastic, and I wouldn't be surprised if Jenks took the opportunity to threaten him again. He had no respect for titles, law, or anything but a pixy sword, and he took his job of keeping my ass above the grass seriously.

Giving me a smile that would have twitterpated Genghis Khan, the vampire took the stairs. I watched his confident pace as he made his way to the sidewalk, shoes clicking smartly, listening to everything, seeing everything. A master vampire. The master of this city. What did he want with me if it wasn't . . . blood?

I ducked inside and shut the door, relieved that Cormel had motioned for his bodyguard and driver to stay put. I didn't want them in my church even if Jenks was with me. Three vampires opened the door for a lot of misunderstandings.

"Matalina?" I said loudly as I padded through the sanctuary. "We have a client." But the pixy woman had already hustled the last of her brood down the hall and out through the chimney in the back living room. It was only the youngest that were giving her trouble, not remembering the drill from last year. They would stay out of the church until Rynn Cormel left, or they'd be cleaning my windows tomorrow.

I scuffed on my slippers by the back door and unlocked it, darting into the kitchen to see if I could do a quick tidy. I elbowed the rocker switch for the lights, already reaching to shove a crumb-strewn plate into the dishwasher before the fluorescent tubes finished flickering to a bright, steady glow. Mr. Fish, my Betta, flipped his tail nervously at the sudden light, and I made a mental note to feed him. Beside him on the sill was a tiny pumpkin that I had bought for Jenks and his kids, hoping that they would go for it instead of the huge pumpkin they'd grown off the compost pile this summer. Chances looked slim since the obnoxious but beautiful vegetable was sitting under the table, warming up. The thing was huge, and I wasn't looking forward to a repeat of last year's fiasco. Pumpkin seeds could be shot with painful accuracy, it turns out.

I loved my kitchen, with its expansive counters, two stoves, and huge stainless-steel fridge that was big enough to hold a goat, at least in theory. There was a heavy antique table against the interior wall holding Ivy's computer, printer, and desk stuff. One side of it was mine, and lately I'd lost all but the last corner of it, having to continually shove her stuff back so I'd have somewhere to eat. I had taken the center island counter for me, though, so fair was fair.

The small island counter was covered in herbs I was experimenting with, last week's mail stacked on a corner and threatening to spill off, and a mishmash of earth-magic spelling hardware. Copper pots and utensils hung over it from a huge rack where the pixies loved to play hide-and-seek among metal that wouldn't burn them. Below the counter was the rest of my spelling stuff jammed together in no particular order, as it was mostly ley line paraphernalia that I didn't know what to do with. My splat gun, with its sleepy-time charms, was nestled in another set of nested copper pots, and my small library of spell books was propped up with my more mundane cookbooks on a low shelf that was open on both sides. Three of them were demon curse books and they gave me the willies, but I wasn't going to store them under my bed.

Everything looked halfway decent, and I flicked on the coffeemaker Ivy had already prepped for breakfast tomorrow. Mr. Cormel probably wouldn't drink any, but the smell might help block the pheromones. Maybe.

Concerned, I put my hands on my hips. The only thing I might have done had I some warning would be to sweep the salt out of the circle etched in the linoleum surrounding the center island counter.

The air pressure shifted and I turned, but my welcoming professional smile froze as I realized I hadn't heard the back door click open.

"Shit," I breathed, tensing as I realized why.

I'd stepped off hallowed ground.

Al was here.

Ten

Jenks!" I shouted, stumbling backward.

I prayed Al would start talking, but his elegant, chiseled features twisted in anger, and he leapt at me, white-gloved hands reaching.

I fell back against the sink. Arms braced, I swung both feet up to hit him square in the chest. Oh, God. I was dead. He wasn't gloating. He wanted to freaking kill me. If I was dead, no one would know he broke his word. Not only was Ceri an idiot for making charms for him, she was wrong, too.

Panic took me when my feet went right through him. Gasping, I fell, sliding down the face of the cupboards to land on my butt. My gaze went to my spell books. *Minias.* My new calling circle was under the counter with my books. I had to get to it.

I scrambled forward. Pain made me slow, and as adrenaline pulsed through me, Al's thick, gloved hand grabbed me by the throat and hauled me up. I choked, ugly sounds making it past my lips. My eyes bulged, and my body went flaccid. He shook me, and the scent of amber rolled over me. "You are a really—*stupid*—witch," he said, giving me another shake with his accented word. "Sometimes, I wonder how you expected your genes to get to the next generation." He smiled, and fear wrapped around my heart as I gazed into his red, goat-slitted eyes and saw his anger. He had nothing to lose. Nothing.

Panicking, I struggled. He couldn't go misty to avoid my strikes and still hold on to me. I had a chance. Al grunted when I scored on his shin, and he let go.

I took a gasping breath of air. My feet hit the floor. Knees crumpling, I screamed when I was jerked back upright by my hair. "I'm going to freaking kill you, Al, if you don't get the hell out of my kitchen!" I vowed, not knowing where the threat was coming from, but I was pissed. Scared. Absolutely terrified.

A velveteen arm went around my neck. A cry slipped from me when his grip on my hair tightened, pulling my head up so I looked at the ceiling. Pain struck through my neck and scalp. I reached backward, and he grunted when I got a fistful of his hair. But he wouldn't let go. Even when I yanked it out by the roots and sent my hands scrabbling back for more.

"Stop it," he said grimly, jerking me into motion. "We have an appointment."

"The hell we do," I panted, finding an ear and digging my nails in. *Where is Jenks?*

Al grunted, tightening his grip until I let go. I wasn't dead. *I wasn't dead.* He wanted me alive. For the moment. *For an appointment?*

"You are going to clear my name," he snarled, bending to mouth my ear as if to bite it off. I fought him until he pulled my hair so hard that tears started. I could smell blood, but I didn't think it was mine. I thought I'd broken his nose when I had flung my head back. I tried to shove against the counter, and Al dragged me away.

"I asked you nicely, but like the spoiled brat you are, you refused," he said. "I don't mind doing it the hard way. You are going to testify to the courts that Ceridwen Merriam Dulciate is limited to teaching one child how to spindle line energy. That the damage is contained. I won't do time for an ex-familiar who would be dead but for you."

My breath seemed to freeze in me. Testify? He meant in the ever-after. He expected me to stand in a demon court? "Why should I trust you?" I panted, fingertips squeaking as he pulled my grip off the counter again.

"It might make things easier," he suggested, sounding almost bitter that I didn't.

Easier? I thought. *It might also make me dead.* I struggled, my slippers sliding on the linoleum as he yanked me backward to the hall. My pulse leapt when the back door opened and the skittering of cat claws rasped. I tried to see, but it was hard with Al's arm around my neck.

"'Bout time, Jenks!" I exclaimed. "What were you doing? Showing him your stump?"

My bravado died at the snarl that rumbled slowly to life and vibrated to my very nerve endings, reaching deep into my psyche and clenching around my primitive brain to reduce me to fight or flight. Cormel? That ugly sound was coming from him?

"Holy shit!" Jenks shrilled, and Al's grip on my hair loosened.

Taking a gasp of air, I twisted, falling away and smacking the flat of my foot square across the demon's right cheek. Al rocked back, his eyes never leaving Rynn Cormel, who was standing in the threshold to my kitchen.

"Get back!" I shouted at the vampire, but he never even looked at me. Al, too, was a hunched shadow ignoring me. Mostly.

"Rynn Matthew Cormel," the demon drawled, a brief shimmer of ever-after cascading over him to leave his nose unbloodied and whole as he straightened. "What brings you slumming here?"

The elegant vampire loosened his coat. "You, in a roundabout way."

I flicked my gaze between them and felt my neck for the new bruise that was bound to show up. Jenks hovered beside me, spilling red dust that puddled on the floor.

"I'm honored," Al said, tension in his voice and posture.

"You're dead," Cormel said. "Morgan is mine. You will not touch her."

Oh, that's nice. Maybe.

Al laughed. "As if you have a say in the matter."

That was even freaking better. My breath came in sharply and I scrambled back when Cormel jumped at Al, arms reaching and an ugly sound erupting from him. A muffled curse slipped from me, and my back hit the fridge. I watched, shocked, as the two grappled, both moving incredibly fast. Al blurred in and out of existence, making the vampire look like he was trying to catch moving sand. I couldn't take my eyes away, and my pulse hammered. If Al won, I was going to be bail money. If Rynn Cormel won, I was going to have to deal with a master vampire hyped up on fear and anger who thought I was his.

"Look out!" I cried when Al got a grip on him, but the vampire twisted with an inhuman bonelessness, dislocating his own shoulder to fix his teeth on Al's neck.

Al screamed and went misty, re-forming to push Rynn backward into the sink. Mr. Fish's bowl teetered, and when the vampire launched himself at Al, his fangs sheened with blood, I darted to rescue the Betta.

Water sloshed as I retreated. Not looking at what I was doing, I shoved the fish onto the back of the counter. My gaze went to the books hiding my scrying mirror. Minias. I could call Minias. *Yeah, one more demon ought to make this farce complete.*

Al hit the wall beside Ivy's computer, and the lights flickered. Gathering my courage, I darted forward, fingers slipping on the cold glass as I found the mirror.

"Oh, God, oh, God, oh, God," I whispered, not remembering the word to invoke the charm.

"Rachel!" Jenks cried.

They were coming right at me. Eyes widening, I curled my body over the mirror and dove out of the way. Al and Cormel crashed into the fridge. The clock above the sink fell, shattering to send the battery rolling into the hall.

Al had Cormel's face in his hands and was squeezing with a supernatural strength, but the vampire's teeth were red. I watched, unable to look away as Cormel reached up and dug his ugly fingers into Al's eyes.

Screaming, the demon flung himself back, but the vampire was after him. The two rolled on the floor, both struggling for control. They were going to freaking kill each other in my kitchen. And wouldn't Ivy be ticked at me for that?

"Jenks?" I said, seeing him hovering at the ceiling, just as captivated as I was.

His face was white, and his wings made a high-pitched whine. "I'll get them apart, you set the circle," he said.

I nodded and shoved my sleeves up past my elbows. The simplest plans were the best.

My heart pounded and Jenks hovered over them. They had regained their feet, struggling like wrestlers, Al's green frock making an odd statement against Rynn's elegant business suit.

"Hey, demon-ass!" Jenks shouted, and Al looked up.

A burst of pixy dust sifted down. Al screamed and went misty. Rynn's hands scrabbled on air, and when Al re-formed, he was hunched over, still rubbing at his eyes.

"Damn you to hell, you burning firefly!" the demon shouted.

Rynn gathered himself, and I sprang into motion. "Get out of the circle!" I shouted, grabbing the vampire's arm and swinging him into Ivy's desk with a crash. The heavy table remained standing, but the faint scent of broken technology mixed with the acidic smell of burnt amber and the rich tang of angry vampire.

The former world leader snarled at me when he found his balance. My face went cold, and I wondered if I'd fare better in the circle with Al.

"Rache!" Jenks shouted, clearly annoyed, and I slapped my hand down on the salt circle.

"*Rhombus,*" I said with relief, and the connection to the ley line out back formed with a satisfying speed. Quicker than thought, a sheet of ever-after rose from the circle I had already scribed on the floor, made strong by my will and the salt I'd used.

Rynn skidded to a halt as the circle formed, his long coat unfurling to brush the impenetrable barrier. On the other side, Al pulled himself upright, howling. "I'll tear you apart!" he screamed, his eyes still watering from Jenks's dust. "Morgan, I'll kill you myself! I will not . . . You can't do this to me! Not again! You are *just* a *stinking* little *witch*!"

I fell back to sit on my butt, carefully pulling my feet to me so I wouldn't accidentally touch the bubble and send it crashing down. "Tag," I breathed heavily, looking around my demolished kitchen. Mr. Fish was quivering, but at least the fish—and Jenks's pumpkin under the table—had survived.

My jaw clenched in fear when I found Rynn Cormel. The vampire was completely flaked out, his pupils wide and his movements sharper and brighter than broken glass. He stood in the corner as far away from me as he could get, and I knew from living with Ivy that he was working hard to get control of his instincts. He held his coat closed, and the hem quivered as he fought his need to leap at me.

"Morgan!" Al raged, and reaching up, he pulled on the rack hanging overhead. Wood splintered and split, and I scrambled up with a gasp when the ceiling cracked, but it was the rack that broke, and stuff went everywhere, rolling until it found the interior of my circle and stopped. But he was contained, and as Al threw a temper tantrum, I worried more about Rynn.

"Are you okay, sir?" I said meekly.

The vampire brought his head up, and fear slid anew around my skull. His presence was thick in the room, his scent filling me inside and out. A tingling had started at my old demon scar, and I saw him swallow.

"Um, I'm going to open a window," I said, and when he nodded, I carefully got up.

Al threw himself at my circle, and I jumped, finding myself sweating when it held firm. "I'm going to kill you, witch," the demon said, panting as he stood before me, the rack broken and scattered over the interior of the circle. "I'm going to kill you, then mend you. I'm going to drive you insane. I'm going to make you beg for your death. I'm going to defile you, cut you from the inside out, put things in you that crawl around and burn your skull——"

"Will you shut up!" I interrupted him, and he howled, his face going red.

"You," I said to Rynn. "You just stay there, will you? I have to take care of this."

I didn't trust his silent posture, but he hadn't ruled the free world by lacking control.

"Mo-o-o-orga-a-a-an," Al crooned, and I turned from scooping up my scrying mirror.

My face lost its expression as I found him with one of my earth charm spell books. "Put that down," I demanded.

His eyes narrowed. "I may not have a lifetime of curses stored in me anymore," he said threateningly, "but I do know a few things by heart."

"Stop it," I said as he swiped an arm across the counter and everything went to the floor.

Jenks landed on my shoulder, sending the sharp scent of broken chlorophyll over me. "I don't like this, Rache," he whispered.

"I said, stop!" I exclaimed as Al sketched a rude pentagram and put my book in it.

"*Celero inanio,*" he said, and I jumped when my charm book burst into flames.

"Hey!" I shouted, suddenly pissed. "Knock it off!"

Al's goat-slitted eyes narrowed. With a stiff motion, he dropped another book in its place. The thump of it reverberated through me. His gaze behind the sheet of black-stained ever-after was heavy with new hatred. I had bested him again. Me. A "stinking little witch."

I stared, thinking before I went with my first gut reaction of calling Minias. I could leave Al there to burn all my books, but with him in my circle, I'd know where he was and be safe that night. Or I could call Minias to drag Al's butt out of here and hope that no one summoned him again before the sun rose. But something in Al's angry expression made me pause.

Behind the fury, he was tired. He was tired of being hauled around and shoved into a little room. He was tired of trying for me and failing. And to have Minias know it, to be carted off under his leash . . . It was almost insulting. Maybe, if I gave Al a night of peace to lick his wounds and his pride, he would grant that same courtesy to me?

The moment hesitated. The kitchen was eerily silent without the noise from the clock, now broken on the floor. Al slowly straightened as he realized something was sifting through my brain, that I was considering just . . . letting him go. "Do you feel lucky, witch?" the demon growled, his lips pulling back from his teeth as he smiled. It was a dangerous smile that went right to my core. But the thing was, even though he could kill me, I wasn't scared of him anymore. As he had said, I had circled the bastard one too many times. He was tired. And by that comment earlier, maybe a little hungry for trust.

Al's eyes slid to the scrying mirror in my hand, and his gaze went introspective as he saw me weighing my options. "One night's truce?" he said inquiringly.

I bit my lip and listened to the pulse in my ears. "Get the hell out of here, Al," I said, not bothering to put any more direction behind it.

He blinked slowly. His features smoothed out, and a real

smile curved over his face. "You're either really smart, or even more stupid than I thought," Al said, then vanished with a dramatic flair of red smoke.

"Rachel!" Jenks shouted, buzzing furiously in my face and shedding dust. "What the hell are you doing? He'll come right back!"

I took a slow breath and straightened. Scrying mirror in my grip, I carefully listened to the church, feeling the air for any sign of demons. My hand ached, and I flexed it, plucking a few of Al's hairs from under my fingernails in disgust. "Let it go, Jenks," I said. Something was shifting between Al and me—had shifted. I didn't know quite what, but I felt different. Maybe because I wasn't whining to Minias. Maybe me treating Al with more respect might just get me a little more respect from him. Maybe.

"You stupid witch!" Jenks was shouting. "Get your lily-white ass on holy ground. He's going to come back!"

"Not tonight he won't." The adrenaline crashed, and I found my knees shaking. My gaze slid to Rynn Cormel, standing in the corner trying to control himself, and I took another even breath to try to slow my pulse and not smell so tempting. The vampire still hadn't moved, but he was starting to look more human. Tired, I slid the scrying mirror back where it belonged between my three untouched demon books. Al had burned a mundane earth charm book.

Rynn took a step forward, jerking to a halt when Jenks got between us and buzzed a warning. The vampire was disgusted. "You let him go," the man said. "With no compulsion. You *do* deal in demons."

The coffee was done, and I crossed the room, trailing my trembling fingers through the plane of the bubble to break it as I passed. I settled against the counter where I could see both the man and the arch to the hallway. Taking a steadying breath, I poured a cup of coffee, and after asking Rynn Cormel with a gesture if he wanted any, I took a sip.

"I don't deal in demons," I said when the first of it slipped down my throat. "They deal in me. Thanks for trying to help, but Jenks and I had it under control." I didn't want him thinking I needed his protection. Vampire protection came at a cost—one I *wasn't* going to pay.

Rynn Cormel's eyebrows rose. "Had it under control? I saved your life."

Jenks huffed. "Saved *our* lives? Your hairy ass! Rachel was the one that saved *yours*. She circled him." The pixy turned to me, missing Rynn's dark expression. "Rache," he fussed. "Get on holy ground. He might come back."

I frowned at him while my free hand prodded my ribs for a possible bruise. "I'm fine. Take a chill pill before you set your dust on fire." The pixy sputtered, and I looked at the master vampire. "Do you want to sit down?"

Jenks made a burst of frustrated noise. "I'm going to check on my kids," he muttered, then darted out.

Rynn Cormel watched him leave. He gauged my fatigue, then eased across the room to sit in Ivy's chair before her cracked monitor. There was a long, bloodless scratch on his cheek, and his hair was mussed. "He was burning your books," he said, as if it was important to him.

I glanced at the pentagram Al had sketched on my counter and the second book sitting in a pile of ash. "He wanted out," I said. "He was burning my books because he was pissed I was going to call another demon to put him in custody. I'm hoping that because I gave him a night of peace he will give me the same." *God help me. I'm trusting a demon to make a moral decision based on respect?*

The vampire's expression shifted to understanding. "Ah-h-h-h-h. You chose the harder, riskier path, but by doing so, it told him you weren't going to rely on another for your safety. That you don't fear him." His head tilted. "You should, you know."

I nodded. I should fear Al. I did. But not tonight. Not after seeing him . . . disheartened. If he was depressed that a stinking little witch kept evading him, then maybe he should stop treating me like a stinking little witch and treat me with some respect.

Deciding Rynn Cormel was fully in control of himself, my shoulders started to relax. "So what did you want to talk to me about?"

He allowed himself a slow, charismatic smile. I was alone with Rynn Cormel, politician extraordinaire, master vampire, and once ruler of the free world. I pulled the sugar closer to the coffee. I was starting to shake, and I was going to blame it on low blood sugar. Yeah, that was it.

"You sure you don't want some coffee?" I said, ladling in a third spoonful of sugar. "It's fresh."

"No. No, thank you," he said, then winced, looking utterly charming. "Ah, I find I'm in the position of being embarrassed," he said, and I caught back my snort. "I came here to assure myself that you were well after your demon attack yesterday, and I see that not only are you fine, but that you're fully capable of protecting yourself. Ivy was not overestimating your skill. I owe her an apology."

Smiling faintly, I pushed the sugar away. It was nice to hear a compliment once in a while. But undead vampires don't get embarrassed. He was a young, sweet-talking, very experienced master vampire, and I watched his nostrils expand as he breathed in Ivy's and my mingled scents.

The vampire shook his head in a very human gesture. "The woman has a will like no other," he said, and I knew he was talking about Ivy besting her instinct to bite me. It was hard when we lived together like this.

"Tell me about it," I said, all of my awe from sitting in my kitchen with Rynn Cormel washed away by the panic of fighting for my life. "I think she uses me to test herself."

Rynn Cormel's gaze came back from Mr. Fish. "Is that so?"

The questioning tone in his voice made me nervous, and I watched him catalog the mixing of Ivy's life and mine. Standing straighter, I gestured with my coffee mug. "What can I do for you, Mr. Cormel?"

"Rynn, please," he said, flashing me one of his famous smiles that had helped save the free world. "I think after that, we should be on a first-name basis."

"Rynn," I said cautiously, thinking this was really weird. I took a sip of coffee and eyed him over it. If I didn't already know he was dead, I'd never have guessed he wasn't alive. "Don't take this the wrong way, but why do you care if I'm okay or not?"

His smile widened. "You're part of my camarilla, and I take my duties seriously."

I suddenly wished Jenks was here. A spike of fear plinked through me, and I became very interested in the whereabouts of my splat gun. Rynn wasn't living, but the sleepy-time charm would drop him as fast as anyone else. "I won't let you bite me," I said, the threat in my voice clear as I forced myself to take another drink of coffee. The bitter smell seemed to help.

Other than his pupils dilating, he hid the effect my fear had on him. I was impressed.

"I'm not here to bite you," he said, pushing his chair back away from me an inch or so. "I'm here to keep anyone else from doing so."

I watched him suspiciously and uncrossed my ankles—getting ready to move if I had to. He had told Al that I belonged to him. Tried to save me from Al because of that. "But you consider me part of your camarilla," I said, not dumb enough to tell him I didn't want his help just yet. "Don't you bite everyone in it?"

At that, he relaxed, leaning forward to push Ivy's keyboard out of the way and put his elbows on the table. An eager light filled him, and I marveled at how alive and excited he looked. "I don't know. I've never had one," he explained, his dark eyes fixed earnestly on mine. "And I've been told I'm charmingly eager in my efforts to start one. A politician can't—it doesn't make for a fair race."

Shrugging, he leaned back, looking very attractive, confident, and young. "And when the chance arose for me to prevent

Piscary's children from being scattered, to take his well-structured, happy camarilla as my own and assert a claim on you and Ivy?" He hesitated, his attention traveling over my demolished kitchen. "It made my decision to retire very easy."

My mouth went dry. *He had retired to get closer to Ivy and me?*

Rynn Cormel's gaze returned to me. "I came here tonight to make sure you were intact, which I can see you are. Ivy said you were capable of protecting yourself, but I assumed her assurances were simply another one of her ways to keep me from meeting you."

I glanced at the empty hall, things starting to fall into place. "That run of hers tonight was fake, wasn't it," I asked, but it wasn't a question.

The vampire smiled, bringing a leg up to rest a foot on his knee. He looked really good sitting there in my kitchen. "I'm pleased Ivy was telling me the truth. I'm suitably impressed. You've been bitten more times than your skin shows."

Again I felt uncomfortable, but I wouldn't cover my neck. That was an invitation to look.

"You have very beautiful skin," he added, and I felt a dropping sensation, quickly followed by a tingling surge.

Damn it, I thought, reining in my emotions. I knew my skin—less than a year old and hiding an unclaimed vampire bite—was like a steak dangling in front of a wolf. Unless the wolf was very well fed, he was going to go for it.

"I'm sorry," he apologized, his voice a wisp of hollow sound. "I didn't mean to make you uneasy."

Yes, you did, I thought, but I didn't say it aloud. I pushed from the counter, needing the false security of more space between us. "Are you sure you don't want some coffee?" I asked, going to the pot to intentionally turn my back on him. I was afraid, but if I wasn't obvious about it, he'd back off.

"I'm in Cincinnati because of you," he said. "Piscary's children owe you thanks for their well-being. I thought you should know that."

My lips pressed tight, and with my arms wrapped about myself, I spun to him, ready for it. The chitchat was over.

"I heard about you and Ivy living together in this church and what she wants from you," he said, and my face flamed. "If you can save her soul after her first death," he continued, "it would be the most significant advance in vampire history since the live-video feed."

Oh . . . that. I hesitated, embarrassed. This was not what I had expected.

The master vampire smiled. "Lacking a soul is why most vampires don't continue past their thirty-year death anniversary," he explained. "By then, the people who loved them and have been giving them blood are either undead as well or simply dead. Blood from someone who doesn't love you is a thin meal, and without a soul, an undead vampire has a difficult time convincing anyone that he or she loves them. It makes it hard to form an emotional bond that is real and not contrived." He shifted, the scent of vampiric incense coming clear to me. "It can be done, but it takes a lot of finesse."

Somehow, I didn't think Rynn Cormel had that problem. "So if I can save Ivy's soul . . . ," I prompted, not liking where this was going.

"It will allow the undead to continue to form auratic bonds with new people, extending their undead existence forever."

I leaned against the counter and crossed my ankles. Sipping my coffee, I thought that over, remembering that when Ivy had bitten me she had taken a portion of my aura along with my blood. The theory went along nicely with my private theory that an undead vampire needs the illusion of a soul or aura about it or the brain will realize it is dead and drive the vampire into the sun to kill it, thus bringing the mind, the body, and the soul back into balance.

"I'm sorry," I said, thinking that the pope would have a coronary at my thoughts. "It can't be done. I don't know how to save Ivy's soul when she dies. I just don't."

Rynn Cormel's gaze roved over the scattered herbs crushed

underfoot, and I warmed, wondering if he knew I'd been experimenting with ways to safely curb Ivy's blood lust.

"You're the one who broke the balance of power between the vampires and the Weres," he accused so very softly, and I felt cold. "You found the focus," he continued, and my pulse quickened.

"My boyfriend—my ex-boyfriend—did that."

"Semantics," he said, waving a hand. "You brought it into the light."

"And I buried it."

"In a Were's body," he exclaimed, showing a hint of anger.

It might have been to cow me, but it had the opposite effect. Hell, I had already bound a demon tonight. I was on top of the world. "If you *touch* David . . . ," I said, setting my cup aside.

But Rynn Cormel only raised his eyebrows, his anger disappearing at the amusement he found in my threats. "Don't try to bully me, Rachel. It makes you look foolish. I'm saying you broke the balance. The artifact is out. Power is shifting. Slowly, with the gentle pace of generations, but it will shift to the Weres."

He stood. I kept my attention off my splat gun, but I could feel it—utterly too far away.

"If you can find a way for the undead to retain their soul, then the numbers of the undead will grow at a similarly slow pace." He smiled, starting to button up his coat. "Balance is maintained. No one dies. Isn't that what you want?"

I put a hand to my middle. I suppose I should've expected this; no good deed goes unpunished and all. "And witches and humans?" I asked.

He looked out my kitchen window and into the dark. "Maybe that's up to you, too."

But what I heard was "Who cares?" Just wanting this to all go away, I said, "I don't know how to do it. You've got the wrong witch."

Rynn Cormel found his hat and, with a graceful swoop, plucked it from the floor. "I think I have the only witch," he said, brushing the matted dandelion seed from it. "But even if you don't find a way, others will see what you accomplished and will build on that. In the meantime, what have I lost by declaring your blood off-limits to all but Ivy? What have I spent in making sure that you and she have a chance to develop a blood relationship free of stress and trouble?"

I stifled a shiver, and my hand rose up to cover my neck.

"It's no effort at all," he said, then put his hat on.

Okay, he was keeping my butt safe from vampires. "I appreciate that," I said grudgingly. "Thank you."

A copper spell pot grated against the salt when Rynn Cormel pushed it aside with the toe of his dress shoe. "That's hard for you, isn't it? Owing someone?"

"I don't—" I started, then grimaced, rubbing my back where a cupboard knob had raked my skin. "Yes," I finally admitted, hating it.

His smile grew to show a slip of teeth, and he turned as if to leave. "Then I expect you to honor that."

"I don't belong to you," I shot after him, and he turned in the threshold, looking good in his long coat and stylish hat. His eyes were black, but I wasn't afraid of him. Ivy was a bigger threat, hunting me slowly. But I was letting her do it, too.

"I meant, I expect you to honor your relationship with Ivy."

"I do that already," I said, clasping my arms about myself.

"Then we are in perfect understanding."

He again turned to leave, and I followed him into the hall. My thoughts went to Ivy, then Marshal. He wasn't my boyfriend, but he was new in my life. And we were having the hardest time getting together to do the simplest thing. "Are you the reason Marshal and I weren't able to get together this afternoon?" I accused. "Are you going to drive him away so Ivy and I will fall into bed together?"

He was in my living room, and from over his shoulder he said, "Yes."

My lips pressed together, and my slippers scuffed the wood floor we had found under the carpet. "Leave Marshal alone," I said, hands on my hips. Kisten's bracelet fell to my wrist, and I shoved it back into hiding. "He's just a guy. And if I want to sleep with someone, I'm going to. You running off men isn't going to send me rushing into Ivy's arms, it's going to piss me off and make me miserable to live with. Got it?"

I suddenly realized I was swearing at a past leader of the United States, and I flushed. "Sorry for barking at you," I muttered as I fingered Kisten's bracelet and felt guilty. "It's been a hard day."

"My apologies," he said, so sincerely that I almost believed it. "I'll stop interfering."

I took a breath and unclenched my teeth before I gave myself a headache. "Thank you."

The sound of the front door crashing open made me jump. Rynn Cormel took his hand from the door and turned to face the hall.

"Rachel?" came Ivy's worried voice. "Rachel! You okay? There's a couple of guys out front in a car."

I glanced at Rynn Cormel. His eyes had gone black. Hunger black. "Uh, I'm fine!" I sang out. "I'm back here. Uh, Ivy?"

"Damn it all to hell," she swore, her boots clunking in the hall. "I told you to stay on holy ground!"

She barreled into the living room, almost pinwheeling to a stop. She flashed red, her short, dark hair swinging as she stopped. Her hand went first to her bare neck, then she forced it down to her leather-clad hip. "Excuse me," she said, her face going pale. "I've interrupted."

Rynn Cormel shifted his weight, and she cringed. "No, you're fine, Ivy," he said, his voice now deeper and measured. He had lightened his usual demeanor to lull me, and it had worked. "I'm glad you're here."

Ivy looked up, clearly embarrassed. "I'm sorry about your men at the car. I didn't recognize them. They tried to stop me from coming in."

My eyebrows rose, and Rynn Cormel's laughter shocked both Ivy and me. "If you bested them, they deserved it and needed the reminder. Thank you for correcting their poor interpretation of your skills."

Ivy licked her lips. It was a nervous habit I didn't see often, and my tension rose. "Um," she hedged, trying to tuck her short hair behind an ear. "I think I ought to call an ambulance. I broke a few things."

Looking like he didn't care, the master vampire eased forward and, very slowly, took her perfect hand in his scarred one. "You're too kind."

Ivy looked at her fingers among his, blinking fast.

"Rachel is a powerful young woman," he said, and I suddenly felt like I'd passed some sort of test. "I can see why you are attracted to her. You have my blessing to cultivate a scion relationship with her, if that is what you want."

My anger rose, but Ivy shot me a look to shut me up. "Thank you," she said, and I got even more mad when Rynn Cormel smiled smugly, knowing I'd held my tongue because Ivy had asked me to. Then I thought, *So what? Why should I care what he thinks if he'll leave us alone?*

Rynn Cormel took another step closer to Ivy, curving an arm about her waist in a familiar fashion that I didn't like. "Would you accompany me this evening, Ivy? Now that I have seen your friend, I understand better. I'd like to . . . try another angle, if you are willing."

Try another angle? I thought, seeing the hinted hunger in him, luring her. *Working on a sequel, are we?* I didn't agree with how vampire society worked, but Ivy took a relieved breath, her eyes positively lighting. "Yes," she said quickly, but then her gaze slid to me.

"Go," I said sourly, glad she hadn't seen the demolished kitchen. "I'll be fine."

She eased closer to Rynn Cormel, her lean, leather-clad body looking fabulous next to his polished refinement. "You're not on hallowed ground," she said.

"Al won't be back." I glanced at Rynn Cormel's light grip on her shoulder. "I'm fine."

Ivy pulled away from him, reaching for me. "He was here?" she said. "Are you okay?"

"I'm fine!" I said, backing up until her outstretched hand dropped. My gaze went to Rynn Cormel, and I didn't like the smile he was hiding.

"I told you not to go onto unsanctified ground," Ivy almost scolded. "God, Rachel, I made you a sign!"

"I forgot, okay?" I shot back at her. "I took it down because it ticked me off, and I forgot. I was so flustered about your *master vampire* paying me a visit that I forgot!"

Ivy hesitated, then said softly, "Okay."

"Okay," I repeated, feeling my anger die at her quick admission.

"Well . . . okay."

I glared at Rynn Cormel, who was adjusting his hat and smiling at the exchange.

"I'll get on hallowed ground," I said, just wanting her to leave.

Ivy took a rocking step toward the door, then hesitated. "What about dinner? You can't order pizza. Al might deliver it."

"Marshal is coming over," I said, looking pointedly at Rynn Cormel as he evaluated the exchange. "He's bringing dinner."

A flash of jealousy passed over Ivy, dying fast. Rynn Cormel saw both its birth and death, and when he met my gaze, I knew he realized Ivy and I had already set up the rules for our relationship—and those rules included other people. Most vampiric relationships did, though that did nothing for my sense of morality.

"I'll see you about sunrise," she said, and the master vampire's eyebrows rose. Ivy gave me a tight-lipped smile and turned to Rynn Cormel.

"Ivy," he said, offering his arm.

"Mr. Cormel," she said back, sounding flustered as she didn't take it. "Um, could you sign your book for me before we go?"

My breath hesitated, and I stiffened. *Oh, God. Not the vampire dating guide.*

Ivy turned to me, her expression eager. I didn't see this side of her often, and it was kind of scary. "You've still got it, don't you?" she asked. "Is it still on your bedside table?"

"Ivy!" I exclaimed, backing up, my face hot. Crap. *Now he knows I've read it.* My thoughts flicked to page forty-nine, and I stared in horror when Rynn Cormel laughed at my expression. "It was so I would stop stomping on her instincts!" I babbled, and he laughed all the more.

Ivy was starting to look ticked, and Rynn Cormel took her arm to escort her out. "I would love to sign your copy," he said as he led her to the back door. "I'm sure Rachel will find it for you, and you can bring it over next time." He smiled over his shoulder at me as he opened the door and the coolness of the night slipped in. "She might want to peruse it first," he added, and my jaw clenched.

"I've already perused it," I said loudly, and the door shut behind them with a soft click.

"God help me," I muttered as I fell back into Ivy's old couch and breathed in the puff of vampire incense that I'd kicked up from the cushions. If she wanted Rynn Cormel to sign her book, she could damn well dig it out from the back of my closet herself. I didn't even know for sure if it was still there. But, staring at the ceiling, I wondered if Ivy might find happiness in a real vampiric relationship with Rynn Cormel. She seemed positively besotted.

My thoughts drifted to Kisten, and I wondered if she felt any of the guilt I did.

The quiet of the church soaked into me, and in the distance, I heard the sound of a car starting up. "Kitchen," I said to myself, and sat up. Yeah, I had told Ivy I'd get on hallowed ground, but I wasn't going to let that mess sit until tomorrow. Tomorrow I was going out with David, and once I knocked some sense into a happy band of demon summoners, I'd have my life back. Such as it was.

I stood in the threshold of the kitchen and sighed at the destruction. Maybe I could pay the pixies to clean it up. But they were tucked into the stump until the warmth of sunrise, so, resigned to the mess, I scuffed in. My back hurt as I picked up the broken clock and set it on the counter. Most of the rack was on the floor, and deciding I'd pile everything up now and sort it later, I went to the cupboard to get the broom.

It was going to be a long night.

Eleven

The moon was shining in the kitchen window as I wiped my footprints off the island counter. I was almost finished with cleaning up. It had taken a twenty-pixy-escort trip out to the shed for my toolbox, but I'd found a metal plate and a few wood screws to tack the rack together. I wasn't going to put anything heavier than herbs on it, but at least it wasn't hanging cockeyed from the ceiling. Yes, I had told Ivy I'd get on sanctified ground, but for some inane reason, I trusted that Al wasn't going to show up, as some weird thank-you for not siccing Minias on him. Tomorrow he'd try to abduct me again, but tonight I was safe. And I never had told Ivy when I'd actually *get* to holy ground. Besides, Marshal was coming over, and the kitchen table was less datelike than the couch.

Tossing the dishcloth onto the table, I knelt before the open shelves under the counter. I had simply shoved everything in there on my first pass through, and it was a mess. If I couldn't hang the smaller spell pots and utensils back up, I'd have to do some rearranging. My splat gun sat in the small spell pot nestled in with the rest on the bottom shelf, right where I'd need it if I was crawling. That was where it would stay. But the ceramic spoons needed a new home.

Gathering up the spoons and long utensils, I arranged them in a glass vase I'd pulled out of the back of a cupboard. I pushed my spell books down and used the vase as a bookend, taking up the space where the book Al had destroyed had been.

Unhappy, I sat back on my heels and considered my smaller library. I'd never be able to replace the book he had burned. Sure, I could pick up another at just about any charm shop, but mine had had notes and everything in it. I wondered if perhaps I ought to move the more valuable demon curse books onto hallowed ground. I'd been lucky Al hadn't destroyed one of them instead. Or maybe I was unlucky, seeing as I still had them.

My fingers tingled as I pulled out the three books in question. I stood, and after running my arm across the counter to make sure it was dry, I set them down.

"Moving them?" Jenks questioned, and I looked to where he was examining my handiwork, his fists on his hips as he hovered at the mended rack.

"Maybe," I said glumly.

His wings made a soft hum, and I swung my hair out of the way as he approached, but he landed on the counter instead. "If that gargoyle weren't up there, I'd say put them in the belfry."

A wince crinkled my eyes as I imagined the extreme temperatures. "He's *in* the belfry?"

Jenks lifted a shoulder and let it fall. "No, but he's on the roof beside the window. Tink's titties, I never see the thing move. One minute he's here, the next he's there, and when he's not asleep, I don't know where he is. At any rate, it might be better than putting them under your bed. Ivy said the guy who blessed the church said the belfry was super holy."

Super holy, eh? Maybe I should sleep up there. Worried, I pushed the books to the corner to make room for the rest of the under-counter stuff. "I don't know. . . ." My nose tickled as I weeded through the stack of herbs I'd been messing with to modify an existing charm to give Ivy a measure of control over her blood lust. It wasn't going well. She didn't like trying them out, taking them on her dates so if it didn't work, I wouldn't have to fight her off. Nothing seemed to have an effect, and I wondered if she was really trying them or just telling me she was. Ivy didn't like my magic touching her, though she thought me blasting anyone else was cool.

Jenks dropped to land beside the curse books. His tiny features were worried as he watched me shake a sheaf of feverfew to get the tansy off it. "You aren't going to keep that, are you?" he asked, and I glanced up from picking cat hair off it.

"You don't think I should?"

"They aren't pure anymore." He kicked a dry stem, making little chips fall off. "You got pieces of rosemary on the coneflower, and coneflower seeds sticking to the dandelions. Who knows what they will do, especially if you're experimenting."

I looked at the pile of dried herbs thinking it would be a lot easier to just chuck it out the back door, but I was afraid that if I did that, I might simply give up. Adapting charms was hard. I could follow a recipe, but my mother was like a gourmet chef, and I had never appreciated that until I tried to do it myself. "Maybe you're right."

Mood souring, I shook out a brown paper bag and shoved a year's worth of gardening into it. The rasping sound cut through the silence, and I felt sick as I wadded the top of the bag down and jammed it all into the trash under the sink. Turning, I deemed the kitchen reasonably clean. The rack was empty, and I wondered if I should just give up on the charm for controlling Ivy's blood lust. Ivy wasn't helping, and it was really hard. Depressed, I slumped into my chair at the table.

"I don't know if I can do this, Jenks," I said, putting my elbows on the table and exhaling with a sigh. "My mother makes it look so easy. Maybe I'll get farther if I mix some ley line magic with the earth charms. I mean, ley line magic is mostly symbolism and word choice, making it more flexible."

Jenks's wings blurred into motion and stopped. Tossing his blond hair from his eyes, he frowned, almost sitting on the demon text and catching himself at the last moment, wings going full tilt. "Mix earth and ley line magic? Isn't that what makes a demon curse?"

Fear slid through me and away. "It won't be a demon curse if I invent it, will it?"

His wings drooped and he seemed to slump. "I don't know. Marshal's here."

I sat up and glanced over the kitchen. "How do you know?"

"He drives a diesel, and one just pulled up to the curb."

A smile curved over me. "He's got a diesel engine?"

Spilling a glittering path of dust, Jenks rose. "Probably needs it to pull his big-ass boat out of the water. I'll get the door. I want to talk to him."

"Jenks," I warned, and he laughed, halfway to the hall.

"About Al being after you. God, Rachel! I'm not your daddy."

I relaxed, then got to my feet and shoved the demon books under the counter, vowing to do some rearranging tomorrow when the sun was up. I heard the front door open before the bell even rang, and a masculine greeting filtered softly back to me in a way that sounded really . . . comforting.

"Is she all right?" came Marshal's soft query from the sanctuary, but I didn't hear Jenks's response. "No, that's cool," he added, clearly closer, and I spun to the hallway at the soft sound of the floorboards creaking and the smell of hot rice.

"Hi, Marshal," I said, glad to see him. "You made it."

Marshal had taken the time to get out of his interview clothes, and he looked good in jeans and a soft flannel shirt of rich blue. There was a folded newspaper under his arm, and he set it and the steam-damp bag on the table before taking off his coat. "I was starting to think the world was conspiring against us," he said. "Jenks said you had a rough early evening."

I glanced at Jenks, wondering what he had told Marshal. I shrugged, arms wrapping around my middle. "I survived."

"Survived?" Jenks landed on top of the rolled-down bag. "We kicked that demon's ass from here to the Turn. Don't sell yourself short, Rache."

Marshal hung his coat on the back of Ivy's chair, pausing to watch Jenks manhandle the bag open. "I like your church," he said, gazing at the kitchen. "It suits you."

"Thanks." A flash of gratitude went through me. He didn't pry, didn't ask why a demon had been in my kitchen, didn't take my hand and peer into my eyes and ask me if I was okay and did I need to sit down, didn't tell me I was going to die young and that I should take up canasta instead. He accepted my explanation and let it go. I didn't think it was because he didn't care either. I think it was because he wanted to wait until I was comfortable and told him myself. And that meant a lot. Kisten had been like that, too.

I will not compare Marshal to Kisten, I thought as I got two plates and the tea bag caddy Jenks used as a dish. Ivy was out on a date. She was able to move on with her life. It would get better, but only if I tried. Only if I wanted it to. And I did. I didn't like being unhappy. I hadn't realized I had been until I started to feel good again.

"Where," Marshal said into the silence as he peered under the table, "did you get such a big pumpkin? It is a pumpkin, isn't it?" the man asked, and Jenks's wings increased their pitch. "It's not one of those squash that looks like a pumpkin?"

"It's a pumpkin," Jenks said, his pride clear. "I grew it myself between the Jamesons' plots and the Davaros statue. Out in the graveyard," he added, as if it wasn't obvious. "We're going to carve it tomorrow. Just me and the kids. Give Matalina a break."

Matalina gets a break, and I get pumpkin guts on my ceiling. I'm sure it would start sedately enough, but it wouldn't be long before they started Pumpkin Wars, the sequel.

"So-o-o-o," I said as I hung up the dishcloth. "How did your last interviews go?"

Marshal edged closer when Jenks got the bag open and the scent of sweet-and-sour came wafting out. "Great." He started removing take-out boxes, and I looked up, suddenly conscious that our shoulders were almost touching. "I got the job," he said when our eyes met, and I smiled.

"Marshal, that's great!" I exclaimed, then gave him a neutral swat on the shoulder. "When do you start?" I added, not looking at him as I turned to fuss with the food. *Maybe that was too much.*

The man backed up a step and ran a hand over the new stubble atop his head. "November first," he said. "But I'll be on salary, so I can go back and forth to sell the business if I need to until classes start up after the winter solstice."

Jenks gave me a warning look, and I scowled at him, bumping the table to make him jump when I went to get a couple of serving spoons. The scent of oil and gas blended with a witch's redwood smell, making Marshal seem like a yummy piece of northern exposure. He dressed differently from anyone I'd spent much time with, smelled different, and had somehow skipped that uncomfortable stage of awkwardness most of my dates had, slipping into my church like he belonged. Not that this was a date. Maybe that was why. I had invited him over without any thoughts of a possible relationship, and we both could relax. But I expected the easy companionship was mostly because he had helped Jenks and me when we had really needed it.

Ivy's chair bumped and scraped as Marshal pulled it to the open spot, and he sighed when he sat down. "It was one of the oddest interviews I've ever had," he said as I rummaged for the chopsticks with my back to him. "They seemed to like me, but I thought they were going to give it to the other guy—and for the life of me, I couldn't tell why. He had developed a swim program for a high school down in Florida, but he didn't have either the dive time or ley line experience, and that's what they were looking for."

I sat down kitty-corner to him and his eyes flicked to the chopsticks.

"Then all of a sudden, they made a decision and offered me the job," he finished.

"All of a sudden, huh?" Jenks said, and I shot him a look to shut him up. Marshal didn't get the job because of Rynn Cormel, but I'd be willing to bet the vampire had been leaning on the university to pick someone else until I had barked at him to get out of my life. Whereupon the university had chosen whom they wanted.

Marshal was still looking at the chopsticks. "It was weird, like I'd done them a favor or something by saying yes." His gaze flicked from the chopsticks to me and he winced. "Uh, I'm going to need a fork."

I laughed and got back up. "Sorry." I felt his attention on me, and feeling sassy, I picked out two forks. Marshal was dishing out the food, and it was nice being with someone who wasn't looking for anything. "You know, since Al showed up, we don't have to hang around here."

"Rachel . . . ," Jenks protested, and I turned, bumping the drawer closed with my hip.

"What?" I complained. "He's not going to come back tonight. I've been on unsanctified ground this entire time."

"And Ivy's going to have fairies coming out her ass when she finds out," Jenks said.

I plopped down, not meeting anyone's gaze. Marshal glanced from me to Jenks, watching us between tapping rice out on our plates. Jenks waved his hand no when Marshal offered, which didn't surprise me. The small pixy wasn't happy, and his wings were turning red as he grew upset and his circulation increased. Annoyed, I set the forks clattering on the table. "He's not going to bother me anymore tonight, Jenks."

"Why? Because you didn't have Minias cart him off when your deluded sense of siding with the underdog told you he was *tired* and he *appreciated you trusting him*? Tink's contractual hell, Rachel. That's nuts. Slug nuts with slime on top. If you die tonight, it's not my fault!"

Marshal continued to serve food, and the spicy scent did nothing to ease my tension. "Ah, Rachel? You want to go roller-skating tomorrow?" he said, clearly not liking Jenks and me arguing. It was an obvious attempt to change the subject, but my ire evaporated, and I uncrossed my arms and decided to ignore Jenks.

"Do you know how long it's been since I've been skating?" I said.

The pixy dropped to his empty tea bag caddy with his arms crossed over his chest, shedding silver sparkles. "According to your mom, not since you were banned for slamming—"

"Quiet!" I said, thumping the underside of the table with my knee, but the antique ash was heavy and Jenks didn't even jump this time. "Don't you have somewhere to go? Gargoyles to spy on or something?" I complained, my face warming. *They wouldn't still remember me at Aston's, would they?*

"Nope," Jenks said. His face was creased in irritation, and then seeing both of us looking at him, he forced himself to relax. "How about putting some of that sake I smell on my plate, Marsh-man," he said suddenly. It was a change of mood I didn't trust, but I'd go along with it.

Looking chagrined, Marshal pulled a worn thermos from his jacket pocket. "It was supposed to be a surprise," he said dryly as he set it between us.

"I'm surprised," I said as I got up to get the tiny, see-through ceramic teacups that Ceri preferred to my thick-walled mugs. They weren't traditional sake cups, but they looked better than shot glasses.

"That will work," Marshal said as I set them down, and he filled them halfway up before carefully tipping his cup over Jenks's tea bag caddy to fill it right to the top.

This isn't like Kisten, I thought, finding a hint of peace as I held my cup up in a toast. Jenks had never hung around when Kisten and I were together. And though Marshal was fun to look at, I was still too raw to be serious. Not having that will-he-won't-he stress to deal with was an unexpected pleasure.

"To new jobs," he said, and we all took a sip, me holding my breath so I wouldn't cough.

"Good stuff," I said, eyes watering and feeling the nasty stuff burn all the way down.

Marshal set his cup down with a careful slowness, the subtle easing of his posture telling me that just that little bit of alcohol had an effect on him. But hell, sake was potent stuff.

Jenks's wings sped up, and the soft slipping of dust ceased.

"Thanks for letting me come over," Marshal said as he took up his fork and arranged his dinner. "My hotel room is . . . empty. And I could use a little normalcy after today."

Smirking, Jenks fanned his wings, sending the scent of rice to me. "She fought off a demon with the help of Rynn Cormel. We ain't normal, Marsh-man."

It almost sounded like a warning, and Marshal's laughter stopped short when he saw my mood go pensive. "Rynn Cormel?" he said, as if trying to figure out if Jenks was kidding him. "The vampire, right?"

I leaned over my plate and took a bite. Good rice sticks together, but I wasn't going to use chopsticks if Marshal wasn't. "Yup," I said when it became obvious that he was waiting for an answer. "He took in Piscary's camarilla, which means he's my roommate's new master vamp, and he came over to find out what my intentions toward Ivy were."

Sort of the truth, but the entire truth was *way* too embarrassing.

"Oh."

It was an uncomfortable utterance, and I looked up to see his brown eyes holding an uneasy wariness—which made Jenks all the more pleased, apparently, if his wing speed was any indication. "It wasn't a big deal," I said, trying to downplay it. "He got in the way more than anything else."

That didn't help at all, and Marshal swallowed to look ill. I sat back, gripping my plate and reaching for my sake cup. "You want to move to sanctified ground? We can watch TV or something. We have cable out there now."

Marshal shook his head. "No. If you say the demon won't show up, I believe you."

A snicker came from Jenks, ticking me off. I took another swallow of sake, following it with the rice and meat. It didn't burn this time, and I thought as I chewed and swallowed. This stank. Marshal wanted to take me skating. What kind of friend makes a guy hide in a church because she's afraid of demons?

Lips pressed, I got up, feeling the men's eyes on me as I plucked my compact from my bag and one of Ivy's fine-line Sharpies from her cup. I had a stick of yew around here somewhere, and the sake was probably a good substitute for wine.

"Uh, Rache?" Jenks questioned.

"I'm tired of hiding in my church," I said, thinking I'd have to get my scrying mirror out to remember what the glyph looked like if I wanted to reproduce the spell to make a calling circle. "It's right before Halloween, for crying out loud."

"Rache . . ."

I wouldn't look up. "If you want to come with us and babysit, fine. Al isn't going to show. Besides, he wants me alive, not dead. And I want to go out."

Marshal's fork scraped as he set it down. "What are you doing?"

"Making something I probably shouldn't." Giving up on doing this from memory, I pulled my scrying mirror out from under the island counter and carefully set it down. I harbored a guilty thought that the thing was beautiful, its crystalline lines of the symbols etched into its surface showing a sharp diamond clarity against the wine-colored depths of the glass reflecting reality in deep shades of maroon. Something this evil shouldn't be beautiful. Ceri had helped me make this one after I broke the first over Minias's head. *Damn it, why is she risking her soul like this again?*

Marshal was silent as he looked at it. "That's a calling circle," he finally said. "I think. I've never seen one like that."

Jenks looked almost cocky when the dust slipping from him turned gold and he said, "That's because it goes through ley lines to summon demons."

I frowned, but the damage had been done. Marshal stiffened, carefully taking a bite of rice and vegetables as if it didn't bother him. Exasperated, I looked at the sake and decided I'd had enough. Of Jenks, not the sake. *What is with him tonight?*

"It doesn't summon demons, just lets me talk to them." *And opens a channel they can travel through.* "Marshal, I'm a white witch. Really." I looked at the pentagram and winced. "The thing is, I've got a demon bent on dragging me into the ever-after, and having a calling circle gives me the option to call someone to pick him up when he shows. He's supposed to be in jail. But everything will be fine tomorrow after I go out with David and beat some sense into whoever is calling Al and releasing him to get me."

It sounded lame even to me, and Marshal chewed his rice, his attention never leaving mine as he weighed his thoughts. His gaze flicked to the calling circle and then swung back to me. "You call it Al?" he asked mildly.

I took a breath, deciding to give him all the drama of my life at once. If he was going to leave because of it, I wanted to know now, not after I started liking the guy. "The smut on my aura I got from using a demon curse to save my ex-boyfriend," I said. *Mostly.* "And the two demon marks were accidents."

Aren't they all? I mocked in my thoughts, but Marshal had taken a sip of his drink and leaned back. "Rachel, you don't have to tell me all this," he said, and I raised a hand.

"Yes I do." Eyeing the sake, I slammed it, wanting a loose tongue for a few minutes. "There is *no way* I'm going to have a boyfriend anytime soon," I said as it burned, "so if you're looking for a fast hop in the sack, you can just walk out the door right now. Actually, you should get out now anyway."

"Uh . . ." Marshal stammered, and Jenks snickered as he drank the last of his sake.

"I have a risky job," I said defensively as I put my arm flat on the table, almost flipping my plate of rice. "I love it. It might make you a target." My jaw clenched. Kisten had died because he refused to kill me when Piscary asked. I was sure of it.

Jenks took flight, and I watched the sparkles as he landed on Marshal's shoulder and sighed. "She's such a drama queen," he muttered a little too loudly, ticking me off.

"Shut up, Jenks," I said carefully so I wouldn't slur. I wasn't drunk, but the alcohol helped. I turned to Marshal. "I got a demon mark when my ex-boyfriend bought a trip through the lines when Al tore my throat open. I have another on my foot because some jackass pulled me through to the ever-after to give me to Al and I had to buy a trip home from another demon who is absolutely nuts and might show up at any time if she remembers me."

"She?" Marshal said, sparse eyebrows high but accepting that.

"I also have a couple of unclaimed vampire scars that make me susceptible to vampire pheromones," I said, not caring what he thought. "If it wasn't for Ivy protecting me, I'd be dead or out of my mind by now because of it."

Jenks leaned toward Marshal's ear and whispered loud enough for me to hear, "I think she likes them, if you ask me."

"I'm trouble, Marshal," I said, ignoring Jenks. "If you were smart, you'd walk out of my church, get in your truck, and drive away. God! I don't even know why you're here."

Marshal pushed his plate away and crossed his arms over his chest. His muscles bunched under his shirt, and I forced my attention from him. I wasn't drunk, damn it, but my eyes warmed. "Are you done?" he asked.

"I suppose," I said, depressed.

"Jenks, do you mind if I talk to Rachel alone?" Marshal asked.

The pixy's expression darkened and he put his fists on his hips, but when he saw me glare at him, he sulkily flew to the door. Ten to one he was going to listen from the hall, but at least we had the illusion of privacy.

Seeing him gone, Marshal leaned across the table and took my hands in his. "Rachel, I met you on my boat, asking for my help to rescue your ex-boyfriend from a group of militant Weres. Don't you think I know you leave a trail of bread crumbs for trouble to follow?"

I brought my eyes up. "Yes, but—"

"My turn," he said, and I shut my mouth. "I'm not sitting in your kitchen because I'm new in town and looking for a curvy body in my bed. I'm here because I like you. I only talked to you for a few hours on my boat, but in that little time, I was seeing you as you. No pretenses, no games. You know how rare that is?" He gave my fingers a gentle squeeze, and my gaze rose. "You never see a person like that on a date, not after a dozen dates. Sometimes, you can spend years with someone and never really know what they're like under the veneer we put on to make ourselves feel better. I liked what I saw when you were under pressure. The last thing I need is a steady girlfriend." He let go of my hand and slid to the back of his chair. "My last one was a nightmare, and I'd just as soon keep things casual. Like tonight. Minus the demon."

He smiled, and I couldn't help but smile back. I'd been around too many guys to take his words at face value, but he was stifling a shudder born from something in his memory. "I don't want you to get hurt," I mumbled, embarrassed now. The quickest way to get a man interested was to say you weren't.

Marshal sat taller. "I'll be okay," he said as he looked out the dark kitchen window and shrugged. "I'm not helpless. I've got a degree in low-level ley line manipulations. I ought to be able to manage a demon or two." He smiled. "Short-term anyway."

This wasn't going well. "I'm not . . . I can't . . ." I took a steadying breath. "I'm still hurting. You're wasting your time."

He looked at the window and the dark square it made. "I told you I'm not looking for a girlfriend. You women are all nuts, but I like the way you smell and you're fun to dance with."

A quiver rose and fell in my middle. "Then why are you here?"

Marshal's eyes came back to mine. "I don't like being alone, and you look like you need to be with someone . . . for a while."

Slowly my gaze dropped and then returned to his. Could I trust that? Seeing my compact, I picked it up, weighed it in my palm, then tossed it into my bag. Somehow I didn't feel like I needed to prove anything to him anymore, and the entire idea had been bad to begin with. God, no wonder I kept getting into trouble. So I couldn't go out? So what?

"You, ah, want to watch a movie?" I said, embarrassed for having bared my soul, though it had left me feeling refreshed.

Marshal made a soft noise and stretched where he sat, looking comfortable and content. "Sure. Mind if I bring my paper in for the classifieds? I'm still looking for an apartment."

"Sounds great," I said. "That sounds really great."

Twelve

It was the softest sound of fabric sliding against leather that woke me. In a pulse of adrenaline, my eyes flashed open and my breath came fast. The scratchy softness of an afghan brushed against my face, and I sat up with a smooth, fast motion.

I was on the couch in the sanctuary, not my bed, and the light coming in the tall stained-glass windows was bright with the sunrise. Across the coffee table, Marshal was frozen halfway to a stand from his chair. His expression was one of shock.

"Wow," he said as he straightened to his full height. "I was trying to be quiet. You're a really light sleeper."

I blinked at him, realizing what had happened. "I fell asleep," I said stupidly. "What time is it?"

With a soft exhalation, Marshal sat back down on the chair where he had spent most of last night. A bowl holding leftover popcorn sat on the table with three bottles of pop and an empty bag of gingersnaps. His stocking feet spread wide, he squinted at his watch. It was analog, which didn't surprise me. Most witches shunned digital. "A little after seven," he said, his gaze rising to the muted TV and the puppets that were dancing there.

"Oh, God!" I moaned, falling back into the warmth of where I had been sleeping. "I'm so sorry."

Marshal had his head down as he adjusted his socks. "For what?"

I gestured to the stained-glass windows past the gently swaying bats. "It's seven."

"I don't have to be anywhere. Do you?"

Uh, not until later. My swirling thoughts slowed. I didn't feel that good, seeing as I still had a chunk of sleep waiting for me somewhere, and I scooted myself up a bit so I wasn't so . . . schlumpy looking.

"Hey, you, ah, want to crash here for the rest of the morning?" I asked, staring at the happy puppets on the TV. Must be a human thing to watch puppets at this hour, because it sure as hell wasn't appealing to a witch. "We have a couch in the back living room. It's darker in there."

Marshal pressed his lips together and shook his head. "No, thanks. I didn't mean to wake you. I was going to leave you a note and slip out. I've been on a human clock for three years. I'm usually up by now."

My face twisted as I imagined that. "I'm not," I complained. "I've got to get to bed."

He smiled as he gathered the empty bottles to take to the kitchen, and I yawned. "Don't bother," I said. "I'll take care of them. If I don't rinse them out, the rani of recycling yells at me."

Smiling, he pulled his hands away and stood, leaving them where they were. "I have to check a few more apartments this morning, but I'll burn through my list in a few hours. You want to get together later?"

A spike of anticipation rose through me, dulled by my sleepy state, but I couldn't help but wonder where this was going. Last night with Marshal had been fun. Comfortable. True to what he had said earlier about wanting a break from a girlfriend, we just sat around and watched TV. I had brought all my runner instincts to bear on him, and though it would be stupid to think that he might not be interested in more later, right now, he just seemed to appreciate the company. God knew I did.

"Sure," I said, carefully, "but David's run out to that witch's house comes first." I was reluctant to move, feeling rumpled and ill from the early hour. I'd thought it had been odd when he'd fallen asleep in his chair at midnight, right during the news, but if he'd been running on a human clock, that would be late for him.

I had intended to let Marshal sleep through the late movie and then wake him, seeing as it was nice having company without having to worry about triggering any blood lust attacks when I got excited in a chase scene. Falling asleep during the slow spots had never crossed my mind. But someone had turned the volume down, so he'd probably woken up at some point and let me keep sleeping. That was nice.

"You need any help? At the house I mean?" Marshal asked, and I smiled up at him.

"Nope."

"Then I'll get out of here," he said, then dropped down to crouch before me. He was way too close, and I drew back with my eyes wide.

"You're funny," he said as he got on his hands and knees and peered under the couch. "I'm not going to kiss you. You're too much trouble to be my girlfriend. Too high-maintenance. My boots are under there."

I grinned in embarrassment as he came up with his boots.

The click of the front door opening shot through me. Marshal got to his feet and turned in one smooth motion, and I bolted upright.

"Ivy?" I called, recognizing the sound of her boots clacking.

Her path ruler-straight and her face placid, she walked past Marshal and me. "'Morning," she said, no clue to her mood in her voice as she vanished into the darkness of the hall. The collar to her jacket was up, and I think she'd been bitten in an intentionally obvious place. My thoughts jerked back to Rynn Cormel, and a feeling of anger burned. He had taken her last night, making his claim in an obvious, indisputable way. I'd known it was coming, and Ivy said it was expected, but it still seemed degrading to me.

Marshal shifted uneasily, and my attention returned to him. He was standing over me, and I suddenly realized what it must have looked like to Ivy. He hadn't been there to give me a kiss, but he had been in the right place for it.

Ivy slammed a kitchen cupboard door shut, and Marshal jumped.

"I'd, ah, better go."

I pulled the afghan up around my shoulders as he started for the front door. Stretching to feel every ache the couch had put in me, I followed him. The pixies were loud outside, and the shadows of their wings showed where they were clearing spiderwebs off the outside panes to help deter fairies from trying to take up residence. My balance bobbled as I came around the coffee table, and Marshal caught my elbow. "Thanks," I mumbled, looking up his considerable height. I didn't like how awkward the early hour had made me, but he looked fine, standing there in his rumpled shirt and lightly stubbled face.

"Kinda klutzy in the morning, eh?" he said, then let go of my elbow when Ivy's boots clattered in the hallway. He stepped back, and I tried not to frown at Ivy. She had Marshal's coat from the kitchen, and she draped it over my swivel desk chair. "Do you want some coffee before you go?" she asked, sounding sincere, but the coat said different.

Marshal cracked his neck, his gaze sliding to his coat before returning to Ivy, who was framed by the hallway opening, her hip cocked, looking predatory in her sleek leather pants and coat. "No, thanks. I have an appointment. See you later, Ivy."

He pulled his coat from the chair, and as it slowly spun, I followed him to the door. Fatigue made my feet heavy, and I yawned, trying to wake up. *God, I must look terrible.*

"'Bye, Marshal," Ivy said, still unmoving. Her face was empty, telling me she wasn't happy. I gave her a pointed look when Marshal paused to put on his boots, and finally showing her ire, she turned and left.

Immediately my tension eased in the dim gray of the foyer. "Don't mind her," I said as Marshal laced his boots up. "She likes you."

"Could have fooled me," he said as he tugged his coat on and the scent of oil, gas, and redwood came to me. "Thanks for last night. I didn't want to sit in my hotel room, and I'm too old for the bar scene. I feel like I'm using you to keep from being alone."

A smile came over me, sort of sad but happy as well. "Yeah, me, too." I hesitated, not wanting to sound pushy, but it had felt good not to be alone. "So, I'll call you later this afternoon when I know my schedule?"

He took a deep breath, exhaling quickly as he gathered his thoughts. "Not if I call you first." Smiling, he opened the door and stepped out onto the stoop. "'Bye, Rachel."

"'Bye," I called after him. I slumped until my back hit the door frame, giving him an unsure smile when he looked up from the sidewalk with his keys in hand. His boots were almost soundless on the walk, and I watched him as the cooler air slipped in to make my ankles chill and a stray curl dance before my eyes. I hoped this wasn't a mistake. I'd had guy friends before, but it usually slipped into something else before it ended.

The human neighbor down the street drove past in his minivan, and when he slowed to check Marshal out, I ducked back inside. Seven o'clock. What was I doing up at seven o'clock? This was a stupid-ass hour to be up.

But I felt good. Sort of melancholy, but good.

The darkness of the foyer was comforting, and I wrapped my arms around my middle as I went back into the sanctuary, grabbing the bowl and bottles on my way to the kitchen. Ivy was in there, and I wanted to know if Rynn Cormel, the charismatic world leader, had taken advantage of my roommate and bitten her.

Squinting at the brighter light and feeling the early hour all the way to my bones, I rinsed the empty pop bottles before dropping them into the recycling bin and slumped into my chair with the last of the popcorn. Ivy was still wearing her coat, sitting poised at her computer and checking e-mail before bed. An open box of flavored cereal was by her keyboard and she chewed slowly. Leaning, I tried to catch a look at her neck, and she jerked back so I couldn't.

"He seems nice," she said, her face emotionless, but I could hear a hint of annoyance.

"He is," I said defensively. "It's nice of you to pretend to like him, by the way. Thanks."

The corners of her eyes tightened. "What makes you think I don't like him?"

Oh, that is just stupid. "Because you never like anyone who pays attention to me," I said, feeling my pulse quicken, angry that she would try to bullshit me.

"I liked Kisten," she said bitterly.

Emotion welled, and I got even more angry that she'd try to make me feel guilty for wanting to move past his death. I tugged the afghan closer, ticked. "The only reason you liked him was because he got me to loosen up and sleep with a vamp," I said sullenly.

"That's part of it," she said mildly.

"And because you knew he was never a real threat," I added. "That if push came to shove, Kisten would back off. You used him."

Ivy stiffened. Her fingers danced over the keys until she hit "send" with an excessive amount of force. "That, too," she admitted softly—irritated. "But *I. Also. Loved. Him.*"

Suddenly I understood what this was about. Leaning back in my chair, I crossed my arms over my chest. "Spending time with Marshal is not betraying Kisten's memory. Don't you dare think badly of me for that. He's just a guy, not my boyfriend. Ivy, you just spent the night with Rynn Cormel. Got a new scar?" I mocked.

I leaned forward to shift her collar, and her arm flashed to intercept me. Her arm met mine in a soft but certain *whap*, and I jerked back, surprised.

"He's my master," she said, her eyes dilating. "It's expected."

But she had turned, and there was a new, carefully given, red-rimmed bite. Something unexpected clenched in me, and Ivy's pale complexion turned a soft blush. *Damn it.*

"Expected, hell. I know you enjoyed yourself," I said hotly. "You enjoyed it, and there's nothing wrong with that, but if you feel guilty about it, don't take it out on me."

Ivy's long hand trembled. My heart gave a hard thump as she pushed from her computer and focused entirely on me in a familiar mix of anger and the sexual domination she used to protect herself. I met her angry expression with my glare, and a twinge came from my neck. I ignored it. The tips of her gold-highlighted hair shifted with her breath, and a feeling of unease rose behind me, like the creepy-crawly things that live under the bed that only kids know are there. The hair on the back of my neck prickled, and my jaw clenched as I fought the urge to turn. She was pulling a vampiric aura. She hadn't done that in almost a year. My own eyes narrowed in anger even as I shuddered and my palms itched. Maybe it was time to remind her that this witch had teeth, too.

"He's protecting me," she said, her low voice swirling like gray silk. "Protecting us."

"Yeah," I said sarcastically. "So he tells me. We're his freaking science experiment." Ticked, I stood. If she was pulling an aura, it was time to leave. And I didn't like the waves of sensation that pulsed down my neck and promised more. "My life is so messed up," I said. I headed for the hallway. I had to get away from everything. Everything. "He's just another dead vamp sucking on your neck," I muttered, feeling every muscle tighten as I passed her.

"And that bothers you?" Ivy said loudly.

I turned before I reached the hallway. Ivy had spun in her chair to face me, her legs still crossed at the knees and her working leathers making her look coy and sleek. Her eyes were black and full. A sudden surge from my scar spilled down my side to pool in my middle, warm and breath stealing. I stiffened, shoving the sensation away. "He's using you!" I said, gesturing angrily. "God, Ivy, don't you get it? He doesn't love you. He can't!"

Ivy gave me a knowing look. Goading. Arching her eyebrows in silent challenge, she succinctly placed a Cheerio in her mouth and crunched through it. "Everyone uses people. You don't think Marshal's using you? That you're not using him to feel safe in the narrow acceptance of your wants?"

"Excuse me?" I barked. "This is about me liking guys and not sleeping with you, isn't it!" I said, and she made a mockingly surprised face. "Damn it, Ivy, I'm going to sleep with who I want, when I want. I want to find a blood balance with you, but your ultimatum of my-way-or-no-way isn't going to wash. I'm *not* going to sleep with you just to make this work, and I'm busting my ass trying to find a way to tone your blood lust down so you don't lose control and we can at least *share something*!"

Ivy set the cereal box down with a sharp tap. "I'm not going to chemically neuter myself so you can continue to hide from who you are."

I almost choked on my outrage. "You've never even tried one, have you!" I sputtered, opening up my charm cupboard to show the slew of uninvoked potions I had been working on. "What did you do with the ones I gave you!" I exclaimed.

Ivy lifted her chin, the rims of brown about her pupils shrinking. "Flushed them."

She was completely unrepentant, and I shook with anger. "You threw them out!" I yelled, furious. "Do you know how long it took me to make them? Did you not *see* the hours I put into modifying them so you'd be in control and could separate your blood lust from love? How can you know what it will do if you don't try it once!"

Ivy closed the cover of the cereal box and stood, pointing one long pianist's finger at me. "How do you know you won't like sleeping with me if you don't try it—once?" she mocked, every word clear and precise.

It was as if her words took the last of my reason. Tugging the afghan up, I got in her face, pissed that I had to look up at her in her boots. "You are not in charge of me," I said, neck flaming, but I was so mad it didn't mean anything. "I am my own person. Don't you *ever* forget it! And right now, I'd rather sleep with Trent than you!"

I turned to leave, gasping when she yanked me back into the room. Adrenaline sang as the world spun, and I found my back against the island counter. A pulse of fear dropped deep, igniting my soul, bringing me alive. Ivy's eyes were black. They were utterly, beautifully black, and they pinned me where I stood. From my scar came a surge that made my knees threaten to give way. I couldn't look from her eyes, and I tried to figure out what had happened. I was . . . I had been arguing with Ivy. Stupid vamp? No, stupid witch.

Suddenly stone cold sober, I stared at her. I wanted her to bite me, but not until I knew she could handle it. Or perhaps more accurately, until I knew I could. And there was the ultimatum that she had thrown down last year: all or nothing. Sex and blood both. Uh-uh. Not like this.

"Back off," I said as I gave her a shove to get her out of my way. "I'm not doing this."

Moving with a provocative slowness, Ivy put her hand on my shoulder and pushed me back, her grip tightening to slow my backward motion until I hit the counter again. A tingling of sparkles lit through my old vampire scar, sending a twin pulse to ignite the one she had given me just this spring. *Shit.*

"I said I'm not doing this," I said, ticked and scared all at the same time. "Ivy, I didn't start this, and I'm not going to sleep with you to share blood. Get out of my way."

"I started this, and you don't have to sleep with me to share blood," she said, utterly still.

I froze. *I don't have to sleep with her?* My gaze rose to meet the faultless black her eyes now were, and she smiled, showing a slip of teeth.

"What do you think Rynn Cormel and I have been doing together for the last two months?" she said softly.

My gaze darted to her new scar and rose to her eyes. A shiver iced through me, between thought and action. *She can separate the two?* "I thought . . . ," I stammered, then mentally kicked myself. Rynn Cormel wanted us to succeed in this. Of course he'd be helping her learn to take blood without mixing it with sex, breaking old habits. My lips parted. *New angle, he said. Not a sexual position, but a new tack? To help her find control?*

Again my attention went to her new bite, now clearly visible as a badge of honor. Of success, maybe? Almost as if she'd heard my thoughts, Ivy leaned closer. "Yes," she said distinctly, hitting the *S* with a sharp sound. "We've been practicing all month, and this morning, I did it. No charms, no drugs, nothing. It was the most frustrating thing I've ever done. It left one part of me satisfied, and the other . . . achingly empty."

I blinked fast to try to gain an understanding of what that meant. Everything shifted, and I held my breath as I became afraid for another reason. It was too easy for me to become drunk on sensation and do something that I'd hate myself in the morning for. But this was something we both wanted. How could it be wrong?

Ivy tilted her head and, smiling, sent her sin-black eyes to drop languorously to my neck, making her intentions clear. Desire pinged through me, and I shuddered, knowing I was lost. Or found. About to be broken, or made whole. Inches away, Ivy pulled in my scent as she closed her eyes, bringing herself to a higher pitch, driving herself crazy with denial even as I stood in front of her. "I can do this, Rachel."

I wanted this. I wanted to feel good. I wanted the closeness with Ivy I knew a bite would bring. I wanted to push away the pain we both felt from Kisten's death with something real. And there was no reason not to.

I shuddered at the barest touch of her fingertip as she brushed the afghan from my shoulders and it pooled at my feet. A shiver took me, born from the cooler air hitting my skin and the heat she was pulling from my core. Vampire incense filled me on a slow intake of breath; it rolled in my soul, flashing up to make her light touch feel like electricity.

"Wait," I said, self-preservation stronger than the remembered ecstasy she could fill me with, a millennium-old payment that evolution had gifted us in return for freely giving what a vampire's soul needed to survive.

And she waited.

My eyes closed. I could feel her breath against my skin, the heat from her body against mine though air stood between us, and the tension making the air tingle against me. I weighed her obvious desire against her slow movements and the fact that she had stopped when I asked. I had to be certain. She said she could do this, but I didn't want to make another stupid mistake. Could she do it? *Could I?* My eyes opened. "Are you sure?" I asked, searching her expression.

She leaned closer, her lips parting to say something, but then her brow furrowed and she stiffened. Dropping her grip on my shoulder, she spun. The clatter of pixy wings shattered the silence.

"Ivy!" Jenks shrilled, and I almost thought I heard her growl. "No! It's too soon!"

I took a deep breath, willing myself to stay upright. I had forgotten the soporific effect vampire pheromones had, and my heart pounded as I propped myself up; I leaned against the counter as I took a deep breath to steady myself.

"It's okay, Jenks," I said, not looking up from my faintly trembling fingers. "Ivy's got a handle on this."

"What about you?" he shouted, darting from her to me. His tiny features were pinched in worry, and I could see a row of faces at the window, watching, until Ivy closed the curtains, sealing us in a soothing blue. "Look at you!" he said, the dust spilling from him turning a pale green. "You can hardly stand up, and she hasn't even touched you yet."

Ivy was standing at the sink, arms crossed over her middle and her head bowed. I didn't want it to end like this. "I can't stand up because it feels that good!" I shouted at Jenks, and he flew backward in surprise. "I'm fine! So you can take your little pixy ass out of here! She stopped when I asked her to wait. She's over there right now, not"—I hesitated, feeling a surge of anticipation rise through me—"not ripping my throat open!"

Ivy's head came up and she gripped herself tighter. Her eyes were absolutely black, and adrenaline made a burning trail from my neck to my middle. Oh, God. This couldn't be a poor decision if we both wanted it so badly. Right? *Please let this be a good decision.*

"I slaked my blood lust three hours ago," she said, her soft voice in contrast with her sharp body language. "I can do this. If it gets to be too much, for either of us, I can stop."

"So we're . . . fine," I stated. "Get out, Jenks."

"You're not fine." Jenks got in my face to break my connection with Ivy. "She is trying to overcome an addiction. Tell her to leave. If she can leave, then maybe she does have enough control and you can try again later. Just not today. *Not today, Rachel!*"

I looked at Ivy standing by the sink, hunched with a need so deep it hurt to see it. I had waited with Kisten, hadn't let him bite me, and now he was dead. I couldn't wait for later if there was a now. I wouldn't.

"I don't want her to leave." I brought my gaze to Jenks. "I want you to."

Ivy closed her eyes and the tension in her face eased. "Get out, Jenks," she said, her voice low and laced with a threat that set my insides quivering. "Or stay and watch, you perverted Peeping Tom. I don't care. Just shut your damn mouth for a fucking five minutes."

He sputtered, rising up out of her way as she pushed herself into motion and came to me. My pulse was racing, and I knew that the more fear I showed, the harder it would be for her to find control. We might not be good at this right away, but we had to start somewhere, and I wasn't going to be the one to fail.

"Ivy," Jenks pleaded. "It's too soon."

"It's too late," she breathed into my ear, her fingers resting lightly on my shoulders. The pounding of my heart was loud, and I could feel my pulse lifting the skin at my throat. Jenks moaned in frustration. After darting into my charm cupboard, he zipped out of the kitchen.

Ivy's touch became liquid heat in his absence. Leaning forward, she traced a path with her fingers across my neck, searching for the unseen scar under my perfect skin. I held my breath, tension rising as she circled for it. This had to be okay. She'd worked hard to find a way around her own desires, and I'd be nothing but a damned tease to say no now.

My air came in fast as her touch turned into a firm grip on my shoulder. I felt her weight shift, and I opened my eyes, surprised at the soothing blue the curtains made. I couldn't see any of Ivy but her hair. She was that close. *God, what is she waiting for?*

"Let me," she murmured, her lips brushing the sensitive skin under my ear, dropping lower, lower, as her head tilted, the blue light making a glint in her hair. I tensed at the sensation, heart pounding. Her hands slid lower, finding the small of my back. Leaning away, she stilled her fingers until our gazes met. "Let me . . . ," she said again, utterly lost in what was to come.

I knew she wouldn't say the entire thing. *Let me take this. Give this to me.* Asking permission was so ingrained into living vampires that if she didn't, she would think she had blood-raped me even if I cut myself and bled into her mouth. I gazed into her pupil-black eyes, seeing her desperate need raw and unhidden instead of the impassive face she usually showed the world. A last strike of fear lit through me at the chance I was taking. A memory of her biting me almost to death in Kisten's van rose and fell. I could feel the tension in her where we touched: her right hand on my shoulder, her left at my back, one hip drifting close to mine. She wouldn't overstep the bounds and would keep the sex out of it. If she didn't, I'd be gone and she knew it. It was a cruel game she played with herself, but I think she hoped that if she waited long enough, I'd come to her.

Maybe she was right. If someone had told me last year that I'd be here now, teasing a vampire into biting me, I would have said they were insane.

My eyes closed. It wasn't worth the effort to try to figure my life out. I had to live it as it came. "Take it," I whispered, locking my knees against the coming rise of feeling.

A sigh came from Ivy, and she pressed lightly into me. Her grip tightened, and with absolutely no hesitation, she tilted her head to meet my neck and sank her teeth.

Ecstasy burned, the pain of the bite shifting instantly into bliss. I took a gasping breath, then held it, stiffening for a glorious instant before catching myself. I couldn't lose myself to sensation. It would all go wrong if I did, and as Ivy's teeth sank deeper, I vowed I wouldn't. Not this time. I wouldn't let this become a bad decision.

Her breath against me came and went in time with the pulls of her mouth, drawing my blood into her to fill her. My hand drifted up to touch her new scar, and I pulled away. In a flash of tension, I brought myself back. "Ivy, slow down," I breathed, needing to know that she could stop. Fear pulsed through me when she didn't, and when I hinted at pushing against her, she pulled her lips from me with a ragged, rough breath. *Thank you, God.* We could do this. Damn it, we could do this!

Pulse fast, I did nothing as we stood, our heads inches from each other. I realized my hands were on her shoulders, and I weighed the sensations flashing through me to gauge Ivy's control and my resolve not to slip into a vampire-pheromone-induced stupor that her instincts wouldn't be able to resist.

Ivy's head was bowed. Her forehead almost touched my shoulder as she steadied herself. Her breath on my broken skin made feeling ebb and flow, building on each other as she tested her will not to move. I felt the warm trickle of what had to be blood turn cool, and still she did nothing though even I could smell it.

She wasn't losing control. She was maintaining it. This probably wasn't the best blood she'd had, but I was taking baby steps, and she was charting a new path. And I was ecstatic.

Ivy scented my acceptance on the very air, and slowly, carefully, until she knew it was welcome, she leaned in again, her lips meeting my neck in a soft pull, turning the cold spot warm again. Tingles shot to my middle and grew.

"Slow," I whispered, not wanting her to stop though fear made me cautious. This was working. I didn't want to tear down this new balance with impatience.

So she lingered, which in hindsight was probably more arousing than simply sinking her teeth again. Her lips moved to the tiny scar she had given me this spring, teasing, luring.

We can do this, I thought, and I let my shoulders ease, glad I was standing under my own power. I let the sensations rise and fall in me as she played, and I listened to my body, making sure she wasn't taking too much. Her vampiric need to dominate was tempered by the love she felt, but she wasn't letting it slide into the erotic. We could do this. And I wondered what might happen if I dared touch her new scar.

My eyes closed as she bent to me again. A soft sound slipped from me as her teeth pressed gently upon the scar, threatening to break the skin. And then her teeth iced in. My knees went weak, but I kept my balance. She was playing with me. Oh, God, I was in the hands of a master, and she was going to take me wherever she wanted.

She bore down, her touch light on my shoulders. Under the cascading sensations was something headier, tingling over my skin like the hum of a power line. It was our auras, blurring about the edges as she took what my soul could spare along with my blood. I remembered feeling it before. I'd almost forgotten.

"Ivy," I whispered. The feel of our auras mingling, almost overshadowing the sensation of her teeth in me. It was building to a rush. An adrenaline rush. I could feel it. There was more here than just exquisite fulfillment.

I pulled away from her, her teeth raking my skin and setting unexpected ribbons of ice scouring my bones. Her eyes flashed open, almost panicked. "I . . . I . . . ," she stammered. She felt it, too, but she looked bewildered. With a swift intake of breath, she tightened her grip. I could feel the edges of our auras mingling, but there was more, dancing just out of my reach.

"Take it," I breathed, and her mouth met my skin again. I gasped, my fingers gripping harder so she wouldn't draw away. The heat of my blood in her mouth hit her, and she pulled again. I breathed heavily, struggling for air, for control. My grip strengthened, and I refused to collapse. We would not fail because of me!

My skin tingled everywhere her aura touched mine, the different charges raking over my aura like silk on sand as the energy of my soul slipped into her along with my blood, coating her being. Vampire pheromones were like liquid sensation, racing through my body to set it alight. I could feel the heat from her own skin rising as well. Something was happening with our auras. And the more I gave to Ivy, the stronger I felt it become.

This, I thought, feeling her aura slip through mine as I gave myself freely and without fear. *I can give this to you.*

And like water through sand, our auras blended into one.

I gasped at the feeling. Her teeth slid across my neck as she pulled away, and she would have fallen but for my hold on her. Eyes wide, I stiffened. Our auras weren't just mixing, they were one. *We had one aura.* In shock, I did nothing as a wash of endorphins spilled into me, into us. Every cell sang with the release. The surge of energy from our auras uniting chimed, resonating in our souls.

My fingers slipped. Ivy staggered away to fall against the table. My head came down as I felt her leave me. "My God," I groaned, and with my unique thought to divide us, our auras separated. It was gone.

I took a gasping breath and slumped against the counter. My muscles wouldn't easily hold me, and my arms trembled. "What in hell was that?" I panted. Torn between laughing at what had happened and being disgusted at how long it had taken us to find it, I brought my head up. Ivy had some 'splaining to do. I hadn't known auras could do that.

But I froze as I saw her crouching by the door in the cool, restful blue of the sunlit curtains. Her eyes were black, and they fixed on me with a predatory strength.

Shit. I was fine, but Ivy had lost it.

Thirteen

vy!" I shouted. Fear took over, and I backpedaled. Ivy moved when I did, her expression one of the lost. I didn't understand. We had done it. We had done it, damn it!

But she was coming at me, silent and with a deadly intent in her. What in hell had happened? She had been okay, and then . . . she wasn't.

My arm came up at the last moment and I knocked aside her hand as it reached for me. Ivy twisted and grabbed my wrist. I had just enough time to gasp before she yanked me forward, leveraging me into losing my balance.

I went down.

She went to drop to a knee, and I rolled. I was just ahead of her move, and I smacked into her feet, knocking her into a front fall. I curled into a ball to avoid her and lurched upright.

I was too slow. Her vampiric speed had her standing, and I rose right up into her grip.

"Ivy, stop!" I exclaimed, and she shoved me backward. My arms flailed and I hit the fridge. Pain hit hard as I tried to keep upright and find my breath at the same time. My eyes watered, and she slowly followed me, carefully placing her boots to just miss the patch of blue-tinted sun glowing through the curtain. She was powerful and lean in her work leathers, walking with grace and a savage, leashed strength. Smiling with her lips closed, she moved, arms swinging as she crossed the few paces between us. She was in no hurry. I was hers.

"Stop," I gasped when I found my first clean breath. "Ivy, you want to stop. Stop!"

My voice brought her to a halt three feet from me, and my heart pounded. A flicker of distress marred her confidence. "Why?" she sighed, her gray silk voice cutting through me.

Faster than I could follow, she pinned me to the stainless-steel fridge. One hand forced my shoulder back, and the other was twined in my hair. My breath came in a pained sound when she jerked my head to the side, exposing my already bleeding neck. *God, no. Not like this.*

Her body pressed into the entire length of mine, one of her boots between my feet. My pulse was fast and I was sweating. I was pushing every button she had, but I couldn't stop. Terrified, I tried to see her, but her grip on my hair wouldn't let me turn. I was scared out of my mind, and a thought of Kisten surfaced and was gone.

"Ivy," I rasped, struggling to see her with my neck craned. "You can let go. Just don't look at me. We can do this. We can do this, damn it!"

"Why?" she repeated in that same calm voice. She pressed harder against me, but her grip on my hair eased, and I turned to her. I felt the blood drain from my face, and Ivy shuddered, drinking my fear in like a blood aphrodisiac.

Her eyes were utterly black. Her face was absolutely expressionless. Perfect and calm, she stared at me, breathing in my fear and feeding her blood lust. It was as if she were dead already, and from the back of my thoughts came another flash of Kisten. I'd seen his eyes like this . . . on his boat.

"Just let go," I whispered, my breath shifting the hair about her face. "We did it, Ivy. Just let go."

A shimmer of distress crinkled the corners of her eyes. "I can't . . . ," she said, her sudden fear making an ugly crease in her forehead as she struggled with herself. "You gave me too much. Damn it, I . . ." Her expression smoothed as her instincts took over. "I want that again," she said, her voice dropping in pitch. It sent a shudder through me, and her grip tightened. "Give it to me. Now."

I could see her conscious thought shutting down to protect her sanity. I was losing her. If I did, I was dead. Panic burbled through my soul as she jerked my head to the side. "Ivy!" I said, struggling to keep my voice calm, but failing. "Wait! You can wait. You're good at that. Just wait. Listen to me."

My heart pounded, but she hesitated. "I'm a monster," she whispered, her words on my skin sending ribbons of sensation through me. Even now, as I saw my life ending, the damned vampire pheromones tried to lie to me. "I can't stop."

Her voice was almost her own again, pleading for help. "You're not a monster." I carefully placed my palm against her shoulder in case I had the chance to push her away. "Piscary screwed you up, and you're getting better. Ivy, we did it. All you have to do is let go."

"I'm not better." Her voice was thick with bitter self-recrimination. "It's the same thing as before."

"It's not," I protested, feeling my pulse slow. "I'm conscious. You didn't take enough to hurt me. You stopped. Just. Let. Go."

I held my breath as she pulled her head from mine to look me in the face. I could see myself in the black depths of her pupils, my hair mussed and tracks of tears I hadn't noticed marking me. I saw myself in her eyes, and I remembered . . . I'd seen myself mirrored in someone's eyes before, as I stood powerless and fearing for my life. I'd lived it.

And suddenly, it wasn't Ivy's lily-white fingers gripping my shoulder, but a memory of someone else's. Fear came from my past, shocking through me. A flash of memory took the place of my reality. *Kisten* . . .

An image of being pinned to the wall of Kisten's boat yanked itself from my unconscious, twining about the reality of my back against the fridge. With a nauseating suddenness, it coated my present in a choking layer of fear and helplessness. A memory I hadn't known existed turned Ivy's eyes into someone else's. Her fingers in my hair became foreign. In my thoughts, her body pressing into me became coated in the alien scent of angry, undead vampire bent on possession.

"No!" I screamed. Ivy's touch had sparked memories I hadn't known even existed. Fear electrified me, and I shoved her away. A burst of ley line energy swarmed out to find her, and I yanked it back, hunching over in agony as the force rolled under the skin of my palms, burning until I finally pushed it back into the line and let go.

My wrist hurt. A vampire had hurt me. I had been pinned against the wall. Someone had pinned me against the wall and . . . Oh, God. Someone had bitten me.

God help me, what had I almost done?

Panting, I pulled my head up to see Ivy slide down the cupboards across the kitchen to the floor. Her expression was unfocused, and she looked out of it.

I pressed against the fridge, holding my upper arm, with helpless tears flowing. Ivy lurched upright, her balance unsure. "Rachel?" she whispered, hand outstretched as if dizzy.

"Someone bit me!" I burbled, the tears coming from nowhere. "On my lip. Tried to . . ." Anguish coated my soul like black tar, and I sank to the floor. "Kisten was dead," I sobbed, knees coming to my chin as I sat against the fridge. *How could I forget?* "He was . . . He was *dead*! The vampire who killed him . . ." I looked up, more scared than I'd ever been before. "Ivy . . . His murderer bit me . . . so I couldn't fight."

Ivy's expression was utterly empty. I stared at her, one hand clenching the opposite arm until it throbbed. God help me. I was bound. I was bound to Kisten's killer, and I'd never even known it. What else had I forgotten? What else was waiting in my thoughts to crush me?

Ivy moved, and I panicked. "Stay there!" I said, heart jumping. "Don't touch me!"

She froze as my reality fought with the lies I had told myself. My tongue ran over the inside of my mouth, fear rising anew as I found the tiny, almost nonexistent scar. *I am bound. Someone bound me.* Nausea rose high, and I felt like I was going to be sick.

"Rachel," Ivy said, and my attention jerked to her. She was a vampire. I had fallen, and I'd never felt my face hit the dirt. Terror made me scrabble upright and move until I found a corner, hand on my neck to hide my blood from her. I had been bound. *I* belonged *to someone.*

Ivy's eyes were black at my fear. Chest rising and falling, she held her fists at her sides. "Rachel, it's okay," she said, her voice low and throaty. "You haven't been bound. I could tell."

She took a step forward, and I flung out a hand. "Stop!"

"I can tell, damn it!" she shouted, then lowered her voice. "I'm not going to bite you. Look at me. I'm not that vampire. Rachel, you are not bound."

Fear spun liquid fibers through me like a spider's web, and I tried to control it. Beneath my fingers, my pulse hammered. It was just Ivy. But she took a step forward, and my will shattered.

"I said stop!" I shouted, pressing into the corner. She shook her head grimly as she took a slow, careful step forward.

"Stop! Stop, or I'll hurt you!" I demanded, almost hysterical. I had let go of the line, but I could find it. I could hurt her with it. I had tried to hurt Kisten's killer, and the vampire had bound me. Bound me so I would come crawling, begging to be bled. *God help me, I was someone's shadow.*

Ivy's hand shook and tears coursed down her perfect face as she reached out and set her fingers upon my shoulder. Her scent poured over me, and her touch reached deeper than my broken memory until it struck the core of my being. My terror dissolved like a filmy gauze. It was Ivy. It was just Ivy, not my unknown tormentor. She wasn't trying to kill me. *It was just Ivy.*

I started to cry. Huge racking sobs shook me. Kisten's murderer had bound me. They would crook their finger, and I would beg, writhe for it. I had fallen, and I never even saw the hole. I was so stupid. I had been playing with vampires. I thought I could keep myself safe, but it was all for nothing now. I hadn't wanted this, but it had happened.

"Rachel, you are not bound!" Ivy said, giving me a small shake. "If you were I could smell it, I could tell. Kisten's killer might have tried, but it didn't take. I would sense it, if it did. Listen to me! You're okay!"

My breath caught, and I tried to stop crying. "I'm not bound?" I said, tasting the salt of my tears as I looked up. "Are you sure?" *Please, God. Give me a second chance. I promise. I promise I'll be good.*

There was a soft hush of sound as Ivy put her arms around me, pulling me into her and rocking me as if I were a child as we stood in our blue-lit kitchen. "You are not bound," Ivy whispered, and I wept tears of relief into her shoulder as I started to believe. "But I'll find out who did this to you, and then I'll make that bastard beg for your forgiveness."

I pinned everything on her soft gray-silk voice pulling me back from the brink. The surety and hot anger in her cut through my confusion. I wasn't alone. Ivy was going to help me. She said I wasn't bound. I had to believe that. Gratitude flowed, and every muscle seemed to relax. Ivy felt it and stopped rocking me.

Suddenly I realized I was standing in my kitchen with Ivy's arms around me. Her pull on my unclaimed scars was gone, and here I was, feeling her warmth, her strength, her determination to protect me. I looked up to find her brown eyes swimming, inches from mine. There was a shared pain in them, as if only now was I able to even begin to understand her.

I licked my lips, trying to figure out what I was feeling. "Thank you," I said, and her pupils widened in a flash. A shocking spark dove to my middle.

There was the clatter of pixy wings, and we both looked to the hallway as Jenks flew in.

"I'm sorry," he gasped, struggling with a full vial. "Am I too late?"

My gaze rose to the open charm cupboard, and then to the vial in Jenks's unsteady grip. From the front of the church came the sound of Keasley's voice raised in worry. "Rachel? Are you okay?"

I reached out to stop him. "Jenks, no!" I cried, guessing Keasley had primed the spell, but Ivy had looked up, and Jenks did a smart backflip.

Ivy got the potion full in the face. Her eyes went unfocused, and as smooth and sweet as fresh laundry snapping on a line, she dropped.

Scrambling, I caught her shoulders and eased her down. Jenks had swiped one of the pacification potions we were experimenting with. But she wasn't supposed to go unconscious. It was far too strong.

Jenks got between us, wings a blur as he hovered by her slack-featured face. Her new bite looked livid, and I thought of mine, feeling what might be shame for the first time. God, I couldn't do this anymore. I had risked everything. There had to be a better way.

"She's out. She's breathing," Jenks said, and I took a relieved breath. Modifying charms was chancy at best, and I could have stopped Ivy's heart.

"It's too strong," I said, glad none of it had hit me. "She's not supposed to go unconscious." Remembering Keasley, I stood to find him standing in the doorway, awkward and unsure in his thin brown pajamas. "You okay?" I asked him.

"I'm not the one with the vamp bite," he said, eyes on my neck, and I refused to cover it. "Jenks said your roommate lost it."

The memory of the last ten minutes smacked me, and I started to waver. *I thought I had been bound to Kisten's killer. I had . . . I could have been bound to Kisten's killer.* "I don't feel so good," I said, my blood dropping to my knees. Dizzy, I took a breath, my muscles going slack and my body starting to slip. I stared at the floor, numb.

"Ho there!" Keasley exclaimed, and then his thin arms

were suddenly around me and he was struggling to get me to the floor without bending his knees.

"I'm okay," I mumbled, clearly not as my legs went akimbo. "I'm okay." Blinking, I sat against the sink cabinets beside Ivy and dropped my head between my knees to keep from passing out. "Jenks," I breathed, and he was on the floor between my feet, looking up.

"She bit you!" he said, silver sparkles mixing with the spots of oblivion making a bid for my consciousness. "I told you she wasn't ready. Why doesn't anyone listen to me!"

"Yeah, she bit me," I said as things started to fall into place. "I freaking wanted her to, and it's none of your damn business—you little winged liar." His wings clattered in anger, but his words died in his throat when he saw my expression. He flew up, suddenly unsure, and I lifted my head, following him.

"Kisten's murderer bit me, too," I said, and he paled, flying up to the counter and out of my reach. "I remembered it," I said, finding the strength to sit up at his show of guilt. "The vampire tried to bind me, and I think you knew it. Start talking, pixy." *I can't do this anymore. I'm playing with fire, and I have to stop.*

In a burst of sparkles, Jenks darted away. Keasley's sneakers on his bare feet moved uneasily, and I stood up, angry and almost out of my mind with frustration. Seeing Ivy on the floor, I gritted my teeth and refused to cry. I was so messed up. My hand gripped my right shoulder until it hurt, the memory of Kisten's death heavy on me. *This isn't fair. This is bloody-hell not fair!*

"You were there, Jenks," I said as I wiped my face to get the hair out of my eyes. "You said you were with me all night. Who bit me? Who gave me the forget potion!" I looked at Keasley, betrayal an angry lump in my gut. "Was it you?" I barked, and the old man shook his head, so sadly that I believed him.

"Rache," Jenks stammered, pulling my attention to him as

he backed up on the counter. "Don't. You were crazy. You were going to hurt yourself. If I hadn't, you'd be dead."

My lips parted, and I tried to breathe. *Jenks had given me the potion?*

I felt like I was going to pass out again. Reaching behind me, I tipped my dissolution vat of salt water over Ivy. Keasley shifted his faded sneakers as it poured over the counter and onto the floor, drenching her. I didn't take my eyes from Jenks as she came to, sputtering.

"You were there," I repeated to bring Ivy up to speed as she scrambled up behind me. "You said you were with me all night. You were there when Kisten's murderer bit me. Tell me who did it!" I screamed, my throat hurting.

My pulse was fast as I stood over Jenks. I was mad. Scared. Terrified he would tell me it had been Ivy. Maybe I was bound, and she couldn't smell it because it had been her. Was that why I had said yes to her today?

Oh, God. Please, no.

Jenks's wings were a blur, but he didn't move, his attention going from me to Ivy as we took three steps to loom over him. My socks were soaked with salt water, and I could hear Ivy's frustration and anger that my magic had dropped her. But Jenks had taken her out, not me.

"I don't know!" he yelped when Ivy smacked a hand on the stainless-steel counter and a splash of salt water hit his wing. "Kisten was dead, really dead, when I caught up with you," he said, shamefaced. "I never saw his murderer. Rachel, I'm sorry. I didn't know what to do. You were crying. Acting crazy. You said Kisten had bitten his murderer, mixed their undead blood to kill them both for good."

Ivy groaned and turned away, and I touched her shoulder, not looking from Jenks.

"But it didn't work," Jenks said, gaze darting between us, "'cause Kisten hadn't been dead long enough, so only Kisten died right away. You were going to go after the bastard to make sure he was dead. Rache, you wouldn't have survived, even if the vampire was almost dead. You'd been bitten. You can't stand up to a dead vampire. You can't."

My jaw clenched, and I closed my eyes, trying to remember as Ivy shook silently beside me. Nothing. Only stark fear and a throbbing in my foot and my arm where someone had gripped me too tightly. It was a pain born almost three months ago, as sharp and real as if I had just been slapped.

"You gave me the forget potion," I whispered to Jenks. "Why?" I gestured helplessly. "Was it worth all this? I want to know who did it!"

"Talk, pixy!" Ivy barked as she spun. Her pupils were dilated, and red spotted her cheeks.

Jenks stood miserably before us, black dust sifting from him. "I had to." He backed up, his wings fanning into motion when his heel hit a napkin. Ivy snatched for him, and he darted away. "I made the spell myself. I put it together and got your blood into it. You were going to go after Kisten's killer!" he exclaimed. "You would have died! I'm only four freaking inches tall. I don't have many options! And I can't lose you now!"

Ivy slumped with her elbow on the counter and her forehead in her cupped hand. Her hair hid her face, and I wondered what she was feeling. Damn it, it wasn't fair. We had done it, managed a balance, and then my memory had to return and screw it all up.

"That vampire would have killed you," Jenks begged. "I thought if you just forgot, time would take care of everything. You're not bound, so everything's okay! It's *okay*, Rache!"

I prayed Jenks was right, but a shiver ran through me as I put a hand to my neck and covered my bites. *God help me, I've never felt this vulnerable.* I had been playing with vampires. I'd believed I had been bound. I couldn't . . . I couldn't do this anymore.

Ivy took a ragged breath. Her brow furrowed, and as she stood upright, I saw an inner pain deep behind her eyes, cemented to her soul. "Excuse me," she said softly, and I jerked when she darted out. She fled with that eerie vampire speed, her feet squeaking on the wet linoleum. I reached out after her, and her bathroom door shut with a loud thump.

I looked at Jenks. *My life sucks.*

Tired, I leaned back against the sink and tried to figure it out. I didn't feel good. I was running on a lack of sleep, lack of food, and lack of understanding. I didn't want to think anymore. I just wanted to hide or cry on someone's shoulder. My eyes pricked with the warmth of tears, and I turned away. I wasn't going to cry in front of Keasley. Ceri and I were arguing. Ivy was hiding. I didn't have any friends to turn to. Depressed, I glanced at the two men, both staring at me with an awkward concern. I had to get out of here.

"Jenks," I said breathily, looking at the salt-strewn kitchen. "I'm going to my mom's. Keasley, I'm sorry. I have to go."

Feeling airy and unreal, light-headed, I pushed past the solemn witch and followed the creeping path of the water into the hallway. I was headed for the door, and I grabbed my bag in passing. I couldn't stay here. My mom might just be nuts enough to understand and sane enough to help. Besides, she might know a charm to reverse a forget potion. And then Ivy and I were going to nail Kisten's killer to a broomstick.

Fourteen

My mom's kitchen had changed since the last time I'd sat at the table eating cereal. A strong herb scent was heavy in the air, though I didn't see any. There weren't any spell pots or ceramic spoons in the sink either, but the redwood smell rolling off of her when she'd answered the door in her fuzzy leopard-print robe told me that she'd been spelling heavily recently.

Now she smelled like lilac, with only the faintest aroma of redwood to mar it. I thought it funny she was trying to hide from me that she was making and selling charms under the table. Like I would turn my mom in? The I.S. wasn't necessarily generous in their pensions to widows—even those whose spouses worked in the Arcane Division—and it probably wasn't enough to meet the soaring property taxes of what had once been a middle-class neighborhood.

The afternoon light coming in the kitchen window was bright as I sat glum and weary, eating cereal out of a cracked bowl in my usual spot. Lucky Charms. I didn't know which was more disturbing, the possibility that the box was the same one from the last time I'd had breakfast here, or the possibility that it wasn't.

My gaze shifted to the pile of supermarket tabloids that my mother loved, and I tugged one out of the pile when MOURN-ING SISTER FINDS KITTY LITTER IN TWIN'S URN caught my eye. Below it was a short article on Cincy's colorful history of grave robbing and how bodies were again turning up missing on both sides of the river. A frown came over me. There was only one reason why cremated bodies were replaced with kitty litter—an offering of mortal ashes kept a summoned demon from appearing out of place, like outside the circle. I usually didn't bother with it, but the demons generally crashed my life, not the other way around.

The reminder of Al prompted me to tug my bag across the table. I hadn't given my mother a reason for showing up and falling into an exhausted sleep on top of my old coverlet on my bed. Depression had replaced my fear at the thought that I'd been bound, and the beginnings of forgiveness to Jenks for wiping my memory had taken hold. He had done the right thing. I could easily imagine the state I had been in, and making me forget had probably saved my life. A witch with a vamp scar couldn't stand up to the undead. Ivy would find Kisten's killer. I'd take care of the demons.

Rummaging in my bag, I pulled out my phone and looked at the screen. I had called Jenks the moment I'd woken up to check on Ivy. She was depressed, he said, which was workable. I wasn't looking forward to going back to the church and trying to patch things up. I didn't know what I was going to say. Despite everything, I was still happy that she was there. Maybe we could just ignore that she'd put four new holes in my neck and that I'd flaked out believing I'd been bound to Kisten's killer. I sighed as I checked the time.

It was just after three, and still no call from Glenn or David. Glenn would get bent out of shape if I bugged him, but David wouldn't.

The clock above the sink ticked, and I listened to the ugly thing while I scrolled through my short list for David's number. Robbie and I had bought the clock for Mother's Day ages ago, when we still thought the bug-eyed witch whose gaze and broom swept back and forth in time with the ticks was cool. There was a spot of white ceramic where the paint had chipped off the broom when it had fallen, and I wondered why she still had it. It was really, really nasty.

My attention went back to the phone when the line clicked open and David's confident hello filled my ear. "Hi, David," I said. "Got anything yet?"

I heard him hesitate, then ask cautiously, "Didn't your mom tell you?"

He knows I'm at my mom's? "Uh, no," I said, scrambling. "How do you know I'm at my mom's?"

David chuckled. "She answered your cell phone this afternoon while you were sleeping. We had a nice chat. Your mom is . . . different."

Different. How politically correct could you get? "Thanks," I said dryly. "I take it we're not going out this afternoon?" If it had been otherwise, I thought she would have woken me. Maybe.

"I've got the claim sitting on my desk," he said, and I heard papers rustling. "Tomorrow at two is the earliest I could nail the woman to a time." He hesitated, then quietly offered, "I'm sorry. I know you wanted to settle this today, but that's the best I could get."

I sighed and looked at the clock again. The idea of hiding in my church another night had all the appeal of painting Trent's toenails. I wouldn't be able to avoid Ivy either. "Two tomorrow is great," I said, thinking I ought to use the time to stock my charm cupboard for an assault on black witches. I'd have to move everything to hallowed ground, though. What a pain in the butt. "Thanks, David," I said when I remembered I was in the middle of a conversation. "I really think it's them."

"Me, too. I'll pick you up tomorrow at one. Get yourself dolled up, will you?" he said, amusement heavy in his voice. "I'm not taking you out in leather again."

My brow furrowed. "Dolled up?" I started, but the line was dead.

I stared at the phone for a moment, then smiled as I closed it and tucked it away. Listening to the quiet house, I ate my pink hearts, saved for last as always. Slowly my mood returned to melancholy. Someone had killed Kisten. That same someone had tried to bind me to them so I wouldn't tear their freaking head off. I had worked so hard to live with Ivy and stay un- bound, and then a faceless monster killed my boyfriend and nearly bound me to it. Just that fast, my life could have been changed beyond my control. *Damn it all to hell. I can't do this. I can't risk it. I can't . . . I* can't *let Ivy bite me again. Ever.*

The thought settled into me like lead. I had been living with Ivy for over a year, and now that we finally got it to work, I get smart? A shiver went through me, rattling the spoon against the bowl. I couldn't play this game anymore. I had briefly lived thinking I had been bound, and they had been the most terri- fying moments of my life, turning me from a confident woman into a terrified plaything with no control over the degradation her life was to become. That the fear turned out to be baseless didn't make the lesson any less real. I could not let a vampire break my skin again. Would not. And I didn't know how I was going to tell Ivy.

Worried, I ate the last spoonful of marshmallows. I listened carefully to the silent house, and once I was sure my mom wasn't coming, I picked the bowl up and drank the sweet milk. My spoon clattered into the empty bowl and I sat back with my coffee, not yet ready to move from the security of memo- ries that muffled my thoughts of the future. There was a small red cloth bag at the back of the table that held the charms my mom had deemed necessary for my Halloween costume. It didn't seem to matter anymore. Unless David's lead panned out and I nailed the demon summoners, I'd be manning the door instead of partying tomorrow. And wearing sexy leather to give candy and cherry tomatoes to eight-year-olds had abso- lutely no appeal.

I sipped my coffee and stared at my phone, willing it to ring. I wondered if I should call Glenn. If my mom was an- swering my phone, he wouldn't tell her anything.

My hand was reaching for the phone when the comfortably

familiar pace of my mom's steps came from the front of the house. I pulled back. No need to worry her more than our coming conversation would. I still had to ask her about reversing a forget potion.

"Thanks for breakfast, Mom," I said as she bustled in and headed for the coffeemaker. She'd been looking for a coat for me, and I could hear it tumbling in the dryer to air out. "I really appreciate you letting me crash here this morning."

She eased herself into the chair across from me, setting her coffee mug gently on the linoleum table, whose pattern was faded by time and scrubbings. "I don't get to be Mom much anymore, especially when you won't tell me what's wrong," she said, her eyes on my two red-rimmed bites, and a stab of guilt made the sweet milk on my tongue go tasteless.

"Um, sorry," I said, shifting my empty bowl away from her sharp gaze. I felt sick. Memory potions were illegal because they didn't break cleanly. Unlike amulets and ley line charms, they created a physical change in the brain to block the memories, and physical changes couldn't be reversed with salt like chemical changes could. I needed a counter-spell.

Gathering my courage, I blurted, "Mom, I need to reverse a memory potion."

Eyebrows high, she looked at my neck again. "You want a Pandora charm? For who?"

She wasn't nearly as mad as I'd thought she'd be. Heartened by that as much as her knowing there was an actual name for what I wanted, I winced. "Me."

My voice had been pensive, and hearing my guilt, my mother's face grew almost scared. "What do you remember now that you had forgotten?" she demanded.

Cradling my coffee in my hands, I tried to warm my soul. The furnace was on against the cold afternoon, but it wasn't able to touch the chill at the pit of my being. My fingers traced the lines of Kisten's bracelet. It was all I had of him—that and the pool table. "Being bitten by the vampire who killed Kisten," I whispered.

Her entire posture melted, and sighing with forgiveness, she reached to take my hand. Her frumpy dress made her look middle aged, but her hands gave her away. I wished she'd stop living like she was nearing the end of her life. It hadn't even started yet.

"Sweetheart," she said, and I pulled my gaze to hers to see it pinched in compassion. "I'm so sorry. Maybe you should forget about it. Why do you even want to remember that?"

"I have to," I said, wiping my eye and pulling out of her reach. "Someone killed him. I was there." I blinked fast, trying to rein in my emotions. "I have to find out. I have to know."

"If you made yourself forget, then you won't like what you find," she said. An old fear unrelated to me simmered in the back of her thoughts, showing in her face. "Let it go."

"It was Jenks—" I started, but she took both my hands, stopping my words.

"Tell me," she said suddenly. "What were you doing when you remembered? What triggered it?"

I stared at her. A hundred dodges flitted through me, but nothing came out of my mouth. And as I sat there, it suddenly occurred to me that I had been spending so much time with my mother these last three months not because of her, but because of me, fragile after Kisten's death. I lost it then, dropping my head onto my folded arms on the table and choking the tears back. This was why I'd come running to my mother, not some stupid charm I knew she didn't have. I had thought with the right spell I could help Ivy. I had thought I could help myself. But now, I couldn't help either of us. We had gotten what we wanted, and it set us back further than if we had let it alone.

I couldn't look at my mom, but there was the scrape of her chair on the linoleum, and an ugly bark of a sob escaped me when her hand landed on my shoulder. Damn it, I had to grow up and be safe, stop reacting when I should be acting. I had to live with a vampire without even the cushion of pretending there would ever be a bite between us, which just might send Ivy away. I wouldn't blame her. But I didn't want her to leave. I liked her. Hell, I probably loved her. And now it was done. We couldn't go back and pretend that there was anything ahead of us.

"Rachel, honey," my mother whispered, close and gentle, with the scent of lilac soothing me as much as her voice. "It's okay. I'm sorry you're confused, but sometimes souls are meant to be together, and the gears just miss. Ivy's a vampire, but she's been your best friend for over a year. You'll find a way to make this work."

"You know?" I warbled, lifting my head to find a shared sorrow in her expression.

"It would be hard to miss those bites," she said. "And if anyone other than Ivy put them there, you'd be in the morgue identifying a body, not sitting in my kitchen pretending nothing is wrong." I blinked up at her as she shifted my hair and made a worried face at my neck. "Jenks called this morning and told me what happened. He worries about you, you know."

My lips parted and I drew out of her reach. Great, who knew what he told her? "Mom."

But she only pulled out a chair to sit beside me, her hand still on my shoulder. "I loved your father with all my being. Don't take potions to forget. It leaves gaps, and then you don't remember why you feel the way you do. It makes things worse."

I hadn't administered it to myself, but that my mother had taken a memory potion was news to me. "You used one?" I asked, wondering if this was why my mom was so nuts, and she turned her lips in, biting them, clearly trying to decide what to say.

"Oh, hell, who hasn't?" she said, then grew sad. "Once," she added softly. "When it got really bad. They never last forever, and there is no charm to bring it all back. The spell to reverse it was lost before we migrated to this side of the lines. Trent might have it, but getting an elf to share spells is like getting a troll out from under a bridge."

I wiped my face, the tears gone. "You know he's . . ."

She smiled, proud of me, as she patted my hand. "Tell me if you get that stingy boy to let you into his library. Honestly, you think he'd have some respect for our family, but he acts like you're the enemy, not his saving grace."

"Whoa, hold up." I tucked a strand of hair behind my ear, then shifted it back forward to hide my neck. All thoughts of Kisten, and Ivy, and everything, were shoved to the back of my mind. "I'm not Trent's saving grace. He's a murdering SOB. I put him in jail once, and I'd do it again if I thought it would stick."

My mother grimaced, her fingers sliding from mine when she drew back. "Small wonder he doesn't like you. You have to stop that. He's going to have something you want someday."

Like a Pandora charm? I exhaled, slumping back into my chair. "Mom . . . ," I complained, and she lifted one eyebrow.

"Life is too short to not be with the people you love," she said. "Even if it scares you."

She was back to Ivy. "Mom, I'm not going to let Ivy bite me again, even if we did okay." She took a breath to speak some words of wisdom, and I interrupted. "Really. She lost it for a minute, and then I made things worse when I remembered Kisten's killer attacking me. I thought—" I ran my tongue along the inside of my lip. "I thought his murderer had bound me, but he didn't." *Thank you, God. I* promise *I will be good.* "It ended okay, but I can't do it again," I finished, my throat tight. "I can't risk it . . . anymore."

A smile of relief creased my mother's face. Her eyes went bright with unshed tears, and she gave my hand a squeeze. "Good," she said. "I'm glad you feel that way. But just because you can't share blood with Ivy doesn't mean you have to end everything with her. She's been too good for you. Made you grow up a little. I like her. She needs you, and you're better with her than without."

I stared as I tried to figure out what she was saying.

"I know I haven't been the best mom," she said as she let go of my hand and looked out the window. "But I'd like to believe I raised you to think for yourself, though you do precious little of it sometimes. I trust you to make good decisions when it comes to the people around you." She smiled. "And what you do with them."

Just where has she been the last ten years? My decisions suck dishwater. "Mom."

"Marshal, for instance," she said, and I stared, shocked. *She knows about Marshal?*

"He's nice," she continued, gazing out the window at nothing. "Too nice to be anything but a rebound guy, but he'd be good for you. Bless Kisten's undead soul, but I was never too keen on him. Two vampires in one room with a witch is asking for trouble. Now, two witches and one vampire . . ." Her eyes danced. "Does Ivy like him?"

God, just kill me now.

"Ivy knows she can't give you everything, you know," my mother continued as if I wasn't blushing so hard I could set hell on fire. "She's wise beyond her years for being able to put aside her jealousy like that. It's so much easier when everyone understands you can love two people at the same time." She flushed. "For different reasons and in different ways."

For a moment, I couldn't speak, trying to process that. There were too many potential problems lying in wait for me to ask. "You know about Marshal?" I finally got out.

Touching her hair as if flustered, she rose and went to the fridge. "He came over about noon to see if you were all right."

Swell. He was here?

My mother pulled a butterscotch pie from the fridge. "We

had a nice talk about you and Ivy," she said as she set the pie on the counter and got out two plates. "We talked about a lot of things. I think he understands now. I sure as hell do. He is coming off a bitch of a bad girlfriend. That's why he likes you."

"Mom!" I exclaimed.

"No, you're not a bitch," she cajoled. "I meant that you're excitable and fun. He thinks you're safe because you're not looking for a boyfriend." She laughed with a knife in her hand. "Men are idiots about women sometimes. When a woman says she's not looking, that's when she is."

"Mom!" *They talked about Ivy and me? She asked him about his girlfriends?*

"I'm just saying that he's like you, in that he gets bored if a relationship is all roses and hearts. It doesn't help that he likes to rescue pretty women. That's probably why he looked you up. He doesn't want a real girlfriend yet any more than you do, but he's not going to sit at home and watch TV. He's taking you out today. You both need a break."

"Mom, stop!" I exclaimed again. "I told you not to set up dates for me, and especially not with Marshal!"

"You're welcome, sweetheart," she said, patting my shoulder. "Get this little fling over with so you can move on with your life. Try not to hurt him, okay?"

I stared at my hands circling my coffee mug, speechless. This was not good. "How did he know where I was?" I asked, depressed. Little fling? I *so* did not need a date right now.

"Jenks was with him."

I exhaled long and slow as I pulled my fingers from worrying at my new bites. *That would explain it*, I thought. The soft scrape of the serving knife on the glass pie dish was obvious and she silently put two slices on plates and licked the serving fork. Still silent, she set the largest piece before me. "Jenks said he knocked Ivy unconscious by accident. It didn't sound like a sleep charm," she said, her voice sharp with accusation.

Embarrassed by my failed attempt at tweaking charms, I

shifted my plate until the pie was pointing at me. This wasn't a topic I really wanted to explore, but it was better than Marshal. "I was trying to modify a sleep charm to give Ivy some control over her blood lust, but she lied to me about trying them out, so the last batch was too strong. Jenks overreacted by hitting her with it in the first place. We were fine. We had everything under control." *By the time he showed back up, that is,* I finished silently.

My eyes came up to see only interest in my mother's gaze. She set a fork in front of me. Her plate in her hand, she leaned against the counter, looking years younger. "You're starting with a sleep charm as your base?" She smiled after seeing my nod and pointed her fork at me. "Well, *there's* your problem. If you're trying to break the hold her instincts have on her actions, you need to make her hyperalert, not sleepy."

I wedged a forkful of pie into my mouth and chewed in thought. The rich tang of butterscotch was sharp, and I ate another bite. Pie for breakfast was one of the perks of a crazy mom. "A stimulant would work better?" I mumbled.

"Guaranteed."

Confidence emanated from her, but I wasn't convinced, and I cringed at the thought of what would happen if it didn't have the desired effect. Besides, it didn't matter anymore. I was going to be the model roommate and never trigger Ivy's blood lust again. That is, if she didn't get mad and leave, ticked at all the time she had wasted on me. But if she stayed, she might someday want a little something to take the edge off. . . .

My mother came to sit across from me, her eyes on her pie. "Throw in a lot of crushed lime. Citrus sends everything deep, and you want to stimulate the complex thought processes, not the surface ones."

"Okay," I said, my gaze flicking to my disguise charms. She was the expert. "Thanks."

Her smile widened, and she became almost teary. "I want to help, honey. I'm sorry if I've been so odd in the past that you felt you couldn't come to me."

I smiled back, feeling warm inside. "I'm sorry, too."

She reached out and patted my hand. "Marshal is worried about you. I'm glad you're being honest with him about how dangerous your life is. More honest than with me, I hope."

Here we go. More guilt. "I didn't want you to worry," I almost whined at my pie. God! I hated it when my voice did that.

Giving my closed fist a sharp tap so that her wedding ring hit my knuckle, she withdrew her hand. "I know how deep in the shit pit you usually are, but tell him before he starts to really like you."

"Mom!"

She sighed then, following it up with a glum "Sorry."

I hid behind a bite of pie. "I'm okay," I mumbled. "We're doing okay."

Again she smiled, becoming my usual mother once more. "I know you are."

We both looked up when the doorbell rang. "That would be Marshal," she said as she rose and tugged her sweater straight. "I told him I'd have you up and ready for your date by three thirty. You still have time before you have to be back on hallowed ground, and a distraction is just what Dr. Mom ordered."

I looked at the pie, then picked up the half I had yet to eat. "Mom," I protested around a full mouth as I followed her down the hall, "I can't. I have to go home and prep for a run. I've got a lead on who might be summoning Al, and I'm going to lean on them tomorrow. Besides, I'm not ready for a boyfriend."

My mother stopped in the long green hallway, surrounded by pictures of my and Robbie's lives, images of the past that she drew strength from. I could see a masculine shadow moving outside on the steps, but my mother put herself right in front of me, filling my world. I was unable to look away from the old regret in her eyes.

"That is exactly why you need to go out with him," she said, her grip on my shoulder tightening to keep me silent. "Prep your spells later. You're strung out to the snapping point, sweetheart. You need to do something different to give your mind a rest, and Marshal is a good man. He's not going to break your heart or take advantage of you. Just . . . go do something with him. Anything." Her mouth quirked. "Well, maybe not anything."

"Mom . . . ," I protested, but she stepped quickly to the door and opened it. Marshal was waiting, and he took us both in, his attention going back and forth, comparing us as we stood side-by-side. Flustered, I set the pie on the top of the hall bookcase and wiped my hands on my jeans. I didn't think it was the pie that had his eyebrows so high. My mother and I looked a lot alike, apart from our hair and how we dressed.

"Hi, Mrs. Morgan," he said, smiling, and then said to me, "Rachel."

My mom smiled like the Mona Lisa, and I rolled my eyes, seeing his big-ass SUV at the curb. "Hi," I said dryly. "I hear you met my mom already."

"Marshal and I looked at your baby pictures while you were sleeping," she said, then stepped back. "Come on in. We're eating pie."

Marshal glanced at the half-eaten slice above our heads and smiled. Cracking his neck, he stepped in just far enough to shut the door. "Thanks, Mrs. Morgan, but if I'm going to get Rachel back to the church before sunset, we really need to go now."

"He's right," I said, not wanting to endure an hour of humiliation at my mother's hand. Besides, the sooner we left, the sooner I could apologize for my mom and he could make his escape. I wasn't going on a date when Ivy was home thinking she screwed up again. She hadn't. We had ended the entire freaking mess in success before Jenks screwed it up. But that didn't mean I was going to let her break my skin again. I had to stop saying a decision was good just because it made me feel better. But being good, really good, really sucked.

"Oh!" my mom chirped. "Your coat. I think you left your bag in the kitchen, too."

She hustled down the hall, and Marshal looked over my shoulder when I heard the dryer door open. I shifted in the reflected green light of the hallway, uncomfortable not knowing what they'd talked about. My pie sat over us, and I wondered if he'd mind if I ate it.

"I'm really sorry about this," I said, sending my attention down the empty hall. "It's my mom's mission in life to find a boyfriend for me, and she doesn't listen when I tell her to stop."

Marshal's gaze shifted over the pictures before him with interest. "It was my idea."

A warning flag went up in me. He had to know what had happened after he left at sunrise this morning. I mean, he *had* talked to Jenks, and the bite marks on my neck were obvious. If it had been me, I would have been halfway to Mackinaw by now.

Marshal's gaze was on my favorite picture of me in the fall leaves when he said, "Jenks wanted me to tell you Ivy said she'll be out late tonight, getting her old friends sugared enough to talk about the night your boyfriend died."

The hesitation before he took a breath told me he had wanted to add something, but he stayed silent. "Thank you," I said cautiously, trying to figure it out.

"She said she'd be back by sunup," he added, and I shifted to make room for my mom as she approached, my coat over her arm, my bag in one hand and a slice of pie on a napkin in the other.

Maybe he thinks he can rescue me? No one is that stupid.

"Thanks, Mom," I said, taking my coat and bag as Marshal flushed and made awkward comments about the pie she was pushing at him. The cooler air coming in had tripped the furnace, and I shrugged into my coat to relish the warmth soaking into me.

My mom beamed, her gaze running over both of us. "I put

your costume charms in your purse," she said as she wound a red scarf around my neck to hide the red-rimmed marks made by Ivy's teeth. "You forgot them Sunday. Oh, and that nice Were called while you were sleeping. He wants to pick you up tomorrow at one. He says wear something nice."

"Thanks, Mom."

"Have fun!" she finished cheerfully.

But I didn't want to have fun. I wanted to find out who had killed Kisten and tried to bind me.

"Wait, wait," my mom said as she opened the closet door and pulled out my battered pair of white roller skates. "Take these. I'm tired of them being in my closet," she said, looping them over my arm and handing me the rest of my pie from the top of the bookcase. "Enjoy yourselves." She gave me a kiss, whispering, "Call me after sunset so I don't worry?"

"Promise," I said, thinking I was an insensitive brat of a daughter. She was scatterbrained, not stupid, and she had put up with a lot of crap from me. Especially lately.

"'Bye, Mom," I called out as Marshal opened the door and preceded me down the two steps and to the walk. He'd already eaten a bite of the pie, and his mouth was full. "Thanks for everything," I added, laughing when Marshal made a noise of bliss. My mom made excellent pie.

"Wow, this is great," he said, turning to give my mom a smile. I felt good all of a sudden. My mom was cool. I didn't appreciate her enough.

I eyed the two vehicles at the curb, my little convertible looking like a drop of red lightning next to Marshal's big, obnoxious SUV. "Marshal . . . ," I started, thinking I really had to get home and work in the kitchen.

Marshal grinned, looking attractive in the sun. "She's going to call me. If I tell her you went home, do you know the grief I'm going to get? I have a mom, too, you know."

I sighed, holding my pie, knowing I'd never get my keys out of my bag with one hand. Taking a bite of pie, I looked at the house. My mom was at the window with the curtain edged aside. She waved but didn't move from the glass. Yeah, it was probably not worth the hassle.

"Two hours," he promised, eyes earnest and caring. "And I'll help you in the kitchen to make up for it."

Waffling, I looked at our cars. I could spare two hours. "You want to take my car?"

Marshal's expression brightened when his gaze landed on it. I had made the red convertible mine with a few feminine touches, but it was still masculine enough to avoid being a chick buggy. "Sure," he said. "I don't mind coming back for my car. The rink isn't far away."

That would make it Aston's, I thought, cringing. They wouldn't remember me. Not from that long ago. "Sounds good," I said, harboring the belief that if we took his car, something would happen and I'd be stranded, unable to get back to my church before sunset. I didn't know how the undead lived, having to be somewhere before sunrise or risk annihilation. I'd better keep a watch on the time. A freaking demon in a roller rink. They'd ban me for life for that.

We angled to my car, and after shoving the rest of the pie into my mouth, I dug my keys out and handed them to him. Marshal's brow rose as he took in the zebra-striped key, but he said nothing. He courteously opened my door, and I slid in, watching him go around to the driver's side. His pie was gone and his mouth was full when he got in with a pained grunt at the tight space, taking a moment to adjust everything to his considerable height. "Nice car," he said when he was settled.

"Thanks. The FIB gave it to me. It belonged to an I.S. agent until Trent Kalamack killed him."

Okay, maybe that was a little blunt, but it would help set the scene for the coming disaster tonight when we would get stuck in traffic and a demon would show up to cause a major incident on the expressway. I hated news vans with a passion.

Marshal hesitated, and the way he looked at the gearshift made me wonder if he knew how to drive it. "Ah, he didn't die in the car, did he?"

"Nope. But I hit him with a sleepy-time charm once and locked him in the trunk."

He laughed at that, the deep, comfortable sound making me feel warm inside. "Good," he said as he put the car into first, jerking us only once as he got us moving. "Ghosts give me the creeps."

Fifteen

The vibration of wheels on varnished wood rumbled up through me, the speed and feel both familiar and exhilarating. Music blared, and the novelty of people skating in costume made the echoing, dingy space seem brand-new. We'd been here for about an hour, going round and round until my mind was numb and my body pleasantly exhausted. Marshal had brushed my hand by accident twice now, and despite his claim that he wasn't looking for anything but casual companionship, my mom's words made me wonder if he was testing the waters.

Together we made the next turn with a comfortable foot-over-foot motion to throw us into a faster pace, and when Marshal's hand bumped into mine again, he took it. I said nothing, but at the slight stiffening in my stance, he let go to pretend to fix the hem of his shirt. Immediately I felt bad, but it really wasn't a date, and I didn't want it to slip into one.

Against the far wall was a huge clock and a sign updated daily stating what time the sun rose. They didn't have a sign saying what time the sun would set, though. My tongue felt the bump on my inner lip, and a flash of fear grew and died. I wasn't bound. I could be out on my own without Ivy protecting me from a faceless vampire appearing and making me beg to be bled. Nothing had changed, apart from me being a little smarter, a little more careful. And as for Al? I was completely safe . . . until the sun went down. *Demon bait.* This was no way to live.

Marshal followed my gaze to the clock before his attention dropped to my hand at my side. "You want to go?"

I shook my head as I fixed my red scarf, then felt guilty I was hiding my vamp bites. I'd never felt shame for them before, but I think it was because I understood for the first time how risky it had been to get them and I was embarrassed to have been that stupid. "No. We've got time yet." Being careful not to touch him, I leaned closer so he could hear me over the music as we passed the speakers. "I need to stop on the way home to pick up some tomatoes and another bag or two of candy. I ran out last year, and when I turned the light off, someone tied condoms to my car's antenna." *Tomatoes, candy, and a complexion charm.*

Marshal's full laugh made me wonder how many he'd tied in his day. There was a distinct glint of devilry in his eyes. "Hey," he said. "Hold on. Let me see if I can still do this." And in a sharp movement of flailing arms, he was skating backward. A turn was coming, and I took his hands to steady him when he bobbled. I let go almost immediately, but just that slight touch had eased the tightness in his jaw.

Now I really felt bad about stiffening when he'd taken my hand earlier, and not wanting him to think I thought he was ugly or anything, I skated closer toward him. I had an idea, and I started to sweat. God, I hadn't done this in years, but if Marshal wasn't afraid to fall and get an I BROKE MY ASS AT ASTON's button, then I wasn't either.

Smiling to hide my nervousness, I leaned forward to be heard over the speakers as we passed them. "Turn around!" I shouted.

"What?"

I grinned. "Stay in front of me, and turn around!"

We were past the speakers, and his eyes were wide as he said, "Okay," and spun.

His back was to me, and I took a moment to look at it, so

wide and broad. Dang, he was tall. My mom had been right. It felt good to get out and do something. If I didn't remind myself of what my life should be, I was going to collapse into a puddle of hopelessness. Balance. It was all about balance.

Pushing my thoughts away, I gingerly put my hands on his shoulders as we took the turn at the outer edge. "Pull me through?" I said as I leaned in so he could hear me over the music. "You're tall enough."

"Oh!" he exclaimed, darting a quick look over his shoulder. "Sure. We've got some straight board coming up."

We were at the speakers, and the music beat into me along with the rumble of the boards. *I should come out here more often,* I thought. Yes, the crowd was mostly human and the music was lame, but it was relaxing. Safe.

Marshal bent at the waist, and when his hands appeared between his knees, I sank to my heels and grabbed them. "Oh, crap!" I exclaimed when I realized too late he had crossed his wrists, and when he pulled me through, he spun me.

"Oh-h-h-h-h no-o-o-o-o!" I gasped, adrenaline pulsing as the world revolved. I scrambled for balance as I ended up facing him. My eyes were wide, and I caught a glimpse of Marshal laughing before he pulled me to him so I wouldn't go down. My wheels aligned, and breathless, I froze, my arms crunched between me and him as I skated backward. I took a breath, then looked up at him. *He was holding me.* "I, uh, wasn't expecting that."

"Sorry," he said softly, gazing at me.

"Liar," I said as the walls raced by. I was in his arms, skating backward, going full tilt. It was kind of how I lived my life. "You, ah, can let go now," I said, but I wasn't moving away, a small, wounded part of me just about dying to stay where I could soak up his warmth and acceptance.

His smile went soft at my awkward conflict, and when his grip loosened, I carefully turned to face forward and slip out of his arms. I probably shouldn't have done a pull-through, but

I hadn't known he was going to turn it into . . . *that*. Crap on toast, I should have left everything as it was.

"Hey," I said nervously, hoping he wouldn't assume I wanted to change our relationship. Not that we really had one. "You're not bad at this. I practically lived here when I wasn't in school. How did you get so good?"

Marshal glanced at the torn stickers on my skates featuring popular bands from the nineties. His brown eyes were crinkled in laughter, and I hoped his eyebrows would grow in soon. "There's not much to do when the tourists leave. You should see what else I'm good at."

I smiled when I imagined what one had to do to keep occupied when snowed in. *Leave him alone, Rachel. He's not looking, and neither are you.*

"So now that you've got the job, you're going to move down here?" I asked.

"Mm-hmm." He was smiling, too, when he looked up from the boards. "I've got a guy who's been looking to buy the business, so it's only a matter of finding a price we both like."

I bobbed my head. "What about your house?"

Marshal shrugged. "I rent. Next trip up there, I'll bring everything back. Providing it's not out on the front lawn or burned."

Remembering what my mom had said about him coming off a psycho girlfriend, I winced. "Sorry. Debbie?" I guessed, remembering her.

He was silent as we took the turn, both of us going foot-over-foot to zoom past a couple dressed up as Raggedy Ann and Andy. "It wasn't anyone's fault," he said when we straightened. "We'd been together for a long time, but the last two years have been a slow-motion crash."

"Oh." The speakers were thundering out loud, fast rock, and I glanced at the clock.

"She wants a trophy husband, and apparently I'm not moving fast enough," he said, with only the faintest hint of bitterness in his voice. "Not to mention she forgot I wasn't working for money to impress people but to go back for my master's. I thought I loved her." Again he shrugged, leaving his shoulders hunched slightly. "Maybe I loved the idea of having her beside me. The same things weren't important to us anymore, and it just . . . died."

I was glad his expression held more regret than anger. "And what's important to you?" I asked.

Marshal thought while we maneuvered around Darth Vader, who was struggling to keep from hitting the wall with his helmet blocking his vision. "Success at work. Having fun doing it. Caring for someone and supporting their interests because you like to see them happy. Having them care about and support yours simply because they want to see you happy."

There was a commotion behind us, and the "ass buster" light at the DJ pit started to spin. Darth had gone down, taking three people with him. I was silent as my thoughts drifted from Marshal's goals to mine, and then to Ivy. God, I hoped she was all right. It seemed so cold to be out enjoying myself when she was trying to find out who had killed Kisten. But it wasn't as if I could go into a den of vamps and demand information. Like I said, she did the vamps, I did the demons.

"Hey," Marshal said, giving me a tentative punch on my arm. "You weren't supposed to go all serious." I smiled up at him, and he added, "You want something to drink?"

I glanced at the clock yet again. "Sure. Sounds good."

Together we angled ourselves past the trio of traditionally dressed witches complete with black hats, arm in arm as they tried to do the cancan. We took the step up together onto the carpeted rest area, and I took a fast breath as my momentum cycled down to nothing in two seconds flat. The air suddenly felt warmer, and the music louder. It was only when I stopped that I realized how fast we'd been going. Again, sort of like my life.

I tucked my hair behind my ear when Marshal leaned in so

I could hear him better. "What do you want?" he asked, his eyes on the line.

Besides to know what the hell is going on? "How about a slushie?" I suggested. "Something green."

"Something green," he repeated. "You got it. Why don't you grab a table?"

I nodded, and he moved to the line, settling in with his attention on the glowing menu. Looking at the clock, I felt like Cinderella. We had lots of time, but I honestly didn't know how vampires did this. Most public places had emergency sun shelters that they charged you beaucoup bucks for. Sacred ground was a little more difficult to come by.

I slid into the hard plastic booth seat with my back to the rink. The minute my mother had said Marshal wasn't going to last was the minute I'd started getting interested. God, I was stupid. I saw what I was doing, and I still couldn't stop it! But I really was starting to like Marshal, and that worried me. I mean, neither of us was looking for a relationship, but that's what made it dangerous. Both our guards were down. That, like me, he enjoyed some excitement in his life wasn't exactly a good thing, 'cause I could give him that dressed in leather and trailing vampire incense. But it was because of that very mind-set that he hadn't given me any grief about the new marks on my neck or the fact that a demon was gunning for me. He hadn't dropped me like a pound of troll turds even after meeting my mom, and that was saying a lot. *My life is a freaking mess.*

My dates with Nick had always centered around talking or watching movies. Kisten had been more extravagant, with dinner at expensive restaurants or trips to dance clubs. But it had been ages since I'd had a date that was a nicely paced, moderate amount of activity that relaxed as well as tired me out. I wanted to just enjoy it, but I couldn't seem to do it without pushing a little bit more to find out just where we were and if things had changed in the last fifteen minutes. *Welcome to my nightmare*, I thought, determined to stop it and let the man be.

I sighed, slumping in the hard plastic. I could be with a guy without thinking about a relationship. I did it all the time. There was Ford, and Glenn, and David. The guy down at the corner market who restocked the ice cream shelves and had those fabulous shoulders . . . But none of them were witches, and as much as I'd like to think otherwise, there was a pull there that didn't exist with a human or Were . . . or even a vampire. Starting a family someday with a witch would be a whole lot easier.

I shifted my skates back and forth, my feet feeling as heavy as my mood now that I wasn't moving. I could see the front door from where I was, and the skate counter. Someone was arguing with the attendant, Chad, and I turned to watch.

Chad had been manning the skate counter even before I had started coming to Aston's in high school. The guy had hair to his elbows and was half out of his mind from past Brimstone use, not giving a crap about anyone but good at his job. The perfect customer-relations person, Chad could do anything up to and including throwing out a patron, and Mr. Aston wouldn't fire him.

One of the men arguing with him was obnoxiously tall, his silhouette, clear against the bright, late-afternoon sky, visible past the glass doors. The other one was shorter but held himself with a stiff formality. My amusement that they were trying to bully Chad faded as I recognized the tall one. Damn it, there couldn't be two such vile, tall people in the world, even on Halloween. That was Jonathan, which would make the other guy Trent Kalamack.

I glanced at Marshal, and seeing that the line hadn't moved, I got up and shifted closer.

Yup, it was Trent, dressed in a suit and tie that looked way out of place with the threadbare carpet and linoleum counters. The thought of a Pandora charm came to me, and I dismissed it. I wouldn't owe him anything.

"I don't care if you're the prime minister of my girlfriend's ass," Chad said, pointing a Brimstone-stained fingernail at Jon. "You're not getting past the gate unless you have skates. See the sign?"

I couldn't see the sign from where I sat, but I'd seen it in the past. The thing was three feet by five and took up the entire wall behind him, lettered in red and outlined in black.

"This is outrageous," Jon said, his voice dripping disgust. "We simply want to talk to someone for five minutes."

Chad leaned back and took a swig of his beer. "Like I haven't heard that before."

Trent's jaw clenched. "Two pairs of nines," he said, clearly avoiding touching anything.

Jon turned, surprise on his angular, hawklike features. "Sir?"

"Just pay him," Trent said as Chad gave Jon a shit-eating grin and dropped two ugly pairs of skates on the counter.

Looking like he'd rather lick asphalt, the tall man pulled a long wallet from an inner coat pocket. Jonathan's feet were way bigger than a size nine, but the point was to get past the gate, not go skating. Trent's fair hair was floating in the breeze kicked up by the skaters when he left Jonathan to pay Chad. His pace faltered as he saw me watching him, and I gave him a little wave. Eyes never leaving me, Trent jerked forward, struggling to get through the turnstile without touching it.

My sarcastic smile went annoyed. *What does he want, anyway?* I thought, wondering if this was about his little vacation into the ever-after; if so, he was going to be sorely disappointed. I wasn't going to work for him, but irritating him was right up on my list of favorite things.

Smirking, I glanced at Marshal. He was going to be there awhile, so when Trent came forward with an intent pace, I simply pushed off the carpet and back onto the boards.

"Morgan!" Trent exclaimed, and I spun to skate backward, giving him a cheeky bunny-eared kiss-kiss. His brow creased, so I started dancing to the music. Oh, God, it was "Magic Carpet Ride," and the entire place was emptying onto the rink.

By the time I had done a circuit, Jon was with him and Trent was lacing up. He was going to come out here? Holy crap, he must be pissed. It wasn't unusual for Trent to track me down when he wanted to wave money at me, but he usually had his act more together than this.

I made another circle, my mind going over our last meeting. I hadn't done anything to tick him off too badly, had I? I mean, irritating him was fun, but the man could kill me if he really wanted. Of course, the nasty little secret of his illegal genetic labs would come out and his empire would come tumbling down, but hell, Trent might do it just to spite me.

My third circuit found Jon standing alone. I quickly scanned the rink, but it wasn't until I looked behind me that I found Trent moving easily and comfortably. *He can skate?* I toyed with the idea of making a race out of this, but there were too many people out there in unsafe costumes, and besides, I'd probably already pushed him to the limit. The guy was a drug lord after all.

Curious, I checked to make sure my scarf was in place, then slowed to let the underweight Arnold pass me so Trent could catch up.

"Rachel," he said as he settled in beside me, and I felt uneasy when he looked at my scarf as if he knew what lay under it. "You are unbelievable. You know I want to talk to you."

"So here I am." I smiled and tucked a curl out of the way. "Besides, I've always wanted to see a world power on skates. You skate really well—for a murderer."

His green eyes squinted and his jaw tightened. I watched him force the tension out of himself. God, I enjoyed pushing his buttons. That he even cared what I thought said volumes.

"I need you to come with me," he said as we took the turn, and I laughed, the sound lost in the boom of the speakers.

"On your suicide mission?" I said. "I'm glad you finally got smart and asked for help, but I'm not going into the ever-after for you. Forget it."

He went to say something, his emotions showing more than usual, but it was cut short as the lights dimmed and the disco ball lit up.

"Couples' skate," Chad said over the loudspeaker in a bored tone. "If you don't have a partner, get off the damned boards."

My eyebrows rose in challenge, but Trent surprised me, sliding closer and looping his arm through mine. His fingers were cold, and my smile faded. Something was seriously wrong. I loved irritating Trent, and I honestly got the impression that he put up with it so he could irritate me back, but this? I'd never felt his skin so cold.

"Look," I said as the music turned slow and the skaters moved closer. "I'm not going into the ever-after. Al is hot for my soul again, and the last thing I need to do is get on his turf, so forget it."

Trent shook his head in disbelief. "I can't believe you call him Al."

"Well, I'm not going to use his summoning name," I said, affronted. We were passing the rest area, and I caught Marshal's eye. He was standing at an empty booth with a concerned look and two slushies. He straightened as he saw me, and I gave him a "just a minute" gesture.

His confusion and disappointment were clear despite the whirling disco lights, then he blinked as he realized who I was with. And then we were past him, headed for the other end of the rink.

"This isn't about the ever-after," Trent said, bringing me back to our conversation.

My lips pressed together, and I wondered if they would ban me again if I ran Trent into the wall. "Yeah, I know, it's for Ceri and her baby. God, Trent. If it had been anyone but Quen."

Trent almost pulled out of my grip, but I held tight, not wanting to look at his face. "Ceri told you?" he said, sounding embarrassed and making me wonder if he had been going to marry her and try to pass the baby off as his own.

I turned, letting him get a good look at my disgust. "Yes. She told me. She's my friend." *Or used to be.* Trent's face went empty of emotion, and I felt a pang of guilt. "Look, I'm sorry. If it means anything, I think Ceri and you look great together and would have really pretty babies, but you and her? Who would be happy there? Really."

He looked away, watching the couple before us dressed up as Bonnie and Clyde. "Rachel," he said as the song went into the last, barf-o-matic romantic verses, "I need you to come to my house. Tonight."

I just laughed and looked at the clock. "No way in hell." Then, deciding that if I didn't give him a reason, he might drug me and cart me off, I added, "Trent, I can't. If I'm not on holy ground by sunset, Al will know it and show up. I won't take the chance. Tell you what, though. I'll come out to see you tomorrow afternoon with a big, *fat* consultation fee, and you'll still get a no out of me."

Fear crossed his face, hidden too quickly for me to think he was trying to manipulate me. "Tomorrow might be too late," he said, his soft voice clear in the cessation of music and rumble of wheels on wood. "Please, Rachel. I couldn't care less, but Quen has asked, and I'll beg for him, not me."

Whoa, wait up a fairy-flipping moment. Suddenly unsure, I halted our motion, dragging Trent to the back corner of the turn where we'd be out of everyone's way. "Quen?" I asked. "Why does Quen want to see me?"

The lights brightened and the popping of the loudspeaker made both of us wince. "It's five straight up, skaters," Chad's voice rumbled out. "Time to award the daywalkers' best costume. Line up, and Aston and his beeyotch will award the lucky dick or dickette a year's pass to the rink."

The people in costume cheered, more than a few patrons falling as they shifted direction to line up. I wanted to get off the boards, but everyone was in the way. Marshal was standing beside Jon, both of them watching us with the attitude of not wanting to be seen together but trying to get information from each other. Marshal looked almost short next to the unearthly height of the obnoxious elf Trent had handling most of his office affairs, and I spared him a glance to try to tell him this wasn't my idea.

"Why can't Quen just come out to see me?" I said when I could hear myself over the excitement, and then it came together. "Damn it, Trent!" I almost hissed. "You stupid businessman. You sent him into the ever-after, didn't you, when I said I wouldn't go."

Anger marred Trent's usual calm. Behind him, Aston, the owner of the rink, skated onto the boards with a dark, wasp-waisted, buxom woman hanging on his arm, clearly under the influence of a bust-enhancing charm. They'd both been drinking, but Aston was a past Olympic skater, and by the looks of it, his companion had been a Roller Derby queen and could probably skate better drunk than sober. Pain charms were illegal in derby competitions; alcohol wasn't.

The noise of the crowd rose and fell as they passed the costumed patrons, people shouting their opinions as to how the contest should end. I rounded on Trent before he could take the opportunity to slink out without hearing my thoughts. "Did Quen go into the ever-after and come out cursed?" I accused. "You don't know what you're doing. Leave the demon stuff to the professionals."

The blood washed from Trent's face, and his chin trembled in anger. "I would, but the professionals are afraid, Morgan, too cowardly to do what needs to be done."

Furious, I got in his face. "Don't you *ever* talk to me about cowardice!" I exclaimed.

But Trent met my anger with his own. "I didn't send Quen into the ever-after," he said, wispy hair floating. "As far as I know, he's never been there. What happened to him is a direct result of your incompetence. Maybe that's why he wants to see you. To tell you to your face that you need to stop trying to live up to your father's name and open a nice charm stall down in Findlay's Market and quit trying to save the world."

I felt like I'd been socked in the gut. "You leave my dad out of this!" I almost hissed, then nearly fell when a spotlight hit us, hot and heavy.

"Congratulations!" Mr. Aston slurred, and I realized everyone was staring at us, cheering. "You've won the daywalkers' best costume!"

He was talking to Trent, and the angry man caught his emotional balance with an enviable quickness, shaking the rink owner's hand with a practiced ease, smiling as he tried to realign his thoughts and figure out what was going on. I could see his fury at me simmering under his pleasant expression. The buxom-spelled beauty giggled, draping a ribbon of entry coupons around his neck, startling me and shocking Trent when she gave him a sloppy, red-lipsticked kiss on his cheek.

"What's your name, Mr. Kalamack?" Aston was saying, gesturing grandly to the watching people.

Trent leaned past Aston to me. His green eyes were almost black with anger. "Quen is asking for you."

Fear slid through me at his formal words. Oh, God. I'd heard that only once before. It had been in the nurse's office at school. I don't even remember the ride to the hospital to find my dad gasping his last.

"Let's all have a round of applause for Mr. Quen, here," Aston shouted, the speaker squealing with feedback. "Winner of this year's daywalker costume contest. If you're afraid of the dark and those who walk in it, go home! The rest of us want to par-ty!"

The music started up, and people began moving to it, round and round in useless circles. I stared at Trent. Quen was dying?

"Sorry, miss," Aston said as he put a hand on my shoulder and sent his bourbon-scented breath over me. "You almost had him beat, but you went overboard with the hair. Rachel Morgan's hair isn't that frizzy. Have a g-good night."

The woman on his arm crooned as she led him away. The spotlight went with them, leaving only Trent and me in the small corner of the rink where the dust bunnies gathered. Looking tired, Trent removed the necklace of coupons and wiped away the lipstick with a white linen handkerchief.

"Quen is asking for you," he said, chilling me. "He's dying, Morgan. Because of you."

Sixteen

I loved my church, but being confined to it sucked dishwater. Up in the belfry, I shoved the last of my spell books onto the shelf with enough force to threaten to knock over the free-standing bookcase I'd found there. Adrenaline struck through me, and I reached for the nicked mahogany wood to keep it from tipping. Catching it, I exhaled, glad Ceri wasn't back from her search for spelling supplies to see my sour mood. Misplaced anger born in guilt accounted for most of it, and as I stood and tucked my complexion amulet back behind my shirt, I resolved to let it go. I wasn't going to go see Quen. It might have been a trick, it might not have. I wasn't going to risk it. It was a good decision, but I wasn't happy with it, adding credibility to my new philosophy that if I didn't like a decision, it was probably a good one.

Thunder slowly grew, rolled, and died, echoing against the surrounding hills that sheltered Cincy to fade into the soft, hissing rain. Exhaling with a deliberate slowness, I sat on the edge of the elaborately carved fainting couch to rest my chin in my cupped hands and look over the small, sparse space. My blood pressure started to drop as the sound of the rain became obvious, shushing against the shingles and dying leaves. The small, hexagon-shaped room had a feeling of open airiness and smelled like coal dust, which was odd seeing as the building had been constructed long after coal was abandoned as fuel.

I'd gotten home before sunset, and guilt had pulled me across the street to Ceri's to apologize. When Marshal and I had gotten back to my mom's, he had seemed relieved to get in his truck and drive away, pensive and deep in thought, and I vowed to back off lest I turn into a needy wanna-be-your-girlfriend twit. I wasn't going to call him, and if he didn't call me . . . it would probably be for the best.

My intent in visiting Ceri had been to apologize for losing my temper and to make sure she was okay. That, and to dig for information about Quen's condition. She was going to see him tonight but said she wanted to teach me how to make a light before she left. It was probably her way of apologizing, seeing as she couldn't say the words. I didn't care if she said them or not, knowing they would come out when the hurt I'd caused her eased enough.

I still didn't agree with what she was doing with Al, but she was trying to live her life the best way she knew. Besides, I made far worse decisions than she did with a lot less power to back them up. And I wasn't going to lose another friend because of stiff-necked pride and a lack of understanding caused by silence.

Ceri was currently looking for a ring of metal for a ley line charm she wanted to teach me, but until she returned, I had nothing to do but stare at Jenks's gargoyle, still not awake but hiding high up in the rafters and out of the rain.

I had seen the quiet, unheated space last winter while avoiding Jenks's brood—before that Ivy's owls had been up·here, briefly, but I'd avoided them, and thus the belfry—but it wasn't until summer and the first rains that I found the beauty in it. Jenks had forbidden his kids from going near the gargoyle, so they wouldn't bother me. Not that it was likely they would venture out of their stump and into the rain. Poor Matalina.

Looking away from the gravel-colored, foot-high critter hunched on a support beam, I quietly moved a folding chair to look out one of the long windows. They were slatted to keep the vermin from getting in and to let the bell's music out. How the gargoyle got in was a mystery that was pissing Jenks off. Maybe he was like an octopus in that he could squeeze through anything.

Hunching to pillow my chin on my arms, which were folded on the sill, I tilted the blinds to see the shiny black night, breathing in the damp air tainted with the scent of roof shingles and wet pavement. I felt warm and secure, and I didn't know why. It was peaceful, almost like a memory was wrapping itself around me. It might have been from the gargoyle—they were said to be guardians—but I didn't think so. The feeling of peace had been there long before he showed up.

I'd moved the folding chair up here this past summer, but the shelf, the fainting couch, and the dresser had been here when I'd found it. The antique dresser had a green granite top and a beautiful, age-spotted mirror behind it. It would make a great spelling counter, easy to clean and durable. I couldn't help but wonder if the space had been used for spelling before. There were absolutely no pipes or wires above or below the high room—which was why I was using candles to light the place—but even so, I was tempted to make this more than a temporary spot to store my spelling books and stir charms when I had to stay on hallowed ground. Dragging everything down to wash it would be tedious, though.

Fortunately Ceri's spell didn't involve much in the way of paraphernalia. The ley line spell wasn't in any of my books, but Ceri said if I could start a fire with ley line magic I may be able to do this. If so, I might take the time to fix it into a one-word quick-spell. Pulling myself up from the slatted window, I wrapped my arms around myself in the damp, candlelit chill and hoped it was easy. The cool factor alone would be enough reason to fix it into my memory.

Ley line magic wasn't my forte, but the idea that I might be able to make a light whenever I wanted had a definite appeal.

I'd once met someone who could use ley lines to hear people at a distance. A faint smile curled the corner of my mouth up at the memory. I'd been eighteen, and we were eavesdropping on the I.S. officers interviewing my brother, Robbie, about a missing girl. The night had been an utter disaster, but now that I thought about it, maybe this was the root of the I.S.'s dislike for me. Not only had we shown them up by finding the missing girl, but we had tagged the undead vamp who had kidnapped her, too.

The faint sounds of Ceri's steps crossing the tree-hidden road drifted through the slatted windows, and I sat up. Ivy was downstairs with her computer and spreadsheets, trying to use logic to find Kisten's murderer. She had gone very quiet at the sight of my complexion amulet, her tight face telling me she was not ready to talk. I knew better than to push her. If she was here, then we were doing okay for now. Jenks was with Matalina and the kids, avoiding the gargoyle. The church was quiet with the three of us doing our separate things. Peaceful.

I heard Ceri come in and call to Ivy, and I rose to pretend to dust the shelves. A fast skittering on the stairs turned into Jenks's cat, bounding in and sliding to a stop when it realized I was up here, standing with her tail crooked and staring at me with black eyes.

"Hey, Rex," I said, and the cat's tail bristled. "What?" I snapped, and the stupid feline darted back out the door. There was a feminine murmur of surprise in the stairway, and I smiled.

Ceri's light steps on the stairs grew loud, and chalk in hand, I looked at the unfinished ash floor to decide how big a circle I wanted to draw. The door to the stair creaked, and I turned, smiling. "Find a ring?" I asked, and she smiled as she held up a flat ring of gray metal. "Found it in Keasley's toolbox," she said, handing it over.

"Thanks," I said, feeling the weight of it in my palm. Rain glistened on her fair hair and spotted her shirt, and I felt guilty for making her come up here. "Really. Thank you. I wouldn't even try this if you weren't helping me."

Her green eyes glinted in amusement in the light from the candles, and something about her tonight flipped my warning flags up. It was as if she was up to something. Her voice was casual, but my instincts had been pinged, and I was watching her.

"I'm going to set a circle," I said over the hush of rain. "Do you want to be in or out of it?"

She hesitated as if to tell me I wouldn't need a circle, then nodded, probably remembering the first time she had taught me how to scribe a demon calling circle and my aura had unexpectedly pooled out. "In," she said, and when she stood to move, I gestured for her to stay. I would draw it right around the couch she had gone to sit on.

"You're fine there," I said, starting my circle a foot inside the hexagonal room's walls. My hair made a red curtain between us, and the feeling of wrongness coming from her strengthened. The hiss of the chalk mixed with the rain, and the breeze slipping past the open slats was chill. I couldn't shake the feeling that there was something she wasn't telling me. Finished, I stood straight and blew my hair out of my way. I met her gaze and narrowed my eyes in challenge. Sure enough, she glanced away.

My heart did a little flip-flop of fear. I wasn't going to do another charm Ceri taught me unless I knew exactly what it was *before* I did it. Finding out belatedly that the spells I'd used to go wolf and turn Jenks human-size were actually curses had been lesson enough.

"This isn't a normal charm, is it," I stated, and she looked up.

"No."

I sighed, slumping to sit backward in the folding chair. My gaze went to the chalk in my hand, and I set it on the green marble top of the dresser with a tap. "It's demonic, isn't it?"

She nodded. "There is no smut for this one," she offered.

"You're not changing reality, you're just pulling on a line. It's similar to how you almost threw raw energy at Ivy. If you can do that, and pull it back into you without hurting yourself as you did, then you should be able to do this. . . ."

Her sentence trailed off at the end, and I flexed my fingers, remembering the pain had lasted only a moment before vanishing in the chaos that had followed. Demon magic. *Damn it back to the Turn.*

"You might not be able to do it," she said, sounding as if she hoped I couldn't. "I simply want to know, and if you can, then you have something that might save your life someday."

My lips pressed together as I thought about it. "No smut?"

She shook her head. "Nothing. You're just modifying energy, not changing reality."

I was tempted, but there was still something she wasn't telling me. I could see it in her subtle motions, my runner training screaming at me. I thought of Quen on his deathbed, and why Ceri was sitting here in my damp belfry instead of with him. It made no sense. Unless . . . "You want to know if I can do this so you can tell Quen. That's it, isn't it?"

Ceri actually flushed, and a pulse of fear slid through me, pulling me straight. "I shouldn't be able to, should I," I demanded, and when she shook her head my gut twisted. "What in hell did Trent's dad do to me?" I said, panicked, and her eyes flashed.

"Rachel, stop," she said, rising and coming to me with the scent of damp silk. "Trent's father didn't do anything but keep you alive. You are you."

Her hands hesitated a bare second before taking mine, but I saw it and the fear slid deeper. "You are the same person you were when your mother birthed you," Ceri said firmly. "And if you can do a magic that no other witch can do, then you should become skilled in it so you can go where others fail. Great power does not corrupt a person, it only brings their true self into the light, and Rachel, you are a good person."

I pulled away from her, and she took a guilty step back.

Mistrust, ugly and unwelcome, trickled through me, and I vowed to purge it right now. I couldn't lose her as a friend. I couldn't. "Promise me you won't tell Quen," I said. She hesitated, and I added, "Please, Ceri. If I'm different, I don't want anyone to know. Let me tell who I want, if I want. Please. Otherwise, I'm just . . . a pawn in someone else's game."

Looking miserable, she clasped her hands before her, and then slowly she nodded. "I will tell no one," she whispered.

Immediately my tension dropped to my gut like lead. I looked at the dresser top where the charm's tools were assembled, and with a tired regret for the lost chance that I could ever live a normal life, I stood. My reflection in the age-spotted mirror above the dresser stared back at me. I took a slow breath. "Do you want to show me first?"

Ceri moved so I could see her reflection behind me. "I can't do it, Rachel."

Swell.

It was as if a door had closed behind me. Before me was a great blackness, but it was wide and sweeping, and I had to believe that somewhere in my future was a happy ending. *This is who I am*, I thought with an overpowering sensation of finality. Wiping my hands on my jeans, I resolutely went to the dresser. *Time to find out what I can do.*

The candle on the dresser was reflected in the mirror, making two. Set to the side was the chalk, the metal disk, a spool of twine, a finger stick, and a vial of grapeseed oil. I had my ley line textbook there, as well, open to the dozen blank pages at the back for notes. At the top of one was a messy LIGHT CHARM BY CERI and the pictorial representations of the hand movements and phonetically spelled Latin that went along with them. I knew Ceri was disgusted that I didn't know enough Latin to read it normally, but I'd been focusing my attention on other things for the last few years—and I didn't expect that to change. But a class in hand gestures might have been in order.

"Well, then," Ceri said as she nervously eased up behind

me. I eyed her candlelit reflection in the mirror, wondering how she was going to teach me a charm she couldn't do herself. The scent of cinnamon and silk mixed with the bayberry candle and the scent of iron from the bell above us. That reminded me of the gargoyle, but he was still sleeping when I glanced up.

"We should tie your base ring up so we get a nice sphere instead of one half inside the dresser," she added with a forced brightness that made my head hurt. "Once it's set, you can't touch it, or you'll break the spell."

"Like any circle?" I guessed.

She nodded, blinking in surprise when she looked up and saw the gargoyle. "Is that . . . ," she stammered, her expression showing wonder.

"It's a gargoyle," I finished for her. "He showed up yesterday. Jenks is ticked, but all he does is sleep." I hesitated. "Should we do this somewhere else?"

Smiling a secret smile now, Ceri shook her head. "No. They're good luck, according to my grandmother. He's fine up there. She had a saying that pixies are to elves as gargoyles are to witches."

I smirked as I recalled how Jenks's kids took to Ceri, and how Ellasbeth's mother, another pure-blood elf, adored Jenks. I didn't have any such "charmed" feelings for the lump of somnolent rock in the belfry rafters, and as far as I knew, neither did any other witch. But then, I was the only witch I knew who lived in a church, which was the only place a gargoyle would stay. Something about the big bells ionizing the air or some such.

"Are you sure this isn't a problem?" I said, pointing up to him.

"No. I'd ask to make his acquaintance and for him to tie up your string if he was awake."

I stared hopefully up at the gray winged shape, but he didn't move. Not even his big fringed ears. "I'll do it," I said, then levered myself up onto the dresser top, and from there to standing. My head was in the bell, and the faint echoes hitting my ear made me shiver. I quickly tied the string to the clapper and got down.

Ceri bit the string to cut it long, then expertly shifted her pale fingers to make a three-cornered sling to set the palm-sized ring of metal into. She let it go, and it swung gently at chest height above the dresser. "There," she said, backing away. "That will make a pretty light."

I nodded, conscious of the gargoyle and wondering if his or her tail curling around the pair of craggy feet had twitched. I didn't like spelling in front of people I didn't know, especially one who had taken up residence without paying rent.

"So the first step is . . . ," Ceri prompted, and I pulled my attention back to her.

"Sorry," I said, gathering myself. "Let me set my outer circle."

Ceri nodded, and I sent my will to the ley line out back. Energy flowed, bright and pure, and I exhaled as the forces balanced in me. I kicked off my slipper and touched my toe to the metallic chalk ring. My trigger word, *rhombus*, echoed forcefully in my thoughts, and a molecule-thin sheet of ever-after swarmed up to arch to a close over our heads. The trigger word condensed a five-minute prep with candles and chalk to a half-second. It had taken me six months to learn to do it.

I winced at the ugly black that crawled over the half-sphere a second later, doing its best to smother the bright gold my aura had colored the typically red sheet of ever-after. The smut was a visual representation of what was on my soul. I felt ugly as I silently scuffed my slipper back on. It didn't seem to bother Ceri, but her smut level was a thousand times thicker than mine. *Minus one year*, I thought, hoping she had really forgiven me for yelling at her.

The gargoyle wasn't in the circle, which made me feel tons better. My hair was starting to float from the currents of energy running through me, and I ran a hand over my curls. "I hate it when it does that," I muttered as I found a loose strand and pulled it free for the charm.

Ceri chuckled a rueful agreement, and seeing her confident nod, I took the strand and turned to the candlelit dresser. I exhaled a puff of air. Calmer, I reached for the oil.

"In fidem recipare," I said, dabbing it on my fingers and running the strand through it to coat it thoroughly. The hair was a conduit to keep the energy flowing into the circle and maintain the light, and the oil with its high smoldering point would keep the strand from igniting.

Ceri's brow was furrowed, but she nodded in agreement, so I carefully coiled the strand so it lay across the ring. A drop of my blood was next, and I hardly felt the prick of the finger stick. The metal ring seemed to be warmer than it should have been when I smeared the blood onto it. "Um, *iungo*," I said, rubbing my palms nervously against each other to wipe off the oil and blood, then, after checking my notations, performed the gesture that cramped my right hand.

"Good," she prompted, easing closer, attention fixed on the dull gray metal.

"Rhombus," I said strongly, holding back a surge of power that wanted to slip my control, allowing only the barest amount to spill forth as I touched the ring.

A second bubble of force sprang up, and the ring of metal shifted to exist both here and in the ever-after, looking unreal and translucent. Like a ghost. I smiled at the black-and-gold sphere hanging there like one of Ivy's glass Christmas balls, the cord bisecting the sheet of unreality as it suspended the metal the charm was in. It wasn't often that I saw the bottom half of a protection circle, and though I knew it was wrong to think the black demon smut marring the glittering golden sphere of my will was pretty, I did. It looked like an aged patina.

"See if you can make it glow," Ceri prompted, but she still seemed worried.

My life is going to change with the creation of light, I

thought. Gut clenched, I said, *"Lenio cinis,"* while watching my fingers awkwardly make the invocation movement. The two had to be simultaneous, otherwise the air would burn up and snuff the spell before the connection spell to bring in more energy to burn was in place. At least, that was the theory.

Anxious, I held my breath and watched the sphere flash before settling to a steady burn. "Oh, my God!" I squeaked when a dropping sensation plinked through me and settled to a steady flow. The power keeping the globe burning rushed through me, and I reached to steady myself against the dresser. I couldn't take my eyes off the burning sphere.

"Breathe!" Ceri said with forced gaiety, and I took a breath and held it. Feeling the energy flow into the ball and become an ephemeral light was just too weird. It was akin to a mental vacuum, or what being in free fall could feel like. It was the oddest thing I'd ever felt, but Ceri was smiling at me through the mirror, her expression pinched and her eyes bright with moisture.

"Do you know what it feels like?" I said, tense, edgy, and excited all at the same time.

Blinking fast, she shook her head. "I can't do this. Rachel . . . be careful."

I swallowed hard. I could do something that no other witch or elf could do, save Lee. *Demon magic.* And it was easy.

And that fast, my life shifted again. I didn't change, but suddenly I was different. A small globe of light had been my signpost. I hoped it was a good portent.

Becoming used to the odd feeling of energy pulling through me quickly, I looked at my light. The glow was not the clear glow of fluorescents, but that of amber. It lit the six-sided room with a black-and-gold haze that seemed darker than the candlelight, but infinitely more far-reaching. Laying heavily upon the empty walls, it brought to mind the late sun close to the horizon that shows from under storm clouds still hanging over you, making everything look like it had a razor-thin shadow, the air full of hidden pressure and the scent of ozone. Demon magic aside, I had created it, and that made it the most ever-lastingly cool thing I had ever seen.

Eyeing it, I licked my lips, wondering. "What happens if I let more energy into it?"

"Rachel, no!" Ceri shouted.

Something dropped from the ceiling, thumping onto the marble top of the dresser with a sharp crack. It was the gargoyle, his red eyes wide and the tuft of lion fur on his tail bristled. I stumbled back, my elbow knocking into my protection circle to make it fall.

"Don't," he said, his voice both high and resonant.

My mouth gaping, I stared at the foot-high person before me as he shook his leathery wings and settled them against himself. Flushing a deep black, he looked at his feet and the new cracks spreading out from them. "Dragon fewmets," he muttered. "I cracked your table. I'm sorry. God in all his grace help me. I am a clay brain."

I bumped Ceri when I took another step back, and she made a small, questioning noise.

His color turned back to a comfortable gray splotch, and he shifted his wings. "Do you want me to fix it? I can."

That shook me, and I remembered to breathe. "Jenks?" I called loudly. "Someone here to talk to you about rent!"

The gargoyle flushed again, everything but the white tuft of fur on the tip of his whiplike tail going black. "Rent?" he squeaked, somehow suddenly looking like an awkward teenager as he hunched his muscular shoulders and shifted from foot to foot. "I don't have anything to pay you rent with. Patron saints berserk us. I didn't know I'd have to pay rent. I never should have . . . No one told me . . ."

He was almost frantic, and Ceri scooted closer with sly amusement. "Be easy, young goyle. I think the landlord would agree to a few months' lodging for what you just did."

"Break the witch's table?" he said quizzically, his big clawed feet shifting with sharp taps. He had really big ears that moved to show his emotion, up and down, almost like a dog's. And the white tufts were adorable.

Smiling wider, Ceri pointed with her eyes to my light, still glowing despite the distractions. "For keeping said witch from frying her synapses," she said. It was my turn to flush, and seeing it, Ceri added, "It's not that big of a circle for the power you're channeling. If you added to it, it might implode and then backlash into you."

My mouth twisted up as an uneasy feeling took me. "Really?"

"Why don't you let it go?" she asked, and when the gargoyle awkwardly cleared his throat, I nodded, separating my will from the line.

I stiffened when the pulling sensation seemed to fall in on itself, blinking when every last erg of power in me was sucked into the ball and the light hanging over the dresser extinguished itself. That fast, the golden shadow-light was gone, and everything looked dull and gray in the glow of the flickering candle on the dresser. Poised, I listened to the rain as the silver metal ring swayed slightly. It seemed colder, and I shivered. Demon magic without cost. This was going to bitch-slap me somewhere. I knew it.

"This is high magic, Rachel," Ceri said, bringing me back to the present. "Beyond what I can do. The chance you will misstep is high, and you can seriously hurt yourself if you jump into experimentation. So don't."

I had a flash of irritation that she would tell me not to do something, but it died fast.

The gargoyle shifted his wings with the pleasant sound of sliding sand. "I just thought it was a bad idea," he said. "The power resonating in that bell is maxed as it is."

"Just so." Ceri turned to the window as Jenks buzzed in through the pixy hole in the topmost window.

"Hey!" he shouted, his wings clattering aggressively, hovering with his hands on his hips as he looked at the awkwardly shifting gargoyle. "It's about time you woke up. What do you think you're doing here? Rachel, make him leave. No one invited him."

"Jenks, he wants to talk rent," I said, but Jenks was having none of it.

"Rent?" he yelped, buzzing his wings to shake the water from them, leaving spots on the granite. "Did you eat fairy dust this morning for breakfast? We can't have a gargoyle here!"

My head was starting to hurt. It didn't help when Jenks landed on my shoulder with the scent of wet garden. I felt a damp spot through my shirt, and I didn't like that he had bared the sword he had taken to carrying around with him since yesterday. Ceri had moved to sit on the fainting couch, her hands resting to either side of her and her ankles crossed as if she were holding court. Clearly it was up to me. "Why not?" I said when I saw the gargoyle had flushed again, shifting from foot to foot.

"Because they're bad luck!" Jenks shouted.

Tired of him yelling in my ear, I flicked him away. "They are not," I said. "And I like him. He just saved me from frying my little witchy brain. At least have him fill out a rental questionnaire or something. You want the city to come down on you for not being an equal opportunity renter? You just don't like him because he slipped your sentry lines. God, Jenks, you should be begging him to stay. You're starting to sound like Trent."

Jenks's wings stopped and he almost fell. Ceri hid a smile, and I felt a moment of amusement. The pixy's features bunched up, then smoothed out. Clearly flustered, he warily dropped to the edge of the dresser top, his wings a blur of motion. Making a show of it, he sheathed his sword. I doubted very much it would have pierced the gargoyle's skin, but everyone in the room probably appreciated it.

"I don't have a form," Jenks admitted, somewhat embarrassed. "We can do it verbally."

The gargoyle nodded, and I backed up a step, sitting beside Ceri when she shifted to make room. It was darker now without my globe, and thunder rolled in a comfortable sound.

"Name?" Jenks shot out. "And your reason for vacating previous residence?"

"Jenks, that's rude," I said, and the gargoyle twitched his tail in a show of acceptance.

"My name is Bis," he said, "and I was kicked off the basilica because I was spitting on the people coming in. Suck-up little Glissando thinks she knows angel dust from dirt and tattled on me."

"Tink's titties, really?" Jenks said in admiration. "How far can you spit?"

My eyebrows rose. His name was Bis? What kind of a name was that?

Bis puffed up in pride. "If we've had a recent rain, I can hit a stop sign from a block away."

"Holy crap!" Jenks's wings lifted him, and he landed closer. "Think you can hit that creepy angel statue from the steeple?"

Bis's color went silver-white to match the fur on his ears and tail, and gold flecks grew in his red eyes. "Faster than you can throw toad shit at a hummingbird poaching your nectar."

"No fairy-ass way!"

"Yes way." Bis settled his wings against himself. The sound was soothing, and my shoulders eased. I think Jenks had found a friend. It was so sweet I could just barf. Except that he really needed one.

"Bis, it's good to meet you," I said as I extended my hand, then hesitated. He was only a foot tall, about half the size of most gargoyles I'd seen from the distant vantage of the road. His hand was too small to comfortably shake even if I wanted to chance those raptorlike claws, but I was willing to bet he was too heavy to land on my wrist in a proper pixylike greeting.

With a surprisingly small whoosh of sound, Bis was in a hopping flight. Jenks jerked back into the air in surprise, and I froze when the gargoyle landed on my wrist. He had gone black again, and his huge ears were bent submissively, like a puppy's. And when his smooth skin touched me, I suddenly felt every single ley line in the entire city.

Shocked, I did nothing as my gaze went vacant. I could sense them, softly glowing in my awareness, like potential unmasked. I could see which were healthy and which weren't. And they sang, like the deep thrum of the earth.

"Holy shit!" I gasped, then covered my mouth, embarrassed. "Ceri," I stammered, turning to her. "The lines . . ."

She was smiling. Damn it, she had known.

The gold flecks in Bis's eyes were whirling slowly, mesmerizing me. "May I stay, mistress witch?" he said. "If Jenks allows me to pay rent?"

He was lighter than I ever would have expected, almost not there. "You can tap a ley line," I said, still in a pleasant shock. My God, the lines were humming with different vibrations, like different bells have different sounds. The university's was heady and deep, and the one out back was a clear ting. From Eden Park was a discordant twang that had to be that ley line some idiot had built a reflecting pond over, turning it weak and almost dead.

Bis shook his head. "No, but I can feel them. They flow through the world like blood and leak from the surface like an unhealed wound."

I took a breath, only now realizing I had been holding mine. "Jenks, he's got my vote to stay. We can work rent out later, but maybe he can do night sentry duty so you can spend more time with Matalina."

Jenks was standing on the dresser, his reflection making two pixies frowning suspiciously at me. "Yeah," he said absently, his thoughts on something else. "That'd be great."

Ceri came forward and made a short, courtly curtsy. "I'm

glad you got kicked off your parapet," she said, smiling. "My name is Ceri. I live across the street. And if you spit on me or my friends, I will turn your wings to feathers."

Bis flashed black and his gaze dropped submissively. "Yes, ma'am."

I looked at Jenks, seeing him asking my opinion with just his expression. I couldn't imagine Ivy would protest. I nodded, enthralled.

"Welcome to the garden, Bis," Jenks said cheerfully. "Rent is due on the first."

It wasn't until half an hour later when I was trooping downstairs to call my mom that I realized I'd taken my protection circle down *after* the gargoyle had dropped through it without a whisper of resistance.

Not before.

Seventeen

Jenks clutched at my ear as David's car cut a sharp right. The small pixy wasn't feeling well, seeing as it was noon and he was missing his afternoon nap. I had told him he could stay home and spit seeds at the creepy statue in the garden with Bis, but he swore so prettily at me that I had invited him along on David's and my run. And I say David's and my run because we both had a vested interest. Now that David had started a real pack, he'd be up for a raise if he could show a significant savings to his company. I just wanted to smack some sense into whoever was summoning Al and freeing him to kill me. *Please don't let it be Nick*, I thought, brow furrowed. The woman who owned the house was a witch, but that didn't mean Nick couldn't be wrapped up with her.

The day was sunny, and I had my shades on. The cool breeze coming in the open window felt good in my hair, which was loose and flowing. The skies promised to be clear, and with the moon just past full, it was shaping up to be an excellent Halloween night. If this was the group that was summoning Al and I could suitably impress upon them the error of their ways, I might risk going out. Marshal hadn't called, but I hadn't expected him to. I think he was backing off after our very quiet car ride back to his truck. Trent had put me in an exquisitely bad mood. Exhaling heavily, I made a face no one could see. *Whatever.*

At least Ceri and I aren't still at odds, I thought, smiling faintly. It felt good to settle that so fast, and I was glad I'd taken the initiative. It wasn't that she'd taught me a new charm that made me feel good, it was knowing that I hadn't lost a friendship. The only thing bothering me now was not knowing what was going on with Quen. I hoped he was all right and that Trent was being a drama queen.

David glanced across the short width of his gray sports car as he slowed at a crossing. The sun glinted on his long black hair, which was pulled back in a casual clip, making him look good. "You should wear a business suit more often," he said, his low voice mixing with the sound of fighting sparrows. We were out in the suburbs, and traffic was light. "You look nice."

"Thank you." I tugged the blah-brown skirt down over my knees. I had on nylons, and they felt icky. My flat-black, no-heel shoes didn't do anything for me either. And the purse that went with this outfit was so not me. At least my splat gun fit in it. David had insisted I look the part if I was coming with him. If he had made me dye my hair and put on brown contacts, I would have thought he was embarrassed to be seen with me.

"It's not the dress," Jenks chimed in, yawning. "She's got a new boyfriend."

I looked askance at him. "Marshal? I don't think so. He bugged out pretty fast yesterday."

Laughing, Jenks darted to David's steering wheel and landed there. "Sure, he's gone now, but he'll be back. Not looking for a girlfriend, my dragonfly's little green turds. That's the oldest line in the book, Rache. Take a smart pill once in a while, huh?"

We had had fun yesterday, until Trent showed up, but I wasn't sure if I wanted Marshal to call. I mean, I knew what was going to happen if he hung around, and I didn't want to go through that crap again. "He's coming off a psycho girlfriend,"

I said, remembering the soft look in his eyes when he had spun me into him. "The last thing he wants is another."

"That's what I'm saying!" Jenks threw his arms up in frustration. "He's just like you, going from one relationship to another to keep from getting bored, and you are going to get so burned on this one that you're going to need skin grafts."

I made an ugly face at him, but he only laughed. David was eyeing Jenks to get him to continue, and the pixy was more than happy to oblige. "You've got to meet this guy," he said, hands on his hips and his wings going full tilt as he walked along the steering wheel when David turned it. He was in the sun now, and his wings glittered. "A normal relationship isn't enough for him, and he's got this white-knight complex on top of that, which Rachel fed when we asked for his help up in Mackinaw. I hope he gets smart faster than her, or he's going to be in a world of hurt. Probably find himself turned into a rat or something."

I didn't appreciate the reference to Nick, and my mood darkened. "Jenks, shut up," I said tiredly, then turned to David. "Have you talked to the ladies about the pack tattoo?"

Jenks snickered. "Nice segue, Rache. From one pain in the ass to another."

"Learn a new word, Jenks?" I needled.

David grinned to show his small teeth. "I've got an appointment for you with Emojin, Cincy's best tat design artist, the first week in April. I'll pick you up."

"April?" I said, my fear and anticipation easing. "I didn't know it would take that long." Maybe with a little luck, they'd forget about the entire thing.

Shrugging, David watched the road. "She's the best, and nothing but the best for my first female alpha."

I snorted and propped my elbow up on the window as I looked out. My schedule was going to be very full in April. Just watch.

Jenks was snickering, and I sent my gaze to the passing

upper-class homes, ignoring him. We were almost there by the look of it, and I'd be glad to get out of the car and take my frustration out on some demon summoners.

"Big lots," I said, seeing the eighty-year-old oaks and shady lawns. The houses were set way back and had iron fences and stone drives.

"The harder to hear your neighbors scream, my dear," was David's answer, and I sent my head up and down in agreement.

Halloween decorations were everywhere—expensive and elaborate displays. Most of them moved, a combination of mechanics and magic that had been found only on locked Hollywood back lots until the Turn. David exhaled loudly as he turned the car onto a cobblestoned, circular drive. "This is it," he said as our momentum slowed and the sound of the tires became louder.

The house was a sprawling ranch with what looked like an inground pool in the back and elaborate landscaping in front. Inside the garage was a black two-seater Beemer, a riding lawn mower, and little else. A basket of cherry tomatoes with a gingham liner was sitting on the steps, a clear indication that the homeowner was Inderlander. I still had to go out and get my tomatoes, and I made a mental note to ask David if he would mind stopping at the Big Cherry on the way home.

Black and orange decorations covered the front porch between the huge Boston ferns and the greyhound statue. They might want to take it in tonight, or someone was going to cover it in tomato. Or worse.

The brakes squeaked as David stopped, and as he put the car in park, Jenks hovered before me. "Be right back," he said, then zipped out the window.

David got out of the car, shutting it with an attention-getting thump. Inside the house, a small dog started yapping hysterically. David looked good in his suit, but also tired. It was just after the full moon, and the two ladies had probably run him hard.

Eager to get my life back, I jumped out of the car and slammed the door.

"Relax, Rachel," David murmured as he came around the car, gripping his briefcase and wrangling his shades into place.

"I am relaxed," I said, then jiggled my feet impatiently. "You want to hurry up?" *Please don't be Nick. Let me have made one good choice in my life.*

David hesitated, his dark eyes flicking to the barking dog visible through a window. "You can't arrest anyone. You don't have a warrant."

I nudged him into motion and up the short walk. "If I'm lucky, someone will take a swing at me, and then I can hit 'em."

Looking askance at me with a wry grin, David snorted. "Just tell me if it was demon damage, and we'll leave. If it is, you can come back and make whoever it is chew his own balls on your terms, but as far as I'm concerned, this is just some nice lady with a crack in her wall."

Yeah, and I'm the cosmetics girl at Valeria's Crypt. "Whatever," I muttered, then tugged my dress straight and checked my complexion charm as we took the stairs to the shady porch. I wanted my Halloween back.

David rocked to a halt on the mat, tilting his head to watch the dog having hysterics through the long window beside the door. "It's not illegal to summon demons."

I huffed as I tucked my shades into that ugly brown purse, right next to the splat gun, the magnetic chalk, and the heavy-magic detection amulet—so far a nice friendly green. "It's illegal to tell them to kill someone."

"Rachel . . . ," he coaxed as he rung the bell and the barking dog jumped up and down. "Don't make me sorry I brought you."

I stared, fascinated as the blond fuzz ball turned somersaults. "Me?" I said coyly.

The little dog yelped, vanishing in the blur of a swinging

foot. I blinked, and my mouth was hanging open unintelligently when the door moved, revealing a middle-aged woman wearing a paisley-patterned dress and an honest-to-God apron. I sure hoped it was a costume, because the fifties look was *not* an attractive fashion statement.

"Hello," she said, sounding like a little-miss-hostess doll. Her eyebrows arched, and I wondered if I had a run in my stockings. She didn't appear as if she was a demon summoner. She didn't appear as if she was in mourning either. Maybe she was the cook.

"I'm David," David said as he shifted his briefcase and shook her hand. "David Hue. And this is Ray, my assistant. We're from Were Insurance."

Ray? As in a little drop of sunshine? I gave him a dry look. I wasn't incognito, here.

"Ms. Morgan," I said, extending my hand, and the woman took it briefly with a noncommittal smile. A wave of redwood spilled from her, telling me she was a witch rather than a warlock, and she'd been spelling heavily lately. I wasn't buying the housewife image—she could probably slam me against the wall. *Better be polite.*

"I'm Betty," she said, stepping back and giving her dog another shove. It skittered sideways and parked its little yappy butt in the archway to the dining room. "Come on in."

David gestured for me to precede him, so eyeing the panting but silent dog happily staring at me, I went in. Betty's skirt swayed as she set a cordless phone on the table by the door between the huge bowl of wrapped candy and the plate of frosted sugar cookies. Orange pumpkins and black cats. *By golly, she bakes, too.*

"I understand you have some water damage?" David prompted when the door shut.

A shiver passed through me as it clicked smartly closed. Everything was clean and bright, lit by a high window. The hall was spacious, and clearly the woman was wealthy. The fact that her husband had just died of a heart attack was no-where on her face or house. Nothing.

Heels clacking, the woman started down the hall. "In the basement," she said over her shoulder. "This way. I have to say I'm surprised you're working on Halloween."

Her tone was slightly sour, and I imagined Betty only offered to be available today as she thought we wouldn't work on Halloween. No one else did.

David cleared his throat. "We like to settle claims fast. Get your life back to normal."

Catch you in a lie, I added, looking at the décor. It was all angles and stark colors that made me uncomfortable. It smelled like hard-boiled eggs. On a long table was a big flower arrangement of lilies and black roses. Okay, so someone had cared.

The rapid patter of the dog's nails at my ankle pulled my gaze down, and the little dog panted happily up at me as if I were his best friend. "Go away," I muttered, motioning with my foot, and he yapped playfully, dancing around my toes.

Betty halted at an unadorned door painted white, and she turned, frowning at him. "Beat it, Sampson," she said roughly, and the cheerful little dog sat at my feet, his banner tail sweeping the tiled floor like mad.

With a last scowl, she opened the door, flicked on the light, and headed down. I looked at David, and he gestured for me to go first. I shook my head, not liking the bare boards and ugly walls after the open whiteness of the rooms upstairs, and sighing, he went first.

Betty was yammering about something, and I took a breath to steady myself. I didn't want to go down there, but that's what I was here for. Frowning, I looked at Sampson. "Everything okay down there, sport?" I asked him, and he stood, his entire backside waving as he ate up the attention.

"Stupid dog," I muttered as I started down. But maybe not so stupid, since he stayed at the top of the stairs in the sun while I followed Widow Betty into the electric-lit blackness underground. Two steps in, I opened my purse and checked the lethal-spell amulet. Nothing. But the heavy-magic charm was glowing brightly enough to read by.

"I don't know how long the wall has been leaking." Betty's voice came echoing up as she reached the bottom and opened up a second door. It was unusual, but they might have had the vamp door for resale value. "I only come down here when I have to store something," she said as she flicked on the lights and the scent of carpet cleaner came drifting up. "I noticed it was wet a few weeks ago, and I ran the extractor over the carpet and forgot about it, but earlier this week, the crack just sort of opened up, and it got a lot worse."

David stepped into the basement, and after a quick amulet check, I halted at the base of the stair. I wasn't ready yet to let that woman get between me and the door. It was really thick, and it had a conventional lock on the outside and a deadbolt on the inside. Nice. Bet it was soundproof. No one likes screams disturbing their Sunday dinner.

Seeing me there, David nodded almost imperceptibly and went to drop his briefcase on the long conference table set up in the middle of the large room. It smelled too clean for Betty to be coming down here only once in a while. Bleach, and maybe that spray that Ivy used on the blood circles this spring. The cinder-block wall under the front door had a crack I could put my pinky in running from floor to ceiling, thinner rays following the mortar lines.

Betty clustered close to David as the clicks of the locks on his briefcase made a tiny echo. He brought out some paperwork, and feeling safer, I meandered to the cracks. My skin crawled when the woman's gaze sharpened on me, even as she started signing papers. If this was water damage, then I was an elf.

There was a back room behind some fake pine paneling. The drop ceiling was low, and the brown indoor/outdoor carpet looked like dirt. No wonder Al liked my kitchen; this would be an ugly place to be summoned into. Past David and Betty at the far end under the high basement windows, an eight-inch-high platform took up the entire end of the room. I looked at the crack in the wall and smirked. Yeah. This had demon-summoning all over it. I'd seen the damage they could do. The water on the floor had probably come from trying to get the blood out of the carpet.

"Ma'am?" David said to get Betty's attention. "Just a couple more places to sign, and I'll take a few pictures. Then we'll get out of here and you can return to your day."

Betty signed where David was pointing, hardly taking her eyes off of me as I flicked a bit of mortar out of the crack to find it dry underneath. "What's she doing?" Betty asked, stiffening.

David took a breath to answer, but I interrupted with a pleasant, "I'm Mr. Hue's demon specialist." This woman wasn't the top person, and that was who I wanted to talk to.

David's lips twitched, and I beamed. Yes, he was irritated, but we had two agendas here, and mine wasn't being met.

"Demon?" Betty said faintly.

"It's state law," I lied. "When the structural integrity of a dwelling has been compromised, it must be inspected for demon damage." Well, it wasn't a law, but it should be.

"I . . . didn't know that," Betty said, turning a new shade of pale.

David frowned, and I surged ahead. "I'd say that by the looks of this, that you have a demon problem, Betty. And a really bad one. This wall is bowing out, not in, as is typical in water damage. And as you can see by the flakes," I said, picking another one out, "the concrete is dry under it. We'll have to run some tests, but I would guess that either someone ran a hose down here to wash out the blood, or a demon urinated all over the carpet. Either one is bad news. Demon urine is really hard to get out."

Betty was backing to the door, and my confidence grew. She wasn't going to do anything. She was scared.

"Rachel," David warned, telling me to back off.

But I couldn't resist. "David, be sure to get a picture of that window. Look, you can see the hose right outside."

"Excuse me," Betty said nervously. "I think I hear my phone ringing."

"And it smells down here, too," I added, wanting to make sure she called her friend the demon summoner and not the I.S. Pretending surprise, I brought out the high-magic charm. It was a bright red, and my fingers glowed from it. "Oh, yes, yes!" I exclaimed, looking at the crack and bobbing my head. "I will definitely have to report this to the demon manifestation department. Big magic within the last few days."

David had his head down and was rubbing his forehead as Betty stared at me with wide, frightened eyes, tense and ready to run. Almost enough. Just one more nail.

"Next time you're going to try to pass off demon damage as something else, Betty, you should wait until after the new moon for the accumulated smut they leave behind to be wiped off. Now you go toddle off and call your grand pooh-bah."

Hand to her mouth, Betty fled. I tensed, not surprised when she slammed the door shut. The sound of the lock was ominous and the patter of her heels on the stairs entirely expected.

"Rachel . . . ," David complained.

"Hey!" I shouted when the lights went out. "Oh, *nice*," I said, fists on my hips and frowning at the ceiling.

"This wasn't the plan," David said, and I heard his briefcase snap shut. Being a Were, his eyes had probably already adjusted to the thin glow coming in the sparse windows, but his approaching shadow was ominous-looking and creepy.

"Yes it was," I said. "You wanted to know if the damage was demonic in origin, and I gave you my opinion."

"I didn't expect you to give it to me in front of her!" he exclaimed, then sighed, sitting back on the table with his case in front of him like a fig leaf.

"Sorry," I said, and I jumped when his hand hit my shoulder. "I know these kind of people, and the head guy won't show unless I call him out. She's phoning him right now. We'll have our chat, and we can all go home and enjoy trick-or-treats tonight."

"Or they'll keep us here until they summon your demon again."

I laughed. "They wouldn't dare. Jenks is outside, and I'm under Rynn Cormel's protection. He'd wipe them out." I hesitated. "Would you be more comfortable waiting above ground?"

David moved to the window, a dark shadow that ghosted like a wisp of fog. "Yes. How do you plan on getting out of here? Blow the door off the hinges? My company won't pay for that."

"I've got Jenks," I said, surprised he hadn't shown up yet. If all else failed, David could boost me out a window. Betty was a boob if she thought we were going to stay here until they chose to deal with us.

I opened my purse to get my phone and call Ivy to tell her I might be a little late this afternoon, and the red light of the high-magic detection amulet blazed forth to make everything a nasty haze. "Four bars on my phone," I said, squinting.

"Someone's here already," David said, coming from the window and joining me at the table. "That dog is having a fit."

Even I could hear Sampson, and I winced at his sudden yelp of pain. The sound of heavy footsteps in the stairwell was clear, and Betty's voice was an irritating, panicked chatter.

"David, if I ever get like that, just slap me," I said, leaning against the table and crossing my arms with my eyes on the door. I didn't know who was going to come through, but I wanted to look confident when they did. The Were chuckled and joined me, then blinked and winced when the lights went on and the lock turned with an oiled slickness. The heavy door opened, and Jenks came in an instant before a slight man in a comfortable pair of slacks and a casual sweater. Behind him was Betty in full hysterics.

"Sorry, Rache," Jenks said as he lit on my earring. "I would have been here sooner, but when I saw Tom Thumb-up-his-ass in the backyard, I stuck with him."

Tom? As in I'm-going-to-arrest-you-for-summoning-demons-in-a-charm-shop Tom? Arms going to my sides, I looked closer. Relaxing, I started to laugh. "Oh, my God. You?" I said, too relieved to be angry. This I could handle. If I could jail city powers, evade master vampires, and outsmart demons, then getting an idiot of an I.S. agent to stop freeing demons to kill me was going to be easy. Finally . . . something was going my way for a change.

Tom stopped at the base of the stairs, ignoring Betty as he glanced from me to David to assess how big a threat the Were was. David calmly clasped his hands before him and waited. Me, I stepped forward as belligerently and obnoxiously as I could.

"Wow," I said sarcastically. "I'm impressed. Congratulations. You had me fooled. You didn't even make my who-wants-to-off-Rachel list. Are you going to kill us now, or sic Al on us when the sun goes down?"

Tom pried Betty's grip off his arm. The woman wouldn't shut up, and it was getting on my nerves. "You don't know when to stop, do you?" he said, clueless as ever. The guy was too young to pull off the amount of domination he was trying for. Trent could do it, but he had the right clothes, not to mention the right demeanor. Slacks and a cardigan sort of ruined it.

"Not when you make a habit of dismissing demons so they can walk Cincy freely," I said. "And don't think you're going to saddle me with the bill for that charm shop. You summoned him. *You're* paying for it."

Tom laughed and came farther in, glancing at the wall before taking an aggressive stance between us and the stairs. I felt him tap a line, and I swung my purse around and brought out my splat gun to casually check the hopper. David shifted his weight and loosened his tie. From the top of the stairway, Sampson's barks grew frenzied.

"Mr. Bansen," Betty said, eyes on the cherry-red gun as she moaned, "I didn't know about the demon investigation. It doesn't say that in the policy!"

"Go upstairs," Tom growled, shoving her hand off him again. "It's not in the policy because she was lying."

David sighed, and I beamed.

"But they know it was a demon!" she wailed.

Tom spun, shouting, "I told you not to put in a claim, you stupid cow. Go upstairs and take that ridiculous costume off. You look like my mother!"

The poor woman fled, her red heels clacking so fast up the stairs I almost felt sorry for her. Sampson went with her, and the tension in the basement eased.

"Having trouble with your neophytes?" I said when an upstairs door slammed. "Jeez, Tom, no wonder you wanted me in your club. That's pathetic."

Tom's lips twisted. Clearly feeling a sting, he gave his head a shake to get the hair from his eyes. "A splat gun? Real witches don't need guns."

"Real witches use all their available resources." David shifted in agitation, and before he could say anything, I said, "Look. I know you've been summoning Al and letting him go to kill me."

"Moi?" he said coyly.

That was just stupid. "Knock it off," I said, taking a step toward him. "You'll live longer."

Tom watched Jenks hovering beside me and backed up. "I know what I'm doing," he said loftily. "He has yet to break my control."

"Really." I sent my gaze to the wall. "What was that from?"

The witch went slightly green, and the scent of bleach seemed to grow stronger. "Someone got careless," he said, not dropping his eyes.

"And you got a promotion?" I guessed. Pity came from nowhere. God! It was right in front of him, and he still didn't get it. "Tom, you are so stupid."

"I'm a visionary," he countered.

"You're a walking corpse. Al is playing with you. You think your little circle is going to keep you safe?" I said, pointing at the stage. "I've circled him every time you sent him to me. It doesn't matter what you told him to do after I catch him. He's mine at that point. And what if I send him back to you instead of the ever-after? Huh? How about that? Think you'd enjoy trying to catch him in this little hidey-hole of a pit you're summoning him into? Or maybe he'll find you in the shower, or asleep?"

The witch blanched. Behind him, David padded with all the stealth of an alpha wolf to the stairs to protect my escape. Jenks was with him, making me feel doubly secure.

"Didn't think about that, didja," I said to knock the precariousness of his situation home. I was a good girl, but I didn't have to be. I'd sent Al back to his summoner before. "You little pissant," I said bitterly, not liking that Tom was probably going to make me do it again. "You don't want to play this game with me. Really, you don't."

Tom drew himself up and David tensed. I couldn't let him think he had the upper hand, and after a look at David to tell him I wasn't close to being stupid, I got in Tom's face.

"Stop summoning him," I said, tapping a line so my hair would float ominously. "If Al shows up to bother me, I'm sending him back, and you'll be cleaning up more than one person hitting a cement wall. Got it?"

Shaking inside, I turned to leave, glad David had the stairs. "And tell Betty not to expect a check for the damage either. Her insurance doesn't cover demons."

Sampson was barking from somewhere as I stomped up the

stairs, Jenks a quiet hum before me and David's steps soft behind. I felt like the cream filling in a cookie, my brain full of fluff and nonsense. What in hell was I doing telling Tom I'd send Al back at him? Tom wouldn't have a chance. He'd be dead in thirty seconds.

Why am I giving him an ounce of thought? He's sending Al to kill me.

I got halfway through the sterile house done in pastels and sharp corners before Sampson was at my heels, panting for attention. "Did she buy you because you matched the couch?" I said bitterly, and the little dog yapped, his tail putting out enough motion to power Cincy for a year. Struck by a sudden thought, I hesitated at the front door to look at my high-magic amulet. It was green; he was just a dog.

"What a nasty little rat chaser," Jenks said from the security of my shoulder as I wiggled my foot to keep him inside when David opened the door.

"He's a saint in fur for putting up with that woman," I said, wanting to pick him up and take him home. I didn't even like dogs. Giving him a last look, I stifled my desire to pat him on the head and just shut the door.

David was eyeing me questioningly, and ignoring it, I schlumped down the stairs and to the car. I wanted to get out of here before Tom found his balls and started after me. In a bad mood, I got in David's car, fastened my belt, and stared out the front window, waiting.

Both David and Jenks were unusually silent, hesitant almost, as they got in.

"What!" I snapped, and Jenks let a little dust slip from him to color David's shoulder.

David shrugged, and after glancing at Jenks he said, "You okay?"

I looked at the house and saw Sampson sitting at the long window, tail still going. "No."

The Were took a breath as he started the car up and put it into drive. "I hope he doesn't call your bluff."

Silently I stared at the Halloween decorations so I wouldn't have to think.

"Uh, it was a bluff, right?" David prompted, and when Jenks's wings hummed nervously, I put on a fake smile.

"Duh, yeah, it was a bluff," I said, and Jenks's wings took on a more normal translucence. But even as I busied myself with changing David's radio from country to something a little more radical, a part of me worried it might not be.

But at least it hadn't been Nick.

Eighteen

I held the black lace top up against me over my black T-shirt, knowing it would take that bust-enhancing charm of mine to fill it out properly and make the thicker lace land in the proper strategically placed spots. It wasn't worth the risk of embarrassment if I had an amulet malfunction, and so I put it back on the rack, reaching instead for something more substantial. Smiling, I pulled out a silky silver-and-black top that would drape fantastically on me, falling right to the top of my hip-hugger jeans. It was a mix of casual sophistication and daring modesty that Kisten would have approved of.

Recalling his blue eyes, I held my smile, though it went decidedly melancholy as I considered the blouse. I didn't need it. I wasn't going anywhere fancy anytime soon.

Ivy drifted up from the next rack over. Her motions edged into vamp speed as she concentrated, shuffling through the clothes using a rating system I had no concept of. We had always enjoyed shopping together, but when I'd suggested that we go out this afternoon, she had agreed with surprising reluctance. I think she knew I was trying to lull her into a good mood before I tried talking to her about yesterday morning. She still hadn't given me any sign of being ready to discuss it, but the longer it took, the more lame my reasoning would sound.

Shopping together wouldn't get her anywhere near a good enough mood to calmly accept my vow that she would never break my skin again, but I had to start somewhere. Much as I hated it, I had to grow up. I couldn't risk my life anymore for something as fleeting as ecstasy, even if it fostered a stronger relationship with Ivy. The fact that we had brought everything back down to normal before Jenks butted in had lost much of its impact, seeing as I had had to hurt her before she could regain control of her blood lust. Jenks had been right that she wasn't ready, and I wasn't going to risk having to hurt her again.

She had done better, fantastically so, but Ivy's instincts were still stronger than her will. That alone wouldn't have been enough to sway my decision—what *had* forced my decision was that terrifying thirty seconds of me thinking I'd been bound.

I had to start making smart, crushing decisions. In a perfect world, maybe we could have done what we wanted without consequence, but it wasn't a perfect world. Just like in a perfect world I'd have been able to go out tonight. But the reality was I couldn't chance it. I didn't trust Tom to be smart.

And being smart sucked, I thought glumly as I looked at the silvery black top. *I had a lot more fun when I was stupid.*

I glanced at Ivy, whose brow was furrowed. Maybe after coffee and cookies . . . with a pint of double-chocolate monkey ice cream nearby in case of emergency.

"This is nice," Ivy said as she held up the same bit of black lace I had just put back. "Not for my costume, but I still like it."

"Try it on," I prompted, and she turned to the nearby dressing room with it. My smile faded when she disappeared behind the door, but we could still talk since her head showed. Tired, I flopped into the cushy chairs they had for bored boyfriends and stared at the ceiling. The long length of my neck pulled at the healing bites, and I shifted the complexion amulet to make sure it was in place.

Ivy silently pulled her shirt over her head and put the new one on. The music from the shop next door thumped like a heart, and I glanced around the moderately busy, trendy mall store. No one had rushed to help us after Ivy glared at the first woman who said hello, and for that I was grateful. How on earth was I going explain to Ivy that the past year had been a waste of her time and that she was never going to get her teeth in me again? Even if our auras had blended? At the very least, she'd get mad. And then leave. And then Jenks would kill me. Maybe if I ignored everything, it might go away. It sounded like a good idea—which meant it wasn't.

The dressing room door squeaked as Ivy came out. Her expression was hopeful as she posed for me, and just that faint glimmer of softer emotion in her eyes turned her beautiful.

"Damn, girl! You look great!" I said enthusiastically, thinking she would look good in anything with the faint, hesitant smile she now wore. The top hung perfectly on her, and the black lace stood out in sharp contrast to her pale skin. "You have *got* to get it. It was made for you." I nodded to further my approval. It was the perfect vampire tease of lace and skin. I couldn't get away with wearing it, but Ivy? Oh, yeah.

Ivy looked down at the black lace barely covering a few key places. A glimmer of silver and red showed where her belly button ring was, and her hand rose to her neck to hide the low scar Cormel had put there. I couldn't help but wonder who she was thinking of as she murmured, "It's nice."

Nice, nice, nice, everything is freaking nice. I didn't watch when she turned and went back into the dressing room. "You're not getting anything?" she asked over the door as the ripping sound of Velcro tore through the pounding music. "This is the third shop and you haven't even tried anything on."

Reclining in the soft leather, I looked at the ceiling. "Budget," I said simply.

Ivy's silence brought my gaze down, and I saw her looking at my neck, a painful self-recrimination pinching her brown eyes. "You don't trust me," she said out of the blue, and her motions, mostly hidden behind the door, stopped. "You don't trust me, and you're ashamed of me, and I don't blame you. You had to hurt me to get me to stop. I'd be ashamed of me, too."

Tension jerked through me and I sat upright. Two nearby shoppers turned toward us, and I stared blankly at Ivy. *What in hell?*

"I said I could do it, and I failed," Ivy said. Her shoulders were bare, and her motions were fast and jerky as she roughly put her T-shirt back on.

I stood, scrambling to figure out what was going on. *I shouldn't have taken her shopping; I should have gotten her drunk.* "You didn't fail. God, Ivy, sure, you lost it, but you caught it again. Don't you even remember what happened?"

Her back was to me as she returned the lacy chemise to its hanger, and I retreated when she came out. It had been . . . fantastic. *But it isn't going to happen again.*

She must have seen it in my face. Ivy stood stock-still before me with the lace top on a hanger, perfectly arranged and ready for the next person. "Then why are you ashamed of me?" she said softly, her fingers shaking.

"I'm not!"

Silent, she pushed past me to hang the shirt where she'd found it with a sharp clink and headed for the door.

"Ivy, wait." I started after her, ignoring the idiot of a clerk cheerfully telling us to come back for the big sale tomorrow. The spell checker at the entryway made a blip at my complexion charm, but no one stopped me. Ivy was already a store down. Her hair was shimmering in the sun coming through the skylights, and I jogged to catch up. Typical Ivy, running away from the emotional stuff. Not this time.

"Ivy, stop," I said as I caught up. "What the Turn gave you that idea? I'm not ashamed of you. God, I'm thrilled at the control you found. Did you not see how much better you did?" *Not that it makes any difference in my decision.*

Head down, she slowed and halted. People flowed around

us, but we were alone. I waited until she looked up, and the pain in her eyes was almost scary. "You're hiding your bites," she said in a low voice. "You've never done that before. Never. It was . . ." She sank down on the bench beside us and looked at the floor. "Why else would you hide my mark, unless you're ashamed of me? I said I could handle it, and I couldn't. You trusted me, and I failed."

Oh, my God. Embarrassment warmed my cheeks as I realized the message I'd been sending. My hand came up, and I pulled the amulet over my head, tugging my hair as it pulled free. Why in hell didn't Cormel's book have anything *useful* in it? "I'm not ashamed of you," I said, throwing the charm into a nearby trash can. I lifted my chin as I felt the spell leave me and my red-rimmed bites appear. "I hid them because I'm ashamed of me. I have been living my life like a freaking kid with a video game, and it took me thinking I was bound to Kisten's killer to realize what I'm doing. That's why I was hiding them. Not because of you."

Her brown eyes were dark with tears she would never shed as she blinked up at me. "You had to slam me into a wall to get me to stop."

"I'm sorry for slamming you into a wall," I said, wanting to touch her arm so she knew how bad I felt. Instead, I sat down beside her, our knees almost touching as I faced her. "I . . . thought you were Kisten's killer." Her expression was pained, and I got mad. "I was having a freaking flashback, Ivy!" I exclaimed. "I'm sorry!"

Ivy's jaw clenched and relaxed. "That's what I'm saying," she said bitterly. "You thought I was Kisten's killer. How bad is that, Rachel, when I turn into something so close to Kisten's murderer that it triggers a memory of . . . that?"

Oh. I slumped back against the hard bench and put a hand to my head as it started to hurt. "He was playing on my scar, Ivy. So were you. My back was to the wall, and I was scared both times. That's all it was. It wasn't you, it was the vampire stuff."

She turned to me, though I was still looking down the hall. "He?" she asked.

I felt my focus blur as I thought about that, weighing what little memory I had regained against my emotions. "Yeah," I said softly. "It was a man. A man attacked me." I could almost smell him, a mix of cold and stone. . . . Old dust. Cold. Like cement."

Ivy wrapped her arms around herself and took a deep breath. "A man," she said, and I noticed her long fingers were clenched about her upper arms with a white-knuckle strength. "I thought it might have been me."

She stood up with her head bowed, and I followed her. Silent, we angled to a coffee cart in an unspoken agreement, and I felt for the presence of my bag. "I told you it wasn't you months ago."

Her posture was heavy with relief, and her fingers shook as she fixed two cups of coffee, handing me one after I paid the woman at the register. It was a comfortable pattern, and I took a sip as we slowly started down the busy corridor for the car. Ivy's posture had shifted, as if a huge doubt had been removed from her soul along with the amulet around my neck. I could walk away from this and leave everything as it was, but I had to tell her now. To wait would make me a coward. "Ivy?"

"Jenks is going to kill me," she said, giving me a quick sideways look. There was a hint of moisture in her eyes, and she smiled bitterly as she wiped it away. "You're leaving, aren't you."

Oh, my God, when Ivy got it wrong, she really got it wrong. I didn't need a boyfriend. I had all the drama I could stand right here. "Ivy," I said softly as I pulled her to a stop among the oblivious people around us. "Sharing that with you was the most intoxicating thing I've ever felt. When our auras chimed . . ." I swallowed hard, having to be honest with her about the good as well as the bad. "It was as if I knew you better than myself. The love . . ."

I sniffed and wiped my nose. "Damn it, I'm crying," I said miserably. "Ivy, as good as that felt, I can't do that again. That's what I've been trying to say. I can't let you break my skin again, not because you lost it or because I don't trust you. But because . . ." I looked up at the ceiling, unable to look at her. "Because I thought I was bound to a vampire, and it was the most frightened I've ever been in my life." I laughed bitterly. "And I've had some pretty scary shit to dig myself out of."

"Then you are leaving."

"No. But I won't blame you if you want to."

I stood where we were in the filtered sun, searching for words so simple that they couldn't be misinterpreted or misunderstood. "I'm sorry," I breathed, but I knew she could hear me over the surrounding chatter of commerce. "I wasn't leading you on. I like you—hell, I love you, probably—but . . ." I gestured helplessly, seeing her expression dark with emotion when I found the courage to meet her eyes. "Kisten died because I was living my life like it had a reset button. He paid the price for my stupidity. I can't keep combining the risk of death with the joy of . . . caring and love. I'm not going to ever share that with you again." I hesitated. "No matter how good it feels. I can't keep living like that. I risked everything to gain—"

"Nothing," she interrupted bitterly, and I shook my head.

"Not nothing. Everything. I risked everything yesterday to gain everything, but it was an everything that I can't have and still keep what I love the most."

She was listening. *Thank you, God. I think I can say it now.*

"The church, Jenks, you," I said. "You as you are. Me as I am. I like me, Ivy. I like things the way they are. And if you bite me again . . ." I shivered and gripped my coffee tighter. "It felt so good," I whispered, lost in the memory of it. "I'd let you bind me, if you asked, just so I would have that forever. I'd say yes. And then . . ."

"You wouldn't be you anymore," Ivy said, and I nodded.

Ivy went silent. I felt drained. I'd said what I had to say. I only hoped we could find a way to live with it.

"You don't want me to leave," Ivy said, and I shook my head. "And you don't want me to bite you," she added, looking at the coffee clasped between her hands.

"No, I said I *can't* let you bite me. There's a difference."

She was smiling thinly when she brought her gaze to mine, and I couldn't help but meet it with my own weak version. "There is, isn't there," she said. Her posture shifted, and she exhaled long and slow. "Thank you," she whispered. I froze when she hesitantly touched my arm and then drew back. "Thank you for being honest."

Thank you? I stared at her. "I thought you'd be pissed."

She wiped her face and put her attention on the skylights to make her pupils contract. "Part of me is," she said lightly. My pulse quickened, and my grip tightened on my cup. Sensing my movement, Ivy looked at me. The ring of brown around her pupils was shrinking, but she was still smiling. "But you aren't leaving."

Wary, I nodded. "This isn't me playing hard to get. I mean it, Ivy. I can't."

Her shoulders lost their stiffness, and she half turned to look at the people around us. "I know. I saw how scared you were when you thought you were bound. Someone tried to blood-rape you."

I recalled my terror, how she had comforted me with security and understanding, telling me it was okay. What we had shared in those brief moments was almost stronger than the blood ecstasy. Maybe that's what she was getting at. Maybe that's what was important here.

Shoulders slumped in an unusual show of fatigue, she leaned forward. With her hair almost brushing my shoulders, she whispered, "If you aren't staying because I might bite you, then you are staying because you like me."

Taking a sip of coffee, she started down the hall, pace confident and slow.

My mouth opened in an O, and I jumped to follow. "Uh, wait a moment, Ivy."

Still she smiled. "You like *me*, not the way the damned vampire pheromones make you feel when I bite you. I can get blood from anyone, but if you keep saying no, then it's me you like. Knowing that is worth the frustration."

She took the lid off her coffee and threw it away as we passed a trash can. I tried to watch her face and my footing to keep from knocking anyone as we neared the main doors and the traffic increased. Her expression was calm and peaceful. The lines of worry and uncertainty that had looked so wrong there were gone. She had found peace. It might not be the peace she wanted, but it was peace. I, though, was never one to leave anything alone. "So . . . are we okay?"

Ivy's smile was full of private emotion. Free arm swinging confidently, she parted the way with her sheer presence and people turned to look at her. "Yeah," she said, looking ahead.

My pulse was fast, and I felt the tension pulling me stiff. "Ivy . . ."

"Shhhhh," she breathed, and I jerked to a halt when she stopped at the doors and turned to put a finger to my lips. Her eyes were inches from mine, and I stared at them, shocked. "Don't ruin it, Rachel," she added, drawing away. "Leave me with a little make-believe to keep myself sane across the hall from you."

"I'm not going to sleep with you," I said, wanting to make that perfectly clear, and the man coming in gave us a once-over.

"Yeah, I know," she said lightly. Pushing the door open, she went outside. "How was your run with David yesterday?"

I looked at her suspiciously as we stepped into the sun, not trusting this. "David wants me to get a pack tattoo," I said cautiously as I pulled the windblown hair from my mouth.

"So what are you getting?" she said cheerfully. "A bat?"

As I walked beside her and told her what I had in mind while we searched for my car, I realized how much our failed blood tryst had been preying on her. She had royally messed up. She had thought I'd been ashamed of her and was going to leave. But we were still friends and nothing had changed.

But as we got into my car and put the top down to enjoy the sun, I found my fingers creeping up to feel the red-rimmed bites, still swollen and sore. Recalling the sensation of our auras becoming one, I shivered.

Well, almost nothing had changed.

Nineteen

The crack of pool balls was pleasant, reminding me of early mornings at Kisten's dance club while I waited for him to finish up with the stragglers and spend some time with me. Eyes shut against the heat of the overhead light, I could almost smell the lingering aroma a hundred partying vampires left behind, mixing with good food, good wine, and just a hint of Brimstone.

No, I didn't have a problem. I wasn't addicted at all. Nope. Not me. But when I opened my eyes and saw Ivy, I wondered.

Doesn't matter, I thought as I went to take my shot and felt the skin around the marks Ivy had put in me pull. This afternoon I might have been scared to tell Ivy she wasn't going to break my skin again, but I'd done it. And it felt good. Like we had really made progress, even though neither of us was going to get what we wanted.

Warming, I focused on the yellow-striped nine as I lined the shot up. So it was Halloween and I was stuck home in jeans and a red top handing out candy instead of wearing leather and lace, bar-hopping with Ivy. At least I was with friends. Holding to my new smart-but-dull-Rachel mission statement, I wasn't ready to trust Tom to do the intelligent thing, and though I was regularly stepping off hallowed ground to raid the fridge, risking a roomful of drunk potential casualties just so I could have a fun night out was a little much.

Ivy agreed, not at all surprised when I told her Tom Bansen of the I.S.'s Arcane Division was the one summoning and releasing Al to kill me. Actually, she laughed, noting, "Least it wasn't crap-for-brains." I was still toying with the idea of filing a demon complaint with the I.S., if only to avoid that spell shop bill, but Ivy said it would be cheaper healthwise to let sleeping demons lie. If nothing happened this next week, I might let it go, but if Al came at me again, I was going to let Tom have it right where it hurt—in the checkbook.

Apart from the annoyance of being stuck home on Halloween, I was in a good mood. Jenks and I were manning the door, and Ivy was in the corner watching a post-Turn comedy classic with lots of chainsaws and a stump grinder. Marshal hadn't called, but after yesterday, I wasn't surprised. My mild disappointment only affirmed my belief that I needed to back off before he slipped into boyfriend status. I really didn't need the trouble.

Exhaling, I tapped the cue ball. It hit the dip by the corner and wobbled into the nine, hitting it perfectly wrong.

The doorbell bonged as I straightened, followed by a chorus of "Trick or treat!"

From under a ceiling of paper bats, Ivy's eyes flicked to mine, and I jerked into motion. "Got it," I said as I propped the cue stick against the wall and headed into the dark foyer with the huge bowl of candy. Ivy had filled the unlit entryway with candles to make it suitably creepy. We had turned the lights off in the sanctuary before midnight to impress the human kids, but now it was all Inderlanders and we didn't bother. A dark candlelit church didn't impress them half as much as a bowl of sugar and chocolate.

"Jenks?" I questioned, and a tight wing hum hit my ear.

"Ready!" he said, then let out an unreal wing chirp to pantomime a squeaky hinge when I opened the door. It was enough to make my teeth hurt, and the assembled kids complained loudly as they covered their ears. Damn pixy was worse than a Were's nails on a chalkboard.

"Trick or treat!" the kids chimed out when they recovered, but it wasn't until they saw Jenks glowing over the candy bowl that their expressions lit in delight, as charmed as the next person by a people-loving pixy. I had to crouch so the littlest one, in a fairy costume with illusionary wings, could reach. She was sweet, wide-eyed, and eager. It was probably the first Halloween she would remember, and I now understood why my mom loved manning the door. Watching the parade of costumes and delighted kids was well worth the sixty bucks I'd spent on candy.

"Ring the bell! Ring the bell!" a kid in a dragon costume demanded as he pointed to the ceiling, and after I set the bowl aside, I reached for the pull, grunting as I yanked the knot almost to my knees. They stared at me in the surprising silence as the rope was jerked back up. An instant later, a deep bong reverberated over the neighborhood.

The kids squealed and clapped, and I shooed them off the stoop, wondering how Bis was handling the noise. In the distance, I heard the faint sound of two more bells from neighboring churches. It was a good feeling—like a distant affirmation of safety and community—and I watched the kids file down to the street to join their moms with strollers and wagons. In the street, vans prowled, creeping slowly amid the flashing lights and flapping costumes. Jenks's carved pumpkin glowed at the base of the stairs like Al's face itself. Damn, I *loved* Halloween.

Smiling, I waited with the door open until Jenks finished lighting the stairs for the youngest. Across the street, Keasley was sitting on his porch alone to hand out candy. Ceri had left at sunset for the basilica to pray for Quen, walking the distance as if in penance. My brow pinched, and as I shut the door, I wondered if things were really that bad. Maybe I shouldn't have refused to see him after all.

"Ivy, you want a game?" I asked, tired of hitting the same balls around. She at least could sink them.

She looked up and shook her head. There was a clipboard

on her drawn-up knees as she sat with her back to the arm of the couch. A broken mug filled with colored pencils was next to her, and she was trying to force spreadsheets and flowcharts to give us the answer as to who killed Kisten. My realization that it had been a man had revitalized her, and her night investigating yesterday had turned up only that Piscary had given Kisten to someone outside the camarilla. That meant we'd be looking for Kisten's killer outside the city, since Piscary wouldn't have given him to a lesser, local vampire. It was only a matter of time though before we'd know who it had been. When Ivy set her sights on prey, she never let go. No matter how long it took.

I ambled over to bug Ivy, since it was her favorite part of the movie and she needed a break. "Just one game," I prodded. "I'll rack 'em."

Ivy's brown eyes were peaceful as she curled her feet under her. "I'm working. Make Jenks big and play with him."

I lifted my eyebrows, and from behind me at the desk still blissfully empty of his kids came Jenks's bark of rude laughter. "Make me big," he scoffed. "No fairy-loving way."

Ivy's attention slid to my wrist, where Kisten's bracelet had been for the last three months, when I handed her the cue. It immediately flicked back to me, accusing, and I tightened my jaw. "You took off Kisten's bracelet."

My pulse increased and I let go of the cue stick. "I took it off," I admitted, feeling the same flash of grief that I had worked through this afternoon when I had placed it in my jewelry box and shut the lid. "I didn't throw it away. There's a difference. Think about it," I finished belligerently.

From behind me came a soft "Uh, ladies?" as Jenks flitted nervously between us. He had no clue what we had talked about while shopping. All he knew was we had left tense and returned with a jar of honey for him and a roll of wax paper for the kids to slide down the steeple on. And that's all he was going to know.

Ivy's expression softened, and then she looked away in understanding. I hadn't thrown the bracelet away, I'd set it aside in memory. "One game," she said as she rose, sleek and lanky in her exercise outfit and the long, baggy sweater she hid half her body behind.

I dropped the chalk into her hand. "I rack, you break."

The doorbell rang, and Ivy sighed. "I'll rack them," she said. "You get the door."

Jenks stayed with Ivy, and content, I swatted aside a low-hanging bat and grabbed the candy bowl. Feeling all was right with the world, I pushed the door open only to have my good mood fade in a flash of annoyance. *Trent?*

It had to be him. He looked his usual self apart from the fact that he was wearing a baggy suit that was three inches too long and shoes that gave him an extra two inches in height. Obviously he had been in costume. My eyes flicked to the KA-LAMACK FOR CITY COUNCIL 2008 button, and he reddened. A sports car idled at the curb, its hazard lights flashing, and the door open. Trent's gaze went from the bats behind me to the bruises decorating the underside of my jaw where Al had gripped me, and finally to my new, red-rimmed bites. Maybe he'd think they were a costume. Maybe.

"What the sweet sugar candy-ass do you want?" I said in irritation, then stepped out of his reach in case it was Al in disguise. My thoughts winged back to Quen, and I fought with the urge to demand that he tell me if Quen was all right and the desire to call the FIB and tell them I was being harassed by a Trent look-alike. I had already said no. He wasn't going to change my mind.

Jenks had darted up at my exclamation, and his wings took on a faint orange glow as his circulation increased. "Hey, Ivy—come here for a sec! I know how you like watching Rache kick the bad guys to the curb."

A trio of witches with glowing wands, chattering madly, dodged Jenks's pumpkin and ran up the stairs shouting, "Trick or treat!" Looking pained, Trent brushed his hair from his eyes and stood aside, clearly agitated. Ivy slid up behind me, and I handed the bowl to her when the three boys left amid thank-yous prompted by their moms on the sidewalk. They jumped the last two steps, and I put my fist on my hip, eager to tell Trent to shove it.

"I want you to come with me," he said before I could speak, his voice terse and his attention darting to Ivy.

A hundred rude responses came from nowhere, but what I said was, "No. Go away."

I moved to close the door, shocked when Trent put his foot in the way. I stopped Ivy's reach to shove him back, and Trent's tanned face reddened. Then, with what must have been a Herculean effort, he pulled his foot back and said in a much softer voice, "Why do you have to be difficult?"

"It keeps me alive," I shot back, "but in this case it's fun, too. I'm busy tonight. Get off my front steps so the kids can get up here." How on earth had Jonathan let him come out here on his own? Trent seldom had an entourage, but I'd never seen him alone.

I shooed him off the steps, and his face took on a whisper of fear. "Please."

Jenks rose up in a column of gold sparkles. "Sweet daisies, I think I'm going to crap my silk undies. The cookie maker said please."

Trent's eyes glinted in annoyance. "Please. I'm asking. I'm here for Quen, not myself, and most definitely not you."

I took a breath to answer, but Jenks was way ahead of me. "Go suck a slug egg," he snarled, unusually defensive. "Rachel doesn't owe Quen anything."

Actually, I sort of did—seeing as he saved my butt last year with Piscary—and the beginnings of shame trickled through me. Damn it. If I didn't go visit Quen, I was going to feel guilty the rest of my life. I really hated this growing-up thing.

Ivy crossed her arms and cocked her hip. Trent dropped his gaze, steadying himself. When he brought his attention back to me, I saw a glimmer of fear, not for himself, but for Quen. "He isn't going to live through the night," he said, the calling children in the street a macabre contrast to his words. "He wants to speak to you. Please."

Jenks saw me hesitate, and in a burst of anger, he lit my shoulder with gold sparkles. "Hell no, Rachel. He just wants to get you off hallowed ground so Al can kill you."

I winced, thinking. Quen had given me information before, and people did weird stuff on their deathbed. Last confessions, that kind of thing. I knew I should stay on hallowed ground, but I'd been on and off it all night. I was going to go. I had to. Quen had known my dad. This might be my last and only chance to find out about him.

Ivy saw it in my face, and she grabbed her coat from the peg. "I'm going with you."

My pulse quickened, and Trent's expression turned confused at my change of heart.

"I'll get your keys," Jenks said.

"We'll take my car," Ivy countered, turning to get her purse.

"No," Trent said, stopping her cold. "Only her. No pixies. No vampires. Just her."

Majorly ticked, Ivy looked him up and down.

The two were going to be at each other's throats before we hit the sidewalk, even if Trent did give in and let her come. "None of you are coming," I said firmly. "Trent doesn't live on hallowed ground—"

"Which is exactly why we *are* going," Ivy interrupted.

"And I can take care of myself easier if I'm not worrying about you." I took a deep breath, my hand coming up to forestall another protest. "Tom isn't going to summon Al. He's afraid I'll send him right back at him." Trent blanched, and I shot him a dry look. "I'll get my stuff," I said, then darted to the kitchen.

Ivy and Jenks were having a hushed argument in the corner when I returned to the foyer, and while Trent watched in silence, I made a point of pulling out my splat gun, checking the hopper, then sliding it into the small of my back. There was a stick of magnetic chalk and the amulets from my run with David earlier, and as Ivy flung her hand in the air and scowled at Jenks, I looped the cord of the heavy-magic detection charm over my head. It would give me a few seconds if Al showed.

"I'll call you in a few hours," I said, and jingling my car keys, I stepped past the threshold and firmly outside the church's influence.

My heart pounded. I heard the excited kids, felt the night. The smell of burning pumpkin was strong, and I waited for a "Hello, Rachel Mariana Morgan" or "Trick or treat, love" in a proper English accent. But there was nothing. Al wasn't going to show. I had taken care of it myself. *Yay, team.*

Jenks landed on my hoop earring, flying up and away when I reached for him. "You're staying, Jenks."

"Smelly green grass farts, I'm not," he said, darting to Trent and forcing him back a startled step. "Ivy and I discussed it, and I'm going with you. You can't stop me, and you know it. And who's going to help you circle Al if he shows up? Trent? He should be begging me to come with you. *He* can't stop a demon." The pixy got in the elf's face. "Or do you have some *special talent* we aren't aware of?"

Tired, I looked at Trent. The young man frowned. "He can come to the front gate, and that's it," he said. With a smooth grace, he turned and started down the stairs.

"Front gate, my dragonfly's green turds," Jenks muttered.

Worry tightened my chest, and my gaze went to Ivy standing alone with her arms over her middle just inside the door. God, I was so stupid, running off to Trent's stronghold to sit with a dying man. But the guilt, and maybe curiosity, were stronger than my fear.

"You know I want to go," she said, and I nodded. Quen had been bitten by a vampire and had an unbound scar. To ask him to overlook Ivy's presence wasn't going to happen.

"I'll call you when I know something," I said. I hesitated before her, not knowing what else to say, and when Jenks landed on my earring, I headed down the stairs. Seeing me going to the carport, Trent rolled down his window and called, "I'll drive you out, Morgan."

"I'm taking my car," I countered, never slowing. "I'm not going to get stuck at your compound with no way home."

"Suit yourself," he said dryly, then rolled the window up. The hazard lights flicked off, and he waited for me.

I looked to Ivy, who was standing beside Jenks's pumpkin. Somewhere between me opening the door to find Trent and me getting to my car, it had gone out. She didn't look happy, but neither did I. "I hope she's okay," I said as I opened my car door.

"I'm more worried about us, Rache," said Jenks.

Getting in, I slammed the door and settled myself. "Tom's a weenie," I said softly. "He's not going to call Al."

Jenks's wings cooled my neck. "What if someone else does?"

I started the car, the engine rumbling to life with the sound of security. "Thanks, Jenks. I really needed that."

Twenty

The long road just off the interstate to Trent's house/corporate office was busy. The two-lane road wound and twisted its way through a sprawling, planned old-growth forest. Having run for my life through it once with dogs and horses chasing me, it had lost much of its appeal.

The ride out here had been fast and quiet once we got out of the city. Jenks had maintained a pensive silence after I suggested he peacefully stay at the outer gate and meet me inside when he managed to slip the guards. That had been a mere five minutes ago, and I missed the pixy already. Worried, I glanced at my shoulder bag on the seat beside me. I'd leave it open so he could duck in when he showed up. I'd be stupid to think Trent didn't expect Jenks to try to circumvent their security, but it would be one way to prove to Trent he was doing himself a disservice by shunning pixies as security specialists. With Quen dying, he was going to have to come up with something.

Quen is really dying? I thought, feeling guilty for not taking Trent seriously yesterday. *And why does he think it's my fault?*

My gaze dropped to the speedometer, and I tunked it down to keep from running into Trent. And as the multistory, sprawling complex of offices and business research buildings came into view, I slowed to a crawl, surprised.

His visitor lot was crammed and overflowing onto the grass. To one side were several white-painted school buses clashing with the ranks of expensive cars and what was clearly a band's tour bus. I looked at the back of Trent's head in the car ahead of me, disgusted. Quen was dying, and he was having a party?

I slowed further, rolling my window down to hear the chatter, hoping Jenks would swoop in. People in costume were everywhere, their movements fast with excitement as they milled around before heading to the expansive front entryway. Trent's brake lights flashed, and adrenaline surged when I hit my own brakes to avoid rear-ending him. I was ready to lose it when I glimpsed a three-foot-tall ghost darting between cars, a harried woman with a clipboard chasing him or her.

It was Trent's yearly Halloween extravaganza, thrown for the obscenely wealthy to mingle with the tragically unfortunate, hoping to tug at heartstrings and make a bold political statement as much as genuinely help them. I hated election years.

My fingers tightened on the gearshift and I crept forward, watching for both people and a parking spot. I couldn't believe there weren't valets, but apparently part of the fun was pretending you were slumming it.

Trent's arm came out the window to point to a service entrance. It was an excellent idea, and I took the left after him, ignoring the DO NOT ENTER sign. A man in a black suit started jogging across the manicured grass to us, but he drew to a halt and gestured for us to continue when he saw who it was. I wasn't surprised. We'd been waved through several informal checkpoints since passing the main entrance three miles up the road.

My gaze scanned the dark grounds as I followed Trent into his private underground parking area, squinting until my eyes adjusted to the electric lights. Another big man in a suit had come forward with the pace and attitude of someone who knew who we were but had to check anyway. This guy had a gun and a pair of glasses I'd be willing to bet were charmed to see through spells. I rolled my window down to talk to him, but Trent parked his car and got out, drawing the man to him instead.

"Good evening, Eustace," he said, his voice carrying over the sound of our cars with a weary cadence that I'd never heard in him before. "Ms. Morgan wanted to bring her car. Can you find a spot for it, please? We need to get to the private floors as quickly as possible."

The big man bobbed his head. "Yes, Mr. Kalamack. I'll have another driver here for Ms. Morgan's car in a moment."

Trent's heel ground into the grit as he shifted to glance at me. His worry was clear in the bright glare of my headlamps. "Ms. Morgan can drive me to the kitchen entrance and you can park mine now."

"Yes, sir," Eustace said, a hand atop the open car door. "I'll have the staff clear out as many people as they can, but it's going to be difficult to get through unless you want pushers."

"No," Trent said quickly, and I thought I heard frustration in it.

Eustace bobbed his head, and Trent touched his shoulder in parting, surprising me. The large man's motions were quick and efficient as he got in the car and drove away. Trent's head was bowed and his steps slow. I moved my shoulder bag to the back when he got in, surprised and a little uncomfortable when he settled wearily into the leather seats to fill my car with the scent of a woodsy cologne and his shampoo.

"That way," he prompted distantly, and I put the car in gear, jerking us.

Warming from the rough start, I let out the clutch and we started forward. My fingers twitched, and I wondered why I cared if he was honest with his feelings to everyone but me. He wouldn't show me any true warmth or depth of emotion. But Eustace probably hadn't put him in jail.

"Take that left," he directed. "It will bring you up to the back."

"I remember," I said, seeing two men waiting for us outside the kitchen entrance.

Trent checked his watch. "The easiest way in is through the kitchen and the bar. If I'm detained, get to the top floor. It's been cordoned off, so no one should be there. The staff is expecting you and will let you through."

"Okay," I said, feeling my hands start to sweat. I didn't like this. I didn't like this at all. I had been worried about Al trashing a bar. What if he showed up here amid Cincy's finest citizens and its most helpless orphans? I'd be lynched.

"I'd appreciate you waiting for me in the common area upstairs before going in to see Quen," he was saying as I pulled up beside the two guys and put the car into park.

"Sure," I said, very uncomfortable. "Is he going to be okay?"

"No."

The emotion in that single utterance was vast, a glimpse of his true emotions slipping through. He was scared, angry, frustrated . . . and blaming me.

The shadow of one of the waiting men fell over the car, and I jumped when he tapped expectantly at the window. The doors had automatically locked, and I fumbled for the button. The moment they disengaged, Trent's door was opened by a second man whose suit and tie screamed security.

The faint thumping of music echoed in the vast underground garage. The dark carried the scent of damp concrete and the tang of exhaust. My door was opened as well, and my ankles went cold in the new draft. I looked up at the man's stoic face, suddenly unsure. I was being rushed into a situation I didn't have control of, and it made me feel vulnerable in a way I hadn't before. *Shit.*

"Thank you," I said, unbuckling myself and getting out. I grabbed my bag from the back, moving out of the way when a smaller man came from the kitchen and settled himself in my seat. He drove away with an ease that assured me he wasn't going to damage my car, leaving nothing but space between me and Trent, who was deep in conversation with the second man.

Again, I saw him in an unguarded moment, the aide's caring and concern pulling a depth of emotion from Trent that I hadn't seen in him before. He was hurting. Deeply.

The two men shook hands, and the security guy took a deferential step back. Trent pushed himself into motion, bothered and hurried as he put a hand on the small of my back and guided me in. The two men stayed outside.

I preceded Trent in. The short aisle opened up to a busy kitchen that had a steamy, fragrant warmth and exotic accents shouted at loud volumes. I could hear the music better, and my step bobbled as I recognized Takata's singing.

Takata is here? I thought in delight when I remembered the tour bus, then quashed it. I was here for Quen, not to be a fawning groupie.

Trent's presence was quickly noted by the kitchen staff, each and every one of them meeting Trent's eyes with an understanding that bit deep, making me almost angry that they cared so much for him. Then I quashed that, too. No one stopped us, and it wasn't until we came out into the extravagant bar tucked under the second floor that we saw the first guest.

"Here we go, Ms. Morgan," Trent said, the professional, congenial air of a host coming over him. "Get upstairs and wait."

I faltered when the heat of the room hit me, the music pounding my insides. "No problem," I said, not sure he heard me. Suddenly I felt vastly underdressed. Hell, even the woman dressed down as a hobo had diamonds on.

One of the bartenders intervened when the first guest approached, and we lost our security escort at the next. News of Trent's arrival went out like a wake, and a ribbon of panic pulled through me. How did he deal with this? So many people wanting his attention, demanding it.

Trent himself begged off from the third guest, promising to

come back as soon as he could. But the slight pause had been his downfall, and the surrounding people in costume closed in like banshees over a wailing infant.

The professional politician hid his annoyance with a grace I had a hard time seeing through. An eight-year-old boy pushed his way through the knees, clamoring for Uncle Kalamack. And at that, Trent seemed to give up. "Gerald," he said to the security escort who had gotten to us too late. "If you would escort Ms. Morgan upstairs?"

I looked up at Gerald, desperate for a way out of the swirling, excited mass of people.

"This way, ma'am," he said, and I gratefully sidled closer, wanting to take his sleeve but afraid to look foolish. Gerald looked nervous, too, and I wondered if it was because of the people he had to politely find a way through or because he'd been told I dealt in demons and one might be crashing the party looking for me.

The music ended, and the first floor exploded into cheers. Takata's gravelly voice echoed over it all with the expected "Thank you," which only made them yell louder. My ears hurt, and when Gerald fell into step behind an hors d'oeuvres lady, I gave up and put my hand on his back. So I looked foolish. Gerald was hotfooting it to the stairs, and if I got separated, I might not get there by myself.

We reached the stairs as the band began a new piece. The amps shook the air, and from the bottom step, I finally caught sight of the band. Takata bounced over the stage as he played his five-string bass, long blond hair caught back in dreadlocks. Expending energy faster than a chipmunk on Brimstone, he pounded the music out, sporting an old-rocker/punk look that only someone very cool could pull off in their midfifties.

My gaze shifted to Trent. He was smiling warmly, his arm around that kid, who was now standing on the arm of a chair so he wouldn't get trampled. Trent was trying to move forward, doing a good job of covering his sorrow and frustration. I could see it, though, in his stance. He wanted to be somewhere else, and a glimmer of his impatience showed when he lifted the child and set him in someone's arms, moving forward all of three steps before he was caught again.

"What a pain in the ass," I whispered, my voice lost in the thundering music. No wonder Trent hid in his forest most of the time.

"Ma'am?" It was Gerald, and he held the velveteen rope aside for me.

Feeling out of place in my jeans and top, I started up, holding the rail since I couldn't take my eyes off the room. It was astounding. Trent's entertaining room was the size of a football field. Well, not really, but the fireplace at the far end was as big as a dump truck. One of those big ones. Takata was on a small stage at the other end with his band, and the dance floor was filled with kids and adults. The ward on the huge opening that looked out onto the deck and pool had been removed, and people moved freely inside and out. Kids were everywhere, running from the hot tub to jump into the big pool and come up shouting from the cold.

I paused at the top of the landing and tried to get Takata to look at me, but he just kept jamming. That never worked except in the movies.

"Please, ma'am," Gerald insisted, and tearing my attention away, I followed him past the second rope and twin security guards into the open walkway that overlooked the party and went on to the cozy living room I knew was ahead.

"If you would, please," Gerald said, his eyes darting from me to the floor. "Stay in Mr. Kalamack's private quarters."

I nodded, and Gerald settled in beside the archway to make sure I didn't wander.

The music wasn't as overpowering up here, and as I went in, I scanned the suite arrangement of four doors opening up onto a sunken lounging pit and a black, wide-screen TV taking up a huge amount of space. Tucked in the back was an open, normal-size kitchen and an informal dining area. Seated at the round table were two people.

My pace bobbled, and stifling a frown, I continued forward. Great. Now I'd have to make nice-nice with two of Trent's *special* friends. Dressed in costume, no less.

Or maybe not, I thought as I got closer. They were both wearing lab coats, and my plastic smile went even more stilted as I realized they were probably Quen's doctors. The younger one had very straight black hair and the tired look of an intern. The other was clearly the superior of the two, older and with the upright posture and stiffness that I'd seen in professionals who thought too much of themselves. I looked closer at the tall woman with her silvered hair back in an ugly bun, then looked again. Apparently Trent had gotten his wish for a ley line witch after all.

"Holy crap," I said. "I thought you were dead."

Dr. Anders stiffened, her face rising to give me a smile utterly lacking in warmth. Glancing at her companion, she shifted her head to get a wisp of her silver hair out of her eyes. She was tall and thin, her narrow face having no makeup or charm spell to make her look younger than she was. She'd probably been born around the turn of the century. Most witches born then were reluctant to show their magic, and that she had become a teacher of it was unusual.

I'd had the distasteful woman for an instructor, twice. The first time she flunked me the first week of class for no good reason, and the second time she threatened to do the same if I didn't take a familiar. She had been a murder suspect I was checking out, and her car had gone over a bridge during the investigation, eliminating her as a suspect. But I'd known she hadn't committed the crimes. Dr. Anders was nasty, but murder wasn't on her syllabus.

Yet seeing her having coffee in Trent's private kitchen, I wondered if she was learning new skills. Apparently Trent had helped her stage her death so the real ley line witch murderer wouldn't target her and she could safely come to work for him.

She reminded me of Jonathan, her disdain for earth magic

as palpable as Jonathan's dislike for me. I ran my gaze over her too-thin form as I neared. It had to be her. Who would want to dress up in costume and pretend to be a woman that plain looking?

"Rachel," the woman said as she turned, her legs crossing now that they were out from under the table. She glanced inquiringly at the heavy-magic detection amulet around my bruised and bitten neck, and my eye twitched when her voice brought back oodles and oodles of good memories of being embarrassed in class.

"How nice to see you doing so well," she continued as her intern glanced between us, weighing our moods. "I understand you managed to break the familiar bond with your boyfriend." She smiled with the warmth of a penguin. "Can I ask how? Another curse, perhaps? Your aura is smutty." She sniffed as if her long nose could smell the blackness on my soul. "What have you been doing to it?"

I stopped three feet back, hip cocked, and imagined how good it would feel to plug my foot in her gut and send her chair crashing back. She had faked her own death, leaving me to try to figure out how to break the bond on my own—the harpy. "The familiar bond broke spontaneously when a demon made me his familiar," I said, hoping to shock her.

The intern gasped, his almond-shaped eyes widening as he sat back in his seat, the tips of his black hair shifting.

Feeling like a smartass, I pulled out a chair and propped my foot on it instead of sitting down. "When the bond didn't work through the lines," I said lightly, enjoying the man's horror, "he forced a tighter connection by making me take some of his aura. That broke the original bond with Nick. It also made him my familiar. He didn't expect that."

"You have a demon for a familiar?" The young man stammered, and Dr. Anders gave him a look to tell him to shut up.

I was tired of this, and as Takata shifted to one of his few ballads, I shook my head. "No. We agreed that because the familiar bonds were unenforceable, so was the deal. I'm no one's familiar but my own."

Dr. Anders's expression changed, her long face becoming greedy. "Tell me how," she demanded as she leaned forward slightly. "I've read about this. You can spindle line energy in your thoughts. Can't you?"

I looked at her in disgust. She had belittled and shamed me in front of two entire classes because I had pursued earth magic instead of ley line skills, and she thought I'd tell her how to be her own familiar? "Be careful what you wish for, Dr. Anders," I said dryly, and she pursed her lips sourly at me. I leaned over my bent knee toward her to hammer my words home. "I can't tell you," I said softly. "If I do, I'm his. Just like you belong to Trent, only a lot more honestly."

A faint flush colored her cheeks. "He doesn't own me. I work for him. That's all."

Her intern was looking nervous, and taking my foot from the chair, I stood and rummaged in my bag. "Did he help you fake your death?" I said as I pulled out my cell phone and checked for messages and the time. *Two A.M.—still no demon, still alive.* She said nothing, and flipping through the menu, I made sure my phone was on vibrate before dropping it away and adding my splat gun. "Then you belong to him," I added cruelly, thinking of Keasley and hoping it might be otherwise for him.

But Dr. Anders sat back, snorting through her long nose. "I told you he wasn't murdering the ley line witches."

"He murdered those Weres last June, though."

The older woman dropped her eyes and anger flooded me. She had known. Helped him, maybe. Absolutely disgusted, I shoved the chair in, refusing to sit with her. "Thanks for helping me with my problem," I added bitterly.

My accusation had unbalanced her, and the woman's face reddened in anger. "I couldn't risk breaking my cover by helping you. I had to pretend to die, or I would have died for real.

You are a child, Rachel. Don't even begin to think to lecture me on morality."

I thought I would have enjoyed this more than I was, and in the soft hush of Takata whispering "I loved you best / I loved you best," I said bitingly, "Even a child would have known better than to leave me hanging like that. A letter would have done it. Or a phone call. I wouldn't have told anyone you were alive." I rocked back, my bag held tight to me. "And now you think I'm going to risk my soul to tell you how to spindle line energy?"

She had the grace to look discomforted. Still standing, I crossed my arms and looked at the intern. "How is Quen?" I asked him, but Dr. Anders touched his arm, stopping his words.

"He has an eleven percent chance of seeing the sunrise," she said, glancing to one of the doors. "If he makes it that far, his chances of surviving rise to fifty-fifty."

My knees went weak and I locked them. He had a chance. Trent had let me drive all the way out here thinking his death was inevitable.

"Trent says it's my fault," I said, not caring if she knew by my pale face that I felt guilty. "What happened?"

Dr. Anders looked at me with that cold, reserved expression she saved for her most stupid students. "It wasn't your fault. Quen stole the antidote." Her face twisted in disdain, and she completely missed the guilty look that crossed the intern's face. "Took it from a locked cabinet. It wasn't ready for testing, much less consumption. And he knew it."

Quen had taken something. Something that likely had tampered with his genetic structure or he'd be in a hospital. Fear slid through me as I imagined the horrors that Trent was capable of in his genetic labs, and unable to wait anymore, I turned to the door Dr. Anders had looked at. "He's in there?" I asked, then headed for it, my pace quick and determined.

"Rachel. Wait," Dr. Anders predictably said, and my jaw

clenched. I reached Quen's door and jerked it open. Cooler air slipped out, softer somehow, with a comforting dampness. The lights were dim and the patch of carpet I could see was a soothing mottled green.

Dr. Anders came up behind me, the sound of her steps lost in the noise from the band. I wished Jenks were here to run interference.

"Rachel," the woman demanded in her best instructor voice. "You're to wait for Trent." But I had lost any respect I might have had for her, and what she said meant nothing.

I jerked to keep from reacting with violence when she grabbed my arm. "Get your hand off of me," I said, my voice low and threatening.

Fear widened her pupils, and suddenly ashen, she let go of me.

From inside the dark room came a raspy, "Morgan. It's about time."

Quen's voice was replaced by a wet cough. It was awful, like the sound of moist cloth tearing. I'd heard it somewhere before, and it sent shivers born in a stifled memory through me. *Damn it back to the Turn, what am I doing here?* Taking a breath, I pushed my fear down. "Excuse me," I said coldly to Dr. Anders as I went in. But she followed, closing the door to shut out most of the music. I didn't care as long as she left me alone.

My tension eased as I took in Quen's shadowy suite. It felt good here, with low ceilings and deep colors. The few pieces of furniture were spaced to leave lots of room. Everything was set up for the comfort of one person, not two. It had an inner-sanctum feel that quieted my thoughts and soothed my soul. There was a sliding glass door looking out onto a mossy stone courtyard, and unlike most of the windows in Trent's fortress, I'd be willing to bet this one was real and not a vid window.

Quen's breathing drew me to a narrow bed in a sunken part

of the expansive room. His eyes focused on me, clearly seeing my approval of his private rooms and appreciating it. "What took you so long?" he said, his words pronounced carefully so he wouldn't start coughing. "It's almost two."

My heart sped up, and I came forward. "There's a party going on. You know I can't resist a party," I quipped, and he snorted, wincing as he worked to keep his breathing even.

Guilt was heavy on me. Trent said this was my fault. Dr. Anders said it wasn't. Hiding my tension behind a false smile, I took the three steps down into the sunken area. It put him below the level of the floor, and I wondered if it was a security precaution or an elf thing. There was a comfortable leather wing chair that had clearly been pulled from a different part of the house, and an end table holding a worn leather journal with no name. I put my bag on the chair, but I didn't feel right sitting.

Quen was struggling to keep from coughing, and I looked away to give him some privacy. There were several hospital-like carts set to the side, and an IV. The IV was the only thing hooked up to him, and I appreciated the lack of the obnoxious beeping of a heart monitor.

Finally Quen's breathing evened out. Braver, I hesitantly sat on the front of the chair with my bag behind me. Dr. Anders hovered on the main level, unwilling to break the mental barrier of the stairs and join us. I solemnly looked at Quen, gauging the marks his struggle had put on him.

His usually dark complexion was pale and wan, and the pox scars the Turn had given him looked stark red, almost as if they were active. Sweat had tangled his dark hair, and lines creased his brow. His green eyes were glinting, brilliant with a fierce passion that twisted my gut. I'd seen that glitter before. It was the look of someone who was seeing around the corners of time to his own death, but he was going to fight it all the same. *Damn it. Damn it all to hell.*

I settled myself, not yet willing to take his small but muscular hand, which lay on the gray cotton sheets. "You look like crap," I finally said, bringing a pained smile to his face. "What did you do? Tangle with a demon? Did you win?" I was trying for levity . . . and failing.

Quen took two slow breaths. "Get out, witch," he said clearly, and I flushed, almost standing before I realized he was talking to Dr. Anders.

Dr. Anders knew who he was talking to, though, and she came forward to look down at us. "Trent wouldn't want you alone—"

"I'm not alone," he said, his voice gaining strength as he used it.

"He wouldn't want you alone with *her,*" she finished, loathing heavy in her words. It was an ugly, ugly sound, and I could tell it bothered Quen.

"Get—out," he said softly, angry that his illness had given her the idea she could assert her will over his. "I asked Morgan here because I don't want the person who sees me take my last breath to be a stinking bureaucrat or doctor. I gave an oath to Trent, and I won't break that. Get out!" A cough took him, the sound, like tearing fabric, slicing through me.

I turned in my chair, gesturing for her to get her ass out of here—she was making things worse, not better—and she backed to the shadows. Stiff and angry, she leaned against a dresser with her arms crossed. I could see her frown even in the dark. The mirror showed her back, making it look like there were two of her. Someone had draped a bit of ribbon over the top to drape down in a smooth arc over the glass, and I realized Ceri had been here before she had gone to pray. *She had gone to pray—walked all the way to the basilica to do it—and I hadn't taken this seriously.*

The distance Dr. Anders put between us seemed to satisfy Quen, and his clenched body slowly relaxed as the jerks of his coughing eased and stopped. I felt helpless, and tension drew my back into an ache. *Why does he want me here seeing this?*

"Gee, Quen, I didn't know you cared," I said, and he smiled, making his stress wrinkles all fold in together.

"I don't. But I meant it about the bureaucrats." He stared at the ceiling, taking three careful, rattling breaths. My panic stirred, settling in a familiar place in my soul. *I've heard this sound before.*

His eyes closed, and I jerked forward. "Quen!" I shouted, then felt stupid when his lids flew open and focused on me with an eerie intensity.

"Just resting my eyes," he said, amused by my fear. "I have a few hours. I can feel things faltering, and I have at least that long." His gaze lingered on my neck, then rose. "Having trouble with your roommate?"

I refused to cover my bites, but it was hard. "Wake-up call," I said. "Sometimes it takes a two-by-four across your head to realize what you want isn't what you'll end up with if you get it."

His head barely shifted. "Good." He took a slow breath. "You're a safer person to be around now. Very good."

Dr. Anders shifted position to remind me she was listening. Frustrated, I leaned closer until the new skin on my bites pulled, smelling pine and sun under the medicinal smells of alcohol and adhesive tape. I glanced at Dr. Anders, then asked him, "Why am I here?"

Quen's eyes opened wider and he turned his head to see me, hesitating as he stifled the urge to cough. "Not 'What did you do to get like this'?" he asked.

I shrugged. "I already asked that, and you got all nasty, so I thought I'd go with something else."

Closing his eyes again, Quen simply breathed, slow and labored. "I already told you why I asked you here."

The bureaucrat thing? "Okay," I said, wanting to take his hand to give him strength, but I felt funny about it, as if he would think I pitied him. That would just tick him off. "Then tell me what you did to yourself."

He took a ragged breath, then held it. "Something I had to," he said on the exhale.

Nice. Just peachy. "So I'm just here to hold your hand while you die?" I said, frustrated.

"Something like that."

I looked at his hand, not ready to take it. Awkwardly I scooted closer, the chair bumping over the low wooden mat. "Least you have good music," I muttered, and the creases in his face eased slightly.

"You like Takata?" he said.

"What's not to like?" Jaw clenched, I listened to Quen breathe. It sounded wet, like he was drowning. Agitated, I looked at his hand, then the journal on the bedside. "Should I read something?" I asked, wanting to know why I was here. I couldn't just up and leave. Why in *hell* was Quen doing this to me?

Quen started to chuckle, cutting it short to take three slow breaths until they evened out again. "No. You've watched death come slowly before, haven't you."

Thoughts of my dad surfaced, the cold hospital room and his thin, pale hand in mine as he fought for breath, his body not as strong as his will. Then Peter as he gasped his last, his body shuddering in my arms as it finally gave up and freed his soul. Tears pricked and a familiar grief stained my thoughts, and I knew I'd done the same with Kisten, too, though I didn't remember it. *Damn it back to the Turn.* "Once or twice," I said.

His eyes met mine, riveting in their gleam. "I won't apologize for being selfish."

"I'm not worried about that." I really wanted to know why he'd asked me here if he didn't want to tell me anything. *No*, I thought abruptly, feeling my face lose all expression. *It's not that he doesn't want to tell me something but that he promised Trent he wouldn't.*

Stiffening on the cool leather chair, I leaned forward. Quen sharpened the focus of his gaze, as if he recognized I'd figured it out. Fully aware of Dr. Anders behind me, I mouthed, "What is it?"

But Quen only smiled. "You're thinking," he said, almost breathing it. "Good." His smile softened his pained features, making him look almost fatherly. "I can't. I promised my Sa'han," he said, and I pushed myself into the back of the chair, disgusted and feeling the bump of my bag behind me. Stupid elf morals. He could kill a person, but he couldn't break his word.

"I have to ask the right question?" I said, and he shook his head.

"There is no question. There is only what you see."

Oh, God. Wise-old-man crap. I hated it when they did that. But I tensed when Quen's breathing became labored over the sound of the faint music. My pulse quickened, and I looked at the hospital equipment, silent and dark. "You need to be quiet for a while," I said, agitated. "You're wasting your strength."

A shadow against the gray of the sheets, Quen held himself still, concentrating on keeping his lungs moving. "Thanks for coming," he said, his gravelly voice thin. "I probably won't last long, and I appreciate you dealing with Trenton trying to cope afterward. He's having a hard . . . time."

"No problem." I reached out and felt his forehead. It was hot, but I wasn't going to offer him the sippy-straw cup on the table unless he asked. He had his pride. His pox scars stood out, and I did take the antiseptic wipe that Dr. Anders silently gave me, dabbing his forehead and neck until he scowled.

"Rachel," he said, pushing my hand away, "since you're here, I want to ask you a favor."

"What?" I asked, then turned to the door as the music rose when Trent entered. Dr. Anders went to tattle on me, and the music faded as the door shut and the light vanished.

Quen's eye twitched, telling me he knew Trent was here. He took a careful breath, then, softly so he wouldn't cough, he said, "If I fail, will you take my position as head of security?"

My jaw dropped, and I pulled away. "Oh, hell no," I said, and Quen's smile widened even as his eyes shut to hide that unsettling seeing-around-corners glint.

Trent came up beside me. I could sense his irritation at me for not waiting for him, and under that, his gratitude that someone, even if it was me, had been with Quen.

"I didn't think you would," Quen said. "But I had to ask." His eyes opened to fix on Trent beside me. "I had someone else lined up if you said no. Can I at least get you to promise to help him when he needs it?"

Trent shifted from foot to foot as his tension looked for an outlet. I went to say no, and Quen added, "From time to time, if the money is right and it doesn't compromise your morals."

The scent of silk and other people's perfume grew stronger as Trent became more upset. I glanced at his frustrated worry, then back to Quen struggling to take another breath. "I'll think about it," I said. "But I'm just as likely to haul his ass in."

Quen's eyes closed in acknowledgment and his hand rolled palm-up in invitation. My eyes pricked again. *Shit. Shit. Shit.* He was slipping. His need for support had surmounted his pride. I hated this. I hated it!

Hand shaking, I slipped my warm fingers into his cool grip, feeling his fingers tighten about mine. My throat closed, and I angrily wiped at my eye. *Damn* it all to hell.

Quen's posture eased, and his breathing evened out. It was the oldest magic in the universe, the magic of compassion.

Dr. Anders began to pace from the window to the dresser. "It wasn't ready," she muttered. "I told him it wasn't ready. The blending had only a thirty percent success rate, and the linkages were weak at best. This wasn't my fault! He should have waited!"

Quen squeezed my hand, and his face crinkled in what I recognized as a smile. He thought she was funny.

Trent left the sunken area, and I relaxed. "No one is blaming you," Trent said, a hand on her arm in solace. He hesitated, then said without emotion, "Why don't you wait outside."

Surprised, I turned to see her indignant shock. "Oh, she's pissed," I whispered so Quen would know, getting my fingers squeezed in return. But I think she heard me, too, since she stared at me with a prune face for an entire three seconds, fumbling for words before she turned on a heel. Pace stiff, she went to the door. There was a flush of drums and light, then the soft smothering of darkness returned. Takata's base thrummed through it like a pulse.

Trent stepped into the lowered pit of Quen's bedroom. In a fast motion of anger, he shoved a piece of expensive equipment off a low cart. The noise of it hitting the floor shocked me as much as his unexpected show of frustrated anger, and I stared as he sat down where it had been to put his elbows on his knees and drop his head into his cupped hands. Trent had once sat and watched his father die, too.

I felt my face blank as I saw him raw and stripped down to the pain in his soul. He was young, afraid, and watching yet another person who had raised him dying. All his power, wealth, privilege, and illegal bio labs couldn't stop it. He wasn't used to being helpless, and it tore at him.

Quen's eyes had opened at the crash, and I found them waiting for me when I turned to him. "This is why you're here," he said, confusing me. Quen's attention slid to Trent, then back to me. "Trent's a good man," he said as if he wasn't sitting right there. "But he's a businessman, living and dying by numbers and percentages. He's got me in the ground already. Fighting this with him is a losing battle. You believe in the eleven percent, Rachel." He took an arduous breath, his lungs moving in an exaggerated motion. "I need that."

The long speech had winded him, and as he labored to catch his breath in wet inhalations, I held his hand tighter, remembering my father. My jaw gritted and my throat closed as I heard the truth in his words. "Not this time, Quen," I said, feeling a headache start and forcing my grip to ease. "I'm not going to sit here and watch you die. All you have to do is see the sunrise, and you're home free."

It was what Dr. Anders had said, and unlike Trent, I saw it as a real possibility. Hell, I didn't believe in the eleven percent, I *lived* on it.

Trent was staring in horror at us as it sunk in. He wasn't capable of living any other way than by his graphs and predictions.

"It's not your fault, Sa'han," Quen said, his gravelly voice carrying a softer pain. "It's a mind-set, and I need her. Because as much as it looks otherwise . . . I want to live."

His face riven, Trent stood. I watched him rise out of the sunken area and walk away, pitying him. I could help Quen—he could not. The door opened and shut, letting in a sliver of life before the uncertain darkness that hid the future cocooned us again in a waiting warmth and smothering stillness. Waiting.

We were alone. I looked at Quen's dark hand in mine and saw the strength in it. The coming battle would be fought by both the mind and the body, but it was the soul where the balance lay. "You took something," I said, my heart pounding at the chance that he might actually talk to me. "Something Dr. Anders was working on. Was it genetic? Why?"

Quen's eyes were bright, still seeing around corners. Taking a breath that it hurt to hear, he blinked at me, refusing to answer.

Frustrated, I took his grip more firmly. "Fine, you son of a bitch," I swore. "I'll hold your stupid-ass hand, but you're not going to die." *God, give us the eleven percent. Please? Just this once?* I hadn't been able to save my dad. I hadn't been able to save Peter. I hadn't been able to save Kisten, and the guilt of his dying to keep me alive was enough to bring me sobbing to my knees.

Not this time. Not this man.

"It doesn't matter if I live or die," he rasped. "But seeing me through this is the only . . . way you'll find . . . the truth," he rasped, his body clenching in pain. It was getting worse. His bird-bright eyes fixed on mine, and the hurt in him was obvious. "How bad do you want to know?" he taunted as the sweat beaded on his forehead.

"Bastard," I almost snarled as I dabbed it away, and he smiled through the pain. "You son of a bitch bastard."

Twenty-one

My lower back hurt, and my arms. They were crossed to serve as a pillow as I lay slumped forward in my chair with my upper body draped on Quen's bed. I was just resting my eyes while Quen had another span of time where he could breathe without my encouragement. It was late, and so very, very quiet.

Quiet? Adrenaline pulsed through me and I jerked upright. I'd fallen asleep. *Damn it!* I thought in panic, my gaze going to Quen. His horrible tearing breaths had ceased, and guilt twisted in me as I thought he had died while I slept—until I realized he didn't have the waxy hue of the dead, but a soft color.

He's still alive, I thought with relief, reaching to shake him back into breathing as I had numerous times that night. The cessation of his labored breathing must have woken me.

But my outstretched hand stopped and tears threatened when I saw his chest rise and fall in an easy motion. Slumping back into the leather wing-back chair, I sent my attention to the wide sliding door that led to the patio. The moss and stones, hazy with the reflected sunlight, grew blurry. It was morning, and damn it all to hell, he was going to make it. Eleven percent chance my ass. He had done it. If he had crossed the eleven percent barrier, fifty was nothing.

Sniffing, I wiped my eyes. There was the softest rattle in

Quen's breathing, and his sheets were sweat soaked. His black hair was stuck to his skull and he looked dehydrated despite the IV, wan with stress wrinkles, making him appear old. But he was alive.

"I hope it was worth it, Quen," I whispered, still not knowing what he had done to himself or why Trent blamed me. I fumbled in my bag for a tissue, forced to use a nasty one with lint all over it. Jenks hadn't shown up, and I hoped he was okay. There was absolutely no sound anywhere. The thump of the music was gone, and I could feel the peace that had settled over Trent's compound. By the light coming from the patio, it looked a shade after sunrise. I had to stop waking up at this hour. It was just insane.

Dropping the tissue in the trash, I carefully scooted my chair from Quen's bed. The soft sound of the legs bumping against my discarded shoes seemed loud, but Quen remained unmoving. His night had been an ugly, painful ordeal.

I was cold, and with my arms wrapped about myself, I tottered out of the sunken pit and headed for the light. The outside pulled at me. I took a last look at Quen to assure myself that he was breathing and then carefully unlocked the patio door and pushed it aside with a swoosh of sound.

Birdsong filtered in, and the cold sharpness of frost. The clean scent filled my lungs to instantly wash out the warmth and darkness of the room behind me. A second look back, and I stepped outside only to jerk to a surprised halt when I ran into the spider-web touch of sticky silk. Disgusted, I waved my arms to clear the doorway of the delicate but effective pixy and fairy deterrent.

"Sticky silk," I muttered as I brushed it from my hair. I thought Trent should get over his pixy paranoia and admit he had an eerie attraction to them, like every other pure-blood elf I'd met. So he liked pixies. I liked double-crunch ice cream, but you didn't see me avoiding it in the grocery store. My thoughts drifted to Bis in the belfry and being able to hear and feel the city's ley lines when he touched me. No, that wasn't the same at all.

Arms wrapped about me in the chill, I watched the steam from my breath catch the sun. The light felt thin and the sky looked transparent. I could smell coffee somewhere, and I gingerly rubbed the soft beginnings of scarring on my neck. My hand dropping, I breathed deep and pressed my feet into the rough stone the patio was tiled with. Dampness soaked my socks, but I didn't care. Last night had been awful. The stuff of nightmares and torture.

I honestly hadn't expected Quen to survive. I still didn't believe he had. After the third time Dr. Anders had stuck her long nose in, I had escorted her out with a twisted arm, telling her if she came back, I was going to break her toes off and jam them up her ass. Quen had gotten a kick out of that. It had kept him fighting for about a half hour. After that, it got really bad.

My eyes closed, and I felt a prickling in my nose from the hint of tears. He had suffered longer and harder than anyone I'd ever seen, endured more than I'd thought possible. He hadn't wanted to give in, but the pain and fatigue had been so great . . . I shamed him into taking just one more breath, bullied him, coaxed him. Anything to keep him alive and tortured though his muscles ached and each breath tore my soul as it tore his body. I reminded him to breathe when he forgot or pretended to forget, disgracing his honor until he took one more. Then another, and another—enduring the torment and shunning the peace that death offered.

My stomach hurt, and my eyes opened. Quen would hate me. The things I said . . . Hatred had kept him alive. No wonder he hadn't wanted Trent in the room. Quen could hate me if he wanted, but somehow . . . I didn't think he would. He wasn't stupid. If I had truly hated him and meant what I'd said, I could have walked out of the room and let him die.

Focus blurry, I stared at the canopy of bare branches above

me to the pale blue of an autumn morning. Though Quen had suffered and won, I was still feeling an inner pain, made worse by my utter exhaustion, both physical and mental. My dad had died the same way when I had been thirteen, and I recognized an ugly ember of anger growing in me that my dad had given up while Quen hadn't. But then the anger shifted to guilt. I had tried to keep my dad alive and failed; what kind of a daughter can keep a stranger alive and not be able to save her own dad?

Watching Quen struggle had brought back every little detail of holding my dad's hand as he died. The same pain, the same labored breathing . . . the same everything.

I blinked, and my focus on the trees cleared in a sudden crystalline thought. *My dad had died* exactly *the same way. I was there. I saw it.*

Socks catching on the rough stone, I turned to the dark room past the open door. Quen had said it didn't matter if he lived or died, but to find the truth, I had to see him through it. He wouldn't break his word by telling me why my dad had died, but he had showed me the connection by forcing me to endure his struggle with him.

The blood drained from my face, and I went colder still. Dr. Anders hadn't concocted whatever Quen had taken, but I'd be willing to wager she'd been modifying it so it would work better. And my dad had died from an earlier version of it.

As if in a dream, I walked from the luminous morning and slipped back into the cocooning warmth of shadow. I left the door open so Quen's unconscious would hear the birds and know he was alive. He didn't need me anymore, and he had shown me what he intended to. What Trent had forbade him to say.

"Thank you, Quen," I whispered as I passed the bed, my pace never slowing. Trent. Where was Trent? He had to know. Trent's father had died first, so whatever had killed my dad, it had been Trent who made the decision to administer it.

Tense, I opened the door and heard the murmur of distant

voices. The common area was empty but for the intern on the couch, his mouth hanging open as he snored. Silent in my socks, I went to the walkway and looked down on the great room.

The comforting sound of conversation and sporadic clinks drew my attention to the stage. It was empty but for the band roadies packing up, doing more talking than anything else. The morning sun lit the aftermath of the party with its scattered glasses, crumb-smeared plates, crumpled cocktail napkins, and decorations in orange and red. The ward on the window was back up, shimmering faintly, and in the far corner by the window, I found Trent.

He was sitting in silent vigil, still wearing the baggy clothes he'd had on last night. I remembered that the big leather chair and small round table beside it was his spot, near the huge fireplace and set where he could see the waterfall that burbled down the cliffs and encircled his backyard pool and deck. Though the rest of the room was a mess, the five-by-eight area he was in was clean and vacuumed. A cup of something steamed beside him.

My chest clenched. Grip loose on the rail, I took the stairs fast in my socks, bent on finding out what he had given my dad that killed him—and why.

"Trent."

The man jerked, pulling his attention from where he had been watching the water ripple on his pool. I wove through the couches and chairs, ignoring the smell of spilled alcohol and hors d'oeuvres crushed into the carpet. Alarm cascaded over Trent as he straightened. Fear almost. But he wasn't afraid of me. He was afraid of what I would say.

Breathless, I came to a stop before him. His face showed no emotion, but his eyes were haunted with a horrible question. Pulse fast, I tucked a strand of hair behind my ear and took my hand off my hip. "What did you give my dad?" I said, hearing my voice as if from outside my head. "What did he die from?"

"Excuse me?"

Anger burst from nowhere. I'd suffered last night, reliving my dad's death and helping Quen survive. "What did my dad die from!" I shouted, and the soft conversation at the stage hesitated. "My dad died from the same thing Quen suffered from, and don't *you* expect me to believe that they aren't connected. What did you give him?"

Trent's eyes closed, his lashes fluttering against skin that was suddenly very white. He slowly leaned back in his chair, placing his hands carefully on his knees. The sun turned his hair translucent, and I could see the ambient heat making it float. I was so frustrated and full of conflicting emotions, I wanted to shake him.

I took a step forward, and his eyes flashed open to take in my clenched jaw and disheveled appearance. His face was empty of emotion, almost scaring me. He gestured for me to take the seat across from him, but I folded my arms over my chest and waited.

"Quen took an experimental genetic treatment to block the vampire virus," he said, his voice flat, its usual grace and subtle flavors lost in the tight grip he had on his emotions. "It makes it permanently dormant." His gaze met mine. "We've tried several ways to mask the virus's expression," he added tiredly, "and though they work, the body violently rejects them. It's the secondary treatment to trick the body into accepting the original modification that your father died from."

I softly bit the scar inside my lip, feeling anew the fear of being bound. I had those same vampire compounds sunk deep into my tissue. Ivy protected me from casual predation. Quen's scar had been tuned to Piscary, and since poaching would lead to a nasty second death simply on principle, Quen had been safe from all but the master vampire. Piscary's death effectively turned Quen's bound scar into an unclaimed scar that any vampire, dead or undead, could play upon with impunity. The risk must have become intolerable for him. He could no longer protect Trent in anything but an administrative way.

Quen took the eleven percent chance, preferring that to a desk job that would slowly kill him. *And since Quen had been bitten while saving my butt, Trent blamed me.*

I sank to sit on the edge of the seat as the lack of food hit me. "You can get rid of the vampire virus?" I said, hope striking me, quickly followed by alarm. Ivy was looking for this. She might risk an eleven percent chance to be free of it. *Not her. I can't do this with her. I know I couldn't survive it again. Not after watching Quen suffer.*

Trent's lips pressed together. It was the first show of emotion he'd let slip through. "I never said it got rid of the virus. I said it masks its expression. Makes it dormant. And it works only in still-living tissue. Once you're dead, it doesn't work anymore."

So even if Ivy took it, it wouldn't eliminate the virus and she would become an undead upon dying. It wasn't a cure for Ivy, and a knot of worry eased. But still . . . Why had my dad risked it?

The leather chair was cold, and I couldn't seem to think, my brain fuzzy from the early hour and too little sleep. My dad had been bitten by Piscary. Was that it?

My head came back up to find Trent staring at nothing, his hands clenched with a white-knuckled strength. "Piscary bound him? My dad?"

"The records don't say," he said softly, not paying attention.

"You don't know?" I exclaimed, and his focus sharpened on me, almost as if he was irritated. "You were there!"

"It wasn't an issue at the time," he said, angry.

Why the blue blazes wouldn't it be an issue?

Pursing my lips, I felt my own anger tighten until I thought I would scream. "Then why did he do it?" I said from between clenched teeth. "Why did he risk it? Even if he had been bound to Piscary, he could have just quit the I.S.," I said, gesturing at nothing. "Or been transferred to another part of the country." People were occasionally bound by accident, and when the cover-up failed, there were ways to avoid being sued. It happened to I.S. employees just like everyone else, and there were options involving large sums of money and generous moving packages.

Trent wasn't saying anything. This was like playing twenty questions with a dog. "He knew the risk, and he took it anyway?" I prompted, and Trent sighed.

His hands unclenched, and he flexed them, gazing at the stark white pressure points standing in contrast to the red. "My father risked immediate treatment because being bound to Piscary compromised his position as . . ." He hesitated, his angular face twisting in an old anger. "It compromised his political power. Your father begged me to let him do the same, not for power but for you, your brother, and your mother."

I stared at Trent as his words and face became harsh.

"My father risked his life to maintain power," he said bitterly. "Your dad did it for love."

It still didn't explain why, though. The jealousy in Trent's gaze gave me pause, and I watched him stare into the garden his parents had created, lost in memory. "At least your father waited until he knew there was no other option," he said. "Waited until he was sure."

His voice was breathy, trailing off into nothing. Tense, I asked, "Sure of what?"

In a soft rustling of silk and linen, Trent turned. His youthful face was hard with hatred. Both our dads had died, but he was clearly jealous that mine had risked death for love. His jaw clenched, and apparently intending to hurt me, he said, "He waited until he was sure that Piscary had infected him with enough virus to turn him."

I took a breath and held it. Confusion blanked my thoughts. "But witches can't be turned," I said, nauseated. "Just like elves."

Trent sneered at me, acting for once as he wanted instead of hiding behind the facade he comforted himself with. "No," he said nastily. "They can't."

"But . . ." My knees went watery, and I couldn't seem to get enough air. My mind shot back to my mother's old complaint of no more children between her and my dad. I had thought she had meant because of my discovered genetic blood disease, but now . . . And her free-thinking advice about marrying for love and having children with the right man. Had she meant marrying whom you loved and having children with someone else? The age-old practice of witches borrowing their best friend's brother or husband for a night to engender a child when they married outside their species? And what of the lovingly retold story of her invoking all my dad's charms for him in college in exchange for him working all her circles. Witches couldn't be turned. That meant . . .

I reached for the arm of the chair, my head spinning as I forgot to breathe. *My dad wasn't a witch? Just who had my mother been sleeping with?*

My head came up, and I saw Trent's bitter satisfaction that my world was going to be rearranged—and I probably wasn't going to like it.

"He wasn't my dad?" I squeaked, not needing to see his nod. "But he worked at the I.S.!" I exclaimed, scrambling for a way out. He was lying. Trent had to be lying. Jerking me around to see how screwed up he could make me.

"The I.S. was fairly new when your father joined," he said, clearly getting a lot of satisfaction out of this. "They didn't have good records. Your mother?" he said mockingly. "She's an excellent earth witch. She could have taught at the university—gone on to be one of the leading spell developers for the nation— if she hadn't been saddled with children so soon."

My mouth was dry, and I flushed when I remembered her slipping Minias a charm to hide his demon scent. And catching her this week reeking of heavy spell casting, only to have it muted a few hours later. Hell, it had even fooled Jenks.

"You get your earth magic from your mother," Trent said, his words seeming to echo in my head, "your ley line skill from your real father, and your blood disease from them both."

I couldn't move, shaking inside. "The man who raised me was my real dad," I said in a surge of loyalty. "Who . . . ," I began, having to know. "You know who my birth father is. You have to. It's in your records somewhere. Who is he?"

Smiling nastily, Trent eased back into his chair, crossing his knees and setting his hands gracefully in his lap.

Son of a bitch . . .

"Who is my father, you freaking bastard!" I shouted, and the roadies at the far end of the room stopped what they were doing to watch.

"I don't want you to endanger the poor man," he said caustically. "You put everyone around you in jeopardy. And how vain of you to assume he wants you to come looking for him. Some things are forgotten for good reason. Shame, guilt . . . embarrassment."

Infuriated, I stood, not believing this. This was a power play for him. A damned power play and nothing more. He knew I wanted to know, so he wouldn't tell me.

My fingertips were tingling, and unable to stop myself, I reached for him.

Trent moved, scrambling up and behind his chair so fast I almost didn't see. "Touch me," he said grimly, the chair between us, "and I'll have you in an I.S. cell before your head stops spinning."

"Rachel," came a raspy voice from the upper level, and both Trent and I turned.

It was Quen, wrapped in a blanket as if it was a death shroud, the black-haired intern at his side, supporting him. His hair was plastered to his skull with sweat, and I could see him wavering as he stood there. "Don't touch Trenton," he said, his gravelly voice clear in the hush, "or I'm going to have to come down there . . . and smack you around." He was smiling at me, but his face lost its pleasure and gratitude as he turned to Trent. "This is petty of you, Sa'han. Far . . . beneath your dignity . . . and standing," he finished breathily.

I reached out as his knees buckled and the intern sagged under the sudden deadweight.

"My God, Quen," Trent whispered. Shock on his face, he looked at me. "You let me think he was dead!"

My mouth dropped open, and I took a step back. "I, uh . . . I'm sorry," I finally managed, chagrin warming my face. "I never said he was dead. I forgot to tell you he was alive is all. You assumed he was dead."

Trent turned his back on me and started for the stairs. "Jon!" he shouted, taking them two at a time. "He made it! Jon, get out here!"

I stood alone in the middle of the floor; Trent's voice echoed against the silent walls with hope and joy, making me feel like an outsider. A door down the hall thumped open and Jon ran down the open walkway to where the intern was lowering Quen—out cold again—to the floor. Trent had already reached him, and the excitement and caring flowing from them hit me deep.

Not even aware I was there, they carried him back to his room and the comfort they shared. I was alone.

I had to get out of here.

My pulse quickened, and I scanned the room, the dregs of the party seeming to soak into me like a stain. I had to leave. I had to talk to my mom.

With single-minded intent, I headed for the kitchen. My car was in the garage, and though my shoulder bag and wallet were upstairs, my keys were likely in the ignition where I'd left them. There was no way I was going up into that room where they were suffused with joy. Not now. Not when I was like this: numb, confused, and mentally slapped by Trent, scorned for not having realized the truth before now. I felt stupid. It had been in front of me all the time, and I hadn't realized it.

The kitchen was a blur, the lights dim and the ovens cold. I hit the heavy service entrance at a run, and the metal door crashed into the wall. Two big guys in tuxes jumped up from the curb at my sudden appearance. Ignoring them, I jogged into the underground lot in search of my car. The cold pavement soaked into me through my socks.

"Miss!" one shouted. "Miss, hold up a moment. I need to talk to you."·

"Like hell you do," I muttered, then spotted Trent's car. Mine was nowhere I could see. I didn't have time for this. I'd take his. Angling to it, I broke into a run.

"Ma'am!" he tried again, his voice dropping in pitch. "I need to know who you are and your clearance. Turn around!"

Clearance? I didn't need no lousy clearance. I jerked the handle up, and the cheerful dinging told me the keys were in the ignition.

"Ma'am!" came an aggressive shout. "I can't let you leave without knowing who you are!"

"That's what I'm trying to find out!" I shouted, cursing myself when I realized I was crying. Damn it, what was wrong with me? Distressed beyond all belief, I slid into the supple leather seat. The engine turned over with a low rumble that spoke of a slumbering power: gas and pistons, a perfect machine. Slamming the door, I put it into drive and floored it. The tires squealed as I jerked forward and took the turn too fast. A square of light beckoned. If they wanted to know who I was, they could ask Trent.

Sniffing, I looked behind me. The big guy had his gun out, but it was aimed at the pavement as the second officer on the two-way relayed orders to him. Either Trent had told them to let me go, or they were going to stop me at the front gate.

I hit the ramp fast, and the undercarriage scraped as I bounced out into the sun. My breath caught in a sob as I wiped my cheeks. I didn't make the next turn properly, and I felt a moment of panic when I drove off the pavement and blasted the DO NOT ENTER sign.

But I was out. I had to talk to my mom, and it was going to take more than two security guards in tuxes to stop me. *Why hadn't she told me?* I thought, my palms sweating and my stomach clenched. Why hadn't my crazy, loony mother told me?

The tires squealed as I took the turns, and once on the three-mile drive out of here, I started to get scared. Was the reason she hadn't told me because she was a little nuts, or was she a little nuts because she was too afraid to tell me?

Twenty-two

The thump of Trent's car door shutting broke the autumn stillness, and the human kids waiting for the bus on the corner turned briefly before going back to their conversations. Someone had smeared a tomato on the street sign and they were giving it a wide berth. My arms wrapped around me against the cold, I tossed the hair from my eyes and headed for my mother's front walk.

The chill from the rough pavement went right through my socks and into me. Driving over without shoes had felt odd, like the pedal was too small. The time spent getting here had cooled me down, too, Trent's comments about shame, guilt, and embarrassment reminding me that I wasn't the only one whose life this touched upon. Actually, I was sort of coming in on the tail end of this drama—an afterthought, an also-ran. I was either the accidental shame of someone's mistake or the result of a planned action whose beginning was covered up.

Neither option left me feeling very good. Especially since my dad had been dead for a long time, leaving plenty of opportunity for the man who'd gotten my mom pregnant to come forward if he wanted. Or maybe it was a one-night fling and he didn't care. Maybe he didn't know. Maybe Mom just wanted to forget.

The kids at the stop had noticed I was in my socks, and I ignored their hoots as I tiptoed up the walk with a hunched posture. The memory of standing at the bus stop rose through my thoughts, of me going in on the same bus that dropped the human kids off. I never understood why my mom had wanted to live in a mostly human community. Maybe it was because my dad had been human, and no one would be as likely to notice he wasn't a witch?

My toes were cold from the melting frost as I reached the porch. Starting to shiver, I rang the bell and heard it chime faintly. Waiting, I looked around, then rang it again. She had to be home; the car was in the drive and it was freaking seven in the morning.

All the kids at the stop were watching me now. "Hey, there's crazy Mrs. Morgan's crazy daughter," I muttered, sliding back the loose piece of siding to get the spare key. "Look, she don't have no shoes! What a skipped track."

But the door wasn't locked, and with a growing sense of unease, I pocketed the key and went in. "Mom?" I called, the warmth of the house obvious on my cheeks.

There was no answer, and I wrinkled my nose. It smelled funny, like burnt metal.

"Mom? It's me," I said, raising my voice and shutting the door hard. "I'm sorry for waking you up again so early. I have to talk to you." I glanced into the empty living room. God, it was quiet in here. "Mom?"

My tension eased when I heard from the kitchen the familiar sound of a plastic photo album page being unstuck. "Oh, Mom," I said softly, and pushed into motion. "Have you been looking at pictures all night again?"

Worried, I strode into the kitchen with my damp socks squeaking against the linoleum. My mom was sitting at the table in a pair of faded jeans and a blue sweater, her hand around an empty coffee cup. Her hair was a comfortable disarray, and the photo album was open to one of our family vacations of sunburned noses and exhausted smiles. She didn't look up as I came in, and seeing one of the stove's burners was roaring full tilt, I quickly went to shut it off, jerking when my foot found an amulet sitting on the floor in the middle of the room.

"Jeez, Mom," I said as I clicked the burner off and felt the heat radiating from the metal rack. "How long have you had this on?" Damn, it was glowing. That's where the hot metal smell was coming from.

She didn't answer, and my brow pinched in concern when I saw the never-used percolator on the counter beside the sink. It was one of those old ones you set atop the stove, and it was the only thing my dad had drunk coffee from. There was an open bag of grounds waiting to be scooped out, and the filters were scattered across the counter.

Double damn, she'd been reminiscing again.

My shoulders slumped, and I picked up the amulet and set it on the table. "Mom," I said, putting a hand on her shoulder to bring her back to reality. "Mom, look at me."

She smiled at me with her green eyes bloodshot and her face blotchy from crying. "Good morning, Rachel," she said lightly, chilling me with how at odds her voice was with her appearance. "You're up early for school. Why don't you go back to bed for a while?"

Shit. This is bad. I'd better call her doctor, I thought, then took a deeper sniff, scenting what the hot metal smell had been covering. My face went cold and I searched her empty expression. It smelled like burnt amber in here.

Alarmed, I looked closer at the amulet I'd picked up, then pulled a chair around so I could sit and see her face-to-face. Al hadn't shown up last night, but what if Tom had sent him . . .

"Mom," I said, scanning her face. "Are you okay?" She blinked at me, and I gave her a little shake, becoming scared. "Mom! Was Al here? Was it a demon?"

She took a breath to say something, then dropped her attention to the photo album and flipped a page.

Fear dove deep, tensing me. Tom wouldn't risk sending Al to me, knowing I could circle him and send him back, so he sent the demon after my mom. *I'm going to kill him. I will freaking kill him.*

"Mom," I said, pushing the album away and closing it. "Was Al here? Did he hurt you?"

My mom focused on me, her gaze clearing for an instant. "No," she said, her voice airy. "Your dad was, though. He says to tell you he said hi. . . ."

Shit, shit, shit . . . Can today get any worse? I looked at the amulet with a new understanding as I recognized it. My mom was never good at making circles, preferring the security of another witch's skills to her own. She had trapped Al with it, or she wouldn't be here. I looked over the room thinking it looked normal, not like the disaster Al usually left in my kitchen.

"Mom," I said, taking her hand off the album and holding it in my lap. "That wasn't Dad." *Whoever Dad was.* "It was a demon disguised as him. Whatever he said to you was a lie. It was a lie, Mom." Her gaze was starting to land on me with some awareness, and both relieved and scared, I asked, "Did he do anything to you? Did he touch you?"

"No," she said, her fingers touching the spent amulet. "No, he didn't. I knew it wasn't really him so I put him in a circle. All night we talked. Talked and talked of before he died."

A chill went through me, and I stifled a shudder.

"We were so happy then. I knew if I didn't keep your demon here, he'd come after you, and I figured you were out having fun. I knew right away it wasn't your dad. Your dad never smiled like that. Cruel and vindictive."

My breath was fast, and I looked at her hands as if they might show a mark from her ordeal. She was okay. Well, she wasn't okay, but she was here and unhurt. At least physically. She had talked to Al all night so he wouldn't come after me. God help her.

"Do you want some coffee?" she said brightly. "I just made some." She looked at her empty mug, clearly clean and never used. Shock flickered over her, then disgust when she saw the percolator and realized the coffee had never gotten made.

"Let's get you to bed," I said. I wanted to ask her about my birth father, but she was scaring the crap out of me. I'd seen it before, but not like this. I had to call her doctor. Find her spells. "Come on, Mom," I said, standing and trying to get her to rise. "It's going to be okay."

She refused to move, and when she started to cry, I got mad at Al. How dare he come into my mom's house and stir her up like this. I should've had her spend the night at the church. I should have done something!

"I miss him so much," she said, the tears in her voice making my throat tighten, and I sank back down. "He loved us all so very deeply."

Reaching out, I held her, thinking life was cruel when the child had to comfort the parent. "It's okay, Mom," I whispered, and her narrow shoulders started to shake. "It's over. The demon did it to hurt you is all. It's over, and he won't do it again. I promise. You can stay with me until they find a way to hold him."

Fear wrapped around my soul and squeezed. I was going to take Al's name to stop this. The other choice was not an option at this point.

"Look," she said around a sniffle, pulling the album to her and opening it up. "Remember this vacation? You got so sunburned you couldn't go on any of the rides. Robbie really didn't mean to hurt your feelings by calling you a crab person."

I tried to close the album, but she wouldn't let me. "Mom, stop looking at these. It just hurts you," I said, then stiffened at the sound of the front door opening.

"Alice?" came a strong, masculine voice, gravelly and resonant, and my heart jumped when I recognized it. "It wasn't me," he pleaded, coming closer. "God, Alice, I didn't tell her. You've got to believe me. It was Trent. And he needs to get his ass out of your house so I can pound him into little pieces of green—"

I stared, my pulse hammering when Takata strode into the room, stiff and angry, his long hands made into fists, his face red, and his dreadlocks swinging. He was in jeans and a black T-shirt that made him look skinny and normal. His words cut off and he jerked to a halt when he saw me holding my mom. His haggard face went ashen, and he said flatly, "That's not your car out there. It's Trent's."

My mother quietly cried, and I took a deep breath. "I couldn't find my car, so I took his." I didn't feel so hot, and swallowing, I remembered his roadies listening to me argue with Trent. And with that, it all fell together.

"You?" I said, my voice a high squeak. There was only one reason he'd have come over here and walk in as if he had a right to. My face flushed, and I would have stood if my mother hadn't clenched her grip on me, keeping me seated. "You!"

Takata's eyes were wide, and he rocked back a step, his long hands up as if in surrender. "I'm sorry. I couldn't tell you. I promised your mother and dad. You don't know how hard it's been."

Hard for you? I stared, horrified and angry. Crap on toast. "Red Ribbons" was about me. My gaze shot to him, reading his guilt. Damn it all to hell, his entire career had been made by putting his fucking feelings of guilt for having abandoned me and my mom out there for everyone to see. "No," I said, moving as my mom rocked back and forth, lost in her personal hell. "You and my mom . . . no!"

My mom started crying in deep racking sobs, and I held her closer, torn between comforting her and shouting at Takata.

"I can't take it anymore," she burbled, trying to wipe her face. "It wasn't supposed to be like this. It wasn't supposed to be like this at all!" she exclaimed, and my grip loosened. "You aren't supposed to be here!" she shouted, standing up out of my arms and looking at Takata. "She's not your daughter. She's Monty's!" she raged, red-rimmed eyes glaring and her hair all over the place. "He gave up everything for her and Robbie when you left to chase your music. Sacrificed his own dreams to support us. You made that choice, and you can't come back. Rachel is not yours! I can't—" Her balance wobbled, and I reached for her. "I want it to stop!" she screamed, and I fell back when she swung blindly at me. "Go away! Go away! Just make it stop!"

Shocked, I backpedaled until I hit the counter, frightened. I didn't know what to do. My mother stood with her arms wrapped around herself and her head down, sobbing, and I was afraid to touch her.

Takata never looked at me. Jaw clenched and eyes bright with unshed tears, he crossed the room and, without hesitation, wrapped his long, wiry arms around her.

"Go away," she sobbed, but he had pinned her arms between them, and it didn't look like she really wanted him to leave.

"Shhhh," he crooned as my mother melted in his embrace, putting her head to his chest and sobbing. "It's okay, Allie. It's going to be okay. Robbie and Rachel belong to Monty. They aren't mine. He's their dad, not me. It's going to be fine."

I stared at his height, measuring it against my own, seeing my tangled curls in his dreadlocks, seeing my lean strength in his limbs. My gaze dropped to his feet in a pair of flip-flops— my feet on someone else's body.

Leaning against the counter, I put a hand to my stomach. I was going to be sick.

"I want you to go," my mom cried, more softly now, and Takata rocked her where they stood.

"You're fine," he soothed, his arms around her but his eyes on me. "It's all going to pass over and nothing will change. Nothing's going to change."

"But he's dead," she wailed. "How could he be here when he was dead?"

Takata's eyes met mine, and I mouthed, "Al." Stark fear melted his expression to one of horror, his attention going to the amulet on the table and then to me. I felt a surge of bitterness. He knew all about me. I knew nothing of him. Son of a bitch.

"Did he touch you?" Takata said, pushing her from him enough so he could see her face. "Alice, did he touch you!"

His voice was high and frightened, and my mom shook her

head, looking where their bodies met. "No," she said, her tone flat. "It wasn't him, and I played along with it until I could get him in a circle. But we talked . . . all night. I had to keep him here so he couldn't hurt Rachel. He wants to use her like a blow-up doll and then give her to someone to pay off a debt."

Oh, this is just what I need.

Tears streaked her face, and Takata pulled her to him again. He loved her. I could see it in his long, expressive face, laced between the heartache. "It's late," he said, his voice starting to crack. "Let me get you to your bed."

"Rachel . . . ," she said, trying to pull from him.

"The sun is up," he said, keeping her from seeing me in the corner. "She's fine. She's probably asleep. You should get some winks, too."

"I don't want to go to bed," she said petulantly, sounding nothing like my mom. "You have to leave. Monty will be home soon, and it hurts him when you come over. He won't admit it, but it does. Robbie is too old for you to see him anymore. He's going to remember you."

"Alice," he whispered, his eyes closed. "Monty is dead. Robbie is in Portland."

"I know." It was a faint, resigned whisper, and I felt ill.

"Come on," he coaxed. "Let me get you in bed. Do it for me. I'll sing you to sleep."

She protested, and he swung her up and into his arms as easily as if she were one of his bass guitars. My mom let her head fall against him, and he turned to me, still plastered into the corner. "Please don't leave," he said softly, then turned and carried her out.

My heart pounded as I stood where I was and listened to their progress through the house, my mom's soft inquiries and his rumbling responses. It grew quiet, and when I heard him singing softly, I staggered to the table, reaching blindly. Numb, I sank into the chair my mother had been sitting in, my head dropping into my hand as my elbow found the table.

I felt sick.

Twenty-three

The acidic scent of tomato soup was comforting, helping to mask the fading smell of hot metal and burnt amber. My stomach rumbled, and I thought it pathetic that I could be hungry when I was so strung out. Course, I hadn't eaten anything last night other than a handful of tiny wieners on sticks and six little squares of cream-topped pumpkin cheesecake.

The soft sound of a wooden spoon thumping the top of a saucepan brought my gaze up from the faded linoleum table, and I watched Takata awkwardly pour the steaming soup into a pair of thin-walled white bowls. He looked funny making dinner—or maybe it was an early breakfast, now—the rock star puttering around in my mother's kitchen, hunting for things in a start-stop motion that told me he had been here before but had never cooked.

My face twisted, and I forced the bitter emotion away. I was sure he had an explanation. The only reason I was sitting here was because I wanted to hear it. That, and because the I.S. was probably looking for Trent's car. And I was exhausted. And he was making food.

Takata's expression was weary as he set a bowl of soup before me, then slid a plate with two pieces of toast beside it. He looked at the amulet I wore to warn me about surprise demon attacks. I thought he was going to say something, but he didn't.

Angry, I took a napkin from the holder on the table. "You know how I like my soup," I said. "With toast." My chin quivered. "You come over here a lot?"

He turned from the stove with his own bowl. "Once a year, maybe. More than that, and she starts leaning on the past too much. She likes to talk about you. She's very proud."

I watched him set his bowl down across from me and sink into the chair, shifting to find a comfortable position on the thin padding. I spared a thought that I could probably chart his visits by his tour dates and her doctor visits.

"Sorry," he said, hesitantly taking a napkin for himself. "I know this isn't much of a dinner, but I don't cook much, and even an idiot can warm up soup."

Ignoring the toast, I tried the soup, and my tension eased as the rich warmth slipped down. He'd mixed it with milk. Just the way I liked it. I glanced up when his pocket started to hum. The tall witch looked discomforted as he pulled a cell phone out and checked the number.

"You have to go?" I said bitingly. I should have just pinned him to the wall and made him talk.

"No. It's Ripley. My drummer." A wan smile curved up his thin lips, making his long face look longer. "She's calling to give me an excuse to leave if I need it."

I took another sip of soup, angry at myself that I was hungry when my life was falling apart. "Must be nice," I muttered.

Giving up on ignoring the toast as a matter of principle, I picked it up and dunked it. So he knew I liked toast with my tomato soup. That didn't mean I shouldn't eat it. Elbows on the table, I looked at him as I chewed. I felt drained, and this was just too weird.

Takata's gaze fell away. "I wanted to tell you," he said, and my heart gave a hard thump. "For a long time. But Robbie left when he found out, and it just about killed your mother. I couldn't dare risk it."

But you could risk having coffee with me ages ago? And you could risk hiring me to work your security last year?

Burying my unreasonable feelings of jealousy, I said, "Robbie knows?"

He looked old all of a sudden, his blue eyes pinched. I wondered whether, if I had kids, they would have green eyes or blue.

"He recognized me at your dad's funeral." Takata grimaced with his attention on his soup. "Our hands are exactly the same. He noticed." Spoon shaking, he took another sip of soup. I silently dunked a corner of my toast.

I felt like such an idiot. God, Takata had asked my opinion of the lyrics of "Red Ribbons" last year, and I hadn't gotten it. He had been trying to tell me, and I had been too dense to see it. But how could I have even guessed? "Who else knows?" I asked somewhat fearfully.

He smiled without showing his teeth, looking almost shy. "I told Ripley. But she has her own past to deal with and she will keep her mouth shut."

"Trent?" I accused.

"Trent knows everything," he muttered. Seeing my unease, he added, "He knows only because his father needed a genetic blueprint to help base your treatment on. Mr. Kalamack could have used Robbie's, but the repair would have been slower and not as perfect. When your dad asked, I said yes. Not just for you, but so Robbie wouldn't have a summer of missing memories."

I made a face, remembering. Or remembering not remembering, maybe.

"So Trent knows I'm your birth father, but not why." Takata leaned into his chair with his tall glass of milk, his long leg hitting the table leg on my side before jerking it back. "It was none of his business," he said defensively.

I couldn't taste my toast anymore, and I set it down. I stared at my soup, took a breath to find my courage, then said softly, "Why?"

"Thank you," Takata whispered.

His eyes were heavy with moisture when I looked, but he

was smiling. He set his glass down and stared out the window at the growing brightness. "Your dad and I met your mother at the university."

I'd heard this before, just not knowing that the other guy had been Takata. "She said she met my dad when she signed up for a ley line class she had no business being in. That she took it to meet the gorgeous hunk of witch in front of her, but ended up falling in love with his best friend."

His smile grew, showing his teeth. "I'd love to know which one of us she considered the hunk of witch."

Confused, I pulled my soup closer. "But my dad, Monty, I mean, was human."

Takata's head was bobbing. "There was a lot more prejudice back then. No, not more, just that no one was as afraid to show it. To avoid getting a lot of flack, he told everyone he was a witch. Until your mother, he would ransack my closet just to smell right."

I thought about that for a moment, then returned to eating.

"Your dad and me?" he continued, his pleasant voice seeming to fill the kitchen and sounding right. "I don't know how we got through those last years without killing each other. We both loved your mother, and she loved both of us." He hesitated, then added, "For different reasons. She thought it was hilarious when her scent charms worked so well that even the instructors couldn't tell he was a human. His ley line skills were more than good enough. It was crazy, the both of us vying for her, and her caught in the middle."

I glanced up and he dropped his eyes.

"But I got her pregnant with Robbie right as my music career started to take off. West Coast take off, not just local stuff. It changed everything." His gaze went unfocused. "It threatened to steal both her and my dreams—what we thought we wanted."

I felt him look at me, and I said nothing, tilting my bowl to get the last of my soup.

"Your dad always blamed me for getting her pregnant when

she could have finished her studies to go on to be one of the premier spell-developers in the state."

"She's that good?" I asked, taking another bite of toast.

Takata smiled. "You won every Halloween contest you ever entered. She continually developed potions to pass the I.S.'s increasingly sensitive detection charms for your dad. She told me once that Jenks thought she was light on the magic, almost a warlock. It wasn't because she was not spelling, but because she was."

My head went up and down, and I wiped the butter off my fingers. Crap, I had forgotten to pick Jenks up at the gate. I hadn't even slowed down long enough for them to get it open. Maybe Ivy would go get him. I wasn't going back there.

"Okay, I got the picture," I said. "I get my earth magic from her. And Trent says you're good at ley lines?"

He shrugged, tossing his head to make his dreadlocks swing. "I used to be. I don't use them much. Least not consciously."

I remembered sitting next to him on the winter solstice and seeing him jump when the circle at Fountain Square closed. Yeah, I probably got my ley line skill from him. "So you got my mom pregnant and decided your dreams were more important than hers and left," I accused.

A deep flush colored his pale complexion. "I asked her to come with me to California," he said, pained. "I promised her we could raise a family and build both our careers at the same time, but she was smarter than me." Takata crossed his arms over his thin chest and shrugged. "She knew something would suffer, and she didn't want me to look back and blame her and the baby for taking my one shot at greatness away."

He sounded bitter, and I picked at what was left of my toast.

"Monty loved her as much as I did. As much as I do," he reiterated. "He wanted to marry her, but he never asked because he knew she wanted children and couldn't give them to her. It made him feel inadequate, especially when I kept reminding him of it," he admitted, tired eyes dropping in old guilt. "So when she wouldn't follow me to California, he asked her to marry him, seeing as she was going to get the child she always wanted."

I watched his face twitch as he relived the memory. "And she said yes," he said softly. "It hurt more than I like to admit—that she stayed with him and that peon I.S. job he took on a dare instead of coming with me and the chance for a big house with a pool and a hot tub. Looking back, I know I had been stupid, but I left thinking I was doing the right thing."

When desire's sold for freedom / and need exchanged for fame / those choices made in ignorance / turn to bloodstained dreams of shame. Son of a bitch.

His gaze flicked to mine and held. "Monty and your mother would be happy. I was going to California with the band. My child would be raised in a loving home. I thought I had cut all the ties. Maybe if I'd never come back it would have been okay, but I did."

I dabbed my finger on the crumbs and ate them. This all felt like a bad dream that had nothing to do with me.

"So I went on to make it big," Takata said with a sigh. "I didn't have a clue how much I had screwed my life up. Not even when your mom flew out to one of the shows one night. She said she wanted another child, and like a stupid ass, I went along with it."

His eyes watched his long hands, carefully arranging the spoon in the bowl. "That was my mistake," he said, more to himself than me. "Robbie had been an accident that your dad stole from me, but I gave him you. And seeing his eager smile when you were put in his arms made me realize how pathetically worthless my life was. Is."

"Your life isn't worthless," I said, not knowing why. "You touch thousands of people with your music."

He smiled bitterly. "What do I have to show for it? Selfishly now, what do I have?" His hands waved in frustration. "A big house? A fancy tour bus? Things. Look at what I could have been doing with my life—all wasted. Look at what your mother and Monty did."

His voice was getting louder, and I looked past him to the empty hall, worried he might wake her up.

"Look at what you are," he said, bringing my attention back. "You and Robbie. You are something real that they can point to and say, 'I helped make that person great. I held that person's hand until they could make it on their own. I did something real and irrefutable.'"

Clearly frustrated, he slumped with his long arms on the table and stared at nothing. "I had the chance to be a part of what life is about, and I *gave it* to someone else, pretending to know about life when all I have is what you can get by looking in other people's windows."

Left looking in the window, red ribbons hide my face. I pushed my plate away, not hungry anymore. "I'm sorry."

Takata met my eyes from under a lowered brow. "Your dad always said I was a selfish bastard. He's right."

I moved the spoon in a figure eight. Not clockwise, not counterclockwise. Balanced and empty of intent. "You give," I said softly. "Just to strangers, afraid that if you give to people you love, they might reject you." My attention came up, pulled by his silence. "It's not too late," I said. "You're only, what, fifty-something? You've got a hundred more years."

"I can't," he said, his expression asking for understanding. "Alice is finally thinking of going back into research and development, and I'm not going to ask her to leave that and start a second family." A sigh shifted his thin shoulders. "It would be too hard."

I looked at him, taking my coffee up but not drinking it. "Hard if she said no, or hard if she said yes?"

His lips parted. He seemed like he wanted to say something but was afraid. Lifting one shoulder and letting it fall, I took a sip and gazed out the window. Memories of struggling to live with Ivy and Jenks lifted through me. Jenks was going to be really ticked I'd forgotten him at Trent's. "Anything worth having is going to be hard," I whispered.

Takata took a long, slow breath. "I thought I was supposed to be the font of philosophical wise-old-man shit here, not you."

He was smiling wanly when I looked at him. I couldn't deal with this right now. Maybe after I had a chance to figure out what it meant. Pushing my chair back, I stood. "Thanks for dinner. I have to go home and get some stuff. Will you stay here until I get back?"

Takata's eyes went wide in question. "What are you doing?"

I set my bowl and plate in the sink before I wadded up my napkin and threw it away. "I have to make up some spells, and I don't want to leave my mom alone, so until she wakes up, I'm going to work here. I need to run back to the church for some stuff. Will you wait until I get back before you leave?" *Can you do that much for me?* I thought bitterly.

"Uh," he stammered, long face empty as he was caught off guard, "I was going to stay until she wakes up so you don't have to come back. But maybe I can help you. I can't cook, but I can chop herbs."

"No." It was a little brusque, and seeing his hurt, I added gently, "I'd rather spell alone, if you don't mind. I'm sorry, Takata."

I couldn't look at him, afraid that he would know *why* I wanted to spell alone. Damn it, I didn't know how to trade summoning names with a demon, but I knew it involved a curse. Takata, though, was wincing for an entirely different reason, apparently.

"Could you call me by my real name?" he asked, surprising me. "It's kind of stupid, but hearing you call me Takata is worse."

I paused at the door. "What is it?"

"Donald."

I almost forgot my misery. "Donald?" I echoed, and he flushed.

He stood, reminding me of how tall he was as he awkwardly tugged his T-shirt down over the top of his jeans. "Rachel, you aren't going to do anything stupid, are you?"

I stopped looking for my shoes when I remembered they were at Trent's. "From your point of view, probably." Al had tortured my mom because of me. There were no marks on her, but the wounds were there in her mind, and she'd taken them for me.

"Wait."

His hand was on my shoulder, and when I stared at him he let go.

"I'm not your dad," he said, gaze lighting on my neck with its bruises and bite marks. "I'm not going to try to be your dad. But I've watched you your entire life, and you do some of the damnedest things."

The feeling of betrayal was rising again. I owed him nothing, and I couldn't see him in my life anywhere. It had been hell growing up having to be strong for my mother because she couldn't handle things. "You don't know me at all," I said, letting a sliver of my anger show.

His brow furrowed, he tried to reach out, then let his hand drop. "I know you will do anything for your friends and those you love, ignoring that you're vulnerable and life is fragile. Don't," he pleaded. "You don't have to take this on all by yourself."

My anger flared, and I tried to rein it in. "I wasn't planning on it," I said bitingly. "I do have resources, friends." My arm came up and I pointed deeper into the unseen house. "But my mother has been tortured for almost thirteen hours because of me, and I'm going to do something about it!" My voice was rising, but I didn't care. "She suffered as that bastard pretended to be my dad. She endured it knowing that if she let him out of that circle or walked away, he might come after me. I can stop him, and I will!"

"Lower your voice," Takata said, and I just about lost it. Jaw clenched, I got in his face.

"My mother isn't going to live her life hiding on hallowed ground because of something I did," I said, more softly now but no less intently. "If I don't do something, next time he might physically hurt her. Or start taking it out on strangers. Or maybe you! Not that I give a flip."

I headed out into the hall. His footsteps were heavy behind me.

"Damn it, Rachel," he was saying. "What makes you think you can kill him when the entire demon society can't?"

I scooped up the keys by the front door where I'd left them, sparing a thought that the I.S. was probably looking for Trent's car by now. "I'm sure they can," I muttered. "I think they simply don't have the guts to do it. And I never said I was going to kill him." No, I was just going to take his name. *God save me.*

"Rachel."

He took my arm, and I halted, looking up his height to find his expression pinched in deep concern. "There's a reason no one hunts demons."

I searched his face, seeing me in it everywhere. "Get out of my way."

His grip tightened. Grabbing his arm, I did a quick ankle tuck and sent him down, resisting the urge to follow it with a fist in his gut—or somewhere a little lower, maybe.

"Ow," he said, his eyes wide as he stared at the ceiling, one hand on his chest as he tried to catch his breath and figure out how he got on the floor.

I looked down at him and his shock. "Are you okay?"

His fingers prodded his lower chest. "Yeah."

He was in my way, and I waited for him to move. "You want to know what it's like to have kids?" I said as he sat up. "Some of it's letting your daughter do stuff you think is stupid, trusting that just because you can't do something doesn't mean she can't. That maybe she's smart enough to get herself out of the trouble she gets herself into."

I felt my focus blur as I realized that's what my mom had done, and though it had been hard and left me knowing more than a thirteen-year-old should, I was better able to handle the bigger dangers my thrill-seeking tendencies got me into.

"I'm sorry," I said as Takata pulled himself backward to lean against the wall. "Will you watch my mom while I take care of this?"

He nodded, his dreadlocks swinging. "You bet."

I glanced past the high window in the door to guess at the time, but at least now I could spell at home. "Get her to my church a few hours before sunset," I said. "If I'm not there, Marshal will be if I can get ahold of him. He's a target now, and you, probably. I'm sorry. I didn't mean to put your life in danger." No wonder he hadn't told me I was his daughter. It wasn't anything that would help extend his life.

"Don't worry about it," he said.

I hesitated, my stocking feet silent on the carpet as I fidgeted. "Can I take your car? The I.S. is probably looking for Trent's." A smile curved his thin lips up, and still sitting on the floor, he dug in his pocket and pulled out his keys to hold them up to me. They were foreign and heavy, keys to who knew what.

"I never thought I'd ever hear you asking for my keys," he said. "It's Ripley's—don't go running any red lights."

I fidgeted some more, then pulled my hand off the doorknob and crouched to see him face-to-face. "Thanks," I said, meaning for everything. "Don't take this like I'm forgiving you or anything," I added, then gave him a tentative hug. His shoulders were bony, and he smelled like metal. He was too startled to do anything back, so I stood and walked out, shutting the door carefully behind me.

Twenty-four

A bright glow from the noon sun filled the kitchen, and I sat with one elbow on the table, my forehead cupped in my hand. The other hand, the one with the demon mark, was firmly on the cool glass of the scrying mirror. From the open kitchen window came the sounds of pixies at play. I was exhausted, having missed out on almost an entire night of sleep. And Minias, the demon from judicial hell, was not being helpful.

"What do you mean, you won't do the curse?" I said aloud so Ivy, sitting on the counter by the sink, could hear at least one end of the conversation. "It was your idea!"

A ribbon of irritation-colored thought slipped through my mind, followed by the eerie sensation of words not mine in my head. *Al cut a deal two days ago. He agreed to stand trial, so he's out on bail.*

"Trial?" I yelped, and Ivy uncrossed her legs in a show of worry. But Al being out for two days would explain how he'd had time to create a disguise to look like my dad. I hadn't wanted to go to the demons but if Ceri twisted the curse, one of us would have to take on the smut—assuming she would still do it—and if I went through the demons, I could negotiate the smut away. That Minias was reneging on our unfinished arrangement ticked me off. "When is his trial?" I asked, trying not to freak out.

I pressed my hand harder into the scrying mirror when Minias's presence seemed to fade while he presumably searched for the answer. I was very glad the calling glyph worked when the sun was up. Actually, this was the best time to use it since Minias couldn't follow the connection and simply . . . appear.

Here it is, came Minias's bothered thought, diving through my idle musings like ice water. *He's down for sometime in the thirty-sixth.*

I closed my eyes and struggled for strength. "The thirty-sixth. Is that this month?" We only had thirty-odd days a month, but they were demons.

No. It's the year.

"Year!" I yelped, and Ivy's face pinched in worry. "This isn't fair! You came to me. I said I'd think about it. I thought about it. I want to do it! He's terrorizing my mother."

Not my problem. Al is functioning within the law, and everyone is happy. You'll get your say in court after he does, and if it's determined he broke his word to you, Newt will put him in a bottle and that will be the end of it.

"I won't survive twenty years waiting for him to come up on the docket!"

It's not an important case, and you'll have to wait, he said. *I'm busy. Is there anything else you want to bitch about?*

"You little will-o'-wisp of a ghost fart," I snarled, borrowing one of Jenks's favorites. "I know who's summoning him. I can't touch him because summoning demons isn't illegal."

You should go into politics and get a law passed, Minias said, and when I took a breath to protest, he snapped the connection.

I jumped, catching a yelp of surprise at the abrupt sensation of half my mind vanishing. It wasn't really, but I'd been functioning with an expanded capacity and was back to normal.

"Damn it all to the Turn and back!" I yelled, then shoved my scrying mirror across the table to thunk into the wall. "Al cut a deal. He's out on bail and free to harass me all he wants.

By the time his ticket comes up on the docket, I'll be dead and he can say anything he wants."

Ivy's expression took on a look of pity, and she drew her knees up to her chin. "I'm sorry." She had been treating me differently since our coffee in the mall. Not standoffish exactly, but a bit hesitant. Maybe it was because our relationship had changed. Or maybe the shift was because I had smacked her into the wall and almost fried her.

"It's not fair!" I exclaimed, standing up and stomping to the fridge. "It's bloody hell not fair!" Furious at my helplessness, I yanked open the fridge and grabbed a bottled juice. "I find out who's summoning Al," I said as I turned and tried to get the stupid thing open. "And then I can't arrest him. I agree to exchange names with Al, and they change their mind."

"We'll work something out." Ivy looked at the archway and put her feet on the floor.

"His court date is in the thirty-sixth," I said, still struggling with the lid. "I don't even know when that is. And I can't get the damn lid off this juice!"

Slamming the bottle down on the center counter, I stormed out, headed for the living room. "Where's the phone?" I barked, though I knew where it was. "I have to call Glenn."

My bare feet slapped on the hardwood floors. The soothing grays and smoky shades Ivy had decorated the room in did nothing to calm me. I snatched up the phone and punched Glenn's number in from memory.

"I had better not get his voice mail," I grumbled, knowing he was working today. It was the day after Halloween and he would have a lot of cleanup to do.

"Glenn here," came his preoccupied voice, and then a startled, "Rachel? Hey, I'm glad to hear from you. How did you do making it through Halloween?"

My first nasty words died in his concern. Leaning against the fireplace mantel, I let my tension go. "I'm fine," I said, "but my mom spent the night with my favorite demon."

The silence was heavy. "Rachel. I'm so sorry. Is there anything I can do?"

I brought my head up when I realized he thought she was dead. "She's alive," I said belligerently, and I heard him exhale. "I know who's summoning Al. I need a warrant for Tom Bansen. He's an I.S. boy, if you can believe it."

There was no answer, and my blood pressure spiked. "Glenn?"

"Uh, I can't help you, Rachel, unless he's broken a law."

My hand, gripping the phone, started to shake. Frustration knotted my stomach, and that combined with the lack of sleep had me at my rope's end. "There's nothing you can do?" I said softly. "Nothing you can dig up on this guy? The coven is either trying to kill me under the I.S.'s blessing or Tom's a stinking mole. There's got to be something!"

"I'm not in the business of harassing innocent people," Glenn said tightly.

"Innocent people?" I said, waving at nothing. "My mom is going to be hospitalized in the funny farm because of last night. I have to stop him now. The freaking bureaucrats have him out on bail!"

"Tom Bansen?"

"No, Al!"

Glenn took a slow breath. "What I meant was if you catch Tom in the act of sending Al to kill you, I can do something, but it's hearsay right now. I'm sorry."

"Glenn, I need some help here! The only options left to me are really ugly!"

"Don't go after Bansen," Glenn said, his voice carrying a new hardness. "None of them, you hear me?" He sighed, and I could almost see him rub his forehead. "Give me today. I'll find something on one of them. That widow is probably a good bet. Her file is as thick as her late husband's."

Frustrated, I spun to the high window and the red leaves still clinging to the tree. "My mother is sedated on her couch, and it's my fault," I whispered, guilt just about breaking my soul. "I'm not going to wait around for him to start on my brother. I have to be proactive on this, Glenn. If I'm not, everyone I care about will be killed."

"I got you a warrant for Trent this spring," Glenn said. "I can do this. Call your brother and get him on holy ground, then give me a chance to do my job. Don't go after Mr. Bansen, or God help me, I'll be knocking on your door with a pair of cuffs and a zip-strip myself."

Head bowed, I tightened my arm about my middle. I didn't like relying on other people when someone I loved was in danger. Let him do his job? That sounded so easy. "Okay," I said, my voice flat. "I won't go after Tom. Thanks. Sorry for barking at you. I had a rough night."

"That's my girl," he said, cutting the connection before I could respond.

Worn out, I hung up the phone. I could smell coffee, and I headed for the kitchen and Ivy's ideas. I wouldn't go after Tom without a warrant—the man would have me in the I.S. lockup for harassment—but maybe I could lean on him a little harder. He obviously wasn't convinced I was a threat. Perhaps if I set fire to his lawn—by accident—he might wait a few days to summon Al again.

I jerked to a stop in the threshold of the kitchen, shocked to find Trent standing between the center island counter and the table, trying to look like he wasn't bothered by the angry living vampire staring at him. The shoes I had left by Quen's bed were cleaned and on the table, and Jenks was on the counter. My face reddened. Crap, I'd forgotten all about him.

"Hey!" the pixy snarled, red sparks dropping from him as he got in my face. "Where the hell have you been? I was stuck in Trent's security office all night!"

"Jenks!" I exclaimed, dropping back. "God, I'm sorry. I sort of drove right by."

"You didn't drive by, you broke the moss-wipe gate!" His tiny features twisted with anger, he hovered before me, the scent of ozone dripping off him like the sparkles he was letting slip. "Thanks a hell of a lot. I had to bum a ride home with greenie-weenie here."

Trent, obviously. Before the sink, Ivy uncrossed her arms, more comfortable now that I wasn't waving my dirty laundry from the adjacent room for him to see. She might have warned me, but I'd been throwing off enough emotion to hit her like a bus.

"Relax, pixy," Ivy said, shifting into motion to hand me my juice bottle with the lid twisted off. "Rachel had a lot on her mind."

"Yeah?" he snapped, wings clattering harshly. "More important than her partner? You left me behind, Rachel. You *left me behind!*"

Guilt hit me, and I flicked a glance at Trent. *Still waving my laundry.*

Wings blurring, Jenks darted into the mended rack when Ivy's eyes narrowed. "She found out her dad wasn't her real dad," Ivy said, "and she was on her way to talk to her mom. Give her a break, Jenks."

Jenks's held breath escaped him in a long, wondering sound, and then his pointing finger dropped. The dust slipping from him thinned to a whisper. "Really? Who's your dad?"

Frowning, I sent my attention to Trent, who still hadn't moved but for shifting his feet, grinding his dress shoes into the grit of salt left on the floor. He looked awkward, soft almost, having changed into a pair of jeans and a green shirt. *Like I'm going to open that topic up with him in the room?*

"Thank you for bringing my partner home," I said stiffly. "The door is down that hall."

Trent didn't say anything as he took in the wonderfulness that was my life. I had saved his friend, father figure, and head of security. Maybe he wanted to thank me.

Ivy's eyes widened for no reason I could see, and before I knew what was happening, she ducked when a flood of pixy children raced in over her head by way of the open kitchen window. Shrieking and yelling, they swirled around their dad, making my eyeballs hurt. Ivy had her hands over her ears, and Trent looked positively agonized.

"Out!" Jenks cried. "I'll be right there. Tell your mom I'll be right there!" He looked at me in question. "You mind if I . . . take a moment?"

"Take all the time you want," I said, slumping into my chair at the table and setting the open bottled juice beside the scrying mirror. I thought about hiding the mirror from Trent, then let it stay in view. My stomach hurt too much to drink anything.

Jenks headed for the kitchen window, hanging back until sure all his kids went before him. "I'm sorry, Jenks," I said morosely, and he touched his forehead in a mock salute.

"No problem, Rache. Family always comes first. I want to hear all about it."

And he was gone.

I puffed my breath out when the ultrasonic barrage vanished. Ivy turned to get a mug from the cupboard. I didn't care that Trent was standing awkwardly within smacking distance, and I put my head on the table beside the mirror. *I'm so tired.*

"What do you want, Trent?" I said, feeling my words come back to me from the table as a warm breath. I had too much to do. I had to figure out a way to put the fear of God in Tom without getting caught. Or I could go for what was behind door number two and try to find a way to kill Al. They wouldn't put me in jail for that, would they? Well, at least not this side of the lines.

Ivy set a cup of coffee by my hand, and I pulled my head up to give her a grateful smile. Shrugging, she sat before her cracked computer, and together we faced Trent.

"I want to talk to you about Quen," he said, his dexterous fingers moving restlessly and his fair hair starting to float in the breeze from the open window. "Do you have a minute?"

I've got until the sun goes down, I thought. *Then I'm going to step out onto unsanctified ground and try to kill a demon.* But I took a sip of coffee and gave him a dry "Let's hear it."

The knock on our front door made me sigh out loud, and I wasn't surprised when I heard it open and recognized Ceri's soft steps as she hastened down the hall. My thoughts jerked back to her offer to help me with the curse herself. I wasn't sure if the offer was still open since we had argued about her making charms for Al. That's not why she was here, though, back from her all-night vigil at the basilica. She was here to learn if the man she loved had lived out the night.

"Rachel? Ivy? Jenks?" she called, and Ivy eased back into her chair. "It's me. Forgive me for walking in. Is Trenton here? His car is out front."

I turned to Trent, shocked at his stark fear. He had casually moved to put the counter between him and the door, and his alarm was hidden behind a professional smile. My mood went utterly black. He was afraid of her and her demon smut, too chicken to admit it openly.

"Back here, Ceri," I called, and the pretty elf breezed in, long white skirt flowing to a stop around her ankles when she saw Trent.

"Quen . . . ," she breathed, her eyes fixed on him, the depth of her feelings painful to see. "Is Quen still alive? Please."

For the first time all day, my smile turned real. Seeing it, Ceri started to cry. Looking like a wronged angel, she wrapped her arms around herself as if letting go would cause her to fall apart. The tears flowed unchecked, making her more beautiful yet. "Thank you, God," she whispered, and Ivy leaned to hand her the tissue box.

My muscles protested as I rose, but Trent beat me to her, coming around the counter to touch her arm. Ceri's head jerked up, her tear-wet eyes a stunning green.

"Rachel saved him," he said, and I marveled at how good they looked together. Almost the same height, both had the same translucent hair and slim build. I glanced at Ivy for her opinion, and she shrugged, looking sour as she crossed her knees and leaned her chair back on two legs until it hit the wall.

Ceri pulled from him. The fear he was hiding hurt her more than an honest reaction would have. Her gaze flicked to me. "I knew Rachel would save him," she said, wiping her face and smiling.

Trent heard a rebuke whether it was there or not, and he stepped back. A thick animosity started to grow in me. Trent was scum. Absolutely pathetic. I didn't have time for him, and I wanted him out. I had too much to do. "You're welcome, Trent," I said bitterly. "Get out."

Trent balked. I knew he felt vulnerable without his lackeys, and I wondered why he had come alone. He backed up when Ivy rose to escort him out.

"Morgan, we need to talk," he said as he maneuvered out of Ivy's easy reach.

"We already talked," I said, the bitterness of frustration closing in. "I don't have time to talk again. I have to figure out how I'm going to keep every last person I care about alive through the night, and I only have six hours to do it. If you don't want to be demon fodder, I suggest you leave." *I'm sorry, Marshal. I never should have said hello.*

Ivy glanced at me for direction, and I shook my head. I didn't want her to touch him. Ivy had a lot of money, but Trent had better lawyers. Her lips pressed tightly, and she let her pupils widen to cow him into leaving. Trent rocked back a step, then gathered his courage, a dangerous look in his own expression.

Ignoring us, Ceri had gone to the stove to fill the kettle, as naturally as if there wasn't an argument going on. "You should trade names with Al," she said, knowing it would make Trent fear her all the more, but not seeming to care. She was proud of it, maybe.

"I tried that," I said, giving my scrying mirror another shove before I wrapped my hands around my warm coffee mug, enjoying how it felt on my fingers. "Al cut a deal. He's out on bail, and he'll kill me before his court date in the thirty-sixth. Year, that is."

Ceri's eyes were so vivid, so beautifully green behind her tears when she turned to me, glowing with the knowledge that Quen was still alive. Nothing could dampen her quiet joy. "You can still twist the curse," she said, a tightening of her jaw showing as she noticed Trent's horror that she could speak of such things so casually. "I told you I'd help you with it, and I will. All you need that you don't have is a focusing object from Al. The smut is almost nil. Nature doesn't give names, so it doesn't care if they are shifted."

I swallowed hard and gave her a grateful look. I hadn't known if she would still help me after I had condemned her for working for Al, and she smiled back, telling me that she was wise enough to set aside differences when real things were threatened. I had saved the man she loved, and she would help me save my family and friends.

Trent looked pale, and I gave him a steady look until his gaze dropped. Maybe now he understood why I did demon curses. No one else was going to save me, and I had to fight fire with fire. But then I went sober in the thought that maybe he had a reason for the things he did as well. Damn it, I was too busy to learn another freaking *life lesson*.

Ivy jerked into motion, startling all of us. Tense and fast, she pulled the trash out from under the sink and started rummaging.

"Uh, Ivy?" I said, embarrassed.

"Remember that hunk of hair you pulled out of Al?" she said, and I jumped up to elbow her out of the way.

"Rachel. Rachel, wait." Ceri pulled me to a stop. "That won't work. Al's hair isn't an accurate sample of his DNA. He's modified it from his original pattern."

Ivy shoved the can back under the sink, slamming the door with a loud bang. Her motions were tight with frustration as she put the taps on full and washed her hands. I fell back against the table, depressed. It would have been so easy. "I should have just killed him," I whispered, then jumped when Ceri touched my shoulder.

"You can't," she said, her voice diving to my core with a terrible certainty. "Newt is the only person who has ever managed to kill a demon, and it made her insane."

Sounds about right, I thought, pulling myself upright. Okay. Next option . . .

Ceri's grip on my shoulder tightened. "You can still do the curse," she said, bringing my head swinging around. "All you need is the sample, and I know where they keep them."

"What?" Ivy blurted.

Looking from me to Ivy, Ceri nodded. "There's a sample of Al's DNA in the archives. There's one for every demon and familiar. The only problem will be how to get it."

Trent's shoes ground into the salt on my floor, his face empty of emotion as he stood in my kitchen, ignored and about as wanted as a fifth wheel.

"Everyone is registered when they become a familiar," Ceri continued, oblivious to his sudden stillness. "They started the practice when Newt went insane and started killing demons. It was the only way to be sure who she really killed."

I looked at Ivy in the pixy-filled silence, hope flooding me. "Where?" I said. Sunset was going to get here really fast. "Where do they keep them?"

"On a patch of holy ground in the ever-after, to prevent them from being tampered with," she said. "I can draw you a map. . . ."

They have holy ground in the ever-after? Pulse quickening, I looked to where I'd once kept my spell books, glad they were in the belfry where Trent couldn't see them. My gaze rose to my calling circle on the table. I had to talk to Minias.

"Ceri, would you help me barter with Minias?" I said, my voice high and sounding as if it was coming from outside of me. Trent's eyes were wide. I didn't care if he thought I dealt with demons. Apparently I did. "I must have something he wants," I said when she hesitated in confusion. "If he won't get the sample for me, he might give me a trip through the lines and I can get it myself."

"Rachel, no," Ceri protested, her loose hair swinging as she reached to take my hands. "This is not what I meant. You can't. You have two demon marks, and if you get a third, someone could trade for all three, and then they'd have you. You promised me you wouldn't go into the ever-after! It's not safe!"

Technically I hadn't, but she was scared, and I pulled out of her grip, surprised. "I'm sorry, Ceri. You're right. It's not safe, but not doing anything isn't safe either. And since the lives of everyone I care about are in the balance, I'm going proactive." I lurched forward, tension demanding I move.

"Wait." Ceri gracefully got in my way. She looked to Ivy for support, but the vampire was leaning against the counter with her ankles crossed, smiling helplessly.

"I have to do something!" I said, then hesitated at an alternative thought. "Trent!" I barked, and he jumped. "Do you have Lee's number?" He stared at me with his wide green eyes, looking odd, and I added, "I want him to teach me how to jump the lines. He knows how. I can learn." I fingered the charm around my neck, nervous. Before sunset. I had to learn before sunset. Damn, I was shaking. What kind of a runner was I?

"He doesn't know," Trent said, his voice distant. "I asked him when you freed him, and it turns out he was buying trips from Al."

"Damn it!" I exclaimed, then took a deep breath. How was I going to get in and out of the ever-after without racking up enough imbalance to make me easy pickings? And all before sunset, 'cause if I didn't do something tonight, Al would be hunting my family.

"I'll get you there," Trent said, and Ceri spun, putting her small white fingers to his mouth. Trent took it in his own hand, holding it, looking at me, not her.

Maybe I can figure out line tripping on my own, I thought, remembering Newt saying I didn't have enough time to figure it out, implying that I could. Time. Time! I didn't have time!

Then I paused when Trent's words hit me. I turned to see his face hard with determination and the fear in his gaze almost hidden. Ceri had dropped back from Trent, and she looked angry.

"I'll get you there and back, but you're taking me with you," he said, and Ceri hissed at him to be still.

I glanced at Ivy when Jenks landed on her shoulder and made her short hair billow with the wind from his wings. "Why?" I said, not believing this.

"I'll pay for it," he repeated, his feet solidly planted on the salt-dusted, faded linoleum. "I'll take the smut. For both of us."

"Trenton," Ceri pleaded. "You don't understand. There's more here than you know."

His eyes flicked to her, and his fear softened. "I understand I can do this. I need to. If I don't, I'll never learn how to live by the eleven percent." His gaze rose to mine, and there was a new light in them. "I'll pay for your trip there and back, but I'm going."

Making a puff of disbelief, I dropped back a step. Why was he doing this? To impress Ceri? "This is stupid," I said harshly. "Ceri, tell him this is stupid."

Trent faced me with his hair disarrayed and his jaw clenched, almost a different man. "I'll pay for your trip, but you are going to keep me alive while I get an elven sample."

My mouth dropped open and I blinked. Ceri fell from her tiptoes and backed away. A hand to her head, she turned her back on us, silent. From Ivy's shoulder, Jenks started to swear with a steady stream of half-heard curses. It was the only noise apart from the wind in the dry-leafed branches and the cheerful shrieks of his children at play.

"Elves were kept as familiars since before the start of the war," Trent said, putting a hand on Ceri's shoulder as she started to shake silently. "If there's a sample in the archives of an elf from over two thousand years ago, I want it."

Twenty-five

The cool chill of sunset seeped in around David's borrowed leather coat, and the smell of grilling burgers made my stomach hurt. I was too worried to eat. Too worried and too tired. Dressed in my working leathers, I sat alone in a folding chair under a tree in the dying autumn garden as everyone pretended everything was normal, clustered at the picnic table to eat their hot dogs before we called a demon into the graveyard.

My fingers played with the charm about my neck, and I felt the soft scar on my lower lip with my tongue. I don't know why I was worried about becoming bound to a vamp. I wasn't likely to live past tonight.

Depressed, I took off the high-magic detection charm. What was the point? My gaze drifted past the swirl of silk and laughter of Jenks's kids to the square of blasphemed ground in the graveyard before that weird warrior angel statue. It was peaceful now, but as soon as the sun set, it was going to feel the touch of demons. I could have called Minias in the kitchen, but I liked the security of hallowed ground close enough to dive into. There was a reason that patch of unsanctified ground existed, and I was going to use it. Besides, trying to cram three elves, three witches, one frightened vampire, a pixy family, and an angry demon into my kitchen was a really bad idea.

Thanks to Glenn, I had a small breathing space. The FIB

detective had dug up something from Betty's past, and though I thought an illegal puppy farm was a thin excuse, the animal protection people had been more than happy to authorize a raid on her house after I signed a paper stating I'd seen her kick her dog. The distraction would keep them too busy to summon Al, so unless someone else summoned him—a prospect not likely the day after Halloween—I had until sunset tomorrow. Telling my mom she didn't need to hide on hallowed ground tonight had been the high point of my day.

David had stopped by earlier to wish me well and loan me his long leather duster. He had left when Quen showed up, looking ill but determined to try to change Trent's mind. I think the Were was rightly concerned that the perceptive elf would see the focus within him.

At any rate, after a hushed argument, Quen agreed to Trent's plan, then spent the next half hour trying to convince Trent to return with him to his compound and prepare. I figured Quen was trying to get him home where he could lock him in a box. Trent must have figured the same thing since he refused to leave and had Jonathan bring over the items on Quen's wish list. Hence the general weirdness of elves eating hot dogs in my backyard.

Quen wasn't happy. I wasn't either. I was going into the ever-after to steal a demon's DNA with a freaking tourist for backup. Just peachy damn keen.

Sensing my frustration, Ivy turned to me from the distant picnic table. I shrugged, and she went back to whatever Jenks was saying. The pixy had been questioning Ceri all day, and I couldn't help but notice that Trent, way on the other side of the table, had been listening with rapt attention. Seeing them there in a noisy bunch trying to pretend everything was normal, I was reminded of my mother's occasional family reunions. Here I was again, watching from the outskirts. It always seemed to be that way. Maybe they had known I was a bastard child.

I smoothed my brow and straightened when Marshal headed

my way with a plate of food. He'd shown up a few hours ago trying to fit in, and doing a damn fine job of it after his initial stammering reaction to finding Trent in my backyard. He had taken over the grilling to stay out of the way yet be in the thick of things. I wasn't quite sure what to think. I wasn't going to repeat old patterns and let this slide into something simply because he was nice looking, fun to be with, and somewhat interested. Especially if Jenks was right and he was here with a white-knight complex and thought he could save me.

"Hungry?" he said, smiling as he put the paper plate on the rickety table beside me and sat in the folding chair beside mine.

His almost-there eyebrows pinched, and I forced a smile. "Thanks." My gut clenched at the smell of the food, but I dutifully pulled the plate onto my lap. It was the first time today we'd been alone. I knew he wanted to talk, and my blood pressure spiked when he took a deep breath. "Don't start," I said, and his brows arched in surprise.

"You're a psychic, too?" he said with a little laugh, and I crunched through a chip. The salt hit my tongue, and my hunger woke up.

"No," I said, seeing Jenks past him. The pixy was watching us with his hands on his hips. "But I've heard this argument before." I crossed my legs and sighed when Marshal took a breath. *Here it comes.*

"The ever-after?" he asked. "Isn't there someone else who can do this? My God, the man has enough money to hire anyone to gather samples for his genetic mapping program."

I stared at my plate because of fatigue, not because of the lie we had told Marshal to hide that Trent was an elf and wanted the sample to revitalize his species. "No," I said softly. "There isn't. This is what I do. Seemingly stupid stuff that most people die doing." I tucked a strand of hair as my frustration grew. "You don't think I know this is one of the most risky things I've ever done? I appreciate your concern, Marshal, but I need that demon sample, and Trent can get me there and back. If you're going to be the voice of common sense and tell me that I'm likely not going to survive, then you need to leave."

My voice had risen, and I exhaled. I knew Jenks and Ivy could hear if they tried. Marshal looked hurt, and I slumped. "Look," I said, lowering my eyes in guilt. "I'm sorry. I really am. You simply knowing me has put you in danger." I thought of Kisten, dying to protect me, and I bit my lip. "Don't take this the wrong way, but I don't even know why you're here."

His face took on a severe cast, and he leaned to block my view of the picnic table. "I'm here because I thought I could talk some sense into you," he said tightly, and my gaze jerked to his at the frustration in his voice. "It's hard to watch someone do something this incredibly stupid, especially when there isn't a damn thing you can do to help them." His fingers found my hands. "Rachel, don't do this."

His fingers, twined in mine, were warm, and I slowly pulled away. *This is so not what I need.* "I'm doing this," I said, starting to get mad.

Marshal's brow pinched. "I can't help you."

I jerked my fingers from him. "I never asked you to help me." *Damn it, Jenks. Couldn't you be wrong once in a while?*

Taking my silence for indecision, Marshal stood. The dry clatter of dragonfly wings intruded, and I stared at Jenks, wondering how he could see people so clearly and I could be so dense.

"Hey, Marsh-man," Jenks quipped lightly. "Ivy wants another burger."

Marshal gave me a faintly sour sideways look. "I was just heading that way."

"It's going to be okay," I said almost belligerently, and he hesitated. "I can do this."

"No," he said with Jenks hovering uncertainly beside him. "It won't. This is bad. Even if you do come back, you're going to be really messed up."

He turned and headed to the grill, his shoulders hunched and his steps slow. Jenks didn't seem to know what to do with his wings as he rose and fell in indecision. "He doesn't know you very well, does he," the pixy said nervously. "You're going to come out of this better than when you went in. I know you, Rache, and it's going to be okay."

"No, he's right," I breathed, my hair moving in my exhaled breath. "This is a bad idea." Hiding in my church for the rest of my life was a bad idea, too, and if Trent was going to pay for my trip in and out of the ever-after, why shouldn't I take him up on it?

Jenks darted away, clearly upset. My gaze landed first on Ivy—who was watching Jenks vanish into the graveyard, which was hazy with dusk—then moved to Quen and Trent arguing. Trent made a sharp motion, and Quen dropped back. The older man's face was dark with emotion, and showing his anger and fatigue, he walked away, hand to his face as he stifled a ragged cough. Trent blew out his breath in relief, then stiffened when he realized I'd seen it. I gave him a sarcastic bunny-eared kiss-kiss, and he frowned. Looked like we were still on for our date.

Quen found his own solitude on my back porch steps, sitting slumped with his knees bent. He looked tired, but nowhere near like he'd been dying last night. Three pixy bucks dropped down a respectful distance beside him, and he started. A faint smile curved over my face as I watched the older man's mood shift from frustrated anger to fascinated relaxation. Yes, something was there. This was more than the usual enthrallment I'd seen humans exhibit when they talked to pixies.

Ivy was watching Quen, too, and when Marshal brought her a burger, she ignored it, getting up and drifting over to the still-recovering elf. The pixies scattered at a sharp word from her, and she sank down beside him. Quen eyed her, taking the beer she handed him but not drinking it. I thought the two of them looked odd together, very unalike, almost adversaries, yet finding common ground in their unusual helplessness.

Pixies were starting to show themselves with sporadic flashes of light hovering close to the ground in the chill, and I followed the low, sleek shadow of Rex padding out from the long grass to make a beeline to Ivy. It wasn't often that the vampire was on her level, and I sighed when Ivy casually picked the cat up and set it on her lap, all the while talking to Quen. It wasn't hard to figure out what their topic of conversation was. They kept looking at Trent and me.

The sun had almost set, and I shrugged David's leather duster closer and dug my toes into the soles of my boots. I was tired. Really tired. Exhaustion had brought me down for a nap earlier, but that hadn't touched my mental weariness. Catching Ceri's eyes, I moved her attention to the setting sun. The woman nodded in acknowledgment, bowing her head as if praying. In a moment, she straightened. There was a new determination to her, a tightening of her jaw and a hint of fear. She didn't want me doing this, but she'd help.

Silence fell at the table when she picked up her five-pound bag of salt and started across the grounds to the blasphemed spot of earth surrounded by God's grace. In a breath, everyone was moving, and I watched in amusement as Quen tried to help Ivy rise, getting an insulted look from her for his trouble. Trent went inside to change, and Marshal grabbed another beer and sat beside Keasley at the picnic table.

I looked up at an unfamiliar wing-clatter and got an eyeful of pixy dust. It was little Josephine, one of Jenks's youngest, with three of her brothers serving as babysitters/guards close behind. She was too young to be alone, but so eager to help maintain the garden and their security that it was easier to watch her from a distance.

"Ms. Morgan," the pretty little pixy said breathlessly as she landed lightly on my offered hand and I blinked her dust away. "A blue car is at the curb, and a lady who smells like you and fake lilac is coming up the front walk. Do you want me to pix her?"

Mom? What's she doing here? Ivy was watching me, wanting to know if we had trouble, and I shifted my finger to tell her we were fine. The exchange was noticed by Quen, which kind of irritated me.

"It's my mom," I said, and the pixy girl's wings drooped in disappointment. "You can pix the next magazine salesman, though," I added, and she perked up, her tiny hands clapping. *God, please let me survive to see Josephine pix a salesman.*

"Thanks, Ms. Morgan!" she chimed out. "I'll show her in." Then she darted over the church to leave a fading sunbeam of sparkles. Her brothers were in hot pursuit, and I couldn't help my smile. It slowly faded as I leaned forward and put my elbows on my knees. *Time enough to say good-bye to my mom,* I thought when the back door opened, and my mother clattered down the back porch steps with a box on her hip. I'd told her what I was doing tonight, and I should have expected she might come over. Quen stood to murmur a greeting to her before he went inside after Trent, and I stifled a surge of annoyance. I didn't like the two of them in my house. Using my bathroom. Sniffing my shampoo.

My mom was wearing jeans and a flowery top, looking younger with her short hair frizzing out all over, only somewhat contained with a ribbon that matched her shirt. Eyes bright, she took in the preparations in the middle of my graveyard with a worried cast to her.

"Rachel. Good. I got here before you left," she said as she waved a distant hello to everyone and headed to me. "I wanted to talk to you. The Turn take it, Trenton has finished baking up to be quite the young man. I saw him in the hall. I'm glad to see you've gotten over your little childhood tiff."

Relief was a warm wash through me when I saw her, her thoughts clearly back together. When I'd left her this morning, she'd been distraught, half out of her mind, but I'd seen her bounce back like this before. Takata clearly knew the right words to say, and I wondered, now that the truth was out, if we had seen the last of her breakdowns. If breakdowns were what they truly were. Living a lie tore at one's being and leaked out in the oddest of places.

My thoughts went to Takata, then my dad. I couldn't be angry at her for loving two men and finding a child to love where she could, and as I stood to give her a hug, an unexpected feeling of peace took root. I was my dad's daughter, but now I knew where I got my ugly feet, my tall height . . . and my nose.

"Hi, Mom," I said as she took me into a hug, but her attention was on Marshal at the picnic table.

"Marshal is here?" she asked as I sat down, her expression wondering.

I nodded, not looking at him. "He's trying to talk me out of it. Bad case of the white-knight syndrome." She said nothing, and alarmed, I looked up. Her green eyes were wide and panic swirled in them. *Not her, too.* "It's okay, Mom," I blurted. "Really."

Dropping the box with a surprising thump, she sank onto the open chair, utterly miserable. "I worry so much about you," she whispered, nearly breaking my heart. Her eyes started to well, and she quickly wiped them. *God, this is hard.*

"Mom, it's going to be okay."

"I hope you're right, sweetheart," she said, leaning to take me into another hug. "It's your dad and Mr. Kalamack all over again, only this time, it's you." Whispering in my ear as she held me, she added, "I can't lose you. I can't."

Breathing in lilac and redwood, I held her. Her shoulders were thin and I could feel every shift of her weight as she reined in her emotions. "It's going to be all right," I said. "Besides, Dad didn't die from going into the ever-after. He died trying to get rid of the vampire virus. This is different. It's not the same thing."

She pulled back, nodding to tell me she had known how he had died all along. I could almost see another brick in her psyche being remortared into place, making her stronger. "True, but Piscary never would have bitten him if he hadn't tried to help Mr. Kalamack," she said. "Just like you're helping Trent."

"Piscary is dead," I said, and her breath came in slowly.

"He is, isn't he."

"And I wouldn't go into the ever-after unless I had a guaranteed way out," I added. "And I'm not doing this to help Trent. I'm doing this to save my ass."

At that, she laughed. "That *is* different, isn't it," she said, needing hope.

I nodded, having to believe it was. "It is. It's going to be okay." *Please let it be okay.* "I can do this. I have good friends."

She turned, and I followed her gaze to Ivy and Jenks in the graveyard, both looking helpless as Ceri directed everyone to their places. We were alone, everyone slowly milling around that weird angel statue in the graveyard and the slab of reddish cement fixing it to the ground. "They do love you," she said, giving my hand a light squeeze. "You know, I never understood why your dad always told you to work alone. He had friends, too. Friends that would have risked their lives for him. Though in the end, it didn't matter."

I shook my head, embarrassed about the love comment. But my mom only smiled. "Here," she said, nudging the cardboard box with her toe. "I should have given these to you before. But seeing how much trouble you got into with the first few I gave you, it was probably just as well I waited."

First few? I thought when my fingers touched the dusty cardboard and a faint tingle of power cramped my joints. I quickly undid a flap and looked inside, and the scent of burnt amber was almost a slap. "Mom!" I hissed, seeing the dark leather and dog-eared pages. "Where did you get these?"

She wouldn't meet my gaze, her brow furrowing as if refusing to look guilty. "They're your dad's," she muttered. "You didn't seem to mind the first ones," she said defensively as I stared at her, aghast. "And not all of them are demon texts. Some are straight from the university's bookstore."

Understanding crashed over me, and I closed the box up. "You were the one who put the books—"

"In the belfry, yes," she finished, standing up and drawing

me to my feet. Ceri was done and we had to move. "I wasn't about to hand them over to an unfamiliar vampire to give to you, and the door was open. I knew you'd find them eventually, seeking out high, lonely spots the way you do. You lost everything when the I.S. cursed your apartment, and what was I supposed to do? Drive over here and give you a demon-text library?" Her green eyes were glinting in amusement. "You would have locked me up."

Oh, my God! My dad had called demons?

Trent came out the back door with Quen, and I felt a wash of panic. "Mom," I pleaded, my pulse racing. "Tell me he never used these. Tell me he was a collector of books. Please?"

She smiled and patted my hand. "He was a collector of books. For you."

My brief relief died, and I froze as she stood to pull out of my grip. My dad had known that I'd be able to kindle demon magic. He had collected a demon library for me. He had told me to work alone. *What in hell had Trent's dad done to me?!*

"Come on, Rachel," my mom said, standing over me and touching my shoulder. "They're ready for you."

I stood, wobbling. A small cluster of people waited at the warrior angel: Ceri, Keasley, Trent, Quen, Marshal, Jenks, and Ivy—the people who impacted my life the most. With my mom at my side, I started walking as she chatted on about nothing. It was a defense mechanism that I saw through to the fear she was struggling to come to grips with.

David's coat enfolded me in the rich, complicated scent of Were, a distant show of support. For all his strength, he'd known he could do nothing and so had given me what he could and vanished in the way of Weres. I shrugged it closer as the hem hissed against the long grass. It needed to be cut, and the dew-wet tips turned the hem a darker brown.

Everyone turned as I approached, and my mom gave me a last hug before falling back to stand with Marshal in the grass. Ceri and Trent were already on the red slab with three concentric circles sketched on it, and eyeing the man's new outfit, I joined them. Trent had put on some sort of black jumpsuit with pockets, and if not for his fair hair poking out from under a close fabric cap, I wouldn't have known it was him at first glance.

"You look like the military guy from a B movie," I said, and he frowned. "You know . . . the token human who gets eaten first?"

"Is that what you're wearing?" he shot back. "You look like a wannabe private eye."

"It's cold over there," I said defensively. "And leather will keep me from getting scraped up if I have to fall down. And if I get hit by a potion, it can't get through." *If I get hit by a demon curse, I'll be dead.* "I can't afford Kevlar and spell-resistant fabric."

Trent gave me an up-and-down look and turned away, miffed. Ivy stepped forward to hand me the satchel that had all my stuff. "I put the map Ceri sketched in there," she said, her pupils fully dilated with worry. "I don't know how helpful it's going to be, but at least you know what direction to go."

"Thanks," I said as I took the light bag. In it was my splat-ball gun with a dozen sleepy-time paint balls, three warmth amulets from Marshal, a scent charm from David I'd loaned him a while back, a small bag of salt, a piece of magnetic chalk, and a couple of other things from my dad's old stash of ley line stuff. Nothing much. Just what I needed to force my summoning name onto Al and take his in return. Soon as I had the sample, I was going to use it.

"And some bottled water," she added. "A few energy bars. And some cream for your neck."

"Thank you," I said softly.

Her attention flicked to mine and away. "Keasley put in a few pain amulets, and I found a finger stick in your bathroom drawer."

"That will help."

"Flashlight. Extra batteries," she added.

There wasn't anything that would help us if we were caught,

but I knew why she was doing this. Trent shifted impatiently, and I frowned. "Hat," I said suddenly as I looked down at the long brown duster. "I need a hat."

Ivy smiled. "It's in there."

Curious, I dropped the bag and unzipped it, digging past Ivy's colored markers that I wouldn't need and Jenks's old toolkit from this spring, when he'd been big. I pulled out an unfamiliar black leather hat and snugged it over my curls. It fit me perfectly, and I wondered when she had bought it for me. "Thank you," I said as I tucked my hair up and out of my face.

Ceri was staring at the horizon. The sun was down, and I knew she wanted to get on with it. "Rachel?" she prompted, and my heart thumped. I almost hoped Trent wouldn't be able to make good on his deal to pay my way and I could bow out of this without looking like a coward. But then I'd be fighting for my life every time someone called Al.

Ivy touched my shoulder, and not caring what anyone thought, I dropped the satchel and took her in a tight hug. Vampire incense filled my senses, and as my eyes closed to keep a tear from leaking out, I breathed it in, feeling not a twinge upon my scars. Misery took me, heartache that this might be good-bye forever. "I'll see you about sunrise," I said, and nodding, she let go.

I couldn't look at anyone, and my throat was tight as I picked up my bag and stepped onto the cement slab. My gaze flicked to Trent. His expression was carefully empty. What in hell did I care what he thought?

Ceri stepped into the first circle, and my eyebrows rose. "I can hold Minias's circle," I said, then swallowed. "Unless you think Newt will show up."

She wrapped her arms around herself, clearly wanting to put herself on hallowed ground, but just as clearly planning to stay where she was. "Minias will follow you if I don't circle him and keep him here until sunrise." Her narrow jaw clenched. "Walk fast."

I looked briefly at my mother as I remembered the mental torture Al had put her through when she had done the same. "Ceri . . ."

"I can do this," she said, fear in her eyes, and I touched her arm. There was nothing this side of the lines that would keep Minias from tattling on us if he knew what we were doing. "Thank you," I said, and she smiled fearfully.

"If spending a night talking to a demon is all I have to endure to keep you alive and help mend the damage the demons did to my species, then it's thirteen hours well spent."

"Thank you all the same," I said, worried.

"I'll close the outermost circle," she said, starting to babble in her nervousness. "That way, no one can interfere. And because Trent will be doing the summoning and bargaining, he will make the inner one to hold Minias. I'll set the middle circle to hold Minias here and keep him from following you once you leave."

"Trent!" I exclaimed, my gaze shooting to him in his cute little jumpsuit, and he flushed. "I can make a stronger circle with one arm tied behind my back."

Ceri shook her head. "Trenton is the one bargaining for the jumps, so he will be the one holding the circle," she said, her smooth features wrinkling as I found fault with her plan. "Keep your mouth shut while he talks or Minias will use it against you."

Ticked, I pressed my lips tight.

"Keep your mouth shut!" Ceri said in a burst of anger, then gestured for Trent to come closer. Sighing, Trent tightened his grip on his backpack and stepped over the outermost chalk line to join us. Ceri pointed for him to stand next to me, and looking nervous, he edged closer yet. I wondered how much of Ceri's temper was actually worry. She was terrified of Newt, and Minias was only a small step from the insane female demon.

Quicker than thought, a shimmering sheet of black ever-after rose up around us along the outermost circle permanently etched out in the reddish cement. There had been a tug on my thoughts when Ceri had tapped the nearby line, and I worked to keep the huge spindle of ever-after I had gathered earlier from unwinding. Trent didn't look happy as Ceri trapped him with the same witch who had turned him in for murder and might just as easily give him to a demon to get rid of one of her own demon marks. *Trust*, I thought suddenly. He trusted me—to some extent anyway.

I took a steadying breath as I looked at the other two circles at my feet. They would make an airlock of sorts. Trent would set the inner circle to hold Minias, but when we left, it would fall. The middle circle, set by Ceri, would hold the demon at that point.

Ceri glanced at Trent and nodded. "Just as we practiced," she said, and Trent set his backpack down and came forward. He glanced once at Quen, then closed his eyes. His lips moved, and I felt an uncomfortable sensation as he slowly tapped a line and set the circle. It was the difference between a sharp tug to remove a splinter and a methodical, painful digging, and I could tell it was bothering Ceri, too. Quen must have been making him practice, since he didn't need candles to set a circle anymore.

"Bartholomew's balls," Ceri muttered. "Can he do this any slower?"

My lips quirked, but my satisfaction at Trent's lesser skills died in a wash of self-pity when his sheet of ever-after rose up. His aura was clean and pure, the bright gold shot through with the sparkles of seeking. Mine would look like a crap-smeared wall next to his.

Jenks, I thought. *Where in hell is Jenks?*

"Ivy?" I said, worried. "Where's Jenks?"

She waved a hand. "He said he was going to make sure his family was safe," she said, and my gaze went over the pixy-empty garden. From the steeple, a pair of unfamiliar red eyes glowed, and my pulse jumped until I realized it was Bis. I felt miserable. Jenks didn't want to say good-bye. I understood that.

Ceri handed Trent my scrying mirror, and I saw his expression close off in the gathering dusk. Damn, the thing was beautiful out here in the gloomy light, the wine-colored glass etched with crystalline lines in the shape of the calling pentagram with all its little figures and symbols. I couldn't tell if Trent thought it beautiful or foul, and I wondered if that was why Ceri insisted he summon Minias. She might be trying to convince him neither she nor I was immoral for what we did, just incredibly stupid.

Swallowing hard, Trent knelt on the red pavement. He set the glass carefully in front of him, and he put a shaky hand on the mirror. My nose tickled, then faded, and when a queer feeling of falling inside out flipped through me, I wasn't surprised when Trent blinked fast several times.

"Trent Kalamack," he said softly, clearly talking to Minias. "I ask for your attention in a matter of traveling the lines and am prepared to pay. I won't pay for you coming over here to discuss it, though. That is your choice, not my request."

Trent blanched at Minias's unheard response. "I'm using Morgan's calling circle," he said as if answering a question, then followed it up with "Standing beside me."

A sudden pop of air pressure hurt my eardrums, and I jumped.

Minias had blinked into this side of reality within Trent's circle. A thin hand held his yellow cap onto his head, and his beautiful green-trimmed robe looked loose and undone. His curly hair was in disarray, and with him was the scent of burnt amber and bread hot from the oven.

The demon had his back to me, but I could see his shock when he realized where he was and spun. "By the two worlds colliding," he swore softly as he looked me up and down. "After sunset and still alive? How did you manage that?"

I shrugged one shoulder as Trent took his hand from the mirror and stood. Her back hunched, Ceri whisked it away.

"You kick your dog one too many times, someone's going to call the animal protection agency," I said, not liking the servile attitude Ceri had adopted in Minias's presence. "Now *that's* an organization you don't want to piss off."

Minias's gaze went to my friends clustered together on holy ground, then Trent—who was trying to look calm—then finally back to me. "An audience?"

I shrugged again. "My friends."

Trent cleared his throat. "This is nice, but we do have a deadline."

My lips pressed. "Which you just blabbed to him, Trent. Way to go."

Trent reddened, and Ceri made a telling face. Minias, though, tugged his yellow robe tightly closed and smiled wickedly at the elf.

"I want to bargain with you," Trent said, casually clasping his hands behind his back to hide their trembling. "I don't want to know your name; I've asked for your presence, not summoned you; and I'm never going to call you again."

Minias reached behind himself for the ornate wire-and-cushion chair that had appeared, tugging it closer until he could sit. "I'll believe that when I see it." His goat-slitted eyes shifted to me, and I forgot to breathe. "Curiosity brought me here. I thought it might have been someone else." His attention landed on Ceri, then slid away. "What could you possibly want, and why in heaven and hell do you think I will help you? A putrid little elf?"

Without hesitation, Trent said, "I want passage in and out of the ever-after for two people, and asylum while we're there. You don't touch us or tell anyone we're there."

Minias's eyebrows rose, and he blinked slowly. "You're going to try to kill Al?" he said softly, and I refused to look away or change my expression. There were ways to solve problems other than killing someone, but if that's what he thought we were doing, then no one would be watching the archive. Right?

In a smooth motion, the demon leaned forward. "I can get you there, but nothing will buy my silence. Two trips in and out," he said speculatively. "You and Ceridwen Merriam Dulciate?"

Trent shook his head, then did a double take to look at Ceri. "You're a Dulciate?" he stammered, and she flushed.

"It means little now," she murmured, her attention down. Minias cleared his throat, and Trent dragged his gaze from her.

"Me and the witch," Trent said, still glancing at Ceri.

"I suppose asking for your soul is out of the question?" the demon said, and I looked at the first of the stars starting to show. We could be here all night. But Trent seemed to have found a cavalier attitude and he turned sideways, as if not really caring whether Minias went along with this or not.

"Stanley Saladin has purchased multiple trips from a demon," he said, his voice carrying an indolent confidence. "Four trips through the lines is not worth my soul, and you know it."

"Stanley Saladin bought line passages from someone trying to lull him into servitude," Minias said. "It was an investment, and I'm not looking for a familiar. Even if I was, I'd buy one, not bother raising one up from scratch. And what makes you think your soul is worth anything?"

Trent said nothing, calmly indifferent until Minias asked, "What do you have that's worth your soul, Trenton Aloysius Kalamack?"

A confident smile curved over Trent. I was shocked at his attitude—he was slipping into this demon-bargaining mode far too easily—but Ceri didn't seem surprised. A businessman is a businessman.

"Good." Trent patted his front for a nonexistent pen. "I'm glad we can talk. I'd like to finish this cleanly, without any marks to be settled at a future date."

Minias's eyes narrowed, and I blanched. "No," he said firmly. "I want a mark. I like the idea of you owing me."

Trent's face went tight. "I can give you the secret of Morgan's parentage—"

My breath hissed in. "You son of a bitch!" I shouted, leaping for him.

"Rachel!" Ceri cried, and I smacked into a front fall when she tripped me.

I scrambled up. My respect for her, not her small hand on my arm, held me back. "That's mine!" I shouted. "You can't buy a trip into the ever-after with my secrets!"

Minias glanced between us. "Add a minor demon mark, and you have your curses."

"Make it settled at my discretion, not yours," Trent haggled, and I jerked from Ceri's grip.

"You son of a bitch!" I yelled, getting in his face. The man had the gall to make an innocent face at me, and losing it, I shoved him into Ceri's outer circle.

He stumbled back, hitting it as if it were a wall. There was a shout of protest, and Quen's toes were suddenly edging near the salt ring. He was ticked, and Ivy was behind him, her lips pressed into a thin line, ready to take Quen down if he somehow got through the sheet of ever-after.

"You sorry little pissant!" I shouted, standing over Trent in his little black jumpsuit with my borrowed duster edging his legs. "You pay for my trip with information about me? I could have done that myself! I only agreed to protect you because you were paying my way!"

"Rachel." Ceri was trying to soothe me, but I'd have none of it. I reached to grab his lapels, and he rolled to his feet. It was fast, and I tried to hide my surprise.

"I'll accept that deal," Minias said, and I almost screamed.

"Done!" Trent shouted, and Minias grinned. "Back off, Morgan, or I'm taking Ceri with me instead, and you get nothing!"

Seething, I glanced at Ceri. He wouldn't dare. He wouldn't dare ask Ceri to go. I saw her fear, hating Trent all the more for threatening her like that. She'd go if I didn't, if only to try to help her species. "You are foul, Trent," I said as I backed from him. "This isn't over. When we're done here, we're going to talk."

"Don't threaten me," he said, and my blood seemed to burn under my skin. I looked at my mother, shocked to see her be-ing held back by Keasley. Her color was high and she looked one hundred percent pissed. If I didn't make it back, she would make sure Trent would be sorry he had ever put me, and now Takata, in danger. If Trent talked, demons would be coming after him, too.

"Interesting," Minias said, and I spun back to him. "Rachel Mariana Morgan protecting Trenton Aloysius Kalamack? Trenton Aloysius Kalamack paying Rachel Mariana Morgan's way? This isn't a suicide run to kill Al. What, by the two worlds, are you doing?"

I pulled back to the edge of the circle until it buzzed a harsh warning. Shit, I hadn't realized I had telegraphed so much of our intent. Jaw clenched, I glared at Trent. "Get your cookie-ass in there and get your mark so we can get out of here," I de-manded, and Trent blanched. A moment of satisfaction col-ored my anger, and I made an ugly face. "Yeah," I said bitterly. "You're going to wear his mark, and you're going to have to trust that he doesn't just change his mind and cart you off once you're in there with him."

Ceri frowned. "That's rude, Rachel," she said. "He's bound by law to leave Trenton alone for the duration."

"Just like Al's not supposed to hurt me or my family," I mut-tered as I backed away from Minias. My legs were shaking from adrenaline as I gestured to Trent to cross over the middle, uninvoked circle and get on with it. The elf got up, brushed himself off, and, with his thin lips pressed tightly, walked over the chalked line with his chin high.

Ceri knelt to touch the line, and a circle of black rose be-tween us and Minias. For a moment, there were three circles, Ceri holding the outer two and Trent holding the innermost one. Then Trent touched his and it fell to put himself and Minias breathing the same air.

Minias smiled, and Trent went ashen. My own heart pounded in the memory of Al doing the same thing to me.

Crap, was I trying to feel better about myself by dragging those I envied down to where I was?

"Where do you want it?" the demon asked, and I wondered why, unless it was more degrading to look at it every day knowing you asked for it, rather than have it forced on you. I felt the raised circle on the inside of my wrist, thinking I had to get rid of one of these soon.

His eyes never leaving Minias's, Trent shoved his sleeve up to show a lightly muscled arm, toned and sun-darkened. Minias grabbed his wrist, and Trent flinched at the knife the demon suddenly held, jerking only once as he scribed a circle bisected with a single line into him. I thought I smelled the acidic scent of blood and the rich aroma of cinnamon. I glanced at Ivy—her pupils were dilating as Quen looked at her in disgust.

"Tell me of Rachel's father," Minias said, his hand still around Trent's wrist. The mark had stopped bleeding, and Trent was staring at it, shocked that it looked old and long healed.

"Give me the way to cross the lines," he said, his gaze jerking up to Minias's.

The demon's eye twitched. "It's in your head," he said. "Just say the words of invocation, and you and whoever is with you will cross the lines. Now tell me of Rachel's sire. If I don't think it worth the imbalance of four trips through the lines, I'll simply upgrade your mark and give you a second slash."

I fidgeted, and my mother shook off Marshal's restraint. *Damn it, Takata. I'm sorry.* Trent was a bastard. I was going to get him for this.

"The man who raised her was human," he said, staring at Minias. "I found out when he came to my father asking for a cure. I have Morgan's father's medical records, but there's no name on them. I don't know who he is."

Keasley and Marshal looked shocked that my dad wasn't a witch, but my lips parted in wonder. *Trent had . . . lied?* My mother was sagging in relief, and I reached behind me until I touched the wall of ever-after, leaning my hand against it for support. He hadn't told. He hadn't told Minias. Trent had lied.

Minias's attention flicked to me and back again. His grip on Trent tightened. "Who's her birth father?" he asked, and Trent's gaze grew wild.

"Ask her," he said, and my heart seemed to start beating again. "She knows."

"Not enough," Minias said, knowing he was lying. "Tell me . . . or you're mine."

My fear redoubled. Did he expect me to save his ass by blurting it out?

"The man is alive," Trent said, that same wild glint in his eye. "He's alive, and Rachel's mother is alive. Morgan's children will survive carrying the ability to kindle demon magic. And I can make more like her." His smile grew ugly. "Let go of me."

Minias's gaze flicked to me. With a shove, he let go of Trent and took a step back. "The mark stands as it is."

Ceri was crying silently, tears trickling down her face as she stood and watched Trent find his composure. Had Trent just assured him that in a few generations they'd have a crop of highly desirable witch familiars available? Ones that could invoke their curses so they wouldn't have to? God help me, he was slime. Utter slime. He had put demon hit-marks on my potential children before they were even born.

I stood where I was and fought to keep from throttling him. He had spared Takata only because he had found a way to hurt me worse. "Can we go now?" I said, hating him.

Minias nodded, and Trent stepped back. The elf set the inner circle to trap him, and when Ceri dropped hers, he retreated to stand beside us. The scent of burnt amber caught at my throat, and Trent reeked. Knowing Trent's circle would fall when we left, Ceri reinstated the second circle about Minias.

The rising and falling bands of power were making me ill. Minias smiled from behind the two different arcs of reality as if he didn't care that he was going to be trapped in a small circle for thirteen hours until the rising sun freed him. Trent's words must have pleased him to no end.

I picked up my satchel and stood ready. My eyes flicked from Ivy to my mom, and my heart pounded. It was going to be over one way or the other really soon. Afterward, Trent and I were going to chat.

"Be careful," my mother said, and I nodded, gripping the straps of my bag tighter.

And then Trent tapped a line and said a word of Latin.

The breath was pushed out of my lungs, and I felt myself fall. The curse seemed to shred me into thoughts held together by my soul. A tingling washed through me, and my lungs rebounded, filling with a harsh gritty air.

I gasped, my hands and knees slamming into the grass-covered ground and my hat falling off. Beside me I could hear Trent retching.

Stumbling to my feet, I swallowed the last of my nausea and looked past my blowing curls to the red-stained sky and long grass. I wanted to give Trent a swift kick for putting my future kids on the demon's radar, but figured I could wait until I knew I had a future.

"Welcome to the homeland, Trent," I muttered, praying we all got back to where we belonged before sunup.

Twenty-six

Shaky, I fumbled with the satchel's zipper to find the map and orient myself. It was cold, and I pulled my hat lower as the acidic wind pushed the hair from my face and I scanned the image of a dim wasteland glinting under the red-smeared sky. I half-expected to see the ruins of my church, but there was nothing there. Stunted trees and twisted bushes rose between hummocks of dried grass. A red haze glowed from the bottom of the clouds where Cincy would have stood, but here, on this side of the dry river, it was mostly sad-looking vegetation.

Trent wiped his mouth with a hankie he then hid under a rock. His eyes were black in the red light, and I could tell he didn't like the wind pushing on him. He didn't look cold, though. The man never got cold, which was starting to tick me off.

Squinting, I tucked a strand of hair behind my ear and focused on the map. The air stank, and the scent of burnt amber caught deep in my throat. Trent coughed, quickly stifling it. David's duster shifted about my heels, and I was glad I had it, wanting something between me and the greasy-feeling air. It was dark, but the clouds reflecting the glow from the broken, distant city gave everything a sick look, like the light in a photographer's darkroom.

Arms wrapped around my stomach, I followed Trent's gaze

to the twisted vegetation, trying to decide if the red-sheened rocks hiding in the grass were tombstones. Amid the trees was a large, shattered slump of crumbling stone. With a lot of imagination, it could have been the kneeling angel.

Trent looked down at the faint tink of metal at his feet. Bending for a closer look, he thumbed a penlight on. It glowed a sickly red, and I cringed at the revealing light, then leaned so our heads almost touched for a better look. In the scuffed grass was a tiny bell, black with tarnish. It wasn't solid, but made of decorative loops that brought to mind a Celtic knot. Trent's hand reached, and in a wash of adrenaline, I gave him a shove.

"What in hell are you doing?" I all but hissed as he glared at me, and I wished I had hit him hard enough to knock him on his butt. "Don't you ever watch TV? If there is a pretty sparkly thing on the ground, leave it alone! If you pick it up, you're going to release the monster, or fall through a trap-door, or something. And what is it with the light? You want to tell every demon this side of the ley lines where we are? God! I should have taken Ivy!"

A surprised look replaced Trent's anger. "You can see the light?" he said, and I snatched it from him and clicked it off.

"Duh!" I exclaimed in a whisper.

He yanked it back. "It's a wavelength that humans can't see. I didn't know that witches could."

Slightly mollified, I backed down. "Well, I can. Don't use it." I stood and watched in disbelief as he flicked his light on and belligerently picked up the bell. It tinkled faintly, and after knocking the dirt from it, he jingled it again. I could not believe this. Putting a hand on my hip, I glared at the red glow hovering over the broken city miles away. The pure sound was muffled, and he tucked it in a little belt pouch.

"Freaking tourist," I muttered, then, louder, said, "If you've got your souvenir, let's go." I nervously stepped to the more certain dark of a twisted tree. It had no leaves, and it looked dead, the cold, gritty wind having scoured all life from it.

Instead of following, Trent pulled a paper from his back pocket. The penlight came on again, and he shone it on a map. A red glow reflected up on his face, and furious, I snatched the light away again.

"Are you trying to get caught?" I whispered. "If I can see it, and you can see it, what makes you think a demon can't?"

Trent's silhouette grew aggressive, but when the distinctive rustle of something small pushing through grass at a run rose over the soughing of wind in the trees, he closed his mouth.

"You had to ring the bell, didn't you?" I asked, pulling him into the shadow with me. "You had to ring the damn bell." I shivered in David's borrowed coat, and he shook his head in disdain.

"Relax," he said over the rustling of the closing map. "Don't let the wind spook you."

But I couldn't relax. The moon wouldn't rise until almost midnight, but the ugly glow in the sky made everything look like a first-quarter moon was shining. I stared at the heaviest glow, deciding that was north. The memory of Ceri's map swam up, and I turned a little to the east. "That way," I said as I tucked his light in my pocket. "We can look at the map when we find some broken buildings to hide the glare behind."

Trent tucked the map into his pocket and shrugged his pack over his shoulders. I nervously shifted my bag to my other arm, and we started out, glad to be finally moving if only to warm up. Grass hid the low spots, and I stumbled three times before we'd gone thirty feet.

"How good is your night vision?" Trent asked when we found a reasonably level swath that ran exactly east to west.

"Okay." I wished I had brought my gloves, and I hid my hands in my sleeves.

Trent still didn't look cold as he stood before me, his cap making his outline radically different. "Can you run?"

I licked my lips, thinking of the uneven footing. I wanted to say "Better than you," but quashing my irritation, I said, "Not without breaking something."

The red haze from the clouds lit his slight frown. "Then we walk until the moon rises."

He turned his back on me and started off at a fast pace. I jumped to keep up. "Then we walk until the moon rises," I mocked under my breath, thinking that Mr. Elf had no idea of the situation. Wait until he saw his first surface demon. Then he'd put his little scrawny elf ass behind mine where it belonged. Until then, he could find the dips in the grass and snap his freaking ankle.

The wind was a constant push, and my ears ached with it. My head slowly bowed until I had to force myself to look up and past the ever-moving shadow of Trent's back. He kept a constant motion just above my comfortable pace as he ghosted forward with a minimal amount of movement through the waist-high grass and past the occasional tree. Slowly I started to warm up, and watching him, I started questioning my decision to wear David's long leather duster. My legs were protected from the dry ache of the gritty wind, but it set up an unnerving hush against the grass that Trent's jumpsuit barely touched.

Things were no better when we left the grass behind and slipped under the canopy of a mature, twisted forest. The ground vegetation was sparser, but now there were tree roots. We passed what might have once been a lake, currently covered in a thick bramble, the thorns lapping the edge of the forest like waves.

I finally called for a halt when the trees gave way to chunks of concrete and occasional patches of thick grass. Trent stopped his unrelenting pace and turned. The wind was a cool brush against me, and breathless, I pointed to what looked like a crumbling overpass. Without a word, he angled to a slump of rock underneath.

Hand on my side and my thoughts on the water and energy bars Ivy had packed for me, I followed, sinking down beside Trent on the cold rock and glad for something solid behind me. I'd been fighting the feeling of watching eyes since we found the forest. The sound of my satchel's zipper was a striking point of normalcy in the red-smeared existence around us, with its greasy wind and heavy clouds.

Trent held his hand out for his light, and I gave it to him. He turned away to study the map as I scanned the terrain behind us. There had been a twisted silhouette at the dry lake, the vaguely human-looking figure furtive and fleeting. Trent's cupped hand hid much of the light, and his red-tinted finger traced our probable path from where we arrived to where Ceri had indicated the demons had their access to their database. Why it wasn't in the city bothered me, but she had said they had put it on holy ground to prevent demonic or familiar tampering.

The map Ceri had sketched had an eerie feeling of familiarity, with an undulating line indicating the dry river and marks showing where old bridges crossed. It looked like Cincy and the Hollows. Why not? Both sides of reality had a circle at Fountain Square.

Turning away, I dug in my pack. "You want a drink?" I said softly as I brought out a bottle, and when he nodded, I handed it over. The crack of the plastic seal shot through me, and Trent froze until he was sure the wind was still blowing and the night was still.

In the ugly red light, his eyes were black when they met mine. "Guess what's on the patch of holy ground they store their samples on?" he said, tapping the map and Ceri's star.

I looked at the map, then past him to the crumbling remains we had yet to venture into. In the nearby distance, glowing in the early moonlight, were spires. Really familiar spires.

"No . . . ," I whispered, tucking a curl back behind an ear. "The basilica?"

The wind ruffled the edges of the map while Trent drank, his throat moving as he downed the water. "What else could it be," he said as he tucked the empty bottle into his sack. The sound of sliding rock jerked him straight, and my pulse pounded.

Trent clicked off his "special light," but there not a hundred feet away in the sickly red haze was a twisted, hunched silhouette—staring at us with arms hanging slack at its sides. Its feet were shod, and leggings rose past the thin shins. An elbow-long cape fluttered in the cold wind. It turned a bare head to the east as if listening, then back to us. Waiting? Testing? Trying to figure out if we were food or foe?

A shudder rippled over me that had nothing to do with the steadily dropping temperature. "Put your map away," I whispered as I eased to my feet. "We need to move."

I thanked God it didn't follow.

This time, I was in front, tension making me almost glide through the ruins as Trent lagged, tripping on sliding rock and swearing when he slipped as he struggled to keep up with my fear-driven pace. We didn't see any more surface demons, but I knew they were there by the occasional rock slide. I didn't question why I found it easier to navigate the sharper shadows that the red moonlight made on the ruins than the natural slump of tree and grass. All I knew was that our presence had been noted and I didn't want to linger.

My first glimpse of the moon shook me, and I tried not to look again after my first, shocked stare. It had become a sickly, red-smeared orb, bloated and hanging over the broken landscape as if in oppression. The moon had always looked silver the few times I had opened my second sight and gazed into the ever-after from the security of my side of the lines. The clear glow of our moon must have been overpowering the red-smeared ugliness I was looking at now. Seeing it with my feet really on alien soil, coated with red like my soul was coated with demon slime, brought to a sharp clarity just how far from home we really were.

We fell in and out of a slow jog as the terrain permitted, traversing the broken, slumping buildings and the occasional line of trees showing where boulevards once were as we went deeper into the remains of concrete and frost-rimmed lampposts, heading for the spires. I started to wonder if the thin, hunched figures that were becoming increasingly bold were elves or witches that hadn't crossed over. Escaped familiars, perhaps? They had auras, but the glow was loose and irregular, like torn clothing. It was as if their auras had been damaged from trying to live in the toxic ever-after.

Worry tightened my brow as we wove through twisted metal that might have once been a bus stop. *Was I poisoning myself by being here?* And if so, how come Ceri was okay? Was it because she hadn't been allowed to age while a familiar? Or maybe Al had kept her healthy by resetting her DNA to the sample on file? Or maybe she never came up to the surface?

A falling rock slid almost to my feet, and I cut a sharp left, betting that there would be an open street after the broken building in front of me that would lead right to the basilica. I didn't think we were being corralled. God, I hoped we weren't.

Trent followed very close, and our progress slowed as we slipped through a narrow passage. His breathing was loud, and my shoulders eased when we emerged from the broken alley onto a clear street. Chunks of adjacent buildings littered the way, but little else. At Trent's nervous nod, we started forward, skirting the larger debris that might hide a skinny surface demon.

My gaze rose up the broken spires as we approached. There were only carved gargoyles perched on the lower ledges, not real ones. Whether they'd abandoned the ever-after along with the witches and elves or they had never existed here, I didn't know. Apart from the missing gargoyles, the building looked relatively untouched, much like their version of Fountain Square. I wondered if it was because it was holy, or because they had a vested interest in keeping it intact. Trent halted beside me as I looked appraisingly at the door, then he turned to watch our backs.

"You think a front door is open?" I said, wanting to be inside. Though if it was like the one in reality, the only holy ground was limited to the expanse where the altar was.

A rock slid behind us. Head jerking like a startled deer's, Trent took the stairs two at a time and tried all the doors. None of them opened, and seeing that there were no locks on the outside, I started for the side door. "This way," I whispered.

He nodded, moving fast as he joined me. I couldn't help the flash of memory of me cold-cocking one of his fiancée's body-guards on the front steps to get in to arrest Trent. I still thought Trent owed me a thank-you for breaking the wedding up. Him being a drug lord and murderer notwithstanding, being married to that cold fish of a woman would have been cruel and unusual punishment.

Trent took the lead, and I followed at a slower pace, watching the street when another slide of rock echoed through the ruined city. The sickly moon had risen over the buildings, the red glare making holes where there were none and disguising the real ones. My fingers itched. I wanted to unroll the ever-after in my thoughts and flash enough light to send all the surface demons running, but I had to reserve my spindle to do Ceri's charm. That is, if I didn't need it between then and now to save my skin.

The familiar sight of the twin stairways to the side door was a shock. It was exactly the same, and the untouched state of the cathedral made the rest of the city look twice as broken. "Trent," I whispered, my knees weak. "Why do you think everything is sort of parallel? I've heard Minias say 'When the two worlds collide.' Is the ever-after a mirror of our reality?"

Trent slowed as his eyes fell from the moon to land upon the expanse of trees growing where the side parking lot would have been. "Maybe. And it's ruined because of the demons?"

I jumped at a sharp click of stone. "Maybe their Turn didn't go very well."

"No," he said, easing forward silently. "The trees where we crossed were more than forty years old. If things went bad at the Turn, then they would be only that old. Elves left two thousand years ago, and witches five. If the ever-after is a reflection of reality, the similarities should have ended when we diverged, and they seem to mirror each other up to almost today, perhaps. It doesn't make sense."

He took the nearest of the concrete stairs carefully, and I followed, watching behind me instead of my footing. "Like anything makes sense here?"

Trent tried the door. It was locked. My lips pressed tight, I set my satchel down to find Jenks's lock-picking kit. The sound of sliding rock quickened my cold fingers, and Trent's gaze flicked everywhere as he waited. I wanted to get off the street like yesterday.

I found the kit, and after tucking it under my arm, I zipped my bag closed. A branch in the nearby trees waved wildly, and a black something hit the earth. *Shit.* Trent put his back to the door, watching. "Do you think that maybe more than the buildings are parallel?" he asked as I crouched before the lock. God, I'd give just about anything for Jenks.

"You mean like people?" I wiggled my fingers for his *special light* and he handed it to me.

"Yes."

I shined the light on the lock, sighing at its corroded state. Maybe I could kick the door in? But then we couldn't shut it. My thoughts went to Trent's question, trying not to imagine a demon with the morals of Trent. "I hope not." I stood, and his attention jerked to me. "I'm going to try to pick the lock," I said. "Watch my back, okay?"

Damn it. I didn't like where I was, but I had no choice.

Trent hesitated as if hearing more than I was asking, then faced the trees.

I took a slow breath and tried to ignore the soughing of the wind and the grit that was making my eyes ache. The case Jenks had bought to hold his tools was soft on my cold-numbed fingertips, and I fumbled at the ties holding it closed. Nice quiet ties instead of a noisy zipper. The man was a thief at heart and had thought of everything.

The kit came silently open, and in a flash of light that rocked me back, Jenks darted out.

"Holy crap, Rachel!" the small pixy swore, shaking himself so the glowing dust lit my knees. "I thought I was going to be sick. You bounce around like a grasshopper when you run. Are we there yet?"

I stared slack jawed, slowly losing my balance and falling to sit on my butt.

"The basilica?" Jenks questioned, seeing Trent standing speechless over us. "Damn, that's more freaky than a fairy's third birthday party. Oh, hey, nice jumpsuit, Trent. Didn't anyone ever tell you the guy in the jumpsuit always gets eaten first?"

"Jenks!" I finally managed. "You shouldn't be here!"

The pixy flexed his wings, landing on my knee and running a careful hand over one of the lower ones to straighten it out. The light from him was clean and pure, the only thing here that was really white. "Like you should?" he said dryly.

I glanced at Trent, seeing by his tight features that he had already figured out the problem. "Jenks . . . Trent only bought four trips. With you along, we only have one left."

Trent turned from the forest, clearly angry. "That last remaining trip is mine. I'm not responsible for your backup's stupidity."

Oh, God. I was stuck in the ever-after.

"Hey, you stupid-ass elf," Jenks exclaimed, rising up in a burst of gold glitter.

There was a collective rustle from the shadowed trees, and I got to my feet. Neither Jenks nor Trent noticed, seeing as Jenks currently had a drawn sword pointed at Trent's eyeball.

"I am Rachel's backup," he continued, the glow from him making a spot of normal color on the scratched side door to the church. "I come with her and am included with her trip as much as her shoes and her hair scrunchy. Human law doesn't count our existence, so neither should demon. I'm an accessory, Mr. Elven Magic," he said bitterly. "So don't get your dancing tights in a twist. You think I'd endanger Rache's life by using her pass to get here if I wasn't sure we both had a way out?"

Please, please let him be right.

Jenks saw my fear, and his wings increased their pitch. "I don't count, damn it! I didn't use up one of your trips!"

Trent leaned forward to say something nasty, but a huge chunk of rock slid into the nearby street, interrupting him. All three of us froze, and Jenks dampened his glow.

"Back off, Jenks," I said, cursing myself. "If there's only one trip left, Trent gets it."

"Rache, he can bargain for more! He should have included me anyway—"

"I'm not going to ask Trent to bargain with anyone else. He gets it!" I said, fear bubbling through me, black and thick. "He made the deal. You changed it."

"Rache . . ." He was scared, and I held out a hand for him to land on it. *Damn it all to hell and back.*

"I'm glad you're here," I said softly, stifling a jerk at a rock plinking down. "Trent can have his lousy trip. He got us here, we can get ourselves back. That's what we do. And that's even if we need to. If Minias doesn't know you hitched a ride, we probably still have two jumps out."

Jenks's wings had turned a dismal blue. "Pixies don't count, Rachel. We never do."

But he counted to me.

"Can you get the lock?" I said to change the subject. "We have to get off the street."

The pixy made a smug noise and dropped to the corroded lock. "Tink's tampons!" he swore as he dug through the rust and slowly vanished inside, leaving a faint glow. "This is like crawling through a sand hill. Crap, Matalina's gonna kill me. The only thing worse than blood is rust."

I really hoped I'd get the chance to hear Matalina ream him out. I really did.

Worried, I put my back to the door and sent out a silent prayer that the surface demons would hold off a little longer. I couldn't set a circle or draw on a line, though I felt a strong one nearby, from across the dry river where Eden Park would be.

If I tapped it, a demon would come to investigate. My gaze slid to Trent. I wasn't going to ask him to renegotiate for more trips out of here. But fear clenched my stomach. *Damn it, Jenks.*

Trent's hands twitched, and he looked worried. *Why am I doing this again?* "How's it coming, Jenks?" I muttered.

"Gimmie a minute," came a faint call back. "There's a lot of corrosion. And don't worry about the trip home, Rache. I saw how Minias did it."

Hope was a surge of adrenaline, and I met Trent's startled gaze. "Can you teach me?"

Jenks emerged from the lock, landing on the handle to shake the rust from himself in a burst of wing movement. "I don't know," he said, his voice stronger. "Maybe if elf-boy let me use the charm to go back and I could compare it to coming here."

"No," Trent said grimly. "I'm not renegotiating because your sidekick tagged along."

Anger made my face burn. "Jenks is not a sidekick!"

Jenks rose up to land on my shoulder. "Let it go, Rache. Trent couldn't buy a clue if he had a million bucks in a dollar store. I saw what happened when Minias shoved us through the lines. The ever-after is like a drop of time that got knocked out, sitting alone by itself with no past behind it to push it forward and no future to pull it along. It's hanging to us by the ley lines, sort of. Your circles aren't made up of differing realities, they're made up of the stretchy stuff that's holding us and the ever-after together, keeping the ever-after from vanishing like it should. But, ah, I hear things coming, so why don't we go in?"

A drop of time? I thought, pushing the door open to see a smothering blackness. The scent of dry paste met me, and when a guttural cry broke the wind's hush, fear slid all the way to the bottom of my soul and wrung every breath of courage from me. It had been distant, but there had been a definite echo of movement from all around us.

"Go," I hissed at Trent, and the elf dove in. I snatched up my pack and followed, moving as if the monster under the bed was ready to reach out and grab my ankle. Trent stopped in the middle of the doorway, and I plowed into him. We fell in the dim light coming through the door, and as Jenks swore and told us to shut it, I breathed in a heavy dust and tried to get up.

Trent managed it first, slamming the door and cutting off the moonlight. It was warmer inside, without the wind. I couldn't see at all, and I listened to his fingers scrabbling at the lock and his breath, loud and harsh in the blackness. *Holy crap, we just made it.* Frozen, I waited for a thump at the door, but it never came.

"You guys look stupid on the floor like that," Jenks said, shaking himself until he glowed. "I'm going to check the doors. If this really is the basilica, I know exactly where they are. Back in a sec."

The pure glow from him darted off to leave a fading ribbon of falling dust. God, I was so glad he was here.

A red haze from Trent's penlight eased into existence. His face was haggard and dust streaked, and his jumpsuit was filthy with a white, ashlike film. The light did little to illuminate anything else, and we got to our feet. *Mr. Elf has a get-out-of-jail-free card, and I don't.* Frankly, I'd rather have Jenks.

"I've got a brighter light," he offered. "You want to wait to use it until we hear back from . . . Jenks?"

My brow eased slightly, and I felt a little more charitable. "That is an excellent idea," I said, wishing he'd shine what light we did have around a little more. Especially upward. No one in the movies ever looks up until the saliva starts dripping down.

I was digging out my own light when the formidable sound of the power thunking on echoed through the church. Both Trent and I fell into a crouch when the glare of electric lights burst into existence. Blinking, we rose, our gazes traveling over the inside of the small cathedral.

Time, I thought again as my lips parted. *The ever-after is a splash out of time? Held to us by the ley lines and being dragged along? So why is it so parallel?*

I had no idea, but the basilica looked like the one I'd dragged Trent out of. Well, sort of. A dingy yellow foam covered the inside of the stained-glass windows to block any light from entering or escaping. The pews had been shoved to the back of the sanctuary in a pile of half-burnt varnished wood. Smoke and fire damage marked the walls and ceilings. The christening well . . . God save me. It was full of what looked like blackened bones and hair, utterly defiled. An ugly stain of black ringed it. Blood? I wasn't going over to look.

My eyes finally went up, and tears pricked. The beautiful woodwork was still there, and the chandeliers, faintly tinkling. A haze of white was slipping from them in a fog, the flow of electricity shaking loose the dust to sift down on the tiled floor gouged by a past fury.

Trent moved, and my gaze shot past him to the altar. It stood on a raised stage, and it, too, was covered in black stains. Something really ugly had happened. I felt my expression twist, and I shut my eyes. Either the sanctity had been broken or it had been defiled by witches or elves. If it was a different time, how far ahead were we?

I refused to look at the defiled altar as I followed Trent onto the stage. I thought I felt a shiver pass through my aura as I stepped onto holy ground, and when I looked at Trent, he nodded.

"It's still holy," he said, glancing at the altar. "Let's find the samples and get out of here."

Easy for you to say, I thought bitterly, not trusting Jenks's opinion that he didn't count.

The dry clatter of pixy wings intruded, and my relief was almost a pain when Jenks shot in from the back rooms. My easing of tension was short-lived, though, as he landed on my extended fist, gray and clearly shaken.

"Don't go out there, Rachel," he whispered, the clear tracks of tears showing strongly on his rust-dusted face. "Please, don't go out there. Stay here. Ceri said the samples were here on holy ground. You don't *need* to go anywhere else. Promise me. Just promise me you won't leave this room."

Fear made a lump at my core, and I nodded. I'd stay here. "Where are the samples?" I said, turning to see Trent running his hand over the woodwork as if he was looking for a secret panel. The yellow foam on the windows seemed to soak up the light. My breath hissed in and Trent froze at the sound of nails. Something was crawling on the outside of the glass.

"My God," I said, retreating to the altar to put my back against it as I looked up. "Trent, do you have any weapons? Like a gun?"

He looked at me in disgust. "You're here to protect me," he said as he closed the distance between us and stood beside me. "You didn't bring a weapon?"

"Yeah, I brought a weapon," I snapped as I brought my splat gun out and aimed it at the ceiling where the sounds were coming from. "I just thought that since you're a freaking murderer you might have a gun, too. God, Trent, please tell me you brought one?"

Jaw clenched, he shook his head no, but he touched a wide side pocket in his jumpsuit for reassurance. He might not have a gun, but he had something. Fine. Mr. Kalamack had a secret weapon he didn't want to share. I hoped he wouldn't have to use it. Heart pounding, I watched the yellow foam and tried to slow my breathing. How were we going to do this while under attack? If I set a circle for protection, real demons would be all over us.

"Jenks?" I called out when a new scrabbling started from the other side of the church. Shit, there were two out there now. "Can you hear a hard drive or anything? Ceri said they stored everything by computer. We need to do this fast."

Face gray, Jenks rose up on a thin sparkle of gold that took on an amber tint. It was almost as if the red glow from outside was seeping in. "I'll look."

He darted off, and hands sweating, I tracked the sound of that second set of nails as it traveled over the ceiling to where the first was digging. The first seven uglies through would be taking a nap, but unless they were cannibals and ate their dead, there were probably going to be a lot more surface demons coming at us than I had sleepy charms for.

The two scrabbling sounds joined, and I stiffened at a sharp crack followed by a thump. There was a cry, then the desperate raking of claws on stone and glass all the way to the ground. I listened, not moving or daring to breathe. *A gargoyle?* I thought. There were gargoyles here? They were fiercely loyal to their churches and would defend them against attack. It was the only explanation, unless both had fallen, but it had sounded as if it had only been one.

Trent sighed in relief, but I kept staring at the high windows, not trusting that it hadn't simply been two klutzy surface demons and that more wouldn't be coming. "I think we're okay," he said, and I just looked at him in disbelief.

"Wanna bet?"

"Guys? Over here," Jenks called out as he hovered before a white statue of Mother Mary. "There's an electronic whine coming from under it."

Giving Trent a last look, I tucked my splat gun into my pants at the small of my back and left the altar to join Jenks. The pixy had sunk down to sit on the statue's shoulder, looking somehow right in between her heart and her halo. Trent had come with me, and before I could say anything, he stretched to put his hands on her knees, clearly planning to shove her over.

"No!" I exclaimed, not knowing why except she was the only thing in here on the ground floor not marked up and defiled.

But Trent scowled, and as I grasped his shoulder to jerk him back, he reached out.

Pain raced through my arm and into my chest, cramping my muscles like an electric shock. I heard Trent yelp, and I must have passed out because the next thing I knew, I was laying on the floor four feet back with Jenks hovering in front of me.

"Rachel!" he cried, and I put a hand to my aching head, my arm moving slower than it should have as I propped myself up. "Are you all right?"

I took a breath, then another. My roving gaze found Trent sitting cross-legged and holding his head. His nose was bleeding.

"Stupid-ass elf," I muttered, feeling my heartbeat. "You stupid-ass elf!" I shouted, and Jenks flew backward, smiling in relief.

"You're okay," he sighed, the sparkles sifting from him turning a clear silver.

"What in hell is wrong with you!" I yelled, my voice echoing against the distant ceiling. "You don't think it's protected?"

Trent looked up. "Jenks was sitting on it."

"Jenks is a pixy!" I exclaimed to burn off some angst. "No one takes them into account because they don't know how dangerous they are, you dumb crap of a businessman. You are *completely* out of your element, so just sit there, okay? You got me here, now let the professionals work, or your insufferable smarter-than-thou attitude is going to get us killed! I said I'd protect you and get you home, but I need you to stop doing stupid stuff. Just . . . *sit there and do nothing*!"

The last was shouted, but I was really mad. "God help you!" I swore as I got up and shook the last of the cramping out of my hand. "Now I have a headache! Thanks a hell of a lot!"

Jenks was grinning, and my brow furrowed at my unprofessional show of anger. "'Bout time you put him in his place," he said, and my frown deepened.

"Yeah," I muttered as I creakily moved to the statue and stood before sweet Mother Mary and her smug smile with my fists on my hips. "But how are we going to get to the samples?"

Jenks's wings increased their pitch, and I looked at his expression of satisfaction. Immediately I felt my own expression ease. "You already have a way in?" I asked.

He nodded. "There's a crack in the base small enough for a mouse. I'll get them."

My breath slipped from me in an audible sigh. The magic protecting the statue didn't recognize him. He didn't count. The thing was, he did count. He counted a lot, and he was going to save my butt again. "Thanks, Jenks," I whispered.

"Hey, that's what I'm here for," he said, then darted behind the statue and was gone.

I had a trip home. I really thought I might. Maybe.

The silence was loud as I turned to find Trent still messing with his nose. The scent of blood seemed to pull whispers from the shadows at the christening pool, and though I knew it was my imagination, it was freaking me out. Going to the limit of the holy ground, I sat on the top step, remembering standing here at Trent's wedding. Right before I arrested him. I could feel Trent's presence behind me but didn't turn. He was silent for about six heartbeats, and then I heard him rise. From outside at the base of the front doors came scratching, a soft digging sound that gave me the willies. It started and stopped as if afraid, but the door was a lot thicker than the glass windows.

I forced my breathing to stay even when Trent stopped five feet from me and just stared. Swinging my waist pack around, I took out my last water and downed it. My splat gun was next to it, and bringing it out, I sighted down it at the front door.

Trent looked me up and down. "Is that all you're going to do?"

My pulse quickened, and I gazed at the front of the basilica where the scratching was coming from. "I might have a snack later if nothing comes through those doors."

Jenks's voice came echoing up, sounding hollow. "I found a terminal!" he shouted. "It's in a cement room with no doors. I squeezed in through the wiring. Tore my freaking wing. Tink's dildo, I'm leaking enough dust to be a lightning rod. It's going to take me some time to hack in and figure out their system, but I can do it."

I pulled my satchel with my spelling stuff closer. If Jenks was using Tink's name in vain, he was okay. The sun would rise at seven and Minias would be free. If we weren't out of here by then, it was going to get a whole lot nastier, holy ground or not. A wooden door and a maybe-gargoyle wouldn't stop a real demon. Not by a long shot.

Trent sighed, easing himself down to sit on the stairs with his knees almost up to his chin.

And now we wait.

Twenty-seven

I flipped my splat gun out of my waistband, letting it spin like a gunslinger's pistol before aiming it at the distant door. The scratching there had quit hours ago, shortly after the sound of a large rock hitting the pavement shook the dust from the ceiling. Apparently, the gargoyles *were* still around. That had made me feel secure enough that I'd managed to grab a few winks a couple of hours ago while Trent stood guard.

The watch—on loan from Ivy—about my wrist said it was twenty minutes to sunrise. Twenty minutes before all hell was going to break loose, and here I was playing gunslinger. Trent would be able to pop out when things got rough with his freaking "magic word," but I had a circle drawn beside the altar for Jenks and me to hide in if worse came to worst. It ought to hold until Newt showed. My spelling supplies to take Al's name were in it, just waiting for the focusing object. I was going to work the curse as soon as Jenks found the demon's DNA. If I didn't survive, at least everyone I cared about would be safe. *Hurry up, Jenks.*

"Bang," I whispered, then pulled the gun back to me and tucked it in at the small of my back. I was dying to go out and see what had hit the street before the front door. Tired, I glanced at the statue, then Trent sitting slumped with his back against the defiled altar. He had nodded off for a few hours around midnight, trusting I'd keep him safe.

This was taking it right to the wire—and that was assuming I had a ride home. Crap, I was tired of this. The theoretical charm shop Jenks sometimes mocked me with was looking mighty good right now. Sure, I had been all spit and indignant righteousness when I told Trent that Jenks hadn't used my ride home to get to the ever-after, but the last few hours before sunrise were dragging deep across my soul, and I feared that I was living in a fairy tale if I expected Minias to accept that Jenks was a hair scrunchy and deserved a free ride.

Trent felt me looking at him and woke up. His eyes were puffy from the grit and tired, and his face showed his strain. I looked away and stretched for my hat, dropping it onto my head and pulling it low so I couldn't see him. Exhaling, I forced the tension out. Maybe I could figure ley line traveling out if there weren't demons breathing down my neck like the last time. Until Jenks came up with Al's cellular sample, there was nothing else to do. I'd been trying to piece it together all night.

My eyes shut and I made my muscles relax. If Jenks was right, ley lines were what kept the ever-after connected to reality. All I had to do was learn how to use them, and Jenks and I would be home free. *Sure. Easy stuff.*

Like I had a hundred times already tonight, I reached a thought out to the nearest line but didn't tap it, afraid a demon would sense me doing it. I lingered there, feeling the energy rush past my consciousness like a red-sheened, silver ribbon. It suddenly occurred to me that the energy was flowing one-way, into our reality. Was the ever-after shrinking? Its substance flowing into our reality like water is drawn to puddle up from a small drop into a larger one? Maybe that was why the ever-after was all broken up.

Tension filtered back, tightening my muscles one by one as I tried to remember what it had felt like when I'd been carried along the lines of energy. The thought of Ivy had brought me home once.

My face warmed. Newt had said I loved Ivy more than the

church. I wasn't going to deny it, but there were all kinds of love, and how shallow would I be if my anchor to reality was a hunk of real estate? It was the people who were there that made it mean something.

The flush cooled as I remembered the feeling of my soul breaking apart and how Newt had held my consciousness until I had a body again. Had the shift between realities fractured my soul or just my body?

I moved my knees to feel they'd stiffened. My eyes opened, and I stared at the new rings of dust under the chandeliers. I couldn't even smell the burnt amber on me anymore, and that bothered me. I jumped when Trent sat down beside me. I had forgotten he was here. Pulse pounding, I shifted down an inch or two, wondering what he wanted. Getting antsy, was he?

"I, uh, want to thank you," he said, when it was obvious I wasn't going to break the awkward silence.

Surprised, I glanced at Ivy's watch. *Tickity-tock, Jenks.* "You're welcome."

He pulled his knees up, which made him look odd in his black jumpsuit. "Don't you want to know what for?"

Expression neutral to maintain the facade that everything was going according to plan, I gestured at the broken cathedral. "For keeping you alive on this magic carpet ride?"

He looked at the shattered room. "For stopping my wedding."

Blinking, I cautiously offered, "You didn't love her."

His gaze had dulled, and his hair was white with dust. "I didn't have the chance to find out."

Trent wants to love someone. Curious. "Ceri—"

"Ceri wants nothing to do with me," he stated. He let his knees fall to stretch his legs down the stairs, his usually collected features scrunched up. "Why do I need to marry someone anyway? It's politics, that's all."

I stared, seeing him as a young man in a position of power being asked to marry, have children, live a nice quiet life of hidden intrigue and public showmanship. *Poor, poor Mr.*

Trent. "That didn't stop you with Ellasbeth," I said, pushing for more.

"I don't respect Ellasbeth."

Don't respect or don't fear her? I ran my gaze up from his boots to his cap. "You're welcome," I said. "But I arrested you to put you in jail, not to save you from Ellasbeth." Jenks had helped Quen steal the evidence that Trent had murdered the Weres, and the FIB had to let him go. And yet Trent was taking the last ride out of the ever-after instead of sticking around and helping us bargain for two more trips. Ah, well. It really wasn't his problem, was it.

A faint smile quirked his lips. "Don't tell Quen, but the jail time was worth it."

My smile grew to match his, then faded. "Thank you for bringing Jenks home," I said, then added, "And my shoes. Those are my favorite pair."

Looking askance at me, he almost smiled. "No problem."

"But I don't appreciate you putting my future kids on the demon radar," I said, and his expression became questioning. God, he didn't even know he had done it. I don't know if that made it better or worse. Jaw tight, I added, "Telling Minias my kids will be healthy and possibly able to kindle demon magic?"

His jaw dropped and I clasped my knees to my chest. "Idiot," I muttered. He hadn't even known what he had done.

My gaze slid to my watch, then the foam-covered windows. The light outside would be growing red and sickly, the wind rising. The gargoyles might have been able to keep us safe in here at night, but as soon as the sun rose, they would be dormant. Even worse, not only was I not going to have time to do the spell, I was likely not even going to get the sample. I had a bad feeling Minias would show up the moment he was free. *Come on, Jenks.*

Trent's boots scraped the decayed carpeting to show the wood underneath. "Sorry."

Yeah. That makes it all better.

"If there's only one trip out, I'll try to get you back," he said suddenly.

Surprise washed through me, almost a hurt, and I jerked my head up. "Excuse me?"

He was staring at the front door, looking as if he had a bad taste in his mouth. "We couldn't have done this without Jenks. If Minias considers him a person, I'll try to arrange two more trips out. If I can."

I took a breath, having forgotten to breathe. "Why? You don't owe us anything."

His lips parted and closed, and he shrugged. "I want to be more than . . . this," he said, gesturing to himself.

What in *hell* was going on?

"Don't get me wrong," he said, glancing furtively at me and away. "If it comes to sending you home and being a hero, or being a bastard by sending myself home and saving my species, I'm going to be a bastard. But I'll try to get you home. If I can."

My breath came and went, and I tried to wrap my thoughts around what had changed in him. It had to be Ceri. The woman's complete disdain for Trent was starting to get to him; she didn't excuse his actions and saw right through his surface attempts at making up for his past—thinking the attempts made him worse, not better. Her soul was black, her past filthy with unimaginable deeds, but she carried herself with a noble strength, knowing that though she broke the law with impunity, she was loyal to those she owed allegiance to and loved. And perhaps Trent was seeing it for the first time as a strength, not a weakness.

"She's not going to ever love you," I said, and his eyes closed.

"I know, but someone might."

"You're still a murdering bastard."

His eyes opened, a spot of green in the dusty gray surrounding us. "That's not going to change."

That I could believe. Needing to move, I rose and went to

stand before the statue. "Jenks?" I shouted. "We're running out of moonlight!" It was too late to do the curse. We were down to snatch and run.

"You aren't so lily white yourself," Trent said. "Stop throwing stones."

Stiffening, I spun. "I got my demon smut trying to save my butt. Nothing died."

With a soft huff, Trent pulled his knees to himself and turned on the top stair to face me. "Such a nice friendly witch, helping the FIB and little old ladies find their familiars. How many bodies are at your feet, Rachel?"

Heat hit me, and my breath caught. *Oh. That.* There were bodies in my past. I lived with a vampire who had probably killed people and I willingly accepted that. Kisten's hands hadn't been clean either. Jenks had killed to keep his children alive, and would do so again without thought. I had intentionally killed Peter, though he had wanted to die.

"Peter doesn't count," I said, hip cocked, and Trent shook his head as if I were a child. "You murder people outright," I said indignantly. "You killed three Weres for *business* last summer and were going to let my friend take the blame. Brett only wanted to belong to something." That it still hurt surprised me.

"We are exactly the same, Rachel. We're both prepared to kill to protect what we care for. It simply comes up a lot more often with me. You murdered a living vampire to protect your way of life. That he wanted to die was simply a pretty bow around it."

"We are nothing alike," I said. "You kill for business and profit. I did what I had to do to keep the balance between the vamps and the Weres." Full of indignant anger, I looked down at him as he sat on the stairs. "Are you saying I shouldn't have?"

Smiling beatifically, Trent said, "No. You did the right thing. Exactly what I would have done. What I'm saying is that the rest of us would appreciate it if you would stop working against the system and start working in it."

"With you?" I said caustically, and he shrugged.

"Your talents, my contacts. I'm going to change the world. You can have a say in it."

Disgusted, I turned my back on him, arms crossed over my chest. Demons were about to chew our noses off, and he was still trying to woo me into working for him. But here I was, doing just that. God, I was such an idiot. "I already have a say in it," I muttered.

"Rache?" came a warbling call from the statue, and my heart jumped. "I got Al's."

I backed up a step, pulse fast when Jenks burst from behind the statue trailing a thin ribbon of gold dust. "I looked for your sample," he said, dropping a pinky-nail-size ampoule of black sludge into my grip. "But you don't have one. I guess you weren't Al's familiar long enough. If Al ever tries to reverse the curse, he's going to have to get a sample from you."

"Thank you," I said, dizzy as I looked at the little drop of nothing in my hand that was Al. I'd risked my life for this. Heart pounding, I looked at Ivy's watch—ten minutes to sunup. I was going to use it now.

"Get Trent's sample," I said, lurching to the circle already scribed out on the wooden floor where the carpet had been burned away. I wasn't going to tap a line and set it unless we were interrupted. At that point, it wouldn't matter if I rang the damned bell.

Trent followed, and I almost smacked into him as he tried to get a look at Al's blood. "That's it?" he said, and I pulled back from his reaching hand. "It's over five thousand years old. It can't be any good."

Jenks's wings snapped aggressively. "It's magic, you big cookie fart. If you can read a DNA sample off a nasty mummified elf corpse, then Rachel can use a five-thousand-year-old drop of blood for a demon curse."

I dropped to my knees inside the circle and set the precious vial aside to brush the dirt from a swath of burned oak.

"What about my sample?" Trent asked, his voice tense, as if we might betray him in the last hour. His eyes were very green, and I watched the emotion pass behind them.

"I haven't been able to find one." Jenks dropped an inch in altitude. "I can't just type in ancient, pre-curse elf. It would help if I had a name."

Trent glanced at me, his face tight with sudden nerves. "Try searching for Kallasea," he said, and I slowed. *Kallasea? An older version of Kalamack, perhaps?*

"Give me a sec," Jenks said, and darted away.

Nervous as much from what I was doing as from Trent watching me do it, I sent my gaze over my stuff. White candle to serve as my hearth fire—check. Ugly big-ass knife—check. Two candles representing Al and me—check. Bag of sea salt—check. Ungodly expensive piece of magnetic chalk that I wasn't going to use—check. Little five-sided pyramid made out of copper—check. Ceri's written instructions and phonetically spelled Latin curse—rolled up like a scroll and shoved in the bottom of my bag—didn't need it. I had memorized everything while sitting on the steps of the basilica's altar.

Feeling Trent's eyes on me, I pinched the wick of the white candle, muttering, *"Consimilis, calefacio,"* as I let it go. The spindled power in me dropped, making me glad I was lighting one candle to function as a hearth fire instead of lighting the two candles individually by magic. The flame flickered like a spot of purity amid the defiled air, and I held my breath and counted to ten. No demon showed up. Just as I had expected, they wouldn't know I was here as long as I didn't tap a line. I could do the spell.

Trent's hesitant movements just outside my vision stopped. "What are you doing?"

My jaw tightened, but I said nothing as I took my bag of salt and carefully spilled it out into the shape of an elongated figure eight. It was a modified Möbius strip. This curse was one of the few I'd ever seen that didn't use a pentagram, and I wondered if it was a completely different branch of magic. Maybe this wouldn't hurt so much.

"Rachel?" Trent prompted, and I sat back on my heels and puffed a curl that had escaped my hat out of my way.

"I've got ten minutes, and I'm going to do the curse that will keep Al from being summoned out of the ever-after."

"Now?" he said, wonder bringing his manicured eyebrows up. "You said demons could feel you tap a line. They'll be on us in seconds!"

Fingers trembling, I carefully placed the pyramid of copper where the salt lines crossed. "Which is why I'm going to do this without the protection of a circle," I said. "I have enough ever-after spindled inside me to do it." Ceri said I did. I trusted her. Though twisting a curse without a circle had me really, really nervous.

Trent's soft boots shifted in a show of protest, and I ignored him as I dug through the bag looking for the stick of redwood I had forgotten to pull out earlier. "Why are you risking it?" he said. "You're doing a demon curse before the sun comes up. In the ever-after. In a defiled church. Can't you do this when you get home?"

"*If* I get home," I accused. He was silent, and I set the flat piece of wood beside Al's sample. "If I don't make it, I want to die knowing my friends won't be taking the punishment Al has aimed at me. He'll be trapped in the ever-after." I eyed him. "For ever after."

Trent sat down where he could watch both me and the statue. Satisfied he wouldn't say anything else, I balanced the tongue-depressor-like stick of wood on the pyramid, the two ends hanging over the open loops of the Möbius strip. I was trying really hard not to think about what he had said about twisting a curse this close to sunup. This was bad. I mean, really bad.

"Okay," he said, startling me, and I looked up, incredulous that he thought I was waiting for his permission.

"Well, I'm glad I have your approval." Fingers shaking, I took the red candle for Al and placed it in the loop farthest from me, setting it with the word *"alius."* The gold one I set in my loop with the word *"ipse."* Gold. My aura hadn't been its original gold in a long time, but to use a black candle would just about kill me.

I poured a handful of salt into my grip, and after muttering a few words of Latin over it to give it meaning, I mixed it back and forth before dividing it equally and sifting it around the base of each unlit candle with the same words. Quickly, before Trent could distract me, I lit the candles with the hearth candle, again using the same words a final time. They were set three ways with the same strength and were immutable. It was a very secure beginning.

"Who taught you how to light candles with your thoughts?" Trent asked, and I jumped.

"Ceri," I said brusquely. "Will you be quiet, please?" I added, and he stood, stiffly going to stand beside the statue and out of my sight.

I felt my blood pressure drop, and moving slowly so as not to unbalance the stick of redwood, I snapped the tip of the ampoule off and tapped three ruby-black drops from it onto Al's side of the stick. The scent of burnt amber rose, almost chokingly thick. My eyes watered while I fumbled for the ceremonial knife. Almost done. It wasn't that difficult a curse, and hardly any magic was involved. The tough part had been in getting the samples. And I had mine right here.

While Trent watched from behind, I pricked my index finger. My heart pounded at the sudden jolt, and I massaged three drops out to land on my end of the stick. My shaking increased as I pushed out a drop more of blood and smeared it on the red candle. The curse was done but for the invocation. No demon would sense what I had done. I wasn't tapped into any line. The energy would come from the spindle in my chi. I looked at my watch, then Trent. I had to do this. I didn't like it, but I liked my other choices even less. Taking a deep breath, I closed my eyes. *"Evulgo,"* I whispered to start it.

I had used this word before. I had a feeling it was to register the curse, a feeling that strengthened when a wave of disconnection slipped over me and I felt the eerie sensation of being in a large room with hundreds of people, all talking at once and ignoring everyone. My heart was pounding. I could feel the curse strengthening in me, winding its way through my DNA, becoming me, pulsing with the force of an unheard heart. Dizzy, I opened my eyes.

Trent was standing above me. There was a faint glow of yellow surrounding him. I looked at my hands, seeing my aura for the first time without the aid of the scrying mirror. It was beautiful, gold and pure. No smut. I could have cried, seeing it. If only it would last, but I knew it was only because things were in flux.

"Are you okay?" he said, and I nodded. I had to finish this before I chickened out.

Mouth dry, I turned the stick a hundred and eighty degrees to move his sample to my loop and vice versa. *"Omnia mutantur,"* I whispered, invoking the curse.

All things change, I thought, then jumped when a feeling of being peeled out of my skin rippled over me. My hands shook, and when I looked, my aura was gone. It just . . . wasn't there.

"I had no choice," I said to Trent in explanation—maybe apology—then clenched my gut when the imbalance hit me.

Pain struck deep, doubling me over, and I pushed violently away in a panic. My foot scattered the curse as I curled into a ball, and I smelled extinguished candle.

"Jenks!" Trent shouted. "Something's wrong!"

I couldn't breathe. Bent into myself, I tried to open my eyes. My face scraped against the decaying carpet, and I grunted as I tried to find control. My head felt like it was splitting in two, and I cracked my lids, desperate to see. That made it worse. Oh, God, the imbalance was stronger than anything I'd ever felt before.

"Rache, you okay?" Jenks said, inches from me as he hovered over the carpet.

I got one clean breath in before the pain hit me again. I didn't want it, but the imbalance would kill me if I didn't take it as my own.

"Hold her!" Jenks shouted. "I can't help her, damn it! Trent, hold her before she hurts herself!" he demanded, and I sobbed when I felt Trent's arms go around me to keep me from rolling down the stairs.

"I take it," I gasped, my head exploding and my chest cramping. "I take the damn curse."

Like a light switch cutting off, my muscles quit seizing, and I sucked in a ragged breath of air that tasted like candle smoke. I took another breath, then another, content to simply exist without pain. Slowly my muscles relaxed, leaving only my throbbing head. Trent was sitting behind me with his arms wrapped around me. My face was wet, and Trent let go when I moved to wipe the dampness and carpet off my cheek. Slow and lethargic, I looked at my hand to make sure it had been tears and not blood I wiped away. My head hurt that badly.

"I'm okay," I rasped, and Trent's hold dropped. I heard him slide away and get up. Jenks was watching us from a railing, his face pale and pinched. "Did any demons show up?" I asked him, and he shook his head.

Utterly wiped, I shifted myself farther from Trent, embarrassed and trying to find some semblance of self again. I had done it. Damn it, it hurt so much that it had to have worked. I looked at my hands, both wanting to and fearing I might see an alien aura. They were shaking. My aura was again hidden, and I was too afraid to ask Jenks if it was mine, or Al's, or nonexistent.

I looked at Jenks, and he smiled. "It's yours," he said, and my eyes closed as a lump grew in my throat. I pushed the emotion down. We had a run to finish.

"Do you have Trent's sample?" I asked. "We have to get out

of here." I'd cry later over what I had done to myself. Right now, we had to leave.

"It's coming," he said. "I found it under 'Kallasea.' Female elf installed in . . . three fifty-seven B.C., if I did my subtraction right. They mark everything from when the elves abandoned the ever-after. Your court date wouldn't have come up for five years." The pixy laughed. "That's what organized justice will do to you. Rome didn't fall. It was strangled in red tape."

"Bring it to me!" Trent shouted, and both Jenks and I jumped.

"All right, all right," he muttered as he zipped to the statue. "Don't have a hairy fart."

They mark the years the same as us, I thought, shoving things into my bag and hesitating when I couldn't find Al's sample. Where in hell had it rolled to?

"Got it!" came a faint call, and Jenks burst back out in a glitter of gold sparkles. A new ampoule was in his grip, with a faint amber tint to the glass. Trent gazed hungrily up at him, looking like Rex following a pixy toddler. "Once I had a name, it was as easy as pulling the wings off a fairy," Jenks said smugly. "You got anything sweet in your backpack? I haven't eaten in hours. Damn, I'm as tired as a pixy on his wedding night."

"Sorry, Jenks. I didn't know you were coming, or I would have brought something."

Trent was shaking, the impatient man snatching up his pack and holding out his hand. "I have some chocolate," he said. "Give me the sample and it's yours."

We were going to do it. We were going to get out of here. Provided the curse Trent bought from Minias worked. If it didn't, Jenks and I were really screwed.

Jenks snapped his wings together with a loud crack in anticipation. "Excellent!" he said, then froze in midair. "Uh, Rachel?" he said, every last speck of dust vanishing from him. "I don't feel right."

"Can it wait until we get home?" I said, checking Ivy's watch. Crap. The sun was up.

There was a soft puff of displaced air, and my head jerked up. Someone had just popped in. *Shit.* But when I scanned the room, it was empty. "Jenks?" I said, feeling cold.

Trent stared at me, one foot on the stairs. "Where's your pixy?"

Had someone cursed him into nothing? I stared at the fading cloud of dust, my heart clenching in fear. "Jenks!"

Trent lurched up onto the stage. "Where's my sample? He's gone! He used the last curse and left us here!"

"No!" I protested. "He wouldn't! How could he? He doesn't even know it!"

"Then why isn't the curse working?" he shouted. "It's not working, Rachel!"

"You're asking me?" I snapped back. "I'm not the one who bargained for it. Maybe we need to go back to where we came in. Don't blame my partner if you made a bad bargain!"

Trent gave me a murderous look. Silent, he took the stairs and headed for the side door.

"Hey!" I shouted. "Where are you going?"

He never slowed. "To put distance between us before someone tracks you down. If surface demons can hide from demons, so can I. I never should have trusted you. Trusting a Morgan killed my family. I'm not going to let it kill me."

The harsh red glare of the sun spilled in when he yanked the door open. Squinting, I glimpsed a flash of purple, prestorm sky. A gust sent my hair flying and atomized the dust circles. Then the door swung shut, cutting off the light and wind.

Heart pounding, I knelt to shove the last of my curse stuff into my bag. "Jenks!" I shouted, clueless as to where he'd gone to. "We gotta go!"

Pulse fast, I ran out after Trent. The light was blinding after the soft glow of electric lights. "Damn it, Trent," I shouted as my feet hit the concrete stoop. "I can't get you home in one piece if you run off like that."

Arms pinwheeling, I skidded to a stop on the narrow landing outside the door. There in the shade of the trees was Minias with three of those demons in red. Trent was slumped on the ground before their feet. He wasn't moving. Crap on toast, they'd known we were here the instant Minias had been slung back home with the sun.

Hand fumbling for my splat gun, I turned to retreat, only to run into Minias's chest.

"No!" I shrieked, but I was too close to do anything, and he pinned my arms to my sides. He was in the sun, and I could see his pupils, slitted like a goat's, and the red of his irises, so deep that it almost looked brown.

"Yes," he said, pinching my arms until I gasped in pain. "What, by the two worlds, have you been doing, Rachel Mariana Morgan?"

"Wait," I babbled. "I can pay. I know stuff. I want to go home!"

Minias sent one eyebrow rising. "You are home."

There was a pop from under the trees, and Minias grimaced as he looked toward it.

"That witch is mine!" came Al's distinctive voice, and Minias wrapped a possessive arm around me. "She's got my mark!" the demon raged. "Give her to me!"

"She wears Newt's mark, too," Minias said. "And I have possession of her."

A ribbon of panic pulled through me. I had to do something. I didn't think Al knew I had his summoning name, or he'd be yammering about that, not the lousy mark he had put on my wrist. I had to get out of here. I had to reach my splat gun.

Grunting in effort, I wiggled and twisted. Minias swung me around. My legs folded awkwardly under me as he slammed my ass onto the concrete. I reached for the cement, trying to find my feet and run at the same time. But Minias put a hand on my shoulder, pinning me. A wave of something flowed from him, and I stiffened as I struggled to breathe through the sensation of every last erg of ley line power being pulled from me. It was the opposite of Al's line-overload punishment, and it felt like rape. I struggled to flee, but his hand on my shoulder pinched harder.

Minias looked down at me, and the scent of amber flowed from him as his gaze took on an inquisitive hue. "Trying to steal Al's name to prevent him from being summoned out was a good idea. Bad idea to attempt to implement, though. No one has ever gotten past that statue."

They didn't know. They didn't know I had done it, and my success gave me a burst of hope. Soon as they figured it out, Al was going to be pissed, but if I could escape, I'd be okay. I could tap a line and hit Minias with it, but he'd probably just pull it out from me again, and my soul was still ringing from his first invasion. If I was going to escape, it'd have to be physically.

Gathering myself, I tried to break free, but he knew what I was going to do before I did it. The moment I had my feet, he simply jerked me off balance, into him. His yellow-clad arm wrapped around me, tightening until I almost couldn't breathe.

At least I can see now, I thought as I spat the hair out of my mouth. The wind was worse with the sun being up, and my hair was gritty and my lips tasted of burnt amber. The red light hurt my eyes. No wonder witches had left to live in an unpolluted world—fleeing a dying ever-after to exist among humans. *Stay hidden, Jenks. Wherever you are.*

Al was striding out from under the trees, his white-gloved hands in murderous fists. "That witch is mine!" he spat. "I'll fight this all the way through the courts."

"Newt owns the courts," Minias said coolly. "You want the witch, you can buy her like anyone else."

They were going to sell me?

Al stopped at the base of the stairs, frustrated. "My mark came first!"

"And that means what?" Minias sniffed, and a pair of wrap-around glasses appeared on his face. "Give me permission to jump you underground through the lines," he said to me. "It's disgusting up here."

My chest hurt, and I wondered if the earth charms in my gun were still good. "No."

From the gray slump that was Trent came a raspy "Never."

One of the demons nudged him with his foot, and a shocking scream burst from Trent, quickly stifled and turned into a ragged gasp of air. Pity filled me as I remembered the agony of Al forcing me to hold more ever-after than I could bear. It felt as if your soul were on fire. Tears warmed my eyes, and I shut them when Trent passed out and the ugly sounds stopped.

"This one at least is mine," Minias said. "Tag him as a novelty and work up a brief history so the collectors will be interested. Don't take a lot of time. Rachel Mariana Morgan will be the high-ticket item."

"You can't auction her off. She's mine! I've been grooming her for over a year," Al threatened, and the tails of his green velveteen coat flapped as he strode up the steps. His chiseled face was hard, and he squinted as if his tinted glasses were ineffective. "I marked her first. Newt's claim is secondary. This is my *job*!"

My teeth clenched, but I could do nothing when Trent and the demon who had touched him into unconsciousness vanished.

"The courts will decide," Minias said, yanking me out of Al's reach.

Al's strong jaw clenched and his hands turned into fists. I wasn't all that joy-joy about it either, and I struggled when Minias gave me a shake and said, "Let me jump you."

I shook my head, and he shrugged, tapping a line. He was going to try to stun me the same way they had stunned Trent. I felt it coming, and I opened my thoughts to take it, gasping as ever-after energy roared into me. I spindled it, panting with the effort.

Minias's eyebrows furrowed, and he turned to Al. "You ass!" he shouted. "You taught a witch how to spindle a line as well? You lied to the courts? Dali can't help you now."

Al jerked back a step. "I did not," he said indignantly. "They never asked. And I bound her to condition as tight as the elf's. What is the *problem* here! I have *control* of the situation!"

I had two demons fighting over me. Seconds, maybe. I reached for a line. Minias felt it.

"Bloody hell!" he swore. "She's trying to jump!" he shouted, shaking me. "Now how do we contain her?"

I touched the line, willing it to take me, my thoughts on Ivy. But a thick white-gloved fist swung to meet my temple. It ripped me from Minias's grip, and I fell, my hands getting between me and the cement at the last moment, palms scraping. Someone's foot slammed into my gut, and gasping for air, I rolled into the basilica's side door. Unable to breathe, I stared at the ugly red sky and felt the wind on my face.

"Like that," Al snarled. "Leave catching familiars to the experts, Minias."

I felt Minias pick me up, my arms dangling. "Holy sweet spit, she's still not out."

"Then you hit her again," Al said, and another burst of pain sent me into nothing.

Twenty-eight

My head hurt. Actually, the entire right side of my face hurt, not just my head, a deep, throbbing ache that seemed to come from the bone and pulse in time with my heart. I was slumped facedown on something warm and softly yielding, like the mats at the gym. My eyes were closed, and words whispered at the edge of my awareness, fading into the hum of a distant fan when I concentrated on them.

I shifted my head to get up, slowing when my neck complained. I put a hand to it and pulled my legs under me to find an upright position. The sound of my leather pants scraping the floor was soft, the echoes nonexistent. My eyes opened, but I couldn't see a difference. One hand on my neck, one sort of propping myself up, I tugged David's coat out from under me and took a slow breath. I was wet—my hair damp and the taste of salt water on my lips. The cool certainty of charmed silver rested upon my wrist. *Swell.*

"Trent?" I whispered. "Are you here?"

There was a rough *harrumph,* chilling me.

"Good evening, Rachel Mariana Morgan."

It was Al. I froze in panic, trying to see. There was a click six feet in front of me, and I scuttled backward, crying out in surprise when my back hit a wall. Fear was a sharp goad. I tried to rise, and my head hit the ceiling a mere four feet up.

"Ow!" I yelped, falling down and moving like a crab until I

found a corner. My pulse hammered, and I strained to see. Everything was black. It was as if my eyes were gone.

Al's low, mocking laugh grew in depth, then faded with a bitter sound. "Stupid witch."

"Stay away," I demanded, pulse hammering and my knees to my chin. I wiped the last of the salt water from my face and pushed my hair back. "You come near me, and I'll make sure you never engender any little demons. Ever."

"If I could touch you," Al said, his accent clear and precise, "you'd be dead. You're in jail, love. Want to be my shower buddy?"

I wiped my face again, slowly letting my knees fall from my chest. "How long?" I asked.

"Have you been here?" Al murmured lightly. "Same as me. All day. How long will you remain? Just until I get out, and then I'll be back. I'm looking forward to joining you in that tiny box of a cell you're in."

Fear slid through me, then was gone.

"Feeling better?" he almost purred. "Come over here by the bars, love, and I'll rub your aching head for you. Rub it right off your skinny little shoulders."

Hatred nearly dripped from his soothing voice, still so elegant and refined. Okay. I was in jail. I knew why I was in jail, but why was Al? Then I winced, wondering if I could have pissed the demon off any more. He'd warned me not to tell anyone I knew how to spindle line energy. And then I went and did it in front of Minias. They had caught Al in a lie of omission, and I didn't think he could put any kind of spin on it to make it look good.

Squinting to try to make the black haze take shape, I began to move with my hand outstretched, making a point of staying far from Al's voice. My ears strained to catch the echo of my breathing against the maybe-walls, but I heard nothing. A soft touch of fabric on my searching fingers jerked me to a stop, then I reached out. It was a warm body that smelled like blood and cinnamon. "Trent?" I whispered worriedly as I crouched closer and sent my hands over him. *They had put us there to-gether?* "Oh, God. Are you all right?"

"For the moment," he said. "Do you mind not touching me?"

His very awake tone shocked me, and I jerked back. "You're all right!" I exclaimed as the warmth of embarrassment turned to a mild anger. "Why didn't you say anything?"

"What would be the point?"

I eased back and sat cross-legged as I heard him shift. I couldn't see, but I guessed he was leaning into the opposite corner. It was the best place in the cell, seeing as it was far-thest from Al. I think.

A shiver rose through me, and I stifled it. Al was there. I was here. I wished I could see. "What are they going to do with us?" I asked Trent. "How long have you been awake?"

A faint exhalation gave evidence of a sigh. "Too long, and what do you think they're going to do with us?"

There was the slosh of water in a plastic bottle, and I grew ten times more thirsty.

"We were caught," Trent said, his gray voice empty of hope. "I woke up here."

Al cleared his throat dryly. "There's a small question being debated right now as to the legality of my claim on you," he said, and I wondered why he bothered, except that he was probably bored and didn't like being ignored. "You had to go and show them that you could spindle energy. They don't even care that I nullified the threat, deciding to drop me here and let me 'think about what I've done.' Soon as I'm summoned out, I'll pop back in, throttle you to death, then throw your dead carcass on Dali's floor and claim I was handling it and they owe me restitution for interfering."

He still didn't know I had his summoning name and couldn't be pulled across the lines, but my brief relief died. What did it matter? He'd find out soon enough. My thoughts flicked to Jenks, and my heart seemed to fall to my gut. We'd been so close. God, I hoped he was okay.

The jiggling of water against plastic drew my hand up, and fumbling, I found the container Trent was extending for me. I didn't bother wiping the top before I took a swig, and I grimaced at the unexpected taste of burnt amber. "Thank you," I said, then gave it back. "This is your water. From your pack. We have our stuff?" My eyes widened in the dark. "Do you have your light?"

I heard Trent shift his feet. "Broken. Yours, too. For the psychological effect, I'm sure, seeing as that's all they did, apart from putting the bands of charmed silver on us and dousing us in salt water."

"Yeah," I said, feeling wet and icky. "I figured that part out." Not bothering to search for my bag, I mentally catalogued what I had shoved into it. Nothing, really. And with the band of charmed silver around my wrist, I couldn't even light the candle. But then my eyebrows rose, and moving carefully, I felt the small of my back. My lips parted when I felt the cool plastic. They left me my splat gun? Pulse fast, I drew it, aiming where I had heard Al's voice. "Maybe," I said as I thumbed the safety off, "they don't think we're a threat."

"Maybe," Al said, "they don't care if we kill each other. You hit me with that, and I won't kill you when I get out, but just play with you. Until you die screaming."

My hand shook just a little, and I strained to see in the dark.

"Just because you can't see doesn't mean I can't," Al said. "It won't land at this distance, witch, but by all means, waste them. It will make it far easier to beat you into submission when I get in there."

He wasn't getting out, but I put the safety back on and tucked the gun away at the small of my back. I wasn't enough of a fool to think the demons had put me here without knowing I had viable charms on me. They'd taken everything I could use to escape but left me a way to protect myself. Was it a test, or just their twisted version of reality TV? I slumped and leaned my head against the wall. Most likely it was a matter of letting us settle this demon to witch, and if I beat him, Newt would have a better legal shot at me.

The light band of silver around my wrist felt heavier than any chain. I didn't even try to tap a line and figure out how to jump out of here. I was caught, and it looked like I wasn't going to get out of it this time.

"Almost sundown," Al said from the darkness, his voice eager. "A few moments and I'll be free. You were a fool thinking you could pin me in the ever-after by taking my summoning name. No one has ever gotten past that bitch of a statue. No one ever will."

Sundown. He seemed pretty sure someone would summon him out. When they didn't, he was going to be royally ticked, and I scooted back even farther.

A quiver in the middle of my chi started. I froze, my hand to my lower gut. I'd never felt anything like this hollow ache before. And it was growing worse. "I don't feel so good," I whispered to Trent, but it wasn't like he cared.

Al made a harsh bark of laughter. "You shouldn't have drunk that water. It had been exposed to the sun."

"I'm fine," Trent said, his soft voice darker than the warm air that surrounded us.

"You're an elf," Al said with disdain. "Elves are little more than animals. They can eat anything."

I groaned, pressing a hand to my stomach. "No," I said breathily, looking downward. "I really don't feel good." *Oh, God. I'm going to spew in front of Trent.*

But every muscle in my body shook as a sneeze ripped through me instead.

Minias? I thought as I wiped an arm under my nose. But there was nothing in my mind but my own thoughts.

"Bless you," Trent said sarcastically.

I sneezed again, and the ache in my middle grew. My eyes widened and I flung a hand out to smack against the floor for balance. I felt like I was falling. My insides were falling. Panicking, I reached out to grip Trent. "Something's wrong," I rasped. "Trent, something's really wrong. Are we falling? Tell me you feel like you're falling." I was going to throw up. That's all there was to it.

From across the unseen hall came a roar of anger. "Damned mother of us all!" Al swore, then he swore again as he hit his head, by the sound of it. "You little whore! You stinking ashed little whore! Come here. Come here where I can reach you!"

Struggling to focus on nothing, I shrank from the sound of him hitting the bars and his fingers scrabbling for me. Every move I made seemed to be made a moment after I willed it, the neurons not firing as fast as they should.

"How did you get past the statue!" Al raged, his voice hurting my ears. "It's not possible!"

"What's wrong with me . . . ," I panted, and Trent made an ugly noise, trying to get my grip off his arm.

"You're being summoned out, you little bitch," Al spat. "You've got my summoning name. And it's being used. How did you get my name! You've been unconscious all day!"

I felt like my middle was gone and I was only a shell. I tried to see my hand, but there was nothing. And then my face went utterly cold. "This can't happen. Minias said it couldn't happen. I'm not a demon. It shouldn't work for me! I'm not a demon!"

"Apparently," Al said, slamming into the bars in time with his words, "you're so damn *close*, it doesn't *matter*!" There was another grunt, then he shouted, "Someone get me out of here!"

Pain pulled me double and my hair pooled on my knees. Oh, God, it was going to kill me. I felt like I was going to be split in two. No wonder demons were pissed when they were summoned.

"Rachel," Trent was saying, his hand on my back, leaning over me as I gasped for air. "Promise me you'll get my people whole. Promise me you'll use the sample! I'll die content if you promise me you'll use the sample!"

Sample? I don't even have the sample. I pulled my head up, not seeing him, then seized as my aura seemed to soak inward to my core, pulling my flesh along with it. Agony burned through my mind, and whimpering, I stopped fighting it. I *wanted* to leave, didn't I?

It made all the difference in the world.

The pain vanished. A silver thread of intent pulled through me, and before I could marvel at the heavenly absence of pain, I was whole, my lungs trying to work but not quite managing it yet. I was on my front, facedown. Or at least I would be when my aura finished rising through me, putting the idea of flesh around my soul again. I panted when my lungs formed, and I stared at the shadowy plywood floor two inches before my face. I could see. And it smelled like . . . bleach?

There was a soft murmur of incantation, and the scent of ash and candle mixed with the reek of burnt amber flowing from me. I looked at my hand in front of my face, seeing the bright glow of my aura. I could see it. I shouldn't have been able to.

I took another breath and the haze of gold faded to nothing. The incantation dissolved into a collective gathering of breath. I was in someone's basement. I had been summoned out under Al's name. It wasn't possible. This was so wrong. Confused, I looked up past the stringy length of my damp curls to see a cluster of black-robed figures safe on the other side of a glowing-hot sheet of ever-after.

"Lord demon," a young, masculine voice said, and my head jerked up as I recognized it. "Are you . . . well?"

Twenty-nine

Y ou!" I raged, my confusion vanishing as I saw the youthful, clean-cut features of the I.S. officer standing before the long conference table in Betty's basement.

Angry, I gathered myself and stood, hunched until I knew I wasn't going to hit the green-tinted ever-after over my head. I was on that low stage, standing in the middle of a large circle filling the cave of a pentagram. Greenish white candles marked the corners, which were hazy as they existed both here and in the ever-after. A tarry black sludge marked the limit of my cell. Horror trickled through me as I realized they had used blood to draw the circle, not salt. *Damn it, I'm at the center of a black circle*.

My gaze went to the crack in the wall, and I felt the assembled people draw back. There were six of them, including Tom Bansen. Music thumped in through the ceiling, a low bass that sounded like a heartbeat, and I thought I recognized it. The stench of bleach and mold told me Betty had been cleaning, but it didn't begin to push out the reek of· ever-after I had brought with me. God, I needed a shower in the worst way.

Tom's eyes were wide as they took me in: my long duster white with ash and dried salt, my hair a tangled mess, and the dust and grit from the ever-after coating me. There were five men in front of him, all in those hokey black robes. Their hoods made them look like a joke, but these people had been intentionally summoning Al and letting him go, knowing he was going to try to kill me.

Furious, I took three steps, almost running into the arc of ever-after I was trapped behind. Claustrophobia clenched my heart and I took a sharp breath. "Let me out!" I yelled in frustration, feeling the energy cramp the muscles of my hand when I got too close. That had never happened before, even when I had been in someone else's circle. God help me, what had Trent's father done to me? I'd kill him. I'd freaking kill Trent for this.

"I said, let me out!" I shouted. I was helpless. For all my skills, I was completely helpless. The little pissant had me trapped with a stupid circle. "Let me out, now!" I said again, giving in and smacking the shield between us. It hissed and burned, and I held my hand to me as the pain shocked me to my senses. I was not a demon. This had to be a mistake. Al had said I wasn't one. My mom was a witch, and Takata was a witch, and that meant I was a witch. *One who can kindle demon magic and be summoned with a name?*

From behind the living wall of trembling acolytes, Tom bowed his head. "Of course, lord demon, Algaliarept, after the formalities have been observed. We have prepared."

My next snarl died, and I steeled my face to show no emotion. I glanced down at myself, then back at him. *He thought I was Al in disguise?*

A slow smile came over my face, which seemed to scare them more than my anger had. If they thought I was Al, they were going to let me out. After all, I had to go kill myself. "Let me out," I said softly, still smiling. "I won't hurt you." *Much.*

My voice had been low, but inside, I was seething. The FIB wanted proof that Tom was sending Al to kill me? Okay. I was willing to bet I was going to get it. Seeing me calmer, Tom bowed, still looking stupid. No wonder Al got off on being summoned. This was sickening.

"As you will," the man said. "We have everything you demanded." He gestured, and two of the men peeled off and went to the back room that I'd never looked into. "I apologize for the delay. We had an unexpected interruption last night."

"The animal control people? How pathetic," I said, and Tom paled. I smiled, enjoying watching him squirm. Al was right. Information was power.

"There won't be any more delays," Tom stammered, his underlings whispering among themselves. "Once you show us the curse, you may go."

You may go, I thought, stifling an angry snort. *I'm going to go put my foot right up your ass, that's where I'm going to go.*

The conference table had a drape of red velvet on it, but I hadn't noticed the three nasty knives, the head-size copper pot, or the three candles until the two outermost guys had left. The pot and candles were ominous enough, but the knives made my gut clench. They had everything but the goat. Nervous, I plucked the damp cuffs from my wrist as I had seen Al do with lace. My eyebrows rose when I realized the band of charmed silver was gone, and I reached for a line, finding it. *Thank you, God.*

"You don't care that I'm going to go murder one of your own?" I asked, fishing for the incriminating words.

"Rachel Morgan?" A hint of disgust crept into Tom's voice. "No. I thought you appeared as her again to taunt me. Kill her and I'll get a raise."

Son of a bastard . . . Anger burned, and I pointed at him, my scraped palm on my hip. "I showed up as her because she's better than you, you puking, stinking excuse for a witch!" I shouted, then drew back when the circle hummed a warning.

"We are unworthy," Tom said sullenly.

Yeah, like I really believed he thought that.

The door to the back room swung open, and I lifted my attention over Tom to see two men wrestling with a frantic, tied woman. My gaze darted to the knives and the bowl, then to her bandaged wrists and the blood on the floor holding me. *Shit.*

She was scared, fighting them though her ankles and wrists were bound with duct tape and she wore a gag. "Who is that?" I demanded, struggling to hide my fear. *Oh, my God. She is the goat.*

"The woman you requested." Tom shifted in his sneakers to look at her. "We had to go out of the city to find her. Again, my apologies for the delay."

Her bare arms were brown from the sun, and her long red hair was bleached by it. Shit on toast, she looked like me, but younger, her limbs lacking the definition of my martial arts practice. Her fear redoubled as she saw me, and she shrieked, starting to fight in earnest.

"Don't hurt her!" I demanded, then shifted my expression to one I hoped looked lascivious enough. "I like untouched skin."

Tom flushed. "Ah, we couldn't find a virgin."

The woman's eyes glistened with tears, but I saw the hint of fury in her. I quite honestly thought that Al wouldn't care if she was a virgin or not. "Don't hurt her," I said again, and the two men wrestling her out dropped her on the floor, standing with their arms crossed above her.

She looked like me. What Al had been going to do with her was sickening. *Please let her be the first one. . . .* "Let me out," I said, standing at the arc of ever-after. "Now."

The acolytes shifted with an excited tension. They wouldn't know what hit them.

"Let me out!" I demanded, not caring whether I sounded like a demon. Hell, maybe I was one. My head hurt, but I didn't touch it. *Let this be a mistake. Let this all be a big mistake.*

Tom looked at the woman, and the first hints of remorse at what he was going to allow to happen to her flickered in his eyes. But he turned away, greed pushing the guilt out. "Do you vow to show us how to successfully perform the spell we want and leave us unharmed, exacting your toll on that woman instead of those who called you?"

I vow you'll never see the outside of a cell again. "Oh, yeah," I lied. "Anything you say."

The idiots behind him smiled and congratulated each other.

"Then be free," Tom said with laughable showmanship, and with the six of them clapping once in unison to indicate their agreement, their collective circle fell.

I shuddered as the prickling vanished, realizing how much it had bothered me to be helpless like that. It hadn't been anything like being in Trent's cage.

The smarter acolytes backed up a step, reading in my posture that they were going to be hurting in the morning. I reached behind me to the splat gun, putting one foot on the circle so it couldn't be invoked anew. "Tom," I said, smiling, "you are so stupid."

His confusion showed, and when I brought out my gun, he jumped to the side.

I shot three of them before anyone else had the smarts to move.

The room seemed to flow into motion. Shouting in fear, the three men left standing scattered, looking like frogs with their silly black robes streaming behind them. The woman on the floor was crying behind her gag, and I shot over her as she rolled to her hands and knees and tried to get to the metal door at the stairway out of here.

A tingle of ever-after prickled through my aura, and I left the raised stage, heading for the nearest guy. They were setting a net, basically an undrawn circle that took three or more proficient ley line witches to hold. He was on his knees, wide-eyed and scared, and when he saw me coming at him, he increased the volume of his voice, screaming Latin at me.

"Your syntax sucks!" I shouted, then grabbed the copper pot off the table and threw it at him. Yeah, I was ticked, but if I didn't get him to stop talking, they might have me.

He ducked, and in the instant he was distracted, I plowed into him.

Yanking him up by his shirtfront, I drew back to slug him, my balance shifting forward when something hit me from behind. Yelping, I let go and stood up, trying to get out of my coat. It was smoldering, covered in green goo.

"Hey! This is *not* my *coat*!" I shouted, turning to see Tom winding up again.

The guy I had pulled up from the floor skittered away, and swearing, I remembered my gun and just shot the poor sucker. He dropped like a bag of flour, sighing as his nose broke and blood soaked the ugly carpet. Poor Betty. She was going to have to get out the Shop-Vac again.

The woman screamed, and I spun at the piercing sound. My look-alike had gotten her gag off and was curled up at the door with her hands and feet still bound. I could hear Sampson on the other side, yapping and trying to dig his way through. The sound of her fear dove to the primitive part of my brain and set my adrenaline flowing.

"Please let me out," she sobbed, trying to reach the knob with her bound wrists. "Someone please let me out!" She saw me looking at her, and she scrabbled harder. "Don't kill me. I want to live. Please, I want to live!"

I was going to be sick. But her fear turned to wonder, and her eyes tracked behind me. My skin prickled, and when her mouth opened in a little round O, I threw myself to the floor.

A small explosion shifted the air, and my ears rang. Pulling my gaze up from the damp carpet, I saw another puddle of green goo slowly sliding down the dark paneling, eating away at it. Damn, what had Al taught them?

I rolled, intuition telling me there was another one coming.

"You idiot!" I shouted as I leapt to my feet, cursing my habit of talking during fights and righteous sex. "You want a piece of me? You want a piece of *this*? I'll shove it down your damn throat!"

In an inexcusable act of cowardice, Tom pushed the last ac-olyte at me. The man fell at my feet, begging for mercy. So I shot him with a sleepy-time potion. It was all the mercy I had right now.

Pissed, I spun to Tom. "You're next, little man," I snarled, taking aim. I squeezed the trigger, and a sheet of green-tinted ever-after rose up around him.

I leapt forward, pinwheeling to a stop when I realized I was too late. Tom had reset the circle I had been summoned into, putting himself in its center. One of the candles had been knocked over, and it rolled off the stage, trailing melted wax and a thin plume of smoke.

The insufferable man panted, confused, as he put his palms on his knees to catch his breath. "You broke your word," he panted, brown eyes savagely bright. "You can't do that. You're mine." He smiled. "Forever."

Hands on my hips, I faced him. "If you summon demons, you lousy, stinking piece of crap, you'd better be sure the right one shows up before you let her out."

His face lost all expression, and he turned to the stage. "You're not Al."

"Ding, ding, ding," I mocked. "Give that man a prize!" In-side I was shaking, but it gave me an obscene amount of plea-sure to watch Tom realize his life had just run full tilt into a pile of demon dung the size of Manhattan. "You have the right to remain silent," I added. "Anything you say I'm going to put in my moss-wipe of a report, and you'll fry faster."

Tom went a beautiful shade of green.

"You have the right to an attorney, but unless you're a hell of a lot richer than this basement looks, you're one royally screwed witch."

His mouth opened and closed, and his gaze darted behind me to the woman by the door. "Who are you? I called Al-galiarept," he whispered.

My breath hissed in. "Shut up!" I shouted, hitting his bubble with a side kick. "Don't say that name!" It was my name now.

Oh, God, it was my name, and anyone who knew it could pull me into a circle. What would happen when the sun came up, I couldn't even guess.

Tom stared. "Morgan? How did you . . . You killed Algaliarept! You killed a demon and took his name!"

Hardly, I thought. I took a demon's name and killed myself. Maybe Ivy had been right and I should have just tried to knock off Al. My demise might have been quicker that way. None of this lingering mess to deal with. "Not so tough without your wand, are you, eh?" I said, hearing an intercom buzzing somewhere, barely audible over the woman sobbing by the door. Tom had drawn himself straight, and I pushed on his bubble, appreciating not being burned by it. "Nice," I said, then, frustrated, I hit his barrier with my foot again. The man stumbled back, almost knocking into his circle and sending it down. I started pacing, limping around him as the intercom hummed. "Get used to it, Tom. You're going to be in a cage for a long time."

But Tom's look went crafty, reminding me he knew how to trip to a line. I stared at him, and his smile grew. He wouldn't. Al was his demon contact, wasn't he? He wouldn't risk it. Al would feel it and be on him in a second. But Al was in jail, so maybe it didn't matter.

"No!" I shouted, desperate to keep him from jumping. Steeling myself, I put my left hand on the barrier and pushed. I knew what it was now. I had taken his circle before, and with one candle missing, this one was compromised. I could do this. *How am I going to do this?*

My aura burned, and teeth clenched, I stared at him from around the lank strands of my hair, panting as I tried to absorb his power. Take control of the line he had tapped. All of it.

I felt something shift, as if the entire field had gone see-through. I looked at Tom. His eyes were wide; he had felt it, too. And then he was gone. His aura-laced shield of ever-after vanished and I fell forward.

"Damn it all to hell!" I shouted as I caught my balance. I

turned, seeing that poor woman watching me, her sobs temporarily halted. The intercom was still humming, and I stood with my hip cocked and my good hand to my forehead. I could have had him, but I had monologued. Damn it, I was not going to do *that* again.

But the woman was still cowering by the door, and forcing a smile, I headed toward her, grabbing the smallest knife in passing to cut her bonds. The intercom finally quit buzzing, a blessed relief.

The woman's gaze widened in panic. "Stay away!" she screamed, scrabbling back. From behind the door, Sampson barked furiously.

The utter terror in her voice stopped me cold, and I looked from the knife in my grip to the bodies laying around. There was a sharp scent of ozone in the damp air, and the scent of blood. Her wrists were bleeding around the duct tape. What had they done to her?

"It's okay," I said, dropping the knife and kneeling to be on her level. "I'm one of the good guys." *I am. Really, I am.* "Let me get the tape off you."

"D-Don't touch me!" she shrilled, her green eyes wide when I reached out.

My hand dropped to my middle. I felt filthy. "Sampson!" I shouted at the door. "Shut the hell up!"

The dog went silent, and my tension eased in the new quiet. The woman's pupils were huge. "All right," I said, backing up when tears kept slipping down her cheeks. "I won't touch you. Just . . . stay there. I'll figure this out."

Leaving the knife within her reach, I searched for a phone to call for reinforcements. Someone's bowels had let go, and it was starting to stink. The intercom began buzzing again, leading me right to it. It was one of those intercom phone systems, and ticked, I thumbed the circuit open. "Betty, is that you?" I shouted into it, releasing some tension.

"Are you okay down there?" came her worried voice. I

could hear the TV on in the background over the music. "I heard screaming."

"He's tearing apart that woman," I said, trying to make my voice lower and winking at the girl. Her whimpering stopped, and her green eyes were wet and beautiful. "Get off the damn phone! And turn the music down, will you?"

"Well, so-o-o-orry," she muttered. "It sounded like you were in trouble."

The line clicked, and the buzz of an open phone line hummed out. My gaze went to the woman, who was sniffing loudly. Hope was in her expression and the knife was in her still-bound hands. "Can I get the tape off you now?" I asked, and she shook her head no. But at least she wasn't screaming. Shaking, I punched in the FIB's number and Glenn's extension.

The ringing phone was picked up immediately, and Glenn's preoccupied "Glenn here" never sounded so good. I sniffed back a tear, wondering where it had come from. I didn't remember starting to cry. "Hey, hi, Glenn," I said. "I got Tom to voluntarily admit he was letting Al go to kill me. Even got a motive. Could you come over and pick me up?"

"Rachel?" Glenn gasped. "Where are you? Ivy and Jenks think you're dead. The entire department does."

My eyes closed and I sent a silent prayer of thanks out. Jenks was with Ivy. He was okay. They both were. I bit my lip and held my breath against the tears. A big bad-ass runner doesn't cry. Even when she finds out she's a demon. "I'm in Betty's basement," I said, keeping my voice low so it wouldn't warble and give away how upset I was. "There are five black ley line witches down here out cold, and at least one upstairs. You're going to need some salt water to wake them up. He tried to make some poor girl into a goat," I said, tears starting to flow. "She looks like me, Glenn. They picked her because she looks like me."

"Are you okay?" he asked, and I forced myself to stop.

"I don't know," I said, feeling my life end. "I'm sorry for dumping this on you, but I can't go to the I.S. I think Tom's doing this with their blessing." I looked at the last spot I'd seen him in, hatred briefly overpowering tears from the adrenaline crash.

"She's alive," Glenn said off the phone. "No, I'm talking to her. You got the house number? You got the number?" There was a crackle of static, and he was back. "We'll be there in five minutes," he said, his deep voice soothing. "Sit tight. Don't move unless you have to."

I slumped to the floor with the phone to my ear. I felt worse than the woman, who was chewing at her duct tape. "Sure," I said listlessly. "But Tom is gone. Watch Betty. She may look stupid, but she probably knows some nasty stuff." I felt dizzy. "Anyone who kicks their dog is nasty."

Glenn sighed in frazzled frustration. "I'm on my way. Damn it, I'm going to have to leave this phone. Talk to Rose until I get there, okay?"

I shook my head, drawing my knees to my chin. "No. I have to call Ivy."

"Rachel . . . ," he warned. "Don't hang up on me."

But I did. The tears slipped down, cleaning the grit of ever-after from my face, but nothing could clean the shame from my mind. A demon. Trent's dad had made me into a freaking damned demon?

Miserable, I sat where I was with my knees to my chin. A light touch on my shoulder jerked my head up, and the woman, who had freed herself, jumped back. Her eyes were wide, and she was shaking in her jeans and red top. "I thought you killed them," she said, her gaze darting over the destruction. "They're asleep?"

I nodded, only now realizing what my attack on them must have looked like. Relief cascaded over her, and she dropped down in front of me, looking like she needed a shoulder to cry on but was afraid to touch me again. "Thank you," she said, shivering. "You look just like me."

I sniffed back my tears and wiped my face. "That's why they kidnapped you."

Her head bobbed. "You're stronger, though." Smiling, she flexed her bicep. Her smile faded, and she clutched her knees to her chest. "How did you get in that circle? You must be a really powerful witch." She hesitated. "Are you?"

My eyes shut and I clenched my teeth. "I don't know," I said, eyes damp when I opened them. "I really don't know."

Thirty

Glenn's black car wasn't my style, but it was nice in an FIB sort of way. The back was full of file boxes, which made it hard to recline my seat enough to close my eyes and take a nap as he drove me home. The clutter was unusual. Glenn usually kept his car as tidy and together as himself, rigorously fastidious.

I was so tired, but sleep was impossible. Tom had gotten away, and now he had a vested interest in seeing me dead. My look-alike was safe in custody and would be headed home as soon as the med guys checked her out. She told me she was going to take some martial arts classes so Tom couldn't hurt her again, and that, combined with Sampson sitting on her lap in the back of a cop car, assured me she'd be okay.

My fingertips were sore from the burn I'd gotten by trying to take Tom's compromised circle, as was my palm from scraping it in the ever-after. I winced when I toggled the switch to crack the window, but the pain was worth hearing the sounds of the kids playing hide-and-seek in the dark, the squeals and shouts of protest coming in unseen soothing me. My eyes shut, and I tried to follow the car's path by its motion. When it got out that an I.S. operative had been summoning demons and letting him go to trash charm shops and terrorize citizens, the I.S. would have to publicly disapprove of Tom, dissolving his contract and moving his name from payroll to most-wanted. Privately, he would likely get a nasty slap and a boot out the door as they tried to disguise his public failure to tag me. I wasn't on their active list, but I knew they wouldn't mind seeing me on a granite table. But at least I wouldn't have to pay for the damages to the charm shop anymore.

The whine of Glenn's window cracked my eyelid, and the increased wind made my almost-dry hair flutter against my cheek. My red curls stank, the scent of burnt amber obvious in the tight confines of the car. No wonder Newt was bald.

Glenn cleared his throat, sounding decidedly peeved, and I shut my eyes. I knew he wasn't happy with me, thinking I'd taken on the entire coven without letting even my roommates know. "This wasn't my idea," I said, bracing my knee against the door when we took a turn. "I didn't mean to do this. It just happened."

Glenn cleared his throat again, this time in disbelief, and I opened my eyes and sat up. The passing streetlights lit his face to make him look older than he was. Tired. "Backup would have increased your chances of getting that wacko," he said tightly, accusingly. "Now he'll be twice as hard to find."

Guilt warred with fear, and my teeth clenched. I couldn't tell him I had been summoned into Tom's basement from the ever-after and I thought I was a demon. My elbow went to rest against the door, and I cupped my chin in my hand. "It was an accident," I muttered. "I was working on something with Trent—"

"Kalamack?" The FIB detective glanced from the road to me and back again, his dark hands gripping the wheel tighter. "Rachel, stay away from him. He holds a nasty grudge and has a lot of money."

Crap, I miss my dad. My breath came and went. Maybe I could give Glenn some of the truth. "I was helping Trent with an ongoing project—"

"The same thing that killed your fathers?" he asked, and I shrugged.

"Sort of. I was in the ever-after, and I got pulled into a demon's summons by mistake. I showed up in Al's circle, and when I got out, I let them have it." *Breathe in, one two three. Breathe out, one two three four.* "Trent is still stuck there."

"In the ever-after? Damn it, Rachel," Glenn whispered, and I stared, drawn by the unusual curse coming from him. "Does anyone else know he went there voluntarily?"

Glenn's worried expression came at me in flashes of street-light, and my eyebrows rose. I'd never dreamed this might look like me getting rid of Trent. Though the press labored under the assumption that we were secret lovers, everyone in a uniform knew we hated each other. That I continued to take his money was just weird. "His bodyguard," I said, not know-ing how Quen was going to react. "Ivy and Jenks. My neighbors—the ones that don't exist?" I finished dryly.

Glenn's grip shifted, and I knew he wanted to reach for the radio and call something in.

"It was an accident," I finished, putting my knees together as I said it again. "What was I supposed to do? Let them bleed that woman to death?"

"There are always options . . . ," he cajoled as we turned down my street.

"Tom admitted he called Al with the intent of letting him go to kill me. Said he would get a raise. The girl heard him. Ask her." I dropped my chin back into my hand and stared at the passing night. Fear gripped my heart at a recurring thought. I had been summoned out of the ever-after like a demon. Would I be drawn back into it when the sun rose?

A huge ache filled me. I just wanted to go home, surround myself with the people I loved, and hide, reassuring my sub-conscious that I was alive and home, even if I might be dragged back to that hell of an existence in a few hours. That Trent was still there, trapped in a tiny black cell waiting for a horrible, degrading future, didn't help.

I didn't like Trent. Nothing could excuse his murdering, drug-lord past, and I'd seen nothing that convinced me he would change that part of himself. But it bothered me; all the good and bad he had done shouldn't end so uselessly. I was shocked to realize that I cared what happened to him. He was responsible for a lot of good, even if it was for selfish reasons.

Staring out the window as we passed Keasley's dark house, I rubbed my arm, almost able to feel Trent's grip there, his last chance to touch someone lingering on me still. He hadn't asked me to save him. He hadn't asked me to stay and fight. There'd been no anger or frustration that I was going to be free, pulled to where he couldn't follow and leaving him to suffer both our punishments.

In the moment when everything had fallen from him, he'd asked me to make sure his people survived. His words had been free of the guilt I now felt. He only sought the reassurance that his people would live, that his life would amount to more than running drugs and murder.

Well, there was no way *I* was going to make sure the elves survived. He could do his own dirty work. I'd simply have to rescue him so he could do it himself. Crap on toast, I really needed to talk to Ceri.

My church was ahead, all lit up, with light streaming out of every window to run across the black grass. Even before we got close, I saw a pair of red eyes blink at me from the topmost nook and a wing shift in salute. Bis knew I was back, and I sent a silent thank-you to his kin who had kept me safe in the basilica last night. They hadn't known me or my plight, but they'd saved me, and I owed the gracious, noble beings my life. I'd pay Bis's rent myself just to keep him around.

The familiar taillights of my car were in the carport; someone had driven it home for me. Quen, maybe? Four streaks of greenish light swirled around the steeple and dropped down to Bis, and when one veered off to dart toward us, I pulled myself together and lowered the window completely. It had to be Jenks. *Please, let it be Jenks.*

My eyes warmed with unshed tears as his familiar wing-clatter battered against my ears and Jenks darted into the car.

"Rachel!" he gasped, looking good in his black thief outfit. "Tink's contractual hell, you did it! You're here! God almighty, you stink. I wish you were smaller; I'd slap you so hard you'd land in next week! I could have killed Trent when he shoved me back with that sample."

I shook my head in confusion. "He didn't shove you back. He said you took the curse and left us."

The pitch of his wings hesitated, and he dropped to my fingers. "How, by my bloody daisies, would I do that? I didn't do anything. I felt like my insides were being pulled through a snail's back door, and I showed up in the basilica to scare the holy crap out of some poor woman." He glanced at Glenn, the sparkles shifting from him turning to red. "Uh, hi, Glenn."

My throat was tight, and my hand shook as he stood on it. I wished I was smaller, too. Trent's reaction to Jenks's absence had been too genuine to be fake, and why bother lying? Maybe pixies were like demons, in that they couldn't stay on the wrong side of the lines when the sun rose? "Did Quen get the sample?" I asked, thinking of Trent's request. "Is it safe?"

The pixy was beaming. "Yeah, I gave it to Quen." A burst of light exploded from him, and Glenn winced. "When you didn't show, Quen took the sample to Trent's. He tried to take Ceri with him, but she said you'd need her when you got back. Holy crap, I have to send one of my kids to tell her you're here. *I* knew you could figure out how to jump the lines. Did you show up at the basilica, too? How come you called Glenn and not us? We would have picked you up."

He rose from my hand when it started shaking violently. Neither man commented on it, but Jenks's excitement cut off with a worried expression. He thought I'd learned how to jump the lines. He didn't know I had been pulled back by riding Algaliarept's summons. "You're not listening to the FIB channels, are you," I said, and Jenks's eyes widened.

"No . . . ," he said, his stance turning suspicious. "Why?"

Glenn pulled to the curb before the church and shoved the car into park. "We kept everything off the airwaves," he said as he leaned over the backseat and groped for his coat. "We didn't want the I.S. to show up."

"Rache?" Jenks said warily, hovering as I hid my hands so he couldn't see them shake. "What did you do?"

I looked at the church, wanting to be in it but too tired to move. "Tom and I had a chat."

A flash of pixy dust lit the car, and Glenn jumped. "Damn it, Rache," Jenks swore. "Why didn't you call us! I owe him his left nut between his teeth."

Guilt and fear mixed, and it came out as anger. "I didn't have a choice!" I shouted, and Jenks hovered backward to land on the dash. He said nothing as I fumbled to open the door. Planting my feet on the pavement, I wearily stood to look up at the church. The night was cool, and I shifted uncomfortably in my damp underwear. Crap, I was tired.

Jenks's wings were a silent blur as he flew too close to me. Not landing on my shoulder, he whispered, "I didn't want to leave you, Rache." Guilt lay heavy in his voice. "I must have gotten sucked out when the lines closed. But I knew you could figure it out. You'll never be stuck in the ever-after again."

This last was said with heavy pride, and I swallowed, using the excuse of shutting the car door to avoid looking at him. To tell him what had really happened was too hard. Seeing his eager face and happy stance, I was afraid. Jenks was too excited to pick up that things were being left unsaid. Things that were really going to screw my life—and by association, theirs—up.

"Ivy!" Jenks said suddenly. "I gotta tell Ivy you're back. Damn, I'm glad you're here."

My breath caught as he darted to my shoulder and I felt the cool touch of pixy wings on my face. "I thought I'd lost you," he whispered. And then he was gone.

Bewildered, I stared at the sifting dust he had left in his wake. Behind me was the thump of a closing door, and I turned to see Glenn coming around to the walk.

"A-Ah," I stammered, "thanks for the ride, Glenn. And everything else."

The streetlight lit his face as he pressed his lips together, making his small mustache stick out. "Mind if I walk you in?" he asked, and I felt a moment of quickly dampened alarm. Jenks might not have been listening, but Glenn had been. His investigative flags were raised, and if I didn't invite him in, he'd have to choose between our friendship and a warrant. He wanted to know how I had ended up in Tom's basement. And seeing as I needed all my friends right now, I nodded in surrender.

Arms held to myself, I looked back into the car for my nonexistent bag. Glenn had put my splat gun in a brown paper bag to get it past the evidence guys and out of the basement, and I felt stupid holding it when Glenn handed it to me. I looked up at the softly lit sign with our names on it, and I wondered if this entire partnership had been such a good idea. Bis blinked at me from his high perch, and I pushed myself into moving. A part of me was waiting for him to try to keep me out, and when he didn't, I felt better.

"You want some coffee?" I said to Glenn as my feet moved silently on the cracked sidewalk. Heaven knew I did.

My head jerked up as the church door was flung open and Ivy took two hurried steps onto the stoop before seeing me. Her pace slowed, but she continued on, her arms wrapped around herself as if she was cold. Shadows disguised her face, but her posture held worry and fear. Jenks was with her.

"See?" he said, as proud as if he had pulled me back from the ever-after himself. "I told you! She figured it out, and here she is. Safe and back where she belongs."

Ivy hit the sidewalk and kept coming. Her attention flicked briefly to Glenn, then fixed on me. "You're here," she said softly, her gray-silk voice carrying an entire twenty-four hours of fear and worry.

She pulled herself to a stop a few steps away, and her hands fell to her sides as if she didn't know what to do with them, afraid to reach out. She turned to anger instead. "Why didn't you call us?" she said, finally reaching hesitantly out and taking that stupid paper bag from me. "We would have picked you up."

My heart heavy, we headed to the steps. Jenks flew between us trailing a faint silver dust. "She went by herself to kick some black-witch ass," he said, and Ivy's gaze sharpened.

"You went to Tom's?" she said. "We're a team. It could have waited a few hours."

I took a breath, and then, right there at the foot of the stairs, I gave her a hug. She stiffened for an instant, then her hands went around me and the crackle of brown paper sounded against my back. Vampire incense grew strong, and my eyes closed as I breathed it in. Immediately my muscles relaxed and the prick of tears grew hot. I'd been so scared, with no way home and a lifetime of degradation facing me. She was my friend, and I could give her a freaking hug if I wanted to.

Ivy's stiffness grew, and I let go of her with one hand so that we stood more shoulder-to-shoulder than front-to-front. She was nervously watching Glenn for his reaction, but I couldn't care less. "I didn't go after him," I said as she helped me up the stairs. "It sort of happened."

The door was open, and in the darkness of the foyer and the confusion of two dozen pixies swirling around us and Glenn, I pulled her attention to me by taking her arm. "I'm so glad to see you," I whispered. "I don't know what's going to happen at sunrise. I need your help."

"What?" she said, concern replacing all her fear-based anger.

But Jenks had cleared the room of his kids, and I pressed my lips together, trying to tell her that I had to talk to her alone. Or at least without Glenn listening.

Her perfect oval face went blank, and I saw her understanding. She turned her upper lip in as she thought, and I let go of her arm. "You want some coffee, Glenn?" she asked suddenly.

My shoulders eased. We'd get Glenn out of here fast by pretending everything was okay. And frankly, I needed to pretend everything was okay—if only for a few minutes.

Glenn's brow rose suspiciously at the offer, but he ambled in after us. He did a good job of hiding that he knew we were trying to get rid of him, but he looked like a cop when he settled himself at the table. Telling Ivy he didn't mind waiting for a new pot, he arched his eyebrows at me and crossed his arms over his chest—and stared. He wasn't going to leave until he heard it all.

Jenks was hovering over my shoulder like there was a string between us. My worry crashed down as I slumped into my spot at the table and tried to decide where to start. The familiar noises of Ivy making coffee were incredibly soothing, and my eyes scanned the kitchen, marking the empty spots where I had moved spelling supplies into the belfry.

A sudden clenching of my chest took my breath away. I was a demon. Or so close to one that it didn't matter. That I had made a human my familiar should have been the first clue. I felt filthy, like the smut on my soul was leaking off and staining everything I loved.

And as Glenn eyed the basket of cherry tomatoes with avarice and prattled on about how he liked a good strong cup of coffee while he waited for me to get on with it, I felt the bolts of my life lock the door to my past. I had only one way to go, and it was going to be hard as hell. Logic said there was no way to rescue Trent. He had accepted his failure and asked me to save his species. But I didn't live or die by percentages, and I wouldn't sit and accept it. It would prey on me forever.

"I . . . I have to talk to you," I said, and the conversation cut off with the startling suddenness of a kite smacking headfirst into the ground.

Ivy turned from the coffeemaker, arms over her middle and her face pale. The pitch of Jenks's wings faded to nothing as he landed on the napkin holder. Glenn's breath slid out of him in anticipation, and I steadied myself, trying to find a way to say what I needed to without telling them what Trent's dad had done to me.

"You didn't get back here on your own," Ivy guessed, and Jenks's wings stopped. "Did you have to buy another mark?" I shook my head, and Ivy's relief turned to a wary suspicion, then horror. "Where's Trent?"

Oh, God, she thought I had bought my freedom with Trent. Everyone would. Vision blurring, I shook my head, my gaze on a series of lines indented into the table, realizing they were Ivy's name in a careful, preschool print.

Why am I here? I thought as I tried to find a way to tell them what I was. I was a demon, and I was likely going to be pulled back into the ever-after in a few hours.

I was a demon, but they were my friends. I had to believe that they wouldn't turn me away. My head hurt, and taking a slow breath, I looked up. "Jenks, could you clear out your kids?"

His wings increased in pitch, and Ivy winced. "Sure," he said, his unease obvious as he made a series of three whistles. A smattering of complaints rose, and the room went silent as the children left. Jenks rubbed his wings together in a harsh discord, and three more darted out from under the sink and were gone.

My gaze dropped, and I pulled my knees up to my chin, grasping my shins awkwardly so my heels almost slipped off the chair. I wanted to be mad at Trent for everything, but this wasn't his fault. I thought of my demon scar, and a bitter anger lifted through me. *I'm a demon; I ought to just accept it.*

But I wouldn't. And I didn't have to.

I looked up to fasten on Ivy's stillness. Her face was empty of emotion, but her eyes were swimming. "I got out," I said in a monotone. "Trent didn't."

The soft creak of the back door closing brought Ivy's head around, and I looked to the hallway. Ceri was standing in the threshold, her filmy white dress edged in purple and green floating about her bare feet, and her hair wild. Tears marked her face, and she looked beautiful. "Rachel?" she warbled, guilt and fear heavy in her voice.

And with that, I realized that Ceri had known. She had known I was a demon, and that was why she hadn't wanted me to go to the ever-after, lest I figure it out myself.

My face bunched up, and I held my knees tighter. "Why didn't you tell me?" I asked.

She took three steps in and stopped. "Because you aren't," she said, pleading. "You are a witch, Rachel. Never forget it."

It wasn't her words but the vehemence she said them with that convinced me she'd rather believe a happy lie than a harsh truth. Damn it, she had known. I could almost pin the moment she'd realized it. She'd been treating me differently ever since Minias had pulled the focus from me and put it into David. No, it had started before that, with the scrying mirror.

My eyes must have given me away, for she strode across the room with a familiar righteous anger. "You are a witch!" she shouted, spots of color showing and her hair flaring out magnificently. "Close your mouth! You are a witch!"

Jenks was hovering in questioning shock. "Why wouldn't she be?" he asked, and Ivy slumped. I looked at her and bit my lip, tears of frustration slipping from me. I think Ivy had figured it out.

"I'm a witch," I said, continuing the lie. But Ceri hadn't touched me yet.

"I didn't want you to go," Ceri said, standing helplessly before me.

Unable to bear it, I put my feet on the floor and took her hand. It was cold, and she didn't pull away. "Thank you," I whispered. "Am I going to stay here, or will I be pulled back?"

Ivy moaned softly, turning to grip the sink and look into the black garden. Ceri glanced at her, then at Jenks's confusion, and finally, back to me. "I don't know," she said softly.

Jenks rose up high, his wings clattering aggressively.

"Someone better tell me what the hell is going on, or I'm going to pix the lot of you."

Blinking fast, Ivy turned, one arm wrapped around her middle, the other holding her head. "You said Rachel twisted the curse. She has Al's summoning name," she said to the floor. "She didn't buy a way back and she didn't learn how to travel the lines. She was pulled back to reality when Tom summoned Al."

"So?" Jenks said acerbically, then hesitated, dropping to the table. "Oh. Shit."

A flash of fear took me, and the shame of being summoned into someone else's circle.

"Rachel is not a demon," Ceri said, and Glenn finally got it, his broad shoulders turning sideways as he gaped at me.

"No," I said bitterly, twisting in my chair and not looking at anyone. "I'm a witch whose blood can kindle demon magic, and who has been integrated into their system so well that I'm bound by their rules of summoning."

"No, you aren't."

I wanted to believe Ceri, but I was afraid to. "Then what am I?" I whispered. She had to know. She had lived among them.

Ceri's face went frightened. "You are what you are."

My gaze met Ivy's to find a sliver of fear.

I couldn't take it anymore. Rising, I ran to the bathroom, slamming the door and slumping onto the closed toilet, miserable. There was a commotion in the hall: worried voices and frustrated accusations. A tear slid down, and I let it. I should cry. I should be crying my freaking eyes out. I think my dad had known, too. Why else would he have asked Cincinnati's top ley line instructor to flunk me, then collect a library of demon texts for me?

"Rachel?" came Jenks's voice amid a close clatter of pixy wings, and I pulled my head up.

"Get out!" I shouted, lashing out with a flick I knew would never land. "Damn it, you stupid pixy, get out!"

"No!" he exclaimed, getting in my face. "Rachel, listen to me. You smell like a witch. Well, you stink like the ever-after right now, but when you wash it off, you'll smell like a witch. And come sunup, you will be here. You won't be pulled to the ever-after. I won't let you!"

His expression was desperate, and I listlessly extended a hand for him to land on. I held my breath and caught my misery back behind a throat-hurting gulp. He landed on it, flying up briefly when Ivy barged in, sending the door swinging into the wall.

"God save you!" I exclaimed, jumping. "I shut the door because I wanted to be alone!"

Ivy's usually placid face was pinched with worry. Tension had pulled her shoulders up, and her movements to tuck her short hair behind an ear were sharp. "You are not a demon," she said, her words precise. "You're sitting in a church. No demon can do that. Glenn said you lied to get out of that circle, and nothing happened to you. You weren't held accountable. You're not a demon, and you won't be pulled back when the sun comes up."

Exhausted in mind and soul, I looked up at her, wanting to believe, but too afraid to do so. "I hope so," I whispered, knowing they wouldn't like what I was going to say next. "But if I was, it would make rescuing Trent easier."

Thirty-one

I t was quiet now, just the small agitated ticks of Jenks tapping his foot against Ceri's porcelain teacup to mar the stillness. I felt bad about screwing up everyone's lives, but in a few hours I'd either be dead or a permanent fixture in the ever-after. Settling this with a happy ending was still a possibility, but the odds were looking really slim. I was hoping for it of course, but honestly, what were the chances?

Glenn had left to get my mother after I'd kicked everyone out of the bathroom to take a shower, so it was just the four of us now, the mood tense and the feeling of harsh words yet unsaid heavy in the air. God, I was tired. The cup of coffee in my grip wasn't helping at all. A bowl of baked cheese crackers was within my reach, and I put one in my mouth. The sharp cheddar flavor bit at the sides of my mouth, and I slowly chewed. Grabbing a handful, I ate them one by one, feeling guilty that I was clean and eating cheese crackers when Trent was in a cell.

Seeing me moving, Jenks took to the air to try again. "Why?" he said belligerently, a thin trace of red dust spilling from him to pool on the table as he landed in his best Peter Pan pose. "Why do you give a fairy's hairy ass about what happens to Trent?"

I rubbed my finger over Ivy's dented signature, feeling the past. She had been innocent once. So had I. *So Trent can tell*

*me what the hell his dad did to me? Because I need him to say
that I'm not a demon? So he can find a way to reverse it?* "Because if I don't," I said softly, "everyone will think that I
bought my freedom with his life." Jenks snorted, and my blood
pressure rose. "Because I promised I'd get him home," I said
more forcefully. "I'm not going to let him rot there."

"Rachel . . . ," Jenks cajoled.

From her computer, Ivy glowered at him. "She promised to
get him home if he paid for her way there and back. I don't like
it any more than you do, but you're going to shut up and listen.
If we can find a way, we'll do it."

"But he didn't get her home," Jenks protested. "She did that
herself. And who cares if he rots in the ever-after?"

Ivy stiffened, and Ceri silently watched, evaluating.

"I care," I said, pushing the crackers away and trying to get
the cheese out of my teeth.

"Yeah, but Rache—"

"He's not home!" I shouted, ticked. "That was the deal!"

Jenks's feet hit the table, and he turned his back on me.
Wings still, he bowed his head.

Ceri eased into the chair beside me and set an open spell
book on the table. There was a pair of glasses perched on her
nose and a pencil between her teeth. The pixies had braided
her hair while I had cried in the shower, and she looked decidedly studious. She had reddened when I noticed her new
glasses, but I hadn't said anything. I think she was proud that
she was aging again and needed them.

Frankly, I was surprised Ivy was siding with me. I'd like to
think that it was because she considered holding to one's word
important, or because she thought Trent was worth going back
for on his own merits, but the truth was Trent's absence would
cause big problems in Cincy's underground power balance.
Rynn Cormel flexing his muscles and reasserting control was
something she wasn't looking forward to. It's harder to fall in
love with a man when he's killing people.

Glancing up, I blinked at the odd figure Ceri was idly tracing over and over on the yellow legal pad she had on the open spell book. I was sure the glyph was from a demon curse; there was a faint haze of black emanating from it. I caught her gaze, and she winced, drawing a circle around it to contain whatever force she had drawn into existence before crumpling the paper up, dropping it into her empty teacup, and setting fire to it with a ley line charm.

Jenks sputtered at the black flame, but Ivy stopped his budding harangue with a hissed comment I didn't quite catch.

"What if I learn how to jump the lines?" I said, searching for the first hints of a plan. "If I could get in undetected, that would be half the battle. Maybe more. Simple snag and drag." It wasn't, but I could build on the idea.

Ceri took the end of her pencil and crushed even the ash to dust. "Learn how to trip the lines before sunrise? No. I'm sorry, Rachel. It takes decades."

Ivy leaned past her cracked monitor. "Why sunrise?"

The pretty elf's shoulders drooped. "That's when the lines will close to summoning travel and they will make a decision. Right now, Trent's probably still in holding, but as soon as they're sure no one will be pulled out of negotiations, he will be sold."

Sold. It was an ugly word, and I felt my face twist. Seeing it, Ceri shrugged. "Anything you want to do, you need to do before someone buys him, or you will be dealing with a specific demon, not a committee. Committees are difficult, but a single demon is tenacious where a committee will only want to make sure they all get something."

This was wrong. Really wrong, and I sighed when Jenks swore at Ivy, dramatically crossed his chest as if making a promise, then flew to my cracker bowl.

"Trent doesn't have a great deal of value as a familiar," Ceri was saying, her eyes down in what looked like embarrassment, "but it's not often that a potential familiar stumbles into the ever-after without a preexisting claim by another demon. There are a lot of demons who will pay, not caring that there will be a long downtime to bring him up to usefulness. That's what Al does to make his bread and butter."

I hesitated, thinking it might explain why Al was so hot for Nick and then me. "He trains familiars?" I asked, and Ceri shook her head. She had begun to doodle again, and I stared at the pair of tortured eyes taking form on the yellow paper, trapped behind lines of blue.

"In a manner of speaking," she said softly. "He finds suitable candidates, instructs them enough to make them profitable, then tricks them into the ever-after to be sold for his gain. Al is good at it, and he's made an exceptional life selling people to those unwilling to cross the lines to get their own."

Jenks's wings clattered and Ivy clicked her computer off, not bothering to pretend to be working anymore. "He's a slave dealer?" she asked, and Ceri drew a slumped figure of a man at the base of a tombstone.

"Yes. Which is why he's so angry you have his summoning name. It takes finesse to build a list of people who know his name and are potential familiars. Not to mention the effort invested in the pre–soul stealing stage, the drudgery of building them up and teaching them something to increase their value, maintaining the balance of having enough people know his name without having so many that it becomes tedious. And then there's the risk that after all the smut he takes on building up a potential familiar, he will take a loss if they don't bring in a high enough price."

I snorted, leaning back in my chair and crossing my knees as I thought of Nick. "He's a freaking familiar pimp." Tom had better watch out, or he was going to be next. Not that I cared.

Jenks rose, and a column of silver sparkles fell to fill the bowl like frosting. "Ivy, stealing people is his job. You gotta help me here. Rachel doesn't need to do this. It's stupid, even for her!"

My eyes narrowed, but Ivy stretched casually, her belly button ring showing. "If you don't stop badgering her, I'm going to smack you into the wall so hard you won't wake up for a week," she said. Jenks lost altitude, and Ivy added as she headed over, "Someone has to pull Kalamack's ass out of the ever-after. You think I can do it?"

"No," he protested weakly, "but why does Rachel have to? Trent knew the risks."

He knew the risks and trusted me to get him out, I thought, unable to meet Ceri's gaze.

Ivy leaned with her elbows on the center island counter. "Why don't you stop trying to convince her not to go and start trying to figure out how you can go with her."

"She won't let me!" he shouted.

"No one is going with me," I said firmly, and Jenks let a burst of silver slip from him.

"See!" he exclaimed, pointing.

My teeth clenched, and Ivy cleared her throat in warning. "I said I'd get him out," I muttered, flipping through the sketches that Ceri had drawn of the underground demon city.

"And I'm coming with you," he said belligerently.

I exhaled, trying to get my jaw to relax, but it wasn't working. In the past year, living and working with Ivy and Jenks, I had learned how to trust others. It was time to remember that I could trust myself, too. That I could do this on my own. And I would. "Jenks—"

"Don't 'Jenks' me," he said, landing on the rolled-over seam of the yellow tablet, his wings going for balance and his finger pointed. "We pop in, grab him, and pop out."

"That won't work," Ceri interrupted softly, and Jenks spun.

"Why the hell not? Plan B worked with that fish. It will work for Trent!"

Ceri's eyes darted to mine and then back to Jenks's. "Whoever Rachel buys the trips from will simply snag her. Or tell Newt, who now has a solid claim on her."

I scuffed my foot, almost able to feel the raised, slashed circle on the bottom of it. "What if I just go through Newt?" I threw out there, desperate. "She might forget about it."

Ceri stiffened. "No," she said, and Ivy's expression went

guarded at the woman's almost-panic. "Not Newt. You already wear one mark from her. She's insane. She says one thing, then does another. You can't trust her. She doesn't follow demon law, she makes it."

I flipped to the next sketch, which showed what looked like the layout for the university library, and Jenks moved to my shoulder, where I was able to judge his agitation by the strength of the draft he was making on my neck. It was cold, and I reached back and covered my bites with my hand.

"Minias maybe?" Ivy suggested, and Ceri shook her head.

"Minias is trying to get back into Newt's good graces. Rachel may as well wear a big bow and sing 'Happy Birthday.'"

I flipped the maps closed. "Why?" I asked, eating another cracker. "They fired him."

Ceri's gaze went serious. "Because Newt is the only female demon left. And just like everyone else, he would risk his life for the chance to engender a child. That was his job. They took a vote and he lost. I told you this before."

Her voice had gotten sharp, but her temper was her way of hiding her fear. Excising it, maybe. "You didn't tell me he was trying to seduce her," I said tartly, egging her on for some inane reason. Perhaps I needed the release of yelling at someone, too. "You told me he was babysitting her."

Jenks's wings brushed my neck, tangling in my hair. "He's been with her, what? A few hundred years? What's his problem? Can't get it up?"

Ceri's eyebrows went high, and she replied dryly, "She killed the last six demons she became intimate with. Pulled an entire line through them and—"

"Fried their little kitty brains," Jenks finished.

I looked for Rex in the threshold, but the cat had yet to come out from under my bed.

"Minias is understandably cautious," Ceri said, and Ivy snorted as she pushed her forearms up from the counter and went to the coffeemaker.

"If it's just a matter of getting there, can't Rachel just stand in a line and . . . move?" Ivy asked, her unusual look of ignorance hinting at her fright.

Ceri shook her head, and I dropped the pad of paper onto the table. I remembered the time I had stood in Trent's office, one foot in the here and now, and one in the ever-after. I had been entirely safe, unless Al had got a grip on me and pulled me through. "Not unless there's a demon to pull you through," I said, rubbing the goose bumps from my arms. "And I'm the only one going in. Not you, not you, and not you."

I looked at them in turn, reading Ceri's relief, Jenks's ire, and Ivy's annoyance.

"I don't mind a little demon smut," Ivy said defensively.

"Me either," Jenks chimed in, and Ceri shook her head with a soft no. That Jenks had popped back to reality when the sun had come up didn't bode well. "I'm going with you, Rache," he said loudly. "Even if I have to ride in your armpit!"

Ooh, that's a pretty picture. "You don't get it," I said, trying to burn the image from my consciousness. "There is no reason for you to go!"

Jenks rose up, his wings clattering. "Like hell there isn't!" he yelled, shooting nervous glances at Ivy. "You need backup."

Frustrated, I slammed my hand down on the table, and two pixies shot out of my charm cupboard, shrieking. I hesitated as they flew down the hall and into the night. Great, now Matalina would know Jenks was trying to come with me. The woman wouldn't stop him, but I'd be damned before I took him away from her again.

"I'm not going in there to kick some demon ass," I said softly, trying to be reasonable. "Even with your help, I can't beat off more than one demon at a time with magic, and as soon as they realize I'm there, it's going to be a bunch of demons." I glanced at Ceri, and the pale woman nodded. "I've thought it over, and I can't do it with muscle or magic. I have to do it with trickery, and I'm sorry, but much as I'd like one or both of you there, you can't help me." I looked at Ivy by the fridge, feeling the frustration coming off her in a wave. "You can do more good by staying here and summoning me home." My face burned with shame that I had a demon name, and fear made my voice soft. "Once I've got him."

"This is crap!" Jenks shouted. "Green fairy crap."

Ivy rubbed her temples. "I have a headache," she breathed, one of the few times she had ever admitted to me that she hurt. "Can you at least take Ceri?"

Ceri's rasp of incoming breath was harsh and quick. "No," I said, touching the woman's shoulder in support. "I'm going alone." Jenks bristled, and I leaned over him. "I'm going alone!" I exclaimed. "I couldn't have gotten the sample without you, Jenks, but this is different. And you taking on a bucket of smut so you can hold my hand while I do this isn't going to happen. Don't you get it!" I almost shouted, starting to shake. "Until I met the two of you, I worked alone, even when I *did* have backup. I'm damn good at it, and I'm not going to put you in danger if I don't need to, so drop it!"

For a moment, Jenks said nothing, his fists on his hips as he pressed his lips together and frowned up at me. From the window came a high-pitched hush for someone to be quiet. "So how much is your life worth, Rache?" he asked.

I turned away so he couldn't see my eyes. "I killed Kisten," I said. "I'm not going to risk either of you." My jaw clenched, and the hurt swelled. I *had* killed Kisten—maybe not directly, but it had been my fault.

Ivy's feet scuffed the linoleum, and Jenks went silent. I couldn't love anyone without putting them in danger. *Maybe this is why Dad told me to work alone.*

Ceri touched my arm, and I sniffed back the misery. "It wasn't your fault," she said, but Ivy's and Jenks's silence said different.

"I know how to do this," I said, shoving the pain down. "I was summoned out—like a demon. I can kindle demon magic—like a demon. I have a name registered in their database—like they all are. Why can't I just claim Trent as mine and bring him home? I know he'd go along with it."

"Oh for the sweet humpin' love of Tink!" Jenks shouted, and even Ivy looked discomfited. Ceri, though, put her elbows on the table and dropped her chin into her cupped palm with a thoughtful look on her face. It was the first hint of hope, and my hands grew damp.

"You can't jump through the lines," she said, as if that were the deciding factor. "How will you get there?"

I fiddled with the bowl of crackers, nervous. I had to make a deal with a demon. Damn it, I had to make *another* deal with a demon. The difference this time was that I was making this choice with a clear head, not being forced into it with death as the only other option. So I dealt in demons. So the *hell* what. It didn't make me a bad person. Or stupid. Or rash. It made me dangerous to everyone around me is all. "So I buy a trip," I said softly, knowing I'd never look at demon summoners the same way again. Maybe I'd take them seriously now, instead of writing them off as idiots. Maybe I'd been really wrong to accuse Ceri of not knowing what she was doing.

Ceri sighed, oblivious to my thoughts. "Back to the beginning," she muttered to her legal pad. I looked down at it to see a second pair of eyes, decidedly masculine this time.

"So I buy a trip from Al," I finished.

Ivy jerked, and Jenks took to the air. "No," Jenks said. "He will kill you. He will lie and kill you. He has nothing to lose, Rache."

Which is exactly why it will work, I thought, but didn't say it. Al had nothing to lose, and everything to gain.

"Jenks is right," Ivy said. Somehow she had crossed the kitchen without me seeing and was right over me.

Ceri's expression was thick with alarm. "You said Al is in jail."

I nodded. "They incarcerated him again when they realized I can spindle line energy. But he can still bargain. And I know his summoning name. I can summon him out."

Her pretty little mouth open, Ceri looked at Ivy and then Jenks. "He might kill you!"

"And he might not." Discouraged but seeing no other options, I pushed the legal pad of sketched maps away from me. "I have something he wants, and holding on to it will not do me any good. Giving it to him might get Trent free. . . ."

Ceri gave Ivy a pleading look, and the vampire dragged her chair to the other side of me and sat down. "Rachel," Ivy said, her voice soft and full of pity, "there's nothing you can do. I don't want Trent stuck there any more than you do, but there's no shame in not waging a battle that can't be won."

Jenks stood before me with his head bobbing, but his relief made me even more angry. They weren't listening, and I really didn't blame them. My tension rose, and I scrubbed a hand across my face. "Okay," I said shortly, and Jenks flew backward as I stood. "You're right. Bad idea." *I have to get out of here.* "Just forget the entire thing," I said, looking over the kitchen for my coat. *The foyer . . . I think.*

I headed for the front door with no bag, no wallet, and nothing but my spare keys, which I had stashed in the safe with Ivy's living-will papers. Someone had brought my car home, but I had yet to find my bag.

"Hey!" Jenks said from the table. "Where are you going?"

My pulse hammered, and my steps jarred all the way up my spine. "Eden Park. Alone. I'll be back after sunrise. Unless I'm dragged into the ever-after," I added, sounding dry, sarcastic, and bitter. The clatter of pixy wings following made me tense.

"Rachel—"

"Let her go," Ivy said softly, and he dropped back. "She's never had to deal with a situation there was no way to win. I better call Rynn," she said as she headed down the hall. "Then go to the store to stock up. The shops might be closing for a while. There might be riots if the city has to reorganize the lower power structure. This is going to be a rough week. The I.S. is going to be too busy to pick its collective nose."

I passed through the bat-filled sanctuary thinking I wasn't going to be around to see it.

Thirty-two

It was cold, sitting on the top of the bench's back the way I was, my feet on the seat as I looked out from Eden Park over the gray Ohio River and across the Hollows. The sun was near rising, and the Hollows was hazy with a pinkish-gray mist. I was thinking—waiting, really. Just the fact that I was sitting here was a clear indication that the thinking portion of my life was done. Now I had to do something.

So I sat on the top of the bench and shivered in my short leather jacket and jeans, my boots doing little to stop the cold of a November morning. My breath made little puffs that existed about as long as my racing thoughts did: thoughts of my dad, my mom, Takata, Kisten, Trent trapped in the ever-after, Ivy trusting me to fix this, Jenks wanting to be a part of it.

Frowning, I dropped my eyes and brushed a smudge of dirt off my boot. My dad had brought me up here upon occasion. Usually it was when he and my mom were arguing or she had fallen into a funk, during which she would always smile and give me a kiss when I asked what was wrong. Now I wondered if her occasional depression had come from thinking about Takata.

I exhaled, watching the thought leave me like the mist from my breath and vanish into the collective consciousness. My mother had quietly gone off her rocker trying to divorce herself from the reality of bearing Takata's children while being lovingly married to my dad. She had loved them both, and seeing Takata in Robbie and me every day must have been a self-inflicted torture.

"You can't forget anything," I said, watching the words vanish into nothing. "And even if you do, it always comes back to bitch-slap you in the morning."

The cool mist of the coming day was damp and pleasant, and I closed my eyes against the brightening sky. I'd been up way too long.

Turning where I sat, I looked behind me over the narrow parking strip to the two man-made ponds and the wide footbridge spanning them. Past the bridge was a ragged ley line, unnoticeable unless you were really looking. I'd found it while helping Kisten fight off a foreign camarilla trying to kidnap his nephew Audric last year, and I'd forgotten all about it until feeling its discordant resonance through Bis. Though weak, it would be enough.

Wondering how little Audric was, I wobbled off the bench, slapped the cold from my jeans, and headed across the lot. I ran a hand over the red paint of my convertible in passing. I loved my car, and if I did this right, I'd be back to get it before they towed it away.

I took the bridge with slow steps, looking down for the telltale ripple of Sharps, the park's bridge troll, but he was either hiding in the deeper water or they had chased him out again. To the left was a wide expanse of concrete tucked in the curve of the upper pond. Two statues were cemented into the ground, and hemmed in between them ran the ley line. The faint red visible to my mind's eye was growing weaker as the sun neared rising, but it was still possible to see where it ran, bound by a wolf on one side and a funny-looking guy with a cauldron on the other, both holding the midpoint of the line stretching from one end of the park to the other. It ran over the shallow water, which was why the line was so pathetically weak here. If the pond had been any deeper, the line wouldn't have been able to survive. As it was, it was leaking enough power to make my skin prickle as I found a fairly clean patch of concrete and sat down just outside it.

Taking a rock, I leaned to scratch a sloppy circle right in the line. Even if the sun rose and broke my summons, I could still talk to Al if I stepped into the line, though he'd be under no obligation to stay and listen. I really didn't think getting Al to stay would be a problem.

My heart pounded, and with sweat breaking out to make me cold, I whispered, "Jariathjackjunisjumoke, I summon you." I didn't need the trappings to force his appearance, I only needed to open a channel. And he came—using the name I had chosen for myself.

Al misted into existence in a seated, slouched posture, and I stared, fascinated and repulsed as he took on a gross parody of me. His legs were twisted akimbo, skinny shoulders slumped and bare, carrying red-rimmed scratches that held crusted blood. The slack-jawed face staring back at me was mine, but it was blank and empty, the red stringy curls lank. It was the eyes that were the worst—demon-red, goat-slitted orbs staring at me from my own face.

I hated it when he showed up as me.

"That's nice," I said, easing back from the circle.

A flicker of anger lit through his empty expression, and a shimmer of ever-after coated him. His form grew blockier, more solid. A whiff of lilac came to me, and the clean scent of crushed velvet. He faced me squarely, full of elegance and lordly refinement, sitting cross-legged on the cold cement: lace at his cuffs, boots shining in the light, ruddy complexion clean, and every vestige of a bruise or cut gone.

"I knew it was you," he said, the hatred in his deep voice pulling a shiver through me. "You're the only one who knows it."

I swallowed and tucked a curl behind my ear. "I never wanted your name. I only wanted you to leave me alone. Why the *hell* couldn't you just leave me alone?"

He sniffed, only now looking around with a haughty disdain. "Is that why you're calling me into . . . a park? You want to trade back? Afraid you're going to be drawn back to the ever-after when the sun rises?" His head tilted, and he smiled, showing me his flat, blocky teeth. "You should be. I'm most curious about that myself."

My mouth went dry. "I'm not a demon," I said boldly. "You can't scare me."

The subtle tension in him rose. I saw it in the slight tightening of his fingers. "Rachel, honey, if you're not scared, you're not going to survive." His manner turned cocky and bitter. "Well, you took my name," he said, his noble British accent perfect and precise. "Isn't it pleasant, being at someone's mercy? Trapped by a hack in a little tiny bubble. Is it a wonder we try to kill you?" An eyebrow rising, he turned introspective. "Did Thomas Arthur Bansen escape?"

I nodded, and he smiled knowingly. "Look," I said, glancing at the growing light, "for what it's worth, I'm sorry, and if you'd shut up about poor little you and listen, we might be able to both come away with something. Unless you want to go back to that cell of yours."

Al was silent. Then he inclined his head. "I'm listening."

I thought of Ceri advising me against this, of Jenks ready to risk his life on a run we couldn't win, and of Ivy knowing I was the only one who could get myself out and dying inside as she forced herself to let me do it. I thought about all the times I had brought in black witches, pitying them for their foolishness, telling myself demons were dangerous, manipulating bastards who you couldn't beat. But I wasn't trying to beat them, I was trying to join them . . . apparently. I took a steadying breath. "This is what I want."

Al made a rude noise. As if for a nonexistent audience, he threw a lace-cuffed hand in the air. A hint of burnt amber tickled my nose, and I wondered if it was real or simply my memory inventing the scent.

"I want you to leave the people I love alone, *especially* my mother. I want Trent, unharmed and free from persecution for stealing the elven sample," I said, voice low. "You are all collectively to leave him alone."

His head moved back and forth, and he eyed me over his smoked glasses. "I'll say it again. You are not shy about asking for things. I can't bind anyone's actions but my own."

I nodded, expecting this. "I want that same amnesty for stealing your sample."

"And I want to rip your bloody fucking head off, but it looks like we're both going to be disappointed, now aren't we?" he mockingly crooned.

My breath shook as I exhaled. I glanced at the east, and my pulse quickened. He had tortured my mom, not in anger but to get to me. Never again. "What is it worth to you if I can not only get you out of jail, but have the person who put you there apologize?"

Al sneered. "If you don't have anything constructive to say, you should let me go back to the ever-after and my cell. I had everything under control until you demonstrated to Minias that you could spindle line energy."

"That's what's going to save your ass," I shot back, belligerent. "I have an idea to benefit both of us. You wanna hear it?"

He crossed his arms over his chest, the lace fluttering. "And what is that? Buy a trip in to rescue Trent with your soul?" It was mocking, and my face burned. "It's not worth it," he added. "In a few hours, I'm going to be banished to the surface, my belongings raffled off as novelty items and my living space given to someone else—my reputation destroyed. I'd rather have your head than your soul at this point in my *illustrious* career."

"Good," I shot back, "because you're not going to get it." My heart pounded as I waited for him to get over his pity party. Sure enough, after about five seconds of miffed silence, he turned back to me. In a very small voice I asked, "Is there a system in place for a demon to teach another? Sort of a mentoring position?" *God, help me. Tell me I'm seeing things clearly and unclouded by pride.*

Al threw his head back and laughed. The water surrounding us rippled, and I heard the echo of it come back from the new town houses across the street.

"There hasn't been a demon needing instruction for five thousand years!" he exclaimed. "I'm about to be exiled to the surface, and you want me to take you on as a student? Teach you everything I know for free *just because*?"

I said nothing, waiting as he followed my question to the reasoning behind it, and his ruddy face lost all expression. Eyes peering over those damned glasses of his, he stared as my pulse quickened. "Yes," he said softly, almost breathing the word. "There is."

My hands were shaking, and I wrapped my arms around myself and tucked them under the shelter of my jacket. "And if you said you had taken me on as a student instead of a familiar—because I could twist demon magic—then you wouldn't be in trouble for letting me know how to spindle ever-after in my thoughts."

His head moved almost imperceptibly up and down, his jaw tightening.

"You could tell them that you taught me, then left me here because I was learning more fighting you than I could in the ever-after."

"But I didn't."

His voice was so lacking in emotion, it sounded dead. "They don't know that," I said.

Al's chest rose and fell in a sigh. I could see relief in him, and I wondered what it was like to be a demon and afraid. And how long he would let me live knowing I not only saw it, but had the answer to save him. "Why?" he asked.

I licked my lips. "I want Trent. If I'm your student, wouldn't I be entitled to a familiar? Hell, I made one of my boyfriends my familiar before you broke the bond," I said, attention going everywhere as I tried to hide my shame even though I knew I'd never use another person like that. At least not intentionally.

"Trent is wearing smut that I should have," I added. "He took it voluntarily. That's what a familiar does."

His fingers twitching with a repressed excitement, Al smiled. "And my reputation is restored." The demon glanced to the east and adjusted his glasses to hide his eyes. "They aren't stupid," he said dryly. "They will say it's a convenient story."

This was the really scary part. I had trusted Al to give me a night of peace, but this was entirely different. "Which is why you're going to bring me through the lines so I can speak in your defense," I said, fear clenching my heart. "Then you do what you have to for me to claim Trent as my familiar."

"Trenton Aloysius Kalamack wears Minias's mark," he said quickly.

"But he's wearing my smut of his own free will," I offered, and Al pursed his lips, leaning back until he hit the bubble and jerked forward.

"I would need to buy your familiar's mark from Minias," he mused aloud. Eyebrows rising, he shifted a hand in a gesture of possibility. "But I can do it."

"Then Trent and I come back here, and we all go back to normal."

Al snorted. "Sweet innocence be damned. What about my name?" he asked, making a moot face. "I want that back."

I met his gaze, refusing to give on this. "You won't be in jail."

His eyes narrowed. "I want my name. I need it."

I remembered what Ceri had said about how he made his living. Would I be responsible for the people Al tricked into slavery if I gave it back to him? Logic said no, but emotion said I should stop him if I could. But what about me being summoned into Tom's circle? I didn't want that happening again. "Maybe," I whispered.

His attention bore into mine as he took a slow breath. I didn't know what he was going to come back with. "Rachel," he said, and the simple sound of it made my blood turn cold. Something was there that hadn't been before, and it scared the crap out of me. "I need to know something before I will bargain with you anymore."

Hearing a trap, I edged back, my jeans scraping on the grit between me and the cement. "I'm not giving anything for free."

His expression didn't change. "Oh, not free," he said in a dangerous monotone. "Insight into another's thoughts is never free. You pay for it in the most . . . unexpected ways. I want to know why you didn't call Minias the other night. I saw your decision to let me go, and I want to know why you did it. Minias would have jailed me. You would have had a night of freedom. Yet you . . . let me go. Why?"

"Because I wasn't about to call a mouse of a demon when I could take care of it myself," I said, then hesitated. That wasn't why. "Because I thought if I gave you a night of peace, you might give me the same." God, I had been stupid. To think that a demon would respect that had been dumb.

But a slow, deeply satisfied smile came over him, and his breath quickened. "So softly it starts," he whispered. "Foolishly clever and with an unsurvivable trust. It just saved your miserable life, that questionable show of thought, my itchy-witch." Al's smile shifted, becoming lighter. "And now you will live to possibly regret it."

I shivered, not knowing if I had just saved or damned myself. But I'd be alive, and that was what mattered right now.

"You as my protégée?" he asked, as if trying it on.

I felt dizzy. "Name only," I breathed, putting a hand on the cold cement to ground myself. "You leave me alone. My family, too. Stay away from my mom, you SOB."

"Priceless," Al mocked. "No. If I am taking you, you will be here." He touched the ground by his knee. "In the ever-after. With me."

"Absolutely not."

Al took a breath, then leaned forward with his brow furrowed, as if he was trying to impress me with the weight of his words. "You don't understand, *witch*," he said, hammering in the last word. "There hasn't been the chance to teach someone worth the salt of their blood in a very long time. If we are going to play this game, then we will play it."

He leaned back, and I remembered to breathe.

"I can't claim you as a student if you aren't with me," he said, gesturing flamboyantly, his earlier mood of seriousness replaced with his usual dramatic flair. "Be reasonable. I know you can be. If you try *very, very* hard."

I didn't like his mocking tone. "I'll visit you one night a week," I countered.

He eyed me over his glasses, his gaze rising to the coming sun. "One night a week off, and the rest of the time, you're with me."

My thoughts went to Trent. I could walk away from this right now, but I wouldn't be able to live with myself. "I'll give you one twenty-four-hour period—a full day and night every week. Take it or leave it." *Damn it, Trent, you owe me big.*

"Two," he countered, and I stifled a tremor. I had him over a barrel, having shown him his freedom and the status having a teachable student would bring. Still, he could say no, and then neither of us would have anything. And I was hoping that I might get something else out of him before we were done.

"One," I said, sticking to my original offer. "And I want to know how to jump the lines immediately. I will not be stranded with no way home."

A curious light flickered in his eyes. It wasn't lust, it wasn't anticipation. I didn't know what it was. "We will spend our time as I see fit," he said, then leered, completely wiping out the deeper emotion I'd seen in him. "Any way I want," he added, licking his ruddy lips.

"No sex," I said, heart pounding. "I'm not sleeping with you. Forget it." It was now or never. "And I want that mark of yours removed," I blurted. "Gratis. Call it a signing bonus."

His lips parted and he laughed until he realized I was serious. "That would leave you with only Newt's mark," he said, amused. "Her claim on you would be stronger than mine. Not a healthy place to be, when one is in the ever-after and . . . vulnerable."

Okay. Good point. Backtrack a little. "Then buy Newt's mark for me," I said, shaking inside, "and take it off. You want me as an apprentice, I want some insurance."

Face clouding, he thought about it, and I got really scared when his expression shifted to a devilish delight. "Only if you give me my name back . . . Madam Algaliarept. Do that, and we have a deal."

I shuddered upon hearing the terms come from his lips, and I didn't care that he saw it. His grin deepened. But considering that I wouldn't have to deal with Newt ever again or risk being summoned into Al's circle, it wasn't a bad arrangement. For either of us. "You don't get your name until Newt's mark is gone," I countered.

He looked at me, then turned to the bright horizon, his smoked glasses going even blacker. "The sun is about to rise," he murmured distantly, and I held my breath, not knowing if he agreed or not.

"So are we doing this?" I asked. There was a jogger at the far end of the park, and his dog was barking furiously at us.

"One more question," he said, bringing his gaze back to me. "Tell me what it was like, being trapped in someone's bubble like a demon."

My face screwed up at the memory. "I hated it," I said, and a small noise slipped from him, rising up from someplace deep inside him where only he knew his thoughts. "It was degrading—infuriating that a worm like Tom had control of me. I wanted to . . . scare him so bad he wouldn't ever do it again."

Al's expression shifted when what I had said hit me and I put a hand to my chest. Damn it back to the Turn, I understood him. He hadn't asked because he hadn't known how I felt. He asked so I would see we were the same. *God, help me. Please.*

"Don't do that to me again," he said. "Ever."

My stomach cramped. He was asking for me to trust him out of a circle, and it was the scariest thing I'd ever had to do. "Okay," I whispered. "You got it."

Al looked at the bubble of ever-after over his head and tugged the lace of his cuffs down. "Come here."

At that instant, light spilled over the rim of earth surrounding Cincinnati. My scratched circle was still there, but Al no longer was. Shaking, I dropped the barrier of ever-after and brought my second sight into focus. Taking a breath, I stepped into the line to find him standing right where I'd left him, smiling with his hand extended. Around him, or us, rather, slumped the broken city, grass-choked chunks of pavement standing at odd angles thrusting upward from the earth. There was no bridge or ponds. Just dead grass and a red haze. I didn't look behind me to the Hollows as the wind blew grit into my face.

I was standing in a line, balanced between reality and the ever-after. I could go either way. I wasn't his yet. "One day a week," I said, knees wobbling.

"I give you Newt's mark, you give me my name," Al said, then wiggled his fingers as if he needed me to take them to finish the deal. I reached for it, and at the last moment, Al's glove melted away, and I found myself gripping his hand. I stifled my first impulse to jerk away, feeling the hard calluses and the warmth. It was done. Now I only had to roll with the surprises.

"Rachel!" came a call with the slamming of a car door. "God, no!"

It had been my mom's voice, and my hand still in Al's, I turned, unable to see anything.

Al pulled me into him, and numb, I felt his arm curve possessively about my waist. "Too late," he whispered, his breath shifting the hair about my ear, and we jumped.

Thirty-three

The jump through the line hit me like a bucket of ice water, an uncomfortable slap right from the start with the shock turning into the sensation of being wet where you don't want to be and left dripping. I felt my body shatter—that was the shock—and then my thoughts tightened into a ball around my soul to hold it together—that was the miserable, dripping-wet part. That I was holding my soul together and not Al was a surprise to both of us.

Good, came Al's grudging, almost worried thought rippling over the protective bubble I had somehow made about my psyche. And then came the push back into existence.

Again the bucket of ice water hit my thoughts as he shoved me out of the line. I tried to see how he did it, coming away without a clue. But at least I had managed to keep from spreading my thoughts over the entire continent crisscrossed with ley lines—the stretchy stuff that kept the ever-after from vanishing, if Jenks was right.

I gasped as I felt my lungs form. Dizzy, I fell to my hands and knees. "Ow," I said as I looked at the dirty white tile, then brought my head up at the hammering of noise. We were in a large room. Men in suits were everywhere standing or sitting in orange chairs—waiting.

"Get up," Al grumbled, bending to bodily yank me upright. I rose, arms and legs flopping until I found my feet.

Wide-eyed, I stared at the irate people dressed in a vast array of styles. Al jerked me into motion, and my mouth dropped as I realized we had popped into existence upon what looked like an FIB emblem. Holy crap, it even looked like the FIB reception room. Minus the demons, of course.

Feeling displaced and unreal, I turned to where the doors to the street would have been, seeing only a blank wall and more waiting demons. "Is this the FIB?" I stammered.

"It's someone's idea of a joke," Al said, his voice tight and his accent impeccable. "Get off the pad unless you want someone's elbow in your ear."

"God, it stinks," I said, hand over my nose as he pulled me into a long step.

Al strode forward, head high. "It's the stench of bureaucracy, my itchy-witch, and why I chose to go into human resources when but a wee lad."

We'd come up to a set of imposing wooden doors. There were two uniformed men beside it—demons, by their eyes—looking bored and stupid. They probably had stupid denizens in the ever-after just like everywhere else. Behind us was a rising angry mutter that I recognized from when I tried to sneak thirteen items into a twelve-item-only line.

"Docket number?" the more brilliant of the two asked, and Al reached for the door.

"Hey," the other said, coming to life. "You're supposed to be in jail."

Al grinned at him, his white-gloved grip tightening on the wooden handle, which was intricately carved in the shape of a naked, writhing woman. *Nice.* "And your momma wanted you to have a brain," he said, yanking the door open and slamming it into the guy's face.

I danced backward at the ensuing uproar, but Al took my upper arm and strode forward, nose in the air, buckled shoes snapping, and velveteen coattails swaying. "You, ah, have a way with civil servants," I said, almost panting to keep up. I wasn't about to drag my feet. I'd stormed a few offices myself;

you had to move quickly to get past the red-tape-loving idiots and find someone intelligent enough to appreciate the nerve of barging in. Someone dying for an interruption and the chance to procrastinate. Someone like . . . I peered at the nameplate on the door Al stopped before. Someone like Dallkarackint. Jeez, what was it with demon names?

Wait a sec. Dali, Dallkarackint . . . Was this the guy Al had wanted to throw my dead body in front of?

Al opened the door, shoved me in, then back-kicked the door shut to block out the uproar storming up the hall behind us. I felt a tweak on my awareness and wondered if he'd locked it. It was a thought that grew more plausible when the pounding on the door stayed pounding and didn't turn into a big ugly demon with a broken nose.

Squinting, I caught my balance in the . . . *sand?* Shocked, I looked up as what had to be a fake breeze smelling of seaweed and burnt amber shifted my hair. I was standing in hot sand in the sun. The door had become a small changing hut, and a boardwalk ran from right to left to the surf-soaked horizon. Stretching into the almost green water was a canopy-covered dock. At the end was a large platform on which a man sat behind a desk. Okay, he was a demon, but he looked like an attractive fifty-something CEO who had brought his desk with him on vacation instead of his laptop. Before him in an upright deck chair was a woman in a purple sari. The scrying mirror on her lap flashed in the sun angling under the canopy that shaded the desk. His familiar?

"Wow," I said, unable to look at everything at once. "This isn't real, is it?"

Al straightened his crushed velvet and pulled me onto the boardwalk. "No," he said as our heels clunked on the wood. "It's casual Friday."

My God, the sun sliding under the awning is even warm, I thought as we found the dock and started down it. I suppose if one was a demon and had unlimited power, why not put the illusion of the Bahamas around you at the office? Al yanked me forward when I lagged to see if there were fish in the water, and I yelped when I felt a cascading shimmer cross over me.

"There," Al soothed, and I shoved his hand off me. "Now don't you look proper? Must wear our best when before the court."

My pulse quickened as I realized I was wearing my usual working leathers, my hair back in a scrunchy and my butt-kicking boots on my feet. The purple scarf around my waist was new, though. "If you're trying to make nice-nice, this might not be the best way to do it," I said to Al when the guy behind the desk leaned back in annoyance as he saw us and the woman took her hand from the mirror.

"Relax." Al pulled me further into his burnt-amber scent as we came to a respectful halt on the round rug laid on the rough planks before the desk. "I'm supposed to be exiled this morning. They would have been disappointed if I didn't do something dramatic."

A puddle of gray in the sun-soaked dinghy tied to the dock moved, and my gaze shifted.

Oh, God. It was Trent. He looked washed out and thin as he bobbed on the fake tide in the sun, and when he saw me, hate filled his bloodshot eyes. He had to know I was here to rescue him. Didn't he?

The demon behind the desk sighed, and my attention shifted to him. Somehow he looked right out here in the cool, Brimstone-scented, breezy shade of the canopy, his desk perched over the water with a coffee cup and a stack of files on it. Flip-flops poked from under the dark mahogany desk, and his Hawaiian-print top showed a wisp of hair at his chest. Setting his pen down, he gestured sourly. "Al, what, by the two worlds colliding, are you doing in my office?"

Al beamed as the demon recognized him, pulling himself straight, tugging the lace at his wrists, and scuffing his shiny-buckled boots on the planks. "Elevating your status, Dali, dear."

Dali leaned back in his chair and glanced at the woman silently waiting. "Before or after I sling your ass to the surface?" he said in a bothered tone, his fast voice rough. His eyes flicked to me, and his lips pursed briefly. "You don't have anything left to elevate anyone. And killing her before the courts will not excuse you from teaching her how to spindle line energy and let her run about with no compulsion to keep her mouth shut."

"Hey!" I said, not wanting that to stand without correction. "I was under compulsion to keep my mouth shut. So was Ceri. We were under lots of compulsion." Al gripped my arm and dragged me back a step as I added, "You've no idea the amount of compulsion we were under."

"You misunderstand, my most honorable ass-kisser," Al said, jaw clenched at my outburst. "I'd sooner *die* before giving Rachel Mariana Morgan to the courts. I'm not here to *kill her*, I'm here to demand that the uncommon stupidity charge against me be dropped."

My shock at the honorable-ass-kisser comment was pushed away by the thought of a law against uncommon stupidity, and I wondered how we could get one. Remembering Trent, I nudged Al.

"Oh, yes," the demon added, "and I would ask that my student's familiar be released to my custody. Busy day planned. We could use his help. Must get him trained up, up, up!"

In the dinghy, Trent pulled himself up and sat on the bench, his motions slow as if he was in pain. There was a humiliating red ribbon about his neck. I wondered why he wore it, but upon seeing that his fingers were red and swollen, I decided they weren't letting him take it off.

Dali pushed his papers away and glanced at the woman. "I appreciate your efforts to weasel out of a hundred years of community service, but you've nothing left. Get out."

I turned to Al, seeing his complexion take on a new hue of red. "Community service? You told me they were going to banish you to the surface."

"They are," he growled, pinching my elbow. "Now shut up."

I fumed, but Al was already facing Dali. "I've taken Morgan as a student, not a familiar," he said. "It's not illegal or uncommonly stupid to teach a student how to spindle line energy. I simply didn't think it was worth mentioning . . . at the time."

Dali's eyes widened. On the floor, Trent's hatred grew directed, and I winced. This was looking really bad, and I'd have done anything to have been able to explain. Smiling, Al looped his arm in mine. "Try to look sexy," he muttered, poking me until my back stiffened.

"Student?" Dali blurted, both hands going palms-down on the desk. "Al—"

"She can spindle line energy," Al interrupted. "Her blood can twist demon curses. She took a human as a familiar before I broke the bond."

"Common knowledge," the demon said, pointing irately. "You said something about status. Give me something I don't know, or get the hell onto the surface where you belong."

Al took a worried breath. His face never changed, but I was standing so close, I felt it. And somehow, that was scary. Exhaling, Al nodded once, as a student might to an instructor. It was the first show of respect I'd seen from him, and I grew more frightened yet. His gaze flicked to the woman with the scrying mirror, and Dali's eyebrows rose.

The older demon pressed his lips and gestured for her to leave. She silently stood, set the mirror on his desk with disgust, and then vanished in a pop that was lost in the sound of the wind against the water. "This better be good," Dali grumbled. "I rent her by the hour."

Al swallowed, and I swear I could smell the faintest hint of sweat on him. "This witch can be summoned," he said softly, an arm behind and before him. "She can be summoned through the lines by way of a password." Dali made a puff of air, and Al added in a louder voice, "I know this because she stole mine and was summoned out in my stead."

Dali leaned forward. "That's how she escaped?" He turned

to me. "You *stole* Al's summoning name? Voluntarily?" he asked. I opened my mouth to tell him it was so Al would leave me and my family alone, but Dali had returned his attention to Al. "She was *summoned out*? How did you get out, then?"

"She summoned me in turn," Al said, his voice dropping in pitch. "That's what I'm saying, old man. She integrated her password into our system well enough for it to be used in summoning. She can invoke demon magic. She *accidentally* made her boyfriend her familiar."

"Ex-boyfriend," I muttered, but neither was listening.

"Now are you going to hand me a shovel so I can dig my way out," Al said, "or are you going to banish me to the surface and throw this pretty little ball of chance against the wall of elf-shit and watch it shatter? None of *you* have the finesse for this. Newt, perhaps, if she were sane, but she isn't. And would you trust Newt not to kill her? I wouldn't."

Dali's eyes narrowed. "You think . . . ," he mused.

"I know," Al said, chilling me with what he might have said, and my gaze flicked to Trent, listening in the dinghy. Damn it, Ceri said I wasn't a demon, but this . . . looked really bad. "She is my student," Al said loudly. "I already made the deal; she's mine. But I want her free of Newt's mark to prevent any— misunderstanding. All I want from you is to serve as witness and to set up a safe place for me to do a deal with Newt."

Fear jerked me straight. *He's going to do the deal now? With me here?* "Ah, wait up, boys," I exclaimed, backing up until Al gave me a withering look. "This is Newt we're talking about, right? No way. No freaking way!"

Ignoring me, the demon behind the desk hesitated nevertheless. He reclined with his fingers steepled against the colorful pattern of flowers on his shirt as the wind ruffled his hair, and I was suddenly struck with the memory of me asking Edden to throw me a preserver to get myself out of my personal crapfest just last year. Damn, were we that much alike, Al and I? Using what we had and scrambling to stay alive?

"Call her," Al said as he picked a tin of snuff from an inner coat pocket. A whiff of Brimstone came to me as he delicately sniffed a pinch. "Newt doesn't remember shit about Morgan, but she knows she forgot something. She'll give me the witch's mark in return for her memory, and when she finds out Minias wiped the knowledge from her, accident or not, she'll bloody kill him. That leaves three knowing." His smile grew devious. "Three is a very stable number."

"What about Trent?" I questioned, thinking this was getting more complex than I'd dreamed it would be. "The deal was I get him."

"Patience, itchy-witch," Al muttered between his teeth as he smiled at Dali and put an arm over my shoulders. I shoved his hand off me and glanced at Trent. He had to have known this was all to get him free and that he wouldn't really be my familiar. But his look was one of pure hatred.

The older demon shifted in his chair, and when our eyes met, I stifled a shiver. In a sudden motion, Dali reached for the scrying mirror. Setting it before him, he smiled wickedly at Al. "I'll see if she's cognizant this morning."

My pulse hammered, and my palms sweated. Almost immediately Dallkarackint's brow furrowed in worry, cleared, and then he smiled. "Al . . . ," I whispered, backing up as I remembered Newt's utterly unbalanced, powerful presence tearing apart my living room and mastering three blood circles as she searched my church for who knew what. "Al, this isn't a good idea. This *really* isn't a good idea."

He huffed and grasped my shoulders, forcing me to stand beside him. "You asked for a bloody miracle. Who did you think I'd have to go to for it? Be a good girl and don't slouch."

I fought to get free of his grip, my motions stilling when Newt's androgynous shape misted into existence, bald and barefoot, her high cheekbones flushed and her brows raised in question. She wore a robe that was somewhere between a kimono and a sari, matching Minias's usual outfit, but hers was a dark red, billowing and lightweight. Her eyes were completely black, even the whites, and I remembered the touch of her hand on my jaw and how she had searched my face the first time we had met, comparing me to her sisters. Mouth dry, I tried to get Al between us, not caring if I looked scared. I was.

She slowly turned, her black gaze going from the bobbing dinghy to the ornate desk. "Dali," she said. Her voice had a smooth but masculine edge to it, and the demon took his hand from the mirror. Her attention shifted to Al. "Algaliarept?" she questioned. "Shouldn't you be making a sun shelter about now?" And then her eyes fell upon me.

"You!" she said, stepping forward with a vehement expression and her finger pointed.

Heart pounding, I pressed into Al. Funny how he seemed so much safer now.

"Newt, love," Al soothed, a black haze enveloping his extended hand, and I felt the tension almost crack. "You look *marvelous*. Don't muss your dress. She's here for a reason. Don't you want to hear it before you tear her head off?"

Newt hesitated, and as my pulse hammered in my ears, she graciously sank back into the deck chair Dali's secretary had been in. Dali was still behind the desk, but he was standing now. "Your familiar has something that belongs to me," she said almost petulantly. "I'm assuming you're here to sell her. Trying to buy space in the zoo, are you?"

Dali cleared his throat and came around his desk to offer her a tall glass of what looked like iced tea. It hadn't been there a moment ago. "Al is trying to weasel his way out of debt and thinks it will take that mark the witch owes you," the older demon said as he leaned against his desk, ankles crossed in a subtle show of submissiveness. "Be a dear and sell it to him, love."

She had taken the drink, the ice tinkling faintly as she set it on a round wicker table that showed up the instant she took her hand from the glass. "Since Al wants it, the answer is no."

Al took a step forward, leaving me to feel exposed. "Newt, love, I'm sure—"

With a glance, she stopped him. "I'm sure you have nothing—love," she mocked. "You sold everything down to your rooms to bribe for a late court date and post bail. I'm crazy, not stupid."

My jaw dropped, and I warmed. "You did what?" I exclaimed. Great. I was the student of a destitute demon. But Newt was now looking at me, and I backed up a step.

"She has something of mine," she said. "She wears my mark. Give her to me, and maybe I'll buy your rooms back for you."

At that, Al smiled. Kneeling before her, he took up her drink. "What she has is a memory of you two meeting, of what you learned and no one else but I figured out. Give me the witch's mark," Al whispered as he handed her the glass, "and I'll tell you what that is. Better still, I'll keep reminding you when that bastard Minias doses you into forgetting it—again."

The glass in her grip cracked, and an amber bead of liquid formed and rolled down the side. It was followed by another. "Minias . . . ," she almost growled as she set the glass aside, her jaw tight in anger and her black orbs terrifyingly intent.

Her gaze fell on me, and I went cold. She stood, and Al casually backed up to get between us. "Yes or no, love," he said, putting me behind him.

"Yes," she whispered, and I yelped, shaking my foot when it gave a twinge.

Al steadied me, but his intake of breath shook at our success. "You put it on your foot?" he asked me.

"I didn't have a choice," I said, knees weak. He had done it. That fast, he had gotten Newt's mark switched to him. Now all that was left was to return his name for it, and I'd be free of the mark completely. *This is working*, I thought, glancing at Trent, who was watching in numb shock.

"Tell me what I forgot," Newt said, eyeing me with suspicion.

Al smiled. Laying a finger beside his nose, he leaned into her. "She can invoke demon magic," he said, holding up a finger to forestall Newt's snort of anger. "She has made a human her familiar, though I broke that bond."

"It had better be more than that, Al," she intoned, starting to look pissed as she drew away from Al and looked out over the fake water.

"She stole my name and made it her own."

Newt turned to face him, her expression empty.

"And she was summoned out under it."

Black eyes going wide, Newt sucked in her breath. "I killed my sisters!" she said, and my brief elation at getting her mark shifted to Al twisted into fear. "She can't be kin!"

"Oh, she's kin," Al said, chuckling as he pulled me to him, his grip tightening as I struggled. "Kin born not of us but of the elves. Stupid, stupid elves who forgot and fixed what they broke. You figured it out, and Minias stole the knowledge from you for long enough that I could realize it, too, and get her first."

"She should be mine! Give her to me!"

But Al shook his head as Dali tensed behind his desk, the demon smiling as he breathed in the scent from my hair. I let him, numb and bewildered. Kin? Witches really were kin to demons? It went against everything I'd been taught, but damn it, it made sense!

I jumped at a soft pop of displaced air. Minias burst into existence, his sandaled feet on the old wood. He was wearing his purple robes, and I fingered my belt, starting to think that was the color demons dressed their familiars in when they were pleased with them. "Newt!" Minias exclaimed, drawing back when he realized who else was here, giving Trent barely a glance. "What are you doing here?" he questioned, then paled at her venomous look.

"You made me forget what she is," she whispered. "Come here, Minias."

Red, goat-slitted eyes widening, Minias reared back and vanished.

"Wait!" I shouted, then turned to Al. "I need him. You promised me Trent!"

Al's expression at my outburst was one of pure disgust, and when Newt turned to me, I wished I'd kept my mouth shut. "You want that elf for a familiar?" she asked.

I licked my lips. "He put me in a cage," I said, trying to come up with a reason other than rescuing him. Trent got to his feet, the dinghy rocking until he steadied himself against the dock, whereupon Dali kicked him back to the bottom of the boat.

"He's the perfect familiar for my student," Al interjected smoothly over my head, his grip on my arm telling me to shut up. "Easily hurt, stubborn, prone to biting, but basically harmless. One must learn to ride a pony before tackling the stallion. He owes Minias a favor. I could press the issue since the elf is voluntarily wearing her smut, but honestly, it's easier just to buy a mark." Al smiled with a delicious irony. "Maybe I'll offer to tell him about my new student. That ought to be worth something."

I tensed as Newt's eyes narrowed. "You'll tell me again, if I forget?" Al nodded, and Newt's face grew ugly. "The elf doesn't owe Minias anything. I give his mark to you."

Trent groaned and fell back, his hate-filled expression chilling me.

Dali's brows rose. "I didn't know you could do that."

Newt spun, making her robe unfurl. "He's my familiar, bought and paid for. I can claim anything of his. Even his life."

Al cleared his throat nervously. "That's good to know," he said lightly. "Important safety tip. Rachel, write that down somewhere as lesson number one."

Her lips pressed tightly, Newt pulled her attention from the false horizon and found me. Ice seemed to scum my skin, and I felt myself pale. I had everything I'd come for. I had rubbed out Newt's mark, or at least I would when I gave Al his name back. I had saved Trent—I thought. So why did every instinct tell me everything was about to hit the fan?

"You will teach her?" Newt said to Al, looking at me with her black eyes.

Al nodded and pulled me closer, and I let him. "As if she were my daughter."

Newt dropped back a step, her hands clasped before her and her head bowed. She looked funny, and I got the feeling that something was being settled that I didn't understand. "You're a good teacher," Newt finally said when her head came up. "Ceri was very skilled."

"I know. I miss her."

Her head moved up and down, and then she turned to me. "When you're ready, come to me. Maybe by then I'll have my memory back and I'll know what in hell is going on."

I clenched my hands so no one would see them tremble, but when I took a breath to answer her, she vanished.

Dali's exhale was loud and strong. "I give Minias two days."

Al's shoulders slumped. "He's used to evading her. I give him . . . seven." He shifted uneasily, looking at the sparkles in the surf. "Rachel, collect your elf. I'm tired and I want to wash the cell-stink off me." I didn't move and he gave me a shove in Trent's direction before turning to Dali. "I'm assuming the charge of uncommon stupidity will be dropped?"

Dali smiled. "Yes, yes, take your student's familiar and get out. Are you going to remind Newt as you said you would?"

Al smiled. "Every day until she kills him. Yes."

Unsure, I looked at Trent gazing murderously at me, then Al. "Uh, Al?" I prompted.

"Get your elf, itchy-witch," he said under his breath. "I want to get out of here before Newt remembers a rule or something and comes back."

But Trent was looking at me like he wanted to jam a pen in my eye. Taking a shaky breath, I strode to him, falling into a crouch and extending a hand to help him out of the bobbing boat. A low sound rose from him. I stared at him, frozen, as he lunged at me.

"Trent!" I managed before he got a grip on my throat. My back hit the dock, and he landed on me, pushing my air out.

He was straddling me, his grip cutting off my air—and then he was gone and I could breathe again. I heard a thump, looking up to see that Al had backhanded him off of me.

Trent slumped to the dock, a leg hanging off it and threatening to pull him into the water. Shocked, I stared as he curled into himself and retched over the side.

"Lesson number two," Al said as he yanked me up with a white-gloved hand. "Never trust your familiar."

"What in hell is wrong with you!" I shouted, glaring at Trent as I shook. "You can kill me later, but right now, I want to get out of here!"

I reached out, and this time he did nothing when I pulled him to Al. I didn't know how to travel the lines, but I assumed Al would jump us, seeing as I had just saved his demon ass.

"Thank you," I muttered, very conscious of Dali watching us with calculation.

"Thank me later, itchy-witch," Al said nervously. "I'm popping you and your familiar back to your church, but I expect to see you in fifteen minutes in your ley line with your spelling supplies and a new stick of magnetic chalk. I need some time to, ah, rent a room somewhere."

My eyes closed in a long blink. Al really was broke. Swell. "Can't we start this next week?" I asked, but it was too late, and I felt Trent's grip on me tighten as my body was torn apart by time, then melted back into existence. I was so tired, I could have cried.

I didn't even feel dizzy when the stink of the ever-after vanished. The acidic scent of cut grass hit me, and wavering on my feet, I opened my eyes to the somber gray and green of my graveyard. Slowly I slumped. I was home.

"Dad!" a tiny voice shrilled, and I jerked to find one of Jenks's kids staring at me. "She's back! And she's got Mr. Kalamack!"

Blinking back the tears, I took a deep breath and turned to the church shining in the morning sun. It had to be later than that. I felt like I'd lived a lifetime. Seeing Trent at my feet, I reached to pull him up. "We're back," I said wearily, hauling on him. "Get up. Don't let Ceri see you on the ground like that." It was over. At least for now.

Still on the ground, Trent yanked on my arm. I sucked in my breath and tried to land in a front fall, but he pulled me off balance and I landed on my side instead.

"Trent—" I started, then yelped when he jerked me up, slamming my head into a tombstone. "Hey!" I shouted, then howled when he twisted my arm.

Quicker than I could follow, he slammed my head into the stone again. My vision blurred as the pain swelled, and trying to figure out what the hell was going on, I stupidly did nothing when he wrapped an arm around my throat from behind and started squeezing.

"Trent . . . ," I managed to get out, then choked, feeling my face seem to bulge.

"I won't let you do it!" came his voice snarling in my ear. "I'll kill you first!"

Do what? I thought, struggling to breathe. *I just saved his ass!*

Putting my heels to the ground, I shoved backward, but we only fell over. His grip loosened and I got a breath, and then his grip went tighter.

"Demon kin!" Trent exclaimed, his voice raw and alien. "It was there in front of me, but I didn't believe it! My father . . . Damn him!"

"Trenton!" Ceri's voice came faintly from over the grave-yard as my consciousness started to slip. "Stop! Stop it!"

I felt her fingers trying to wedge between Trent's grip and my skin, and I choked as it loosened again. I couldn't break his hold, and my oxygen-starved muscles were like wet paper.

"She has to die," Trent said, his voice close and rasping in my ear. "I heard them. My father. My father mended her," he agonized, and his grip tightened. "She can start it up again! Not now! I won't let her!"

His arm muscle bunched, and as pain struck through me, I heard my last breath gurgle.

"Let go," Ceri pleaded, and I saw her dress. "Trent, stop it!"

"They called her kin!" Trent shouted. "I watched her take a demon's name. She was summoned out under it!"

"She's not a demon," Ceri demanded. "Let her go!" Her braid slapped me as she bent over us and tugged at his fingers. "Trenton, let her go! She saved Quen. She saved all of us. Let her go! She's not a demon!"

His grip loosened, and as I gasped, retching almost, he shoved me away from him.

I fell against the tombstone that he had hammered my head against, and I held it, fingers shaking as I pulled lungful after lungful of air into me, holding my neck and trying to find a way to breathe that didn't hurt. "She might not be a demon," Trent said from behind me, and I turned. "But her children will be."

I slumped back against the stone, feeling the blood drain from me. *My children . . .*

Ceri was kneeling beside him, her hands on him as she felt for damage, ready to hold him back if he tried to finish the job. But all I could do was sit in the sun and stare. "What?" I rasped, and he laughed bitterly.

"You're the only female witch my father fixed," he accused, taking the red ribbon from his neck and letting it fall to the ground. "Lee can't pass on the cure. It's in the mitochondria. You're the only one who could start it all up again. But I'll kill you first!"

"Trenton, no!" Ceri exclaimed, but he was too weak to do anything.

Staring at him, I felt my reality start to crumble. *God, no. It was too much.*

"Trent," Ceri was saying, kneeling between us, trying to distract him. "She saved us. You have a cure waiting in your labs because of her. We can be whole again, Trent! Kill her, and you stain our beginning. You lose everything! Stop fighting them. It's killing us!"

From under the mat of his hair, Trent seethed, his eyes trying to burn me where I sat. I felt dirty, unclean. Filthy.

"Your father saved her because he was friends with her father," Ceri rushed. "He didn't know what it would do. It's not your fault. It's not her fault. But she gave you the way to make us whole today. Right now." Ceri hesitated, then added, "Perhaps we deserved what happened."

Trent's attention tore from me, landing on Ceri. "You don't believe that."

Ceri was blinking to keep from crying, but a tear slid down, making her all the more beautiful. "We can start again," she said. "So can they. The war almost destroyed both of us. Don't start it up again. Not when we finally have a chance to live. Trent. Listen to me."

I shut my eyes. *Why doesn't it go away?*

In a rush of sound, Ivy and Jenks arrived together, standing over us in shock while Ceri held Trent back from killing me.

"Hi," I croaked, still holding my neck, and Ivy dropped to me.

"What happened?" Ivy asked, and my chest clenched to an unbearable tightness. She didn't know. How could I tell her? "You're back," she added, checking me for damage. "Are you okay? Your mother said you went with Al at Eden Park. Damn it, Rachel, stop trying to fight everything by yourself!"

I opened my eyes at the concern in her voice. I wondered whether I should just stay in the ever-after. At least there, I wouldn't be putting my friends in danger. Kin. *Witches are kin to demons.* Suddenly it was making a whole lot of sense. Demons had cursed elves into a slow slide of extinction. Had it been done in retaliation? Had the elves hit the demons first?

"Rache, you okay?"

No. I wasn't okay, but I couldn't seem to get my mouth to work to say the words. I wasn't a demon, but my children would be. Damn it! This wasn't fair.

"Is it Trent?" Ivy said, her anger rounding on him, and I shook my head. "Get out of here, Kalamack, before I pound you into the ground!"

Ceri's delicate form helped Trent up, and as they hunched into each other, she helped him hobble to the street gate. She turned once, the tears flowing freely from her anger-black eyes. "I'm sorry, Rachel. I-I . . ."

I looked away, unable to bear it. I wasn't ever going to have kids now. Not with anyone. Never. *Stupid-ass elf. Look what they did to me.*

"Rachel," Ivy said, forcing me to look at her. "Tell me what happened."

She gave me a shake, and I stared at her, numb. Jenks was on her shoulder. He looked terrified, like he already knew. "Trent," I started, and tears spilled over. Wiping them angrily, I tried again. "Trent's dad . . . he . . ."

Jenks took to the air and got in my face. "You're not a demon, Rachel!"

I nodded, trying to focus on him. "I'm not," I said, choking on my words. "But my kids will be. Remember last year when I said witches and demons both started in the ever-after? I think the elves spelled the demons, magically stunting their kids and starting the witches, and when Trent's dad fixed me, he broke the genetic checks and balances they put in to keep the demons from having children. Witches are stunted demons, and now demons can come from witches again. From me."

Ivy's hand fell from me, and I saw the horror in her quiet face.

"I'm sorry," I whispered. "I didn't mean to screw up your life."

Ivy sat back, stunned, and the sun blinded me. Tired beyond belief, I looked up to see Ceri helping Trent out of the garden. *What in hell had it all been for?*

Thirty-four

Blue and pink baby booties had replaced the bats hanging in the sanctuary, the store-bought garland draping from one end of the sanctuary to the other. A cutout of a stork stood on the coffee table, and Ivy's piano was covered in yellow and green paper tablecloths. The white cake on it was surrounded by pixies snitching frosting. That is, the ones who weren't clustered over Ceri, oohing over the delicate pair of baby booties and lace collar that Matalina and her older daughters had made.

The happy elf sat across from me in Ivy's chair, surrounded by pixies, wrapping paper, and gifts. She was nearly glowing, and it made me feel good. Outside, the falling rain brought darkness early, but in here, it was warm, comfortable, and full of the peace of companionship.

One month pregnant is way too soon for a baby shower, I thought as I leaned into the cushions while Ceri read the card from my mother, the box on her lap suspiciously similar in size to a humidifier. But watching Ceri's delight, I knew it had been the right thing to do. We needed to celebrate the beginning of a life. The beginning of something.

Ivy was to my left on the couch, crammed into the corner as if she didn't know her limits anymore. She'd been like that all week, hovering but hesitant, and it was driving me nuts. Her gift to Ceri had been the first one opened: an absolutely stunning lace christening dress of intricate beauty. Ivy had gone red at the fuss Ceri had made over it, and I was sure that Ivy had picked the delicate bit of feminine beauty out because she had given up the idea of ever having children herself. Though she never talked about it, I knew Ivy would rather remain childless than perpetuate her vampiric misery upon someone she loved, especially an innocent who was dependent on her for everything.

I squished the crumbs of my cake up with a fork as my eyes drifted to the present Jenks and I had gone in on together, wondering what it said about us. I had bought a set of redwood building blocks, and Jenks had painted garden flowers and bugs on them to go along with the alphabet. He was working on another set for his children, determined they would all know how to read before spring.

The pixies flew up in noisy delight when Ceri got the wrapping paper off and revealed a Dr. Dan's Misty Memories Humidifier with deluxe soothing atomizer built right in to "lull your baby to sleep on the most trying of nights." I was staying out of the way, but my mother went to kneel beside Ceri as the elf seriously unpacked the thermometer and burping cloths she had put in there with it.

"Ceri, this is a lifesaver," my mom was saying as the young-looking elf lifted the green plastic monstrosity out. "Rachel was a fussy baby, but I would just put a bit of lilac into the little cup, and she would drop right off." She smiled at me, looking different with her new hairstyle. "And it's indispensable if your baby gets the croup. Robbie never got the croup, but Rachel, lord love a duck, she'd just about scare me to death every winter with her coughing."

Hearing a story coming on, I picked up a few plates and stood. "Excuse me," I said, beating a tactful retreat into the kitchen as my mom started in on the story of my nearly suffocating. Ceri looked properly horrified, and I rolled my eyes to tell her it was mostly momma drama. Mostly.

I glanced back at the scene of content femininity as the dark confines of the hall took me. My mother had gifted Ceri's baby with a wish for health, Matalina gave the trappings of security, Ivy imparted beauty and innocence, and Jenks and I gave wisdom. Or maybe entertainment.

The kitchen held a cool quietness, and I glanced out at the graveyard and let my vision drift into my second sight to make sure Al wasn't waiting for me. The red-smeared sky of the ever-after mingled with the reality of gray clouds to make an ugly picture, and I shivered though the line was empty. He said he would call first, but I didn't trust him not to just show up and scare the crap out of everyone. Apparently Newt's claim that he had made himself destitute was right, because he said he wasn't going to bring me over until he had a kitchen that wouldn't embarrass him. I wanted my name back and that mark on my foot removed, and I think he was stalling, not wanting to lose that hold on me.

"That was a lovely shower," my mom said from the hallway, and I jumped, startled.

"Holy crap, Mom!" I exclaimed, dropping my second sight and turning. "You're worse than Ivy."

She smiled, a glint of devilry in her as she sashayed in, cake-strewn plates and silverware in hand. "Thank you for inviting me. I don't get to go to too many of these things."

Hearing an accusation in there, I plugged the sink and ran some water. "Mom," I said tiredly as I pulled out the soap, "I'm not having any kids. I'm sorry. You'll be lucky if you even get a wedding out of me."

My mother made a rude sound, part laugh, part wise-old-woman scoffing. "I'm sure you feel that way now," she said as she dropped the forks into the sink. "But you're young. Give it some time. You might feel differently after you've met the right man."

I turned the water off, breathing deeply of the lemon-scented air and slipping my hands into the warm water and washing the forks. I wished she'd drop the facade of what she wanted for what was real. "Mom," I said, voice low, "my children will be stolen by demons for the ability to kindle their magic. I'm not going to risk that." Well, actually, they *would* be demons, thanks to Trent's dad, but there was no reason to tell her that. "I'm not going to have kids," I said, slowly washing the plates.

"Rachel . . . ," my mom protested, but I shook my head, adamant.

"Kisten died because of me. Nick went over the bridge. I've got a standing date in the ever-after once a week once Al gets his act together. I'm not a good candidate for a girlfriend. Can you see me as a mother?"

My mother smiled. "Yes. I can, and you would be a good one."

The tears pricked, and I dropped a handful of clean silverware into the dry half of the sink and ran hot water over them. I couldn't. It was too risky.

Pulling a cloth from a top drawer, my mom took the handful of clean silverware I'd dropped into the sink. "Let's say you're right," she said, "and you don't even adopt or take in a child who needs a home. But what if you're wrong? There's someone out there who's suited for you. Someone who has enough strength or knowledge to keep themselves safe. I bet there's a foxy young man looking right now for a woman who can take care of herself and thinking he can't have anyone either."

I smiled faintly, picturing it. "I'll place an ad, okay?" SWFW looking for SWM. Must be able to fight off demons and vampires, and be willing to put up with jealous roommate. Then I sighed in the thought that that pretty much summed up Nick and Kisten. Nick was a real winner, and Kisten was dead. Because of me. Because he had tried to save me.

My mom touched my arm, and I handed her one of Ceri's teacups.

"I just want you to be happy," she said.

"I am," I said confidently so I could believe it. "I really am." But when I found out who had bitten me and killed Kisten, and then I ripped him apart, I was going to be a whole lot happier.

Maybe Al knew a Pandora charm. Maybe he had a book and I could just read up on it when he was sleeping.

From the sanctuary came the masculine sound of a hello and the excited tinkling of pixy chatter. It was Quen; the party was breaking up. Passing my mom the last dish, I went more melancholy still. I had saved Quen, but not my dad. That sucked.

My mom must have known my thoughts as she gave me a sideways hug. She pulled away, but her damp hands seemed to leave a lasting impression on me. "Don't make such a sad face, Rachel. I loved your dad. But I've been hurting for so long, I forgot how to be happy. I need to . . ."

I nodded, knowing where she was coming from. "Put something good in its place so you can think about him without the pain?"

She nodded, giving me another tight hug as if she was trying to squeeze some of her happiness into me. "I want to help Ceri get her things back home," she said, and I dried my hands. We left the kitchen together, my mother's arm still over me. It made me feel good, like I felt when I was little. Protected. Loved.

But when we entered the sanctuary, my arm fell away. *Takata is here, too?*

The man gave me an awkward wave as he stood by the piano with his fingers in the frosting and pixies sitting on his thin shoulders. I felt a stab of emotion when my mother's demeanor changed and she went to him, delighted. She seemed younger, especially with that new haircut. Her heart was light now that the truth was out, which made me feel bad that it had taken so long for that to happen.

Ceri had her raincoat on, and seeing me standing alone, she excused herself, gathering Quen in her wake as she crossed the room. She was beautiful in her happy contentment, and I glanced at Ivy. The vampire wore a hungry look I understood. It wasn't vampiric hunger; it was the hunger from seeing someone who has what you want but knowing that if you get it, it will break your heart, your life, and your soul.

Neither of us would be having children. It was as if Ceri were having a child for all of us. Poor little baby was going to have so many aunts he or she wasn't going to walk on anything but rose petals.

"Rachel," Ceri said, beaming as she took my hands, "thank you for the wonderful party. I never—" Her expression shifted, and tears deepened the green of her eyes. Quen touched her shoulder, and she straightened, smiling. "I never thought I'd ever do this," she continued. "I thought I was going to die mindless in the ever-after. And now I have the sun, love, and a chance to live and have purpose." Her grip on my hands tightened for a moment, deepening the intent behind her next words. "Thank you."

"You're welcome," I said, feeling the prick of tears as I mourned the loss of my own dreams. "Stop it. You're going to make me cry."

I glanced at Quen as I wiped the corner of an eye. He was stoic, letting the estrogen flow around him as if it couldn't touch him.

Ceri's gaze flicked to him and away. "If it's a girl, we're naming her Ray. If it is a boy, Raymond."

There was a lump in my throat, and I couldn't swallow. "Thank you."

She leaned in and gave me a quick hug. "I have to leave. Trenton wants to poke and prod me with more tests." The young-seeming elf rolled her eyes, and my hand slipped away.

"Then you'd better go." Trent wasn't gunning for me, but I distrusted his silence.

Her smile went stiff, and she whispered, "Be careful with Al. If you're honest with him, he will be less likely to . . . hurt you. And if he gets angry, try singing."

She pulled back, and I glanced at Quen, wondering how much of this conversation was going to end up in Trent's ears.

"Okay. Thanks. I'll remember that." I didn't know how me singing "Satisfaction" would make anything better, but the honesty thing? I could do that.

My focus sharpened on Ceri and she nodded. "I must say good-bye to Mrs. Morgan and Ivy," Ceri said, touching Quen's arm. "Can you give me a moment?"

He gazed at her and said "Yes," but what I heard was "I will give you the world if you but ask."

Ceri smiled and walked away. Quen watched her go, then flushed when I cleared my throat with an attention-getting sound. "Don't worry," I said as I put some space between us now that Ceri was gone. "I won't tell anyone you're twitterpated."

The uncomfortable man stared at a spot behind and somewhat above me. His scar, now defunct and made silent with illegal genetic tinkering, was a white mass of tissue almost hidden behind his collar. "I don't think I thanked you for helping me," he said evenly, "on Halloween night."

I turned so that we were standing shoulder-to-shoulder, both watching Ceri talking to my mom and Ivy. "Yeah, well, no good deed goes unpunished."

He inclined his head, but his expression was blank, and struck by a sudden thought, I blurted, "Hey, you do know that the familiar thing with Trent was just to get him out, right? He's not really going to be my familiar." But there was a new shadow of a mark on my arm, mirroring Trent's. I'd assumed Newt had transferred the mark to Al, but it looked like I had it. Curious.

Quen gave me a half-smile. "He knows." After glancing at Ceri, he leaned so no one but I could see his face. "He tried to kill you because of what his father did to you, accidentally giving the demons a way to reclaim their kin, but you're alive because you saved my life when he could not, then went on to save him at great cost to yourself when he was helpless. If not for that, you, your church, and everyone and everything in it would be razed to the ground."

"Yeah. Okay," I said, nervous and believing him. Trent had a right to hate me. But he owed me big. If I was lucky, he would ignore me. Quen saw Ceri saying her last good-byes, and I jiggled on my feet. I had one more thing to say, and this might be my last chance.

"Quen," I said, the softness of my voice stopping him. "Would you tell Trent I'm sorry that I mishandled things so badly that he had to endure being treated like an animal?" The scarred man looked silently at me, and I grimaced. "I never should have taken Trent into the ever-after. I think it was an ego thing. That I was trying to prove to him that I was stronger or smarter than he was. It was stupid and egotistical . . . and I'm sorry."

The man's leathery, pox-scarred face turned into a smile. Eyes drifting to Ceri, he nodded. "I'll do that." His gaze came back to me and he extended his hand. Feeling weird, I shook it. His fingers were warm, and it was as if I could feel them on me even after he went to join Ceri to guide her slowly to the door.

The two of them left amid a flurry of noise, and much to my relief, they took a nice slice of the pixies with them. I exhaled in the subdued uproar of winged things hopped up on sugar, and my mom and Takata headed my way. She had her purse and coat, and it looked like they were leaving, too.

I leaned against the pool table with a whisper of nervousness tightening my muscles. Takata would never take the place of my dad—I didn't think he was going to try—but he was going to be a part of my life and I didn't know what that meant yet. Again I was startled by how alike we looked. The nose, especially.

"We're going to go, too, sweetheart," my mom said, her heels clicking smartly as they approached. "It was a lovely party."

She gave me a hug, her pink-and-blue goody basket thumping on my back. "Thanks for coming, Mom."

"I wouldn't have missed it for anything." She stepped back, her eyes bright.

At her elbow, Takata shifted awkwardly. "Did you ask her?" he said to my mom, and I looked from one to the other. *Ask me what?*

My mom took my hand, trying to reassure me, but it wasn't working. "I was just about to." Flushing, she met my gaze and asked, "Would you house-sit for me for about two weeks? I'm going out to the West Coast to visit Robbie. He's met a nice lady and I want to meet her."

Somehow I didn't think meeting Robbie's girlfriend would make her turn that particular shade of red. She was going out there to be with Takata. "You bet," I said, forcing a smile until it became real. "Anytime. When are you leaving?"

"We're not sure yet," she said, glancing shyly at Takata. The older rock star was smiling with half his mouth, apparently as amused as I was with my mom's embarrassment.

"Well." My mom settled herself. "I was going to stay to help pick up, but it looks like there isn't much left."

I glanced at the sanctuary, nearly back to normal under the attentions of Matalina and the remnants of her brood. "No, it's okay."

She hesitated. "You're sure?" she said, her gaze flicking behind me to the rest of the church. "It's Saturday. Isn't that the day . . ."

I nodded. "It is, but he's still looking for a set of rooms. I have another week's reprieve."

Takata nervously ran a hand through his unruly hair, and I smiled wryly. "This is the same demon who was trying to kill you, right?" he asked. I could smell the redwood coming off of him. He wasn't happy, but he didn't feel it was his place to say anything. Smart man.

"Yup." When my mom wasn't looking I shot him a look to get him to be quiet. "He sold everything he owns to get me, so he'll treat me okay." *So shut up so my mom doesn't get spastic.*

My mother beamed and gave my hand a squeeze, but Takata looked horrified. "That's my girl," she said. "Always keep a few cards back."

"I will." A feeling of peace filled me as I gave her a hug good-bye. She was a cool mom. We broke, and I looked at Takata, then gave him a hug, too. God, he was tall. He seemed pleased until I tightened my grip on his shoulder, holding him while I whispered, "If you hurt my mother, I will be all over you like mist."

"I love her," he whispered back.

"That's what I'm afraid of."

My mom was frowning at me when I let go of Takata, apparently knowing I'd threatened him. But hey, that's what a kick-ass daughter was for.

Ivy sidled up to me, looking nice in her jeans and sweater. "'Bye, Mrs. Morgan. Takata," she said, clearly trying to get them out. She wasn't one for long partings. "Let me know about the security for this solstice, Takata. I can get you a good price."

Takata started edging backward. "Thanks. I will."

He took my mom's goody bag and escorted her out to the door. Matalina took advantage of the open door and corralled her kids, getting them out of the church on the excuse of taking the leftover fruit cups into their stump now that the rain had slacked off. My mother was chatting cheerfully as the door thumped shut behind them all, and I exhaled, soaking in the welcome silence.

Ivy started gathering the trash, and I pushed myself into motion. "That was fun," I said as I took a pool cue and jerked free an end of the festive banner from above the windows. It fluttered down, and I tugged to pull the other end off.

Ivy came to help me wind it up. "Your mother had her hair differently."

A soft feeling of melancholy slipped over me. "I like it. It looks better," I said.

"Younger," Ivy added, and I nodded. We were working the long banner together, folding it back and forth on the little brackets, getting closer to each other with each bend.

"I haven't made any progress in finding out who killed

Kisten," she said unexpectedly. "Just eliminating people."

Startled, I let the packet go as we met in the middle. Ivy caught it with her vampire reflexes before it unfolded more than two twists and casually folded it up. "It has to be someone outside Cincy," she said, pretending ignorance at my fluster. "Piscary wouldn't give him to a lesser vampire outside of the camarilla, only a higher one. I'm going to try to get into the airline records, but whoever it was probably drove in."

"Okay. Do you need any help?"

Not meeting my eyes, Ivy dropped the packet in the bag and set it aside. "Have you given any thought to talking to Ford?"

Ford? The memory of the FIB's psychiatrist flashed through me, and I warmed. He made me nervous.

"If you could remember anything. Anything at all," Ivy was saying, sounding almost afraid. "Even a smell or sound."

Scared, I felt the inside of my lip for the small scar. The memory of someone forcing my back into a wall rose up from my past. Vampire incense and the agonizing, aching need to be bitten, to feel the icy burning of teeth in me, followed close behind—and the fear that I couldn't stop it. It wasn't a memory of Ivy, but of Kisten's killer. There was nothing to identify whom it had been, only the terror of being forced into something I desperately didn't want.

My heart was pounding, and I looked up to find Ivy at the far end of the sanctuary, her eyes black as she felt my fear and it triggered her instincts. "Sorry," I whispered, holding my breath to get my pulse to slow. Seeing her like that, I wondered how we were going to do this—live in a church together without pressing each other's buttons. That we had been doing this for over a year didn't help. It made things worse.

Ivy grabbed the leftover cake off her piano. Her motions edging into a vampiric quickness, she breezed past me and went into the hall. "Don't worry about it."

I listened to my breathing and counted to ten. Fingers slow, I gathered the bowl of jelly beans from my mom's baby-shower game and followed her. I found Ivy leaning against the sink, her expression mildly peeved. The cake was sitting forgotten on the counter.

"Don't screw this up by thinking too hard, Rachel," she said softly, her voice like silk against the rain. "The question isn't *if* we can do this. It's can we live with ourselves if we *don't try*." She looked up, her eyes a steady brown, but there was a hint of hurt in them. "Don't apologize every time you feel something and accidentally jerk me around. It makes me feel like you've done something wrong. You haven't. You're just being you. Let me take my share of the responsibility. Just give me time to collect myself. Okay? And maybe start wearing your perfume again."

I blinked, shocked that she was actually talking to me instead of running away. "Okay. Yeah. Sure. Um, sorry."

She snorted at that, and clearly wanting to drop it, she found the tinfoil and started wrapping up the leftover cake. It seemed different now, as we silently went about the business of cleaning up the kitchen, both of us not quite walking on eggshells, but peaceful almost, knowing nothing was ever going to happen between us and we could just concentrate on getting along. But when things loosened up into a casual comfort was when I usually had the most trouble with relationships. Sighing, I turned at the sound of pixy wings in the hall.

"Hey, I think Al's here," Jenks said as he hovered between us, and a spike of fear slid through me and was gone. Ivy took a slow breath, but she was smiling as her softly dilating pupils met mine.

"I can't see him, but the air got about three degrees colder in that ley line," Jenks added, then hesitated, his expression going wary when he noticed we were a careful eight feet apart. "Did I interrupt something?" he asked warily.

"No," I blurted. *What is Al doing here? I thought I had tonight off.* "Is it still raining?"

Ever the observant pain-in-the-ass, Jenks flew a circle around Ivy. "Are you sure?" he persisted, laughing. "'Cause it looks like—"

"No," I reiterated as I started for the back door, anticipation of the unknown running through me. *Who would have thought I'd ever go into the ever-after willingly.* "Ivy and I were discussing how I need to go talk to Ford. See if I can remember anything new."

Ivy was right behind me with Mr. Fish. I opened the door to find the rain had settled into a fine mist. I glanced at the Betta, then her. "Uh, Ivy?"

"Take your fish," she said, eyes low as she shoved it at me. "Use him like a canary. If he can handle the toxicity of the ever-after, then you can."

Knowing it would be easier to just accept the fish than argue, I took him. A sneeze ripped through me, and I almost spilled the bowl. "I'm coming!" I shouted, knowing Al was trying to hurry me up. Like the weather wasn't enough of a goad?

Jenks was tight by my ear as I waved one finger at the empty-seeming garden. I couldn't see Al without bringing up my second sight, but he could probably see me. "So you want me to make an appointment for you with Ford?" Jenks asked uncertainly.

Oh, yeah. I squinted, considering it. I wanted to know who'd killed Kisten and tried to bind me, but it was as scary as all hell. Reading on the damp night that the pain was still too fresh, Ivy shook her head and spoke. "Let me see what I can find out my way first. Someone must know something."

A twinge of fear for her joined the fear for myself. "No, I can do this," I said. "Whoever did it is an undead, and it's a lot safer for me to spend a couple of hours on the couch with Ford than for you to poke around in the affairs of the undead."

Ivy's perfect face scrunched up in protest, but before she could say anything, I sneezed again. *Damn it, I'm coming!*

On Ivy's shoulder, Jenks harrumphed. "Like Ivy has ever had a problem poking around underground? We'll be fine. Kisten didn't have me watching his back."

Together they made a determined picture, and I sighed.

"Okay," I said, giving in, then sneezed once more. "I gotta go." Impatient bastard. This was as bad as your date sitting in the drive and beeping a horn. I hated that, too.

I adjusted my grip on Mr. Fish and started down the stairs in the rain. The smell of the dying garden was strong, and my ankles went damp. Behind me, I heard Jenks ask something and Ivy mutter a soft, "I'll tell you later."

"Sorry about leaving you with a mess, guys!" I shouted over my shoulder. God, I felt like I was going off to camp.

"Don't worry about it."

Ahead of me was the line, and as I approached, I let my second sight come into play. Sure enough, Al was standing in it, his coattails shifting as he fidgeted impatiently. The rain wasn't touching him, and he made an inquiring face when I stopped just shy of the line and turned for one last look at the church. It wasn't fear that pulled me around, it was satisfaction.

There was a reddish haze over the church from the overlay of the ever-after, but because I wasn't in the line yet, I could still see Ivy and Jenks standing on the back steps, just at the edge of the rain. Ivy had an arm wrapped about her middle, letting it drop when she saw me look at her. She wouldn't wave, but I knew the thought was there and that she and Jenks would worry while I was gone. Jenks was a shifting drop of silver light from this distance, resting on her shoulder and probably telling her a bad joke full of sexual innuendos. They had found strength together, and I would be back.

I gave them a wave, and with a new confidence in my steps, I tucked my hair behind my ear and turned back to Al. The demon was waiting impatiently, and he made a rather rude gesture, as if he was wondering what my problem was. I smiled, thinking the next twenty-four hours were going to be like no other. Sure, I was going off to the ever-after, but I wasn't scared.

I was free of any favor owed to Newt, confident she would let me be until I went looking for her—like that would ever happen. I had made a hellacious deal with a demon, but the reward was just as great; those I loved were safe, as was I. With Jenks's help, I'd stolen something that no one in the history of the ever-after had, *and* I survived the fallout. I had saved Trent's lousy little elf ass, and with a bit of luck, I might survive that, too. Ceri's baby, and by association the entire elf species, was going to thrive. But that wasn't the best thing. The best thing was what I was leaving behind, knowing I'd be back.

I had my church. I had my friends. I had a mother who loved me, and a dirtbag sort-of-father who was going to make her happy again. So what if my kids, if I had any, would be demons? Maybe my mother was right. Maybe there was someone out there for me who would understand that there was good stuff to balance out the bad. And maybe by the time I found someone like that, I'd be so kick-ass that no one, not even Newt herself, would dare lay a finger on us.

For the first time in a long time, I knew who I was and where I was going. And right now, I was going . . . this way. Happily into the ever-after.

For more sexy,
supernatural adventures
in the Hollows,
don't miss . . .

White Witch, Black Curse

available March 2009
from Eos

The bloody handprint was gone, wiped from Kisten's window but not from my memory, and it ticked me off that someone had cleaned it, as if they were trying to steal what little recollection I retained about the night he'd died. The anger was misplaced fear if I was honest with myself. But I wasn't. Most days it was better that way.

Stifling a shiver from the December chill that had taken the abandoned cruiser, now in dry dock rather than floating in the river, I stood in the tiny kitchen and stared at the milky plastic as if willing the smeared mark back into existence. In the near distance came the overindulgent, powerful huff of a diesel train crossing the Ohio River. The scrape of Ford's shoes on the metallic boarding ladder was harsh, and worry pinched my brow.

The Federal Inderland Bureau had officially closed the investigation into Kisten's murder—Inderland Security hadn't even opened one—but the FIB wouldn't let me into their impound yard without an official presence. That meant intelligent, awkward Ford, since Edden thought I needed more psychiatric evaluation and I wouldn't come in any more. Not since I fell asleep on the couch and everyone in the FIB's Cincinnati office had heard me snoring. I didn't need evaluation. What I needed was something—anything—to rebuild my memory. If it was a bloody handprint, then so be it.

"Rachel? Wait for me," the FIB's psychiatrist called, shifting my worry to annoyance. *Like I couldn't handle this? I'm a big girl.* Besides, there wasn't anything left to see; the FIB had cleaned everything up. Ford had obviously been out here earlier—given the ladder and the unlocked door—making sure everything was sufficiently *tidy* before our appointment.

The clatter of dress shoes on teak pushed me forward, and I untangled my arms from themselves and reached for the tiny galley table for balance as I headed for the living room. The floor was still, which felt weird. Beyond the short curtains framing the now-clean window were the dirty gray and brilliant blue tarps of boats at dry dock, the ground a good six feet below us.

"Will you hold up?" Ford asked again, the light eclipsing as he entered. "I can't help if you're a room away."

"I'm waiting," I grumbled, coming to a halt and tugging my shoulder bag up. Though he'd tried to hide it, Ford had some difficulty getting his butt up the ladder. I thought the idea of a psychiatrist afraid of heights was hilarious, until the amulet he wore around his neck turned a bright pink when I mentioned it and Ford went red with embarrassment. He was a good man with his own demons to circle. He didn't deserve my razzing.

Ford's breathing slowed in the chill silence. Wan but determined, he gripped the table, his face whiter than usual, which made his short black hair stand out and his brown eyes soulful. Listening in on my feelings was draining, and I appreciated his wading through my emotional crap to help me piece together what had happened.

I gave him a thin smile, and Ford undid the top few buttons of his coat to reveal a professional cotton shirt and the amulet he wore while working. The metallic ley line charm was a visual display of the emotions he was picking up. He felt the emotions whether he was wearing the charm or not, but those around him had at least the illusion of privacy when he took it off. Ivy, my roommate and business partner, thought it stupid to try to break witch magic with human psychology in order to recover my memory, but I was desperate. Her efforts to find out who had killed Kisten were getting nowhere.

Ford's relief to be surrounded by walls was almost palpable, and seeing him release his death-grip on the table, I headed for the narrow door to the living room and the rest of the boat. The faint scent of vampire and pasta brushed against me—imagination stoked by a memory. It had been five months.

My jaw clenched, and I kept my eyes on the floor, not wanting to see the broken doorframe. There were smudges of dirt on the low-mat carpet that hadn't been there before, marks left by careless people who didn't know Kisten, had never known his smile, the way he laughed, or the way his eyes crinkled up when he surprised me. Technically an Inderland death without human involvement was out of the FIB's jurisdiction, but since the I.S. didn't care that my boyfriend had been turned into a blood gift, the FIB had made an effort just for me.

Murder was never taken off the books, but the investigation had been officially shelved. This was the first chance I'd had to come out here to try to rekindle my memory. Someone had nicked the inside of my lip trying to bind me to them. Someone had murdered my boyfriend twice. Someone was going to be in a world of hurt when I found out who they were.

Stomach fluttering, I looked past Ford to the window where the bloody handprint had been, left like a signpost to mock my pain without giving any prints to follow. *Coward.*

The amulet around Ford's neck flashed to an angry black. His eyes met mine as his eyebrows rose, and I forced my emotions to slow. I couldn't remember crap. Jenks, my backup and other business partner, had dosed me into forgetting so I wouldn't go after Kisten's murderer. I couldn't blame him. The pixy was only four inches tall, and it had been his only option to keep me from killing myself on a suicide run. I was a witch with an unclaimed vampire bite, and that couldn't stand up to an undead vampire no matter how you sliced it.

"You sure you're up to this?" Ford asked, and I forced my hand down from my upper arm. Again. It throbbed in a pain long since gone as a memory tried to surface. Fear stirred in me. The recollection of being on the other side of the door and trying to break it down was an old one. It was nearly the only memory I had of that night.

"I want to know," I said, but my voice sounded wobbly even to me. I had kicked the freaking door open. I had used my foot because my arm had hurt too much to move. I'd been crying at the time, and my hair had been in my eyes and mouth. I had kicked the door down.

A memory sifted from what I knew, and my pulse hammered as something was added, the image of me falling backward, hitting a wall. *My head hit a wall.* Breath held, I looked across the living room, staring at the featureless paneling. Right there. *I remember.*

Ford came unusually close. "You don't have to do it this way."

Pity was in his eyes. I didn't like it there, directed at me, and his amulet turned silver as I gathered my will and passed through the doorframe. "I do," I said boldly. "Even if I don't remember anything, the FIB guys might have missed something."

The FIB was fantastic at gathering information, even better than the I.S. It had to be since the human-run institution had to rely on finding evidence, not sweeping the room for emotions or using witch charms to discover who committed the crime and why. Everyone was capable of missing something, though, and that was one of the reasons I was out here. The other was to remember. Now that I was, I was scared. *My head hit the wall . . . Just over there.*

Ford came in behind me, watching as I scanned the low-ceilinged living room that stretched from one side of the boat to the other. It looked normal here, apart from the unmoving Cincy skyline visible through the narrow windows. My hand went to my middle as my stomach cramped. I had to do this, no matter what I remembered.

"I meant," Ford said as he put his hands in his pockets, "I've other ways to trigger memories."

"Meditation?" I said, embarrassed for having fallen asleep in his office. Feeling the beginnings of a stress headache, I strode past the couch where Kisten and I had eaten dinner, past the TV that got lousy reception, not that we ever really watched it, and past the wet bar. Inches from the undamaged wall, my jaw began to ache. Slowly I put a hand to the paneling where my head had hit, curling my fingers under when they started to tremble. *My head had hit the wall. Who shoved me? Kisten? His killer?* But the memory was fragmented. There was no more.

Turning away, I shoved my hand in my pocket to hide the soft shaking. My breath slipped from me in an almost-visible cloud, and I tugged my coat closer. The train was long gone. Nothing moved past the curtains but a flapping blue tarp. Instinct told me Kisten hadn't died in this room. I had to go deeper.

Ford said nothing as I walked into the dark narrow hallway, blind until my eyes adjusted. My pulse quickened as I passed the tiny bathroom where I'd tried on the sharp caps Kisten had given me for my birthday, and I slowed, listening to my body and realizing I was rubbing my fingertips together as they silently burned.

My skin tingled, and I halted, staring at my fingers, recognizing the memory of feeling carpet under my fingers, hot from friction. I held my breath as a new thought surfaced, born from the long-gone sensation. *Terror, helplessness. I had been dragged down this hall.*

A flash of remembered panic rose, and I squelched it, forcing my breath out in a slow exhalation. The lines I'd made in the carpet had been erased by the FIB vacuuming for evidence, erased from my memory by a spell. Only my body had remembered, and now me.

Ford stood silently behind me. He knew something was

trickling through my brain. Ahead was the door to the bedroom, and my fear thickened. That was where it happened. That was where Kisten had lain, his body torn and savaged, slumped against the bed, his eyes silvered and truly dead. *What if I remember it all? Right here in front of Ford and break down?*

"Rachel."

I jumped, startled, and Ford winced. "We can do this another way," he coaxed. "The meditation didn't work, but hypnosis might. It's less stressful."

Lips pressed tight, I moved forward and reached for the handle of Kisten's room. My fingers were pale and cold, looking like mine but not. Hypnosis was a false calm that would put off the panic until the middle of the night when I'd be alone. "I'm fine," I said, then pushed the door open. Taking a shaky breath, I went in.

The large room was cold, the wide windows that let in the light doing little to keep out the chill. Arm clutched against me, I looked to where Kisten had been propped up against the bed. *Kisten.* There was nothing. My heart ached as I missed him Behind me, Ford started to breathe with an odd regularity, working to keep my emotions from overwhelming him.

Someone had cleaned the carpet where he'd died for the second and final time. Not that there had been much blood. The fingerprint powder was gone, but the only prints they had found were from me, Ivy, and Kisten—scattered like signposts. There'd been none from his murderer. Not even on Kisten's body. The I.S. had probably cleaned his corpse between when I'd left to kick some vampire ass and my bewildered return with the FIB after I'd forgotten everything.

The I.S. didn't want the murder solved, a courtesy to whoever Kisten's last blood had been given to as a thank-you. Inderland tradition came before society's laws, apparently. The same people that I'd actually once worked for were covering it up, and that pissed me off.

My thoughts vacillated between rage and a debilitating heartache. Ford panted, and I tried to relax, for him if nothing else. Blinking back the threatened tears, I stared at the ceiling, breathing in the cold, quiet air and counting backward from ten, running through the useless exercise Ford had given me to find a light state of meditation.

At least Kisten had been spared the sordidness of being drained for someone's pleasure. He had died twice in quick succession, both times probably trying to save me from the vampire he'd been given to. His necropsy had been no help at all. Whatever had killed him the first time had been repaired by the vampire virus before he had died again. And if what I'd told Jenks before losing my memory was true, he'd died his second death by biting his attacker, mixing their undead blood to kill them both. Unfortunately, Kisten hadn't been dead for long. It might have only left his much older attacker simply wounded. I simply didn't know.

I mentally reached zero, and calmer, I moved toward the dresser. There was a shirt box on it, and I almost bent double in heartache when I recognized it.

"Oh, God," I whispered. My hand went out, turning to fists before my fingers slowly uncurled and I touched it. It was the lace teddy Kisten had given me for my birthday. I'd forgotten it was here.

"I'm sorry," Ford rasped, and gaze blurring from tears, I saw him slumped in the threshold.

My eyes squinted shut to make the tears leak out, and I held my breath. My head pounded, and I took a gasping breath only to hold it again, struggling for control. Damn it, he had loved me, and I had loved him. It wasn't fair. It wasn't right. And it was probably my fault.

A soft sound from the threshold told me Ford was struggling, and I forced myself to breathe. I had to get control of myself. I was hurting Ford. He was feeling everything I was, and I owed him a lot. Ford was the reason I hadn't been hauled in for questioning by the FIB despite me working for them occasionally. He was human, but his curse of being able to feel another's emotions was better than a polygraph or truth charm. He knew I'd loved Kisten and was terrified of what had happened here. "You okay?" I asked when his breathing evened out.

"Fine. Yourself?" he said in a wispy voice.

"Peachy keen," I said, gripping the top of the dresser. "I'm sorry. I didn't know it was going to be this bad."

"I knew what I was in for when I agreed to bring you out here," he said, wiping a tear from his eye that I no longer would cry for myself. "I can take anything you dish out, Rachel."

I turned away, guilty. Ford stayed where he was, the distance helping him cope with the overload. He never touched anyone except by accident. It had to be a crappy way to live. But as I rocked away from the dresser, there was a soft pull as my fingertips left the underside of the dresser top. *Sticky.* Sniffing my fingertips, I found the faint bite of propellant.

Sticky web. Someone had used sticky web and smeared it off on the underside of the dresser top. Me? Kisten's murderer? Sticky web only worked on fairies and pixies. It was little more than an irritant to anyone else, like a spiderweb. Jenks had begged off coming out here on the excuse of it being too cold, which it was, but maybe he knew more than he was saying.

My heartache eased from the distraction, and kneeling, I dug in my bag for a penlight and shined it on the underside of the lip of the dresser. I'd be willing to bet no one had dusted it. Ford came close, and I snapped the light off and stood. I didn't want FIB justice. I wanted my own. Ivy and I would come out later and do our own recon. Test the ceiling for evidence of hydrocarbons, too. Shake Jenks down to find out just how long he'd been with me that night.

Ford's disapproval was almost palpable, and I knew if I

looked, his amulet would be a bright red at my anger. I didn't care. I was angry, and that was better than falling apart. With a new feeling of purpose, I faced the rest of the room. Ford had seen the smeared mess. The FIB would reopen the case if they found one good print—other than the one I'd just made, that is. This might be the last time I was allowed here.

Leaning back against the dresser, I closed my eyes and crossed my arms, trying to remember. Nothing. I needed more. "Where's the stuff?" I asked, both dreading and eager to realize what else lay hidden in my mind, ready to surface.

There was the sound of sliding plastic, and Ford reluctantly handed me a packet of evidence bags and a stack of photos. "Rachel, we should leave if there's a viable print."

"The FIB has had five months," I said, nervous as I took them. "It's my turn. And don't give me any crap about disturbing evidence. The entire department has been through here. If there's a print, it's probably one of theirs."

He sighed as I turned to the dresser and arranged the plastic bags, print-side down. I took up the photos first, my gaze rising to the reflection of the room behind me.

I moved the picture of the smeared, bloody handprint on the kitchen window to the back of the stack, and tidied the pile with several, business-like taps. I got nothing from the handprint apart from the feeling that it wasn't mine or Kisten's.

The picture of Kisten was absent, thank God, and I crossed the room with a photo of a dent in the wall. Ford was silent as I touched the paneling, and I decided by the lack of phantom pain that I hadn't made it. There'd been a fight here other than mine. Over me, probably.

I slid the photo behind the stack. Under it was a close-up of a shoe imprint taken under the bank of windows. My head started to throb, and with that as a warning, I knew something was here, lurking in my thoughts. Jaw tight, I forced myself to the window, kneeling to run a hand over the smooth carpet, trying to spark a memory even as I feared it. The print was of a man's dress shoe. Not Kisten's. It was too mundane for that. Kisten had kept only the latest fashion in his closet. *Had the shoe been black or brown?* I thought, willing something to surface.

Nothing. Frustrated, I closed my eyes. In my thoughts, the scent of vampire incense mixed with an unfamiliar aftershave. A quiver rose through me, and not caring what Ford thought, I put my face on the carpet to breathe in the smell of fibers. *Something . . . anything . . . Please. . . .*

Dear Reader,

I never know how the muse is going to hit me until I actually sit down and write a piece. What follows was, at its beginnings, supposed to be a small, "interview with a demon" sort of work that gave the first glimpse into the demon realm. And the muse laughed at me. The characters of Big Al, my demon, and Ceri, his tortured familiar from the past, were hiding more than I had originally thought, and as I began, I found myself swept away in my enthusiasm to learn just a little bit more. The result being I sheepishly turned in to my editor something that had somehow turned into a full short story.

So, here, for the first time, I'm pleased to present a sneak peak behind the demonic curtain.

Enjoy!

All best wishes,

Kim Harrison

The Bespelled

Kim Harrison

Paperwork, Algaliarept thought in resignation as he blew gently upon the ledger book to dry the ink faster. *Ink that wasn't actually ink, paper that had never been wood,* he thought as he breathed deep for the cloying scent of blood. Though blood made a sublimely binding document, the nature of it tended to slow everything down. Even so, if he could pass this part of his job to a subordinate, he wouldn't. The knowledge of who owed him and what was worth a lot in the demon's world, and familiars were known for their loose tongues until you cut them out. It was a practice Algaliarept frowned upon. Most of his brethren were bloody plebeians. Removing a familiar's tongue completely ruined the nuances of their pleas for mercy.

Resettling himself at his small but elegantly carved desk, Algaliarept reached into a lidded stone box, dipping a tiny silver spoon for his Brimstone and letting the drug slowly melt on his tongue. The small tap of the spoon as he replaced it jolted through him like fire, and closing his eyes he breathed, pulling the air into him over the ashy blackness to bring a hundred faint smells to him as the Brimstone heightened his senses and took his mind into a higher state.

Paperwork has got to be the biggest pain in the ass, he thought as he hung for a moment in the mild euphoria. But as his eyes opened he gazed upon his opulent quarters—the walls draped with dark silk, vases painted with beautifully erotic bodies, richly shadowed corners with cushions and fragrant oil lamps, and underfoot, the rug showing a winding dragon devouring its smaller kin—Algaliarept knew he'd have it no other way. Everything about him would be missing if he worked for another.

The East was where the world's intelligence currently resided, and he quite liked the Asian people, even if they called him a dragon there, and expected him to breathe fire. Apart from the elves making a last stand in the mountains of Europe, Asia was the only real culture in the world right now—thanks to his efforts, mostly. One must create what another will covet.

Dipping his quill, Algaliarept bent to his work again, his brow tightening for no reason he could fathom. He was a dealer in flesh and seducer of souls, skilled in training people in the dark arts enough to make them marketable, then abducting them when they made a mistake in order to sell them to his peers into an extended lifetime of servitude. He was so good at it that he had achieved a status that rivaled the highest court members, reached on his own merits and owed to no one. Yet, as his quill scratched out the interest of a particularly long-running debt, he finally acknowledged the source of his growing feeling of dissatisfaction.

Where he'd once relished watching a potential familiar agonize over wanting more and thinking he was smart enough to evade the final outcome, now there was only an odd sensation of jealousy. Though doomed, the familiar was feeling *something*. Algaliarept, however, was feeling nothing. He'd lost the joy, and the chase had become too easy.

Another page tallied, and Algaliarept reached for a second spoonful of Brimstone while the red ink dried and turned black. As his silver spoon dipped, his moving reflection caught his attention and he hesitated, meeting his own gaze in the gilded mirror upon the desk. Tired, goat-slitted eyes stared back at him. They narrowed, and with a feeling of unhappiness, he watched himself let the black ash sift back into the box. If he wanted sensation, he should go out and take it, not sip it from dust. *Perhaps,* Algaliarept thought darkly as he touched his script to see if it was dry, *it was time to retire for a time.* Begin removing his name from the texts in reality to leave just enough for the occasional summoning instead of the numerous summons he fielded. He was weary of mediocre dealings and fast satisfaction that gave him nothing lasting. He wanted . . . more. Mood soured, he bent to his work. *This can't be all there is,* he thought as he tried to lose himself in the beauty of wants and needs, supply and demand.

Intent on his work, the soft tickling in his nose almost went unnoticed until he sneezed. His hand slammed down on the open Brimstone container, saving it. Shocked, he stared at his door, tasting the air and trying to decide where the sun had just fallen. Someone was summoning him. *Again*, he thought with a sigh, until he realized where it was likely coming from. *Europe*?

Algaliarept's gaze returned to the mirror, and his goat-slitted, red eyes glinted. A slow smile came over his creased face. Inside, a quiver of excitement coursed through him, more heady than Brimstone. It had to be Ceridwen. She was the only one who knew his name across that continent, the only one who could call him there. *Three months*, he thought, his excitement growing as he gazed into the mirror while his features became younger and more refined, taking on the strong jaw she was accustomed to. *I knew she couldn't resist.*

Humming a snippet of music that had never been penned, he shook out his sleeves, watching them turn from the casual silk kimono he appreciated into a stuffy European crushed green velvet coat. Lace appeared at his throat, and his hair slicked itself back. His ruddy complexion lightened, and white gloves appeared. He would be pleasing to her sight even if he thought the outfit ugly. Until she stopped three months ago without warning, Ceridwen Merriam Dulciate had summoned him every week for seven years. He was nothing if not patient, but the lapse did not bode well. That he was excited for the first time in as many weeks did not escape him, but Ceri was special. She was the most devious, intelligent, careful woman he had tried to snag in almost three hundred years, and he never knew what she was going to do.

Art, he realized suddenly. Ceri was art where everyone else was work. Was that where his dissatisfaction was coming from? Was it time to stop simply working and begin making art? But to do that, he needed the canvas before him. It was time to bring her home. If he could.

Standing, he sneezed again, more delicately this time. His thoughts went to a seldom-used curse and he winced, searching his mind until he remembered. "*Rosa flavus*," he whispered, shivering as the unusual curse shifted over him to leave a yellow rose in his grip. Damn his dame, this felt good. He'd bring her home this time. He was anxious to begin.

"Zoe!" he shouted, knowing the three-fingered man-whore would hear him. "I'm out! Take my calls!" And with no more thought, he allowed the summons to pull him from the splash of displaced time he existed in to reality.

He traveled by ley lines, the same force of nature that kept the drop of time he existed in from vanishing. The shock of the line melting him into a thought was a familiar ache, and it was with a sly confidence that he found himself drawn to a spot far up in the mountains of Europe. He never knew for sure where he was going until he got there, but this? Algaliarept smiled as the clean mountain air filled his lungs as he reformed, the stench of burnt amber that clung to him being replaced by the honest smell of horses and cultivated flowers. This was pleasant.

The hum of a binding circle grew oppressive, and Algaliarept found himself in a dusky garden surrounded by dark pines, the sky above them still holding the fading light of the sunset and fluttering blue butterflies. The circle holding him was defined by semi-precious stones inlaid in crushed gravel. Through the haze of energy trapping him came the sound of running water and birds. Music. A small orchestra. Something was badly off. And when his eyes went to the full moon rising above the fragrant pines, his smile faded in a wash of worry. *Is the bitch getting married?*

A soft clearing of a throat turned him around.

"Ceridwen," he said, allowing a sliver of his annoyance to color his words, then he hesitated. She was absolutely stunning in the puddle of nearby lamp light with blue butterflies flitting about her. "Ceri, you are exceptionally lovely." *Damn it to the two worlds colliding, she's getting married. Directly.* He had tarried too long. It was tonight, or never.

The slight, fair-haired woman before him modestly ran her hands over her clearly wedding garb, white and trimmed with her family's colors of maroon and gold. Her fair hair was piled atop her head but for a few strands artfully drawn down. She was pale and lithe, having wide green eyes and a narrow chin. If for no more than that, she would be unique among the predominantly Asian women populating the demon familiar market and bring a high price. But that wasn't why he'd courted her so carefully.

Though her eyes were cast down demurely, she knew she was beautiful, reveled in it, vainly believed it was why he was attentive and kind to her. He'd kept her oblivious to the real reason he stayed pliant to her summons and demands for knowledge when anyone else would have been met with anger and threats years ago for the audacity of being too clever to be caught and therefore was wasting his time. She carried the surname Dulciate. It was one of the most desired familiar names in the demon realm, though if the castle behind her was the level to which the elves had fallen to, there wasn't much left to take revenge upon. Even if she were ugly, he could make more from her then seven skilled familiars. And she was skilled, thanks to him—infuriatingly clever and careful. *Hopefully not careful enough*, he thought, his hands clenching in their white-gloved preciseness.

Behind her on the cropped grass, a round stone table was

strewn with her golden tarot cards, clear evidence that she was upset. She knew he thought little of them, having spent summers striving to break her from their grip, failing even when he proved them false as she sought counsel from a power he didn't believe in. Rising beyond the garden was the gray-walled castle of her family. It was pitiful by the Asian standards he appreciated, but it was the pinnacle of society in this superstitious, cultural wasteland. Where he'd created a society in Asia with science, rivals had inundated Europe with superstition in their attempts to match his gains.

From the balcony walkway, clusters of overdressed women kept watch as the darkness took hold and the butterflies dwindled. As a member of the elven royal house, it was Ceridwen's right to summon demons, expected and encouraged until she took a husband. Tradition dictated that the ruling personage in waiting was to learn all they could of the arcane. It was just as expected that her station would grant her the privacy to do it where ever she wanted. So her fluttering ladies waited in the torchlight, holding Ceri's little dogs as they yapped furiously at him. They knew the danger, and it was a delicious irony that no one listened to them.

Looking closer, he gauged her aura to see if a rival had been poaching on his claim which could explain the three-month lapse. Ceridwen's aura, though, was as he had left it; the original bright blue marred by a light black coating of demon smut that was all his own.

Seeing the yellow rose in his hand, a heavy tear brimmed in her deep green eyes, unusual for the emotionally balanced woman. Her head bowed as it fell, but pride brought it up again immediately. Chin high, she looked behind her to her tarot cards, starting to cry all the more. Her hands stayed stoically at her sides, fisted as she refused to wipe her tears away.

Hell and damnation, I'm too late, Algaliarept thought, taking an angry step forward only to stop short as the barrier she'd summoned him behind hummed a familiar, vicious warning. "Love, what's wrong?" he asked, pretending to be oblivious, though inside, he was scrambling. He had not labored seven years only to lose a Dulciate elf to marriage! "Why are you crying? I've told you not to look at the cards. They only lie."

Crestfallen, Ceri turned away, but her pale fingers straying to touch her tarot cards were still bare of gold, and Algaliarept felt a glimmer of hope. "I'm not your love," she said, voice quavering as she turned the lovers card face down. "And you're the liar."

"I've never lied to you," he said. Damn it, he was not going to lose her to some inane cards! Frustrated, Algaliarept nudged a booted toe at the circle's seam to feel her power repel him. Never had she made a mistake in its construction. It both infuriated him and kept him coming back, week after week, year after year, and now, because of it, he was going to lose her.

"I had to tell you good-bye," she continued as if he hadn't spoken, pleading as she fingered a gold-edged card. "They told me not too, that with the responsibility of marriage, I must sever all ties to the arcane."

Agitated, he gripped his rose until a thorn pierced his glove and the pain stifled his fidgeting. "Good-bye, my love?" He had to make her control lapse—if only for an instant.

"I'm not your love," she whispered, but her gaze was upon the cards. There were no others like them, having been painted by a second-rate Italian painter who had attempted to put the royal family within the artwork. It hadn't pleased him to find out Ceri was on the death card, being pulled away by a demon.

"Ceri, you *are* my unrequited love," he said earnestly, testing the strength of her circle until the stench of burning leather from his shoes drove him back. "Tell me you've not wed. Not yet." He knew she wasn't, but to make her say the words would make her think.

"No." It was a thin whisper, and the young woman sniffed, holding a hand out for a tiny blue butterfly seeking warmth in the fading day. He'd seen them only once before in this profusion, and it was likely the wedding had been planned around the beautiful, fragile creatures. But butterflies like carrion as much as flowers, battlefields as much as gardens.

Algaliarept looked at the yellow rose in his grip, his thoughts lifting and falling as the music rose high in celebration. Fast. He had to work fast. "Why do you hurt me?" he said, squeezing his hand until a drop of blood fell upon it, turning the entire rose a bright scarlet. "You summon me only to spurn me?" He dropped the rose, and she blanched, eyes rising to his bloodied glove. "To say good-bye?" he accused, allowing his anger to color his voice. "Do our seven years mean nothing to you? The skills I've taught you, the music, ideas that we shared from across the sea? It all means nothing? Was I just your demon, your pet? Nothing more?"

Distressed, Ceridwen faced him, the butterfly forgotten. "Talk not to me of love. They are naught but pretty words to trap me," she whispered, but under her misery was a frantic need he had yet to figure out. There was more here than she was saying. Could she be unhappy about the marriage? Was this the key to making her control lapse?

"As you trapped me!" he exclaimed, jerking his hand back when he intentionally burned himself on the barrier between them. Excitement was a pulse when she reached out, concern for him showing briefly. "Ceridwen," he pleaded, breath coming faster, "I watched you grow from a shy, skittish colt to a rightfully proud woman, fiery and poised to take responsibility for your people. I was there when all others grew distant, jealous of your skills. I didn't expect to grow fond of you. Have I not been a gentleman? Have I not bent to your every whim?"

Green eyes deep with misery met his. "You have. Because you're caught in my circle."

"I would regardless!" he said violently, then looked to the darkening sky as if seeking words, though what he was going to say he'd said to untold others. This time, though, he meant them. "Ceri, you are so rare, and you don't even know it. You are so beyond anyone here because of what I've shared with you. The man who waits for you . . . He cannot meet your intellectual needs. When I hear your summons, my heart leaps, and I come directly, a willing slave."

"I know."

It was a faint affirmation, and Algaliarept's pulse raced. This was it. This was the way to her downfall. She didn't desire her husband. "And now you'll abandon me," he whispered.

"No," she protested, but they both knew tradition dictated otherwise.

"You're going to wed," he stated, and she shook her head, desperate as her tiny feet tapped the flagstones, coming closer in her need to deny it.

"That I'm wed doesn't mean I won't summon you. Our talks can continue."

Feigning dejection, he turned his back on her, all but oblivious to the manicured gardens going dark and damp. "You will abandon me," he said, chin high as he probed the circle to find it still perfect. Though he was a demon and could crush an army with a single word, such was the strength of a summons that a simple circle could bind him. He had to upset her enough such that she would make a mistake and he could break it. Until then, nothing but sound and air could get through.

Taking a ragged breath, he dropped his head, his hands still laced behind him. "You will begin with all good intentions," he said, his voice flat. "But you'll summon me into underground rooms where no one can see, and our time together once open and celebrated will become brief snatches circled by guilt instead of precious stones. Soon you will call me less and less, shame dictating that your heart be ruled over by your head, your responsibilities." He took a breath, turning his tone thin. "Let me go. I can't bear seeing what we shared abandoned bit by bit. Make of my heart a clean death."

The clatter of the gravel sliding beneath her shoes sparked through him like lightning, and he grit his teeth to hide his anticipation. One tiny stone, knocked out of place, would do it. "I would not do that," she protested as she faced him, a gray shadow against the dark vegetation.

Refusing to meet her gaze because he knew it would hurt her, he looked at the moon, seeing a few lone butterflies daring the dark to find a mate. Crickets chirped as the music from the castle dissolved into polite applause. "Marry him if you will," he said stoically. "I'll forever come if you call, but I'll be but a broken shadow. You can command my body, but you cannot command my heart." He looked at her now, finding she was clutching a golden card to her chest, hiding it. "Do you love him?" he asked bluntly, already knowing the answer in her frantic expression.

She said nothing as torchlight shined upon her tears.

"Does he make your heart beat fast?" Algaliarept demanded, a shudder running through him when her eyes closed in pain. "Can he make you laugh? Has he ever brought new thought to you, as I have? I've never touched you, but I've seen you tremble in desire . . . for me."

He nudged at the circle with a booted toe, jerking back at the zing of power. Though her face wore her anguish, her circle still held strong, even when her chest heaved, and her grip on her dress dropped, leaving creases in the otherwise perfect fall of fabric.

"Don't hurt me like this, Algaliarept," she whispered. "I only wanted to say good-bye."

"It's you who hurt me," he stated, forcefully where before he had always been demure. "I'm forever young, and now you'll make me watch you grow old, watch your beauty fade and your skills tarnish as you shackle yourself to a loveless marriage and a cold bed."

"It is the way of things," she breathed, but the fear in the back of her eyes strengthened as she touched her own face.

Her fondness for the mirror had always been her downfall, and he felt a surge of renewed excitement. "I will mourn your beauty when you could have been young forever," he said, looking for a crack in her resolve. "I would've forever been your slave." Faking depression, he slumped his perfect posture. "Only in the ever-after does time stand still and beauty and love last forever. But, as you say, it's the way of things."

"Gally, don't speak so," she pleaded, and he tensed when she used the nickname she'd chosen for him. But his lips parted in shock when she reached for him only to drop her hand mere inches from the barrier between them. His breath came in with a shudder, and his eyes widened. Had he been cracking the nut the wrong way? He had been trying to rattle her, make her lose her resolve so he could find a crack in her circle and break it, even knowing that her will would likely remain absolute even when her world was crashing down about her. She would not let her circle weaken, but what if she would take it down voluntarily? Ceri was of royal blood, a Dulciate. Generations of crown-sanctified temptation had created women who would not make a mistake of power. *But she might make a mistake of the heart.*

And the instant he realized why he had failed these seven years, her gaze went past him to the palace, lit up and replete with joy. Her eyes closed, and panic hit him as he saw everything fall apart. *Shit, she was going to walk.*

"Ceri, I would love you forever," he blurted, not faking his distress. *Not now. Not now when he'd found her weakness!*

"Gally, no," she sobbed as the tears fell and tiny blue butterflies rose and fell about her.

"Don't call me again!" he demanded, the words coming from him without thought or plan. "Go to your cold bed. Die old and ugly! I would make you wise beyond all on earth, keep you beautiful, teach you things that the scholars and learned men have not even dreamed of. I will survive alone, untouched, my heart becoming cold where you showed me love. Better that I had never met you." He looked at her as a sob broke from her. "I was happy as I was."

"Forgive me," she choked out, hunched in heartache. "You were never just my demon."

"It's done," he said, making a hitch in his voice. "It's not as if I ever thought you would trust me, but to show me heaven only to give it to another man? I can't bear it."

"Gally—"

He raised a hand and her voice broke in a sob. "That's three times you've said my name," he said, crushing the now red rose beneath his foot. "Let me go, or trust me. Take down the wall so I may at least have the memory of your touch to console me as I weep in hell for having lost you, or simply walk away. I care not. I'm already broken."

Expression held at an anguished pain, he turned his back on her again, shifting his shoulders as if trying to find a new way to stand. Behind him, he heard a single sob, and then nothing as she held her breath. There was no scuffing of slippers as she ran away and no lessening of the circle imprisoning him, so he knew she was still there. His pulse quickened, and he forced his breathing to be shallow. He was romancing the most clever, most resolute bitch he'd ever taught a curse to, and he loved her. Or rather, he loved not knowing what she would do next, the complexity of her thoughts that he had yet to figure out— an irresistible jewel in a world where he had everything.

"Do you love him?" he asked, adding the last brushstrokes to his masterpiece.

"No," she whispered.

His hands quivered as adrenaline spiked through him, but he held perfectly still. He would've given a lot to know which card she held crushed in her grip. "Do you love me?" he asked, shocked to realize he'd never used those particular words to seduce a familiar before.

The silence was long, but from behind him came a soft, "Yes. God help me."

Algaliarept closed his eyes. His breath shook in him, hid excitement racing through him like a living ley line, burning. Would she drop her circle? He didn't know. And when a light touch landed on his hand, he jumped, looking down to find a blue butterfly slowly fanning its wings against him.

A butterfly? he thought in shock, and then he realized. She had broken the summoning circle, and he'd never even felt it go down. *Oh God*, he thought, a surge of what was almost ecstasy making his knees nearly buckle as he turned, finding her standing before him, nervous and hopeful all at the same time. She had let him in. Never had he taken anyone like this. It was like nothing he'd ever felt before, debilitating.

"Ceri," he breathed, seeing her without the shimmer of her power between them. Her eyes were beautiful, her skin holding a olive tint he'd never noticed before. And her face . . . She was crying, and he reached out, not believing when he ran a white-gloved hand under her eye to make her smile at him uncertainly. It was a smile of hope and fear.

She should be afraid.

"Gally?" she said hesitantly.

"Do you really love me?" he asked her as the butterflies swarmed, drawn by the scent of burnt amber, and she nodded, gazing at him as tears slipped down and she hesitantly folded herself into his arms.

"Then you are one stupid bitch."

Gasping, she flung her head up. Pushing from him, she tried to escape, but it was too late. Silently laughing, Algaliarept wrapped his arm around her neck, grabbing her hair with his free hand and pulling her across the garden to the nearest ley line. "Let me go!" she screamed, and gathering herself, she shouted, *"celero inanio!"* sobbing as she flung the entire force of the nearest ley line at him.

With a quick thought, Algaliarept deflected the burning curse, chuckling as flickers of light blossomed to show where the blue butterflies burned before they hit the dew-wet grass. In his grasp, Ceri hesitated her struggles, aghast that he had turned her magic into killing something she loved. "Do that again, and I'll burn anything that comes round that corner," he encouraged, winding his fist in her hair until she began hitting him with her tiny fists.

"You lied! You lied to me!" she raged.

"I did nothing of the kind," he said, holding her close and dragging her out of the circle so that the people now running toward her screams wouldn't be able to trap him easily. "I'm going to keep you forever young and teach you everything I know, just as I promised." She was panting, her struggle hesitating as she waited for the help that wouldn't be able to free her. Closing his eyes, he smelled her hair. "And I'm going to love you," he whispered into her ear as she began to pray to an uncaring god he'd teach her not to believe in. "I'm going to love you within an inch of your life, then love you some more."

Anticipation high, he reached for her inner thigh. The instant his fingers touched her, she screamed, fighting to be free. A fierce smile came over him and his blood pounded in his loins. This was going to be everything he wanted. A distraction for as long as he cared to make it last.

"Let me jump you to my bed so we may begin your tutelage," he said as the bobbing torches came closer.

"No!" she cried out, wiggling as her hair came undone to fall about her face. She looked so much more fetching, her color high and rage making her eyes sparkle.

"Wrong answer," he said, flooding her with the force of the line.

Her eyes widened, her small lips opening to show perfect teeth. Gasping, she bit her lip, trying not to scream. Almost she passed out, and he let up the instant she started to go limp. That she wouldn't scream made him smile. She'd scream before it was over, and finding her breaking point would be . . . exquisite.

"I'm giving you everything you want," he breathed in her ear when she could think again, hanging in his grasp as she panted. "Everything and more, Ceri. Let me take you." He could knock her out and take her by force, but if she gave in entirely to him . . . it would be beyond anything he'd ever accomplished.

The bobbing torches turned the corner, little dogs yapping in overdressed women's arms.

"Stop! For the love of God, stop!" she shouted, and Algaliarept felt a deep surge of satisfaction. Destroying her will would fulfill his every need.

A young man in white and gold pushed past the women, stumbling to a stop, shock in his perfect face. A wailing outcry rose from the nobles behind him, and several turned and ran.

Ceri's bridegroom was perfect, Algaliarept decided bitterly as he held her tighter. The man before him now complimented her in every way, slim, fair—everything Algaliarept was not. And then Algaliarept smiled—she had shunned elven perfection to be with him.

The man's lips parted in horror as Algaliarept's fingers entwined deeper in her hair, jerking her head up to expose the long length of her neck to him. And still Ceri stared at her bridegroom, color in her cheeks as her lungs heaved. Turning, the prince called for magicians.

At the sight of his back, Ceri's hand opened and the card she held fell to the earth. Something in Algaliarept sparked when the devil card fell to the manicured grass. The bent gold glinted in the torch light, but it was easy to see the beautiful maiden being dragged off by an ugly, red-skinned demon. "Take me," she whispered as three magicians stumbled into the clearing, frightened but determined. "I don't want to grow old. You are my demon."

With her acquiesce, it was done. Seven years of labor culminated in one satisfied laugh that made the young man in white pale. But he didn't move to save her.

"You don't deserve her," Algaliarept said, and then, as the magicians moved, he shifted his thoughts to leave. The yapping dogs, the wailing women, everything vanished into the clean blackness of thought. And as they traveled the lines back to the drop of time that had been flung from space itself, Algaliarept touched her soul, ran his fingers through her aura and felt her squirm. She had wanted it. Even with her denials and screams, she wanted it. Wanted him. She was his little blue butterfly, seeking out carrion.

Don't cry, Ceri, he thought, knowing she heard him when her mind seemed to quiver.

He was going to keep this one for himself. Turn the Dulciate elf into a showcase of his talents. No one had ever come willingly, before. He was an artist, and destroying her as he made her into what he wanted, would be his finest masterpiece.

Until I find someone with a little more skill, that is, he thought, knowing that wasn't likely to happen for, oh, probably another thousand years.

PROWL THE NIGHT WITH
NEW YORK TIMES BESTSELLING AUTHOR

KIM HARRISON

DEAD WITCH WALKING
978-0-06-057296-9

When the creatures of the night gather, whether to
hide, to hunt, or to feed, it's Rachel Morgan's job to keep
things civilized. A bounty hunter and witch with serious sex
appeal and attitude, she'll bring them back alive, dead . . .
or undead.

THE GOOD, THE BAD, AND THE UNDEAD
978-0-06-057297-6

Rachel Morgan can handle the leather-clad vamps and even
tangle with a cunning demon or two. But a serial killer who
feeds on the experts in the most dangerous kind of black magic
is definitely pressing the limits.

EVERY WHICH WAY BUT DEAD
978-0-06-057299-0

Rachel must take a stand in the raging war to control
Cincinnati's underworld because the demon who helped her
put away its former vampire kingpin is coming to collect his due.

At Avon Books, we know your passion for romance—once you finish one of our novels, you find yourself wanting more.

May we tempt you with . . .

- **Excerpts** from our upcoming releases.

- Entertaining **extras**, including authors' personal photo albums and book lists.

- Behind-the-scenes **scoop** on your favorite characters and series.

- **Sweepstakes** for the chance to win free books, romantic getaways, and other fun prizes.

- Writing **tips** from our authors and editors.

- **Blog** with our authors and find out why they love to write romance.

- **Exclusive content** that's not contained within the pages of our novels.

Join us at
www.avonbooks.com

AVON *An Imprint of* HarperCollins*Publishers*
www.avonromance.com